Simon Maier

SILVER GREEN

Volume I

Michael Terence
Publishing

First published in paperback by
Michael Terence Publishing in 2020
www.mtp.agency

ISBN 9781800940956

Aro, Niger, Africa, 1491

From the ship, the few crew members who'd been left onboard saw the dawn sky where it met the horizon - a crimson gash, fading at the edges to shades of pink. They could also see that the early light made a perfect path of rippled red on the surface of the ground as it stretched towards the glow of the burning village. An officer on the foredeck later reported that it was like the gateway to hell.

The sound in the village was deafening. Half-naked sailors waved swords with drunken abandon, stabbing at villagers trying but failing to flee. Blood-fevered officers fired their stolen Spanish pistols, now and then hitting some of their own crew by mistake. Many of the pistols, broken beyond use for shooting, were used as clubs.

The invaders wore torn uniforms, villagers' clothing or the skins of animals, still covered with the blood of prior owners. One, a boatswain, had draped a leopard's skin over his shoulders and another, a midshipman, waved a freshly severed tusk. A young apprentice, no more than twelve years' old, carried a dented breastplate as a shield and wore spurs on his raw, bare heels. An old carpenter, wearing a bright yellow dress, wandered about in an opium daze. All the marauders were screeching, shouting or singing ribald songs. Everywhere there was smoke and confusion.

A cousin, trying to protect her, collapsed, his pleading eyes looking up and then becoming sightless. Princess Iheme of the Aro peoples of Niger was unable to scream but, instead, shook in terror. Hearing her name being called out, she turned to see her father, the king, shouting for her as he was dragged away while her weeping mother, arms tightly bound, was pulled along by a length of twine around her neck.

Seven marauders closed in on the girl, throwing their weapons and clothes to the ground. The one at the front of the group began licking his lips as he undid his breeches.

A wind had been rising all the while. The very air seemed to grow dark with purple clouds scudding across the big morning sky and, for the first time, the traders looked up anxiously. They could hear the wind and they could hear the crackling fire. They could also hear a distant howling from what they thought at first were dogs, but one of them whispered that the noise came from wolves and another said no, hungry hyenas. The officer in charge shared their anxiety and ordered everyone to focus, to take valuables, to collect the captives and to organise immediate departure back to the ship.

In the royal hut, the sailors surrounding the princess still advanced despite the bugle call to leave. The girl whimpered and hugged herself. The closest man, now naked, stopped walking, his gibbering leer becoming a sudden, startled look of surprise. Eyes widening in shock, his head jerked back and the girl could see blood gushing from the man's throat. Another man fell forward, a long, thin dagger sticking out of his back. One man immediately knelt and muttered some sort of prayer. The remaining four looked round in confusion and ran. Strong arms, belonging to someone she couldn't see, grabbed the princess who, struggling, finally found her voice to scream.

Whoever was carrying her away began to speak in her own language and it was obvious that he knew who she was. Then, before she could scream again, the man pressed a soft cloth over her mouth and nose. She could smell hibiscus, vanilla and lemon which were pleasant and something unrecognisable which was not.

Just as the rising wind became a violent storm, the dawn sky turned the colour of night.

Qumran, Judean Hills, Imperial Province, Roman Empire, 79 CE

The hills of Qumran were exposed to the already scorching mid-morning sun. Jacob, hiding in the purple shadows of the cave's depths, was cold despite the suffocating heat outside. He could see the shimmering Dead Sea in the distance and the bleached, white salt flats that surrounded it. High above him, on the other side of the gorge, was the lush green of the Ein Gedi oasis with its waterfall sending silvery water, rushing, splashing and gurgling over a sharp edge, hitting a pool far below. The oasis shimmered in the heat like a mirage, but Jacob knew that it was no mirage, for up there lurked death.

Not three weeks before, the Sicarii had slaughtered all those in the small settlement whom they thought were informers. Now, Jacob could just make out a boy of roughly his own age and a few goats whose tinkling bells reminded him of times when he too had tended goats.

Jacob had been waiting for nearly half the previous night and much of a day, as instructed. He knew that the soldiers had to come this way. Or, rather, that's what he'd been told. Now, he was pretty sure that the whole thing had been a total waste of time.

He was not only fed up, but was angry with himself. He'd been stupid and he wasn't often stupid. A few days before, his beloved sica had been stolen. The tall, ragged, old man who'd stolen it had not run away, but had said from a safe distance, 'I need a little of your time Jacob, nothing more. Then you can have your knife back.'

Jacob was used to crazy or drunk people walking the streets of the ruined city of Jerusalem. But nobody had ever stolen his precious knife before.

'Old man,' he remembered calling out, 'return my knife now if you value your life.'

'A conversation is all I seek,' the old man had said calmly. 'I wish you no harm.'

'I will not warn you again,' Jacob had shouted more anxiously. 'Wherever you go, I shall follow. As will others. You'll die for this.'

'Share some wine, listen to me, get your knife back and then leave.'

'Oh yes? And be poisoned? You think me a fool? You think me an idiot?' Jacob considered now that, having allowed someone to steal his precious knife had been both foolish and idiotic.

'This is your last warning, scum,' he'd shouted in the busy street, not only angry but worried. People had stopped to see what the argument was about. 'Give me my knife now or death will stalk you. This is a promise. You really don't wish to anger me further.'

'Just give me a few minutes of your time,' the old man had repeated.

Jacob had walked towards the old man. 'My knife! Give it to me now!' He remembered being suddenly aware that the people had looked curiously at what was going on and had moved closer towards him to get a better view.

'Do you know what I am?' Jacob had shouted, losing his temper.

'Yes, I do,' the old man had replied. 'Do you really wish me to say in public what you are?'

Jacob had realised that even more people had started to gather round. That's all he needed, he'd thought, someone in the hope of a reward to shout for a patrol and declare that there was a young thug in the open, possibly Sicarii, ripe for the picking. In a way it had been fortunate that the old man had already started walking away. Jacob had followed, relieved to leave the prying eyes and greedy hands of the growing mob.

Nearby, in a deserted street next to a ruined tannery that still stank of the urine once used to soak and soften leather, the old man had sat on a large piece of stone from what once had been a marble pillar. He'd beckoned Jacob to sit too which the boy had done, all the time looking around to see if there were enemies about to spring on him. The old man had handed Jacob a small gourd of wine and a leather purse in which the boy had discovered to his temporary delight four silver coins.

'And my knife, camel breath,' he'd said impatiently, his left hand outstretched.

The old man had handed over the sica. 'Run and I shall catch you boy.'

Jacob had clutched the knife. He'd looked around the street trying hard not to seem nervous. 'I don't think you could catch me, old man.'

'I would catch you.'

The wine had been surprisingly good, remembered Jacob, and sweet. He'd insisted that the old man should try some first and Jacob had only drunk the rest after he'd watched the old man for any ill effects.

The old man's instructions had been clear.

'You are needed for a task. Wait. Don't interrupt. Let me finish what I have to say. Then you can speak... I want you to collect something. I want you to collect something that will be in the hills of Qumran. Near a cave. Look.' The old man had drawn a map in the sand with a long finger.

'Wait in the cave marked so,' the old man had told him as he'd scratched a symbol in the dust. The man's accent had seemed local, an Aramaic dialect that most people from Jerusalem spoke along with some Latin phrases thrown in as well.

Jacob, who spoke both languages fluently, had asked, 'Why should I do this?' The old man hadn't replied.

'I do as I please,' Jacob had declared. 'I am Sicarii. I am a daggerman. For ten silver pieces, I may consider your task, but for only four and a small cup of wine, no. And you have a strange way of asking for favours. Who are you?'

'That doesn't matter,' the old man had said.

'Well, blood of any gods, it does to me!' Jacob had stood up ready to run or fight, both at which he was extremely good. 'In my years I've known many who wanted to do me harm. All are now dead.'

The old man had smiled. 'I asked you to hear me and so do me the courtesy of letting me finish.'

'I'm going now,' said Jacob. 'It's not safe on the streets. Thank you for your money and wine, old man.' He'd stood up and had turned to leave.

Jacob recalled with shame and disgust how the old man had also stood up, stepped forward and grabbed the boy's knife throwing arm, holding it in a vice-like grip. Jacob had tried to pull away.

'I mean you no harm,' the old man had said.

'I've heard that before, scum. And for someone who means me no harm, you're hurting me now. If you plan to rob me, I have nothing.'

'I want nothing from you. Apart from a task to be performed.' The old man's eyes had demanded attention. 'I need you to listen though, so shut that mouth of yours for a moment and just listen.'

Jacob had dropped to one knee and he remembered that he'd quickly tried to pull his arm free. But the old man had dropped down too, incredibly fast and had not let go. Jacob had then rolled away forcing the old man to release his arm. The man had stood, smiling at the boy. At a crouch now, Jacob had his sharp, beloved, curved-bladed sica in his hand and then quickly had begun to stand upright, about to throw it. In the second that he'd delayed, the old man had quickly stepped forward and with his right foot had swept Jacob's legs from under him.

'Don't get up, boy,' the old man had growled.

Jacob, suffering a bruised back, grazed shoulder and hurt pride, had considered his options and realised that they were limited when he'd seen that his sica was now in the old man's right hand.

'Can we talk now?' the old man had asked mildly. 'I truly didn't come here to fight you.' Without warning, he had thrown the curved bladed knife so that it had speared a scuttling cockroach that had been close to one of the Jacob's feet. Jacob had picked up the knife, wiping the sharp blade on his leather belt.

'Not bad,' he had said, 'for an old man.'

Jacob had always mistrusted everyone. More or less everyone anyway. Death in ruined Jerusalem was frequent and lives were mostly worthless. He sighed now as he stared across the gorge and remembered looking at the old man with suspicion. He also remembered the dusty, narrow passageway between the two rows of destroyed buildings that had been empty apart from fat rats, healthy from feasting on bodies. The fat rats he remembered had scampered along the edges of the deserted and crumbling houses not yet interested in the old man and the boy.

'Here,' the old man had said calmly, 'take this.' He'd tossed another leather purse to Jacob who had caught it cleanly.

Opening the purse, Jacob had found six more silver coins. He'd whistled. 'Well now,' he'd said. 'Ten silver coins. Clever. But not much use if you plan to kill me.'

'You won't die today,' the old man had said. 'And anyway, you will never die of old age. Listen and it will be worth your while.'

Jacob had stiffened. 'What did you just say? About my old age?'

'Listen and then by all means leave if you still wish to leave.'

'No. You said something else. About my old age. What did you say?'

'Listen and be quiet.'

'Maybe I'll take more silver from you, old man. If I have a mind to.'

The old man had just nodded and crouched down indicating that the boy should sit.

'You know the caves at Qumran?'

Jacob had crouched down too and nodded but had kept looking around the street, just in case.

'The caves are many,' Jacob remembered the old man saying, 'but there is a particular cave marked as I have shown you here. This is the cave you must find in four days' time. See, boy?' The old man had pointed to a symbol he'd drawn in the sand. 'You will know it by this sign.'

Jacob remembered how his head had suddenly hurt.

'Look at what I have drawn here,' the old man had said urgently, ignoring Jacob's discomfort. 'The mark will be clear, exactly like this. Look.' Jacob had looked at the lines in the sand and then back at the old man, where he'd seen a shimmering pale green light around the man's head and shoulders.

'This cave and no other,' the old man had insisted and, looking kindly upon Jacob, had spoken softly. 'The pain will go boy. It will. But listen to me now. In four days' time, soldiers will pass by the caves. Five of them, perhaps six. They will be carrying many scrolls and papyrus writings. I have no interest in them. Neither have you. Wait at the cave and then receive what one of the passing legionaries will give you... Do you understand?'

Jacob, looking at the strange, pale green glow around the man's head and, rubbing his own, had muttered, 'Yes. I... '

'Listen to me because I have little time.'

'Little time? Why have you little time?' Jacob had glanced behind and around him, wondering if armed men or legionaries were about to spring out. The pain in his head had lessened. He had stared again at the green glow around the old man's head and shoulders.

'If nobody stops as the soldiers pass you, then you must speak out.'

'Speak out?'

'Speak out, yes. Shout. Say something. Make yourself known. Without fail. Ask for Flavius. Ask for Flavius Josephus if nobody stops. Understand?'

'Yes, Flavius Josephus. I'm not an idiot.'

'The pain, Jacob,' the old man had said, 'will pass. All things will pass.'

'What in Vulcan's armpit does that mean? And how do you know I have a pain in my head? And how by Caesar's arse do you know my name?' Jacob had rubbed his temples while asking these questions and had thought that the old man hadn't been dangerous at all, but just mad.

'The pain in your head,' the old man had said, 'is what happens when a Silver Green becomes aware.'

'A silver and a green? What is a silver and a green? A tree? The sea? Coins? Figs? Old man, you speak in riddles! I'm going. I have no idea what it is you're talking about and neither do I much care. I'm busy. Things to attend. For the money, I thank you. For your company, I spit at your feet. Farewell.'

The old man's voice had changed to one of urgency.

'Jacob wait. We need you to undertake this task.'

'There's a we? Who is this we?'

'People I work with.'

'For money?'

'Money?'

'You work with these people for money?'

'I get paid, yes, but I do my work for other reasons.'

'What reasons? My head aches, I am thirsty and, in a moment, a few bloodthirsty and very, very bored soldiers will turn that corner and skin me alive. Hopefully you too. Speak plainly and fast. Why must I do this thing that you ask? And... if I do undertake this task, what happens if nobody gives me anything up there in the hot hills? And what is it that I'm expected to receive? And, most important, what will you pay me?'

The old man had held up a hand and Jacob remembered that his pale blue eyes had been bright.

'Sit down.'

Reluctantly, Jacob had done as he'd been told.

'You will receive a package from one of the legionaries or from Flavius Josephus who will be in that party. In the package will be an artefact. A special... item. On the package will be an instruction. For you.'

'An artefact? What in the name of Saturn's nose is an artefact?'

'A special and old thing of great value. One of a kind.'

'Truly great value?'

'Yes, of unimaginable value... but you cannot sell this artefact because nobody would buy it... although someone might try and steal it from you. But you won't let that happen.'

Jacob had looked around, checking for his safety, then spat, the phlegm hitting a large fly that had settled on a cobblestone. He'd looked at the man in the eye and had sneered, 'Then, if this... artefact can't be sold, it's not a right lot of use to anyone, is it?'

The old man had ignored the comment. 'Be at the cave before the moon is high. Remember the day. Remember the cave. Remember the soldiers and remember the name - Flavius Josephus. Keep what is given to you very safe. And tell no one else of this.'

Jacob had snorted, 'So in four days, I just wander up to the hills and I find a particular cave. And then I wait patiently for who knows how long until some of the Roman army's bravest and best lads stroll by as happy as can be in the hot hills, probably singing songs to which babies might sleep?'

The old man had just looked at the boy but had said nothing.

'And then I smile sweetly and politely ask the legionaries to simply hand over a package, wait for them to bow, call me a clever Jew and pat me on my back, invite me to share their wine and bread and then let me go on my way with pleasant hopes for my future life?' Jacob had paused. 'Are you insane?'

'They will not harm you if Flavius Josephus is with them. They would not dare.'

'Old man, I am a Jew. I am Sicarii. I've told you. I'm a daggerman. I hurt people. They will not harm me? Yes, you're quite right. They will kill me!'

'They will not.'

At that moment the old man had seen something over Jacob's shoulder; he had stood, his eyes narrowing. In a second Jacob had been up too, his sica drawn, the curved blade glinting. A unit of the Praetorian Guard, distinguishable by blood red cloaks edged with gold, had been marching purposefully and straight for the old man and the boy. There'd been eight legionaries and a centurion, and they had all seemed battle hardened and grim. Mind you, Jacob thought now as he stared gloomily at the goats on the opposite ridge, all the Praetorian Guard, even the younger ones, looked battle hardened and grim. It was their job to look hard and grim.

Standing next to the old man, the boy had wondered how in the name of any god had the Praetorian Guard known that he was here? Had he been betrayed? Had someone in the marketplace said something to the authorities in the hope of a reward? Had this old man fooled him? Had he, a Sicarii warrior, a daggerman, fallen for the simplest of tricks?

Before Jacob had properly even considered answers to any of these questions, he'd turned to shout at the old man and possibly kill him, but where the old man had stood, there was now nobody.

3

Rome, Italy, 1492

The bells always rang on Sundays but, for some reason, this Sunday was quiet. Gabriella wondered why. She leapt out of the narrow bed in the tiny room high up in one of the palazzo's turrets. Grabbing her grubby clothes, she washed quickly, although it wasn't really a wash - more of a dab from almost stagnant water in a small bowl. She prayed that she would not be late to help prepare breakfast for her master, Cesare.

When she reached the kitchen doors, a pair of large, reddened and rough hands grabbed her hair. The back of her head was punched hard and her nose bled as it met the brick floor.

'Bitch child!' shouted the owner of the rough hands. The massive cook, seemingly as wide as she was tall, spoke in rough, street Italian and with low menace.

'You're late!' Yanking the girl to her feet, the cook grabbed a large butter paddle and smacked Gabriella hard on the back.

'There were no bells,' pleaded Gabriella, her Italian made worse by her gasps of pain.

'I'll give you bells. Get in there.' The cook pushed Gabriella through into the kitchen. Gabriella fell and scraped her forehead so that she now had another cut to go with the two she'd received from the same source the previous day.

Leaning over the girl, spittle falling from her fleshy lips, the massive cook smiled nastily.

'The family's father, his holiness the Pope, is to visit,' she shouted, breathing malodorous breath over the girl's face. 'That's why there were no bells. For your information, the bell ringers are being instructed by the camerlengo at the Vatican. Not that it's any business of yours, you beetle. I should crush you now, like all vermin should be crushed. You will work harder than ever before, bitch. And I am still waiting for the florin I expected to collect yesterday.'

'I told you. I have no more money,' cried the girl.

'Then find some, steal some, sell yourself for some,' bellowed the cook, the veins on her neck ready to burst.

'The Pope? The real Pope?' asked the girl desperately wanting to change the subject.

'Are you a deaf insect as well as a stupid one? Yes, the real Pope.' The cook raised a massive hand as if to hit Gabriella again. Gabriella flinched.

'Why will the Pope come here?' she asked, edging herself away.

'That's not your business, you gizzard.'

The cook looked upwards to a heaven in which she didn't really believe and crossed herself. 'Pope Alexander,' she said for the benefit of anyone overhearing, 'blessed be he.'

Gabriella ducked the slap that she knew would come, tripped once again and then ran out of reach to the sinks where there was a mountain of greasy crockery in grey water and a heap of filthy tankards to wash. She knew that the water would be tepid at best, so the task would take a long time and, if it took too long, then she would be beaten again as she had been almost every day since her arrival.

Other servants were bustling about preparing breakfast dishes and taking newly baked bread out of the ovens. That made Gabriella's mouth water. If she was lucky, later in the day she'd be given a piece of yesterday's bread and some thin vegetable broth with a few globules of fat floating in it.

Gabriella, fourteen years old, had arrived in Rome sixteen days' earlier after escaping from a stonemason in Venice who had tried to rape her. She had lived with the mason's family in a narrow house near the Ponticello dei Sospiri - the Bridge of Sighs. The stonemason had two assistants, one of whom had pulled the panting, half-naked mason away from Gabriella and had beaten him badly. The assistants had insisted that the girl go immediately to Rome with one of their friends, a middle-aged and kindly apothecary. The apothecary arrived almost on cue and the assistants disappeared into the Venetian shadows. Astonished and terrified in equal measure, Gabriella had not much option but to do as she had been told, wondering once again what would become of her.

The apothecary had taken her to where she was now working in Rome and the family's housekeeper, on his recommendation, was content to employ the girl. The apothecary had bought her a few clothes, gave her a smile along with a small bag of florins and then had taken his leave.

Gabriella had wept for the first night and for much of the second.

Then the large cook began beating her regularly and insisted on being paid money almost every other day.

As she began washing the pile of dishes, Gabriella reflected on the fact that some people hated her. Coming from Africa was more than just a disadvantage; here in Italy she was abused, humiliated and called terrible names, but she remained enormously proud of her heritage.

As she picked dead flies out of the greasy water, she thought of how good it had been growing up in her village where she had been the same as anyone else. Well, she smiled to herself, almost the same. She had been, no... she still was... the daughter of the village chief, head of the Aro peoples... and that made her a princess. She absent-mindedly straightened her hurting back and squared her aching shoulders as she knew a princess should.

Her childhood had been very happy. But she remembered how, one beautiful morning, everyone in the village, including her parents, her brothers, her uncles, aunts, friends - all had been captured by the white sailors and taken away or... had been put to death.

She could only half remember what had happened exactly, but she knew that it was the sheer horror of what had happened that stopped her remembering everything. Every day though she remembered a little more detail and it was this growing clarity - and pain - that made her clench her teeth and fists now.

She had only managed to escape with the help of a neighbouring village hunter called Jereiphia. Together the two undertook the long journey from their homeland in Niger through to the land of the Berbers, onwards to the Caliphates, to Mesopotamia, to the cold lands and then to Italy. Jereiphia had been ever watchful and she had felt safe with him. He had called her by her name, Princess Iheme, but in Venice had decided that she should be called Gabriella. Jereiphia had left her with a trusted Venetian gondolier who was paid money to care for her. The great warrior had said his farewells and travelled back to Africa where he had said he was needed. And

Gabriella's friend, her protector, her link with home was suddenly gone. After a few weeks, a stonemason, thinking her an interesting plaything, had stolen her from the gondolier for his own household.

She wiped her eyes with the back of her hands. Once the dishes had been washed and, after one of the scullery maids had set her to work plucking chickens, she was aware that she hadn't seen or heard the bullying cook in the kitchens, which was odd. Ever fearful, she timidly asked one of the pastry chefs where she was.

'Oh, you didn't hear?'

'Hear what?'

'There was a fight outside the side entrance to the kitchens just now,' said the little pastry chef, 'and one of the cooks, that fat cow of a woman, the bully, was killed. With a knife! She's dead.'

Gabriella was shocked and at the same time relieved. She felt guilty at her relief, but then considered that it was the sort of relief when something of which one was afraid is suddenly no more, like a bad dream which, when one awoke, was nothing. She was puzzled though how the fight could have happened and so quickly. The cook was enormous, very strong and had a reputation for managing herself in any confrontation.

'Was she attacked by many people then? A gang perhaps?'

'Oh no, just one man,' said the pastry chef. 'A young man.'

'One person? One person against her?'

'Well,' said the pastry chef, enjoying the drama, 'they say it was a man - tall with fair hair he was - not from round here they think. They do say that he just had a knife, according to one of the palazzo guards anyway. Apparently, it was all over in seconds! And nobody could find the man afterwards. Probably ran away. Some grudge or something. Money maybe. Me, I couldn't care less. Good riddance I say.'

Other servants had gathered round to listen to the little pastry chef, everyone enjoying both the gossip and the drama.

'Goodness knows,' went on the pastry chef proud for once to be the focus of attention, 'not one soul liked the nasty old hag.'

Turning back to her chicken plucking, Gabriella wondered who the young man had been, why he'd been there, what the argument had been about and how he'd managed to get even close to the massive cook. A favourite childhood song came into her head and subconsciously she began to hum it, as she often did when she was thinking.

Suddenly, the huge kitchen was silent. The banging and shouting, the clanking of utensils all ceased. Gabriella, unaware of the silence, carried on humming softly. A scullery maid tried to attract her attention.

'Who is singing?' called out a loud, irritable voice from across the kitchen. Gabriella immediately froze and looked round. She saw the master of the house, Cesare. Seeing that everyone else was standing, she stood up too. Her stomach turned to ice as Cesare, tall, handsome and dressed in beautiful clothes, strode over to her. He looked angry. She looked at the floor.

'You are an interesting child. Singing some strange air… Are you well-fed?'

Gabriella, still looking at her shoes, nodded. Cesare cupped a hand under chin and pulled her face up.

'You look at me when I speak…' He paused. 'You have been beaten? Who did this to you?'

Gabriella said nothing. Cesare looked down at the girl and a thought occurred to him as he stroked Gabriella's face and neck. She squirmed and bit her lower lip.

'Never mind,' he said. 'A good beating never did anyone much harm and… maybe you enjoyed it?'

The girl said nothing.

'Well, we'll see… This evening we have visitors,' Cesare said still stroking her, his hand moving downwards. 'My father, my sister and my brothers. And their wretched families. A family feast in honour of my father, the Pope. You shall serve at table. My father will find you… interesting.'

Cesare frowned. 'My father is… what's the word? Yes… disgusting.' His frown became a smile as he looked round at the very still kitchen staff each one of whom was studying shoes or toes depending on their rank.

'But,' Cesare sighed, turning back to a shaking Gabriella, 'he is my father. I shall probably kill him one day.' Cesare turned to look for the housekeeper, saw her and snapped his fingers. Running to him, the terrified woman stumbled. Cesare first gave her a kick and then some instructions.

'Take this filthy child, wash her,' he said, 'then wash her again. Dress her appropriately and make sure she understands her duties for tonight. And I mean all duties. Capito?' He didn't bother waiting for an answer but looked at Gabriella and leered. 'Yes, all duties,' he muttered under his breath to himself and in a louder voice to the housekeeper, 'Well, go on then you stupid wretch. See to it. Go!'

The housekeeper curtsied to Cesare's retreating back and awkwardly pulled and then pushed a confused Gabriella who was still holding a chicken. Cesare turned at the kitchen door looking at Gabriella again, curiosity in his eyes. He was suddenly aware that everyone was waiting for him to leave. With one sweep of his eyes across the kitchen he swore, but at whom or why nobody was quite sure. 'Miserabili puttane e bastardi,' he shouted and walked out.

Gabriella had been fed more than the usual slops. She'd been instructed in her serving duties for the evening and forced to repeat them back several times. The housekeeper had ensured that the girl was twice scrubbed from head to toe, then dried, powdered and dressed in a soft, white linen blouse, dark blue leggings and blue, flat shoes with a pale blue, suede jerkin on which was sewn the Borgia family crest.

She was now standing, early evening, in the great banqueting hall which had gold fittings, huge floor to ceiling wall mirrors and a beautiful, painted ceiling showing scenes about which Gabriella had no understanding - mostly fat men drinking wine and being fed grapes and other fruits by beautiful ladies dressed in white, flimsy dresses. On one part of the ceiling there was some kind of almost undressed, old man with a beard and a twinkle in his eye surrounded by small, chubby children skipping about. The bearded giant had a big smile on his face, garlands on his head and a huge wine jug in his hands.

Throughout the great room there were fresh bouquets of blue, yellow and white flowers along with silver bowls of glistening fruit, most of which she had never seen before. She recognised the smell of apricots though and that reminded her of times when, as a small child, she had been allowed to attend royal events. She reminded herself again that she was a princess and unconsciously straightened her back and held her head high. She was aware that, despite the laughter and gaiety, there was a sense of nervousness amongst the waiting staff and guests.

Thirty others like her, dressed similarly, were ready to ensure that all the food would be brought quickly to the long table. Gabriella had been tasked with carrying large dishes of roasted vegetables, platters of warm bread of all kinds and then, later, plates of sweetmeats and little cakes covered in sugar. The quantity of food now being brought in was vast.

She could see roasted chickens, probably she thought with a smile including those that she had herself plucked this very morning. There was polenta, pasta, tureens of soups, sauces and gravies, huge dishes of risotto and a gigantic side of beef which took four men to carry on what looked like a wooden door. Enormous rounds of cheeses were brought to the table as well as heavy jugs of ruby red wine. A gigantic boar with an apple in its mouth reminded her of some of the feasts that she had witnessed, wide-eyed, as a child.

The music from the gallery was loud and Gabriella looked up to see six men of various ages and three young women all playing a variety of instruments with seriousness and vigour as if their lives depended on it - which, thought Gabriella, they probably did. One of the musicians caught her eye and winked at her. The lamp behind his head was of green glass and seemed to create a kind of green halo round his head, Gabriella thought. She smiled at him but became serious as one of Cesare's relations walked close by, an ugly woman with a bent back, terrible skin, awful breath, stinking clothes, yellowing lips and brown teeth. She eyed Gabriella coldly with red, watery eyes, then stared with startled surprise above the girl's head.

Gabriella looked round to see what she was looking at but could see nothing unusual.

The reception room just beyond the vast banqueting hall was filling up and the chatter and hoots of laughter were fighting the music. Gabriella was pushed forward to serve small madeira cakes and antipasti bits and pieces as people waited for the Pope to arrive and dinner to be announced.

Twice she nearly fell over others' feet. She had been told to bow her head when serving and to retreat as soon as someone had taken something. Several people said cruel things to her, mostly about her colour. Then, thankfully she thought, dinner was announced by someone with a very loud voice and there was a fanfare of trumpets. People vied for position to line up on either side of the pink carpet that led from the door of the palazzo's reception area through the banqueting hall to the huge dining table.

Papal guards in blue and yellow slow marched before the Pope as he walked or, thought Gabriella, waddled down the carpet accompanied by his family, including Cesare and various dignitaries.

The Pope was fat and squat with several chins that wobbled as he walked. His pig-like eyes looked slyly left and right as he made his way along the carpet. His large hooked nose was covered in purple veins and his thick lips were slippery with saliva. He wore red and white robes with flat-heeled, maroon slippers. Gabriella could see his bejewelled fingers and various brooches made up of fabulous rubies at his throat.

She knew they were rubies, for her father had owned many. She knew very well that fake gems were often dull and lacked the sharpness of the real thing. If the gem was more of a dark red, her smiling father had once said, then it may be a garnet instead of a ruby. She thought of her father and his smile. That made her smile in turn and, once again, she unconsciously stood straighter, exactly as she'd been taught as a child.

'If it's a real ruby,' her father had once said patiently to her, 'the darker stones are worth more than the lighter ones. Check for a consistent and even colour throughout the stone.' She smiled again at the memory.

Suddenly, someone pushed her hard from behind and she nearly lost her grip of the heavy silver salver that she was holding. It was a young child, a brat, of whom there were a few running around everywhere and who seemingly could do as they pleased with impunity. This one, a boy of around five or six years' old had a balloon of mucus from his already grubby nose. The boy's tongue kept flicking at the mess. Gabriella faltered, her reverie gone. The child smirked, made to run off but, instead, turned and moved towards her with a fist raised ready to strike out or to shove a half-eaten jam-filled bun onto Gabriella's outfit. She stepped forward, raised the salver as if to throw it at the brat and the child ran off squealing. Looking up she noticed that a beautiful woman in a silver and pale grey dress was staring at her and frowning. Gabriella felt hot, uncomfortable and suddenly frightened.

Whenever the Pope saw, or was introduced to, an attractive woman or, indeed, man, he licked his thick, wet lips and smiled. For some reason, he glanced up and caught Gabriella's eye and, for a split second or two, he seemed genuinely surprised as if he recognised the girl. A fleeting look of concern crossed his face, or so she thought. Then he turned away and waddled on slowly and importantly, smiling some more at people around him.

The papal procession made its slow way forward as guests were greeted and hands or rings kissed. From time to time, the Pope had a short, whispered conversation with someone. Nobody dared make him hurry up although, after a while, Cesare none too gently touched his father's arm and steered him to the long dining table.

Eventually, everyone was at their place, but not yet sitting. The Pope said grace in a surprisingly slow, thin, reedy voice after which someone asked everyone to sit and the music began again, but quietly now. The feast was under way.

Gabriella was soon busy toing-and-froing with laden wooden boards or huge bowls, trying hard not to bump into other servants or any of the small children who were still freely running around, often throwing food at each other.

At one point, an unpleasant courtier with missing teeth and cross eyes reached out from his chair, grabbed Gabriella by the waist and brought her close. He leered at her while chewing some meat in his open, giggling mouth, but then once again she saw a sudden, surprised and, yes, fearful look in his eyes and he let her go as if burnt.

About three quarters of the way through dinner, Cesare, as master of the house, stood and everyone became quiet. The guests seemed to know that to anger Cesare was to court danger. As he spoke, nobody did anything but watch and listen or pretend to listen. But few people looked at him, wishing upon wish not to catch his gaze. He began a long speech of welcome to his father the Pope, Alexander VI.

People applauded Cesare from time to time at points during the speech when it was obviously prudent to do so. Occasionally someone would clap for that moment too long and the culprit would receive a withering look from the master of the house.

Cesare paid tribute to his friends, his family, some eminent dukes and various members of the church. He mentioned the Borgia and papal support for Aragon and Castile and the unification of Spain and even went into detail about adventures to foreign lands, signalling the virtue of new trade routes. Throughout the speech, only the Pope kept eating, mostly with his mouth constantly open, much to the barely disguised disgust of those around him.

Gabriella listened but, while her Italian was pretty good thanks to the warrior Jereiphia and the kitchen staff here in the palazzo, she couldn't follow everything. She looked around the huge table and at the various guests all listening to Cesare with genuine or, more likely, pretended interest.

She noticed Alfonso of Aragon. She knew it was him because she had overhead him talking to a group of admiring people earlier and his name had been mentioned several times. Alfonso was one of the few people looking directly at Cesare, but the beautiful woman next to him was not. She was the one who had stared at Gabriella earlier and now she was surreptitiously fiddling with a large ring on the middle finger of her left hand. There was a lit lantern behind the woman which seemed to anyone looking to make her hair glow almost orange.

Gabriella saw the woman open the ring and then tap it against the rim of the man's wine glass. Nobody else could have noticed, so deftly was it done. Cesare had just come to the end of his speech and, after yet more applause, someone else stood, acknowledged the holy father - who continued eating - and thanked Cesare for his generous hospitality. A toast was made, everyone applauded yet again, raised his or her glass and drank deeply. The chatter began once more as did the eating, the flow of wine, the music and the laughter.

Gabriella realised that she had been holding her breath since seeing the beautiful woman put something into Alfonso's glass of wine. Suddenly, without warning, the man stood clasping his throat and then staggered forward, collapsing with a great crash onto the table. Plates, cutlery, food and glasses skittered over the table and onto the floor. The spilt wine looked like a pool of blood spreading slowly over the white tablecloth.

The music stopped mid-quaver. There was a moment's hiatus before the room became a scene of absolute panic. Guests screamed and pushed back chairs which fell, guards shouted confusing orders, children - no longer so smug - cried, demanding their mothers. Old women fell to their knees and genuflected. Older men gasped, clutching their hearts or their purses.

Gabriella and the other servants didn't know what to do, so they stood still and did nothing. A few people tried to attend to the fallen Alfonso. Gabriella could see that the Pope and his party were hastily making their way out, urged on by an irate Cesare.

The Pope was still holding and trying to eat an enormous slice of crostata di frutta with bits of apple and several raspberries falling down the front of his robes. Gone was the pomp of his arrival. There were few people around him in the chaos, most of his attendants rushing elsewhere in their own panic. The Pope lost control of the fruit tart and he considered picking it up, but then someone trod on it. For a moment he looked anguished at the loss of the tart but was then pushed forwards and he had no choice but to move on.

Wheezing and holding up his robes so that he could walk more speedily, he waddled as fast as he could and was just about to pass Gabriella. At the same time, a young palazzo guard rushed in from an anteroom and collided with the Pope who staggered back and then forwards onto his knees, almost as if he was about to pray. The soldier stammered profuse apologies and helped the now winded and apoplectic Pope to his feet. Gabriella could hear more mumbled apologies and a great deal of angry and irreligious language from the Pope and his attendants who were now pushing the guard away. The Pope wiped down his hands on his robes, hoisted up his clothing again and, breathing heavily through his wet lips, moved clumsily forwards, glaring all the while at everyone in his eyeline.

The guard who had collided with the Pope immediately approached Gabriella who now froze with fear. She had done nothing wrong! Why was the guard, who seemed angry, armed and huge, coming towards her? He stood close and roughly took Gabriella's left arm.

'Take this,' he whispered urgently, pushing something metallic into her hand. 'Keep it very safe and leave this house now. Now! There will be a woman waiting for you outside. Her name is Maria and you will be safe, but you must go. Go now!' Someone shouted in the guard's direction, calling for him. He looked again at Gabriella for an instant, squeezed the arm he'd been holding and moved quickly away.

Gabriella glanced down and saw a ring in her left hand, a very plain ring of iron or some similar metal with a hexagram pattern raised on the flat surface. It looked to the girl like an ordinary seal. She tucked it inside her tunic pocket and walked slowly towards the banqueting room main door which led to the reception area. As she did so, Cesare Borgia stepped in front of her.

'Oh no, mio caro usignolo - my dear nightingale. Not so fast. The evening for you is not over. Not by any means. This... small disturbance is only a minor irritation...'

The beautiful woman, the woman whom Gabriela knew had been the poisoner, shouted across the room, 'Cesare, you are needed here now! This is your household brother, not mine!'

Cesare turned angrily to look at his sister and nodded reluctantly. He looked back at Gabriella. 'Stay here. Lucrezia, my sister, she... I will see you later. You move, you die.'

As he strode off, Gabriella, now terrified, thought quickly. She could run, but what if the guards stopped her? She could try and hide somewhere in the palazzo, but she had no idea where and anyway they would easily find her.

She shuddered. People were still milling about and there was general chaos as many guests tried to leave. As she was worrying about her fate, guards were carrying out the dead body of Alfonso of Aragon. One of these guards was the one who had given the ring to Gabriella. He frantically indicated with his eyes that she should leave, and fast. Gabriella walked quickly to the other side of the small procession of the guards who were removing the body. Just as she did so, the Pope's attendants came rushing back in, looking anxious and very concerned.

Two guards began to close the doors to the banqueting hall and others were trying to shut the palazzo's great front doors. One yelled, 'Cesare Borgia, keep everyone here! Let nobody leave. Nobody. The Pope, the holy father, has lost the Seal of Solomon!'

4

The Judean Desert, Imperial Province, Roman Empire, 79 CE

Immediately after meeting the old man, Jacob had decided that he needed to get out of Jerusalem. It was, he'd thought, just too dangerous to stay in the ruined city.

From time to time the boy helped the Bedouin by doing all kinds of work, mostly paid for in clothing and food rather than money. He liked the company of these calm people. Their calmness calmed him. And so that's where he'd gone, to a Bedouin encampment where he was known and where he felt safe, some four hours walk from the city.

Like most people in the region, the Bedouin tribes were terrified of the Sicarii, but Jacob doubted that any Bedouin knew that he was or had been in any assassination group. They had taken him, as they did most people, at face value and trust was built or broken. If broken, any trust was like sand in the wind.

Tending Bedouin goats, Jacob had tried to forget about the ragged, old man and his nonsense. Still, he had thought happily, he'd got ten silver coins that he hadn't had before and that was always a benefit no matter how odd the encounter. He'd nearly lost his treasured sica though - and had almost been caught by the ferocious Praetorian Guard. He remembered thinking that the old man had been clever, but Jacob had resolved to have vengeance. He'd been determined that the old man would suffer either at Jacob's own hands or those of other Sicarii.

As he stared out over towards Ein Gedi, Jacob remembered very well that after a day of running after sheep and goats, his back had ached. He'd shared a tent with three Bedouin elders there being little spare space in the camp. Apart from their short conversations, the elders hadn't bothered him, and he'd always been courteous to them. This evening he'd had the tent to himself while the elders had met others for their discussions and hookah pipes.

The tent had been lit by two large, honey wax candles that had smelt sweet and had reminded Jacob vaguely of childhood. He'd yawned and had decided that hunger lost out to tiredness. He'd begun to undo his belt, when he'd heard a slight noise. Turning he'd seen once again the tall, old, ragged man standing by the tent's entrance.

Jacob's knife had been in his left palm within seconds. The old man hadn't moved.

'You…! You bastard! How did you find me?'

'It's my job to find you,' the old man had said quietly, 'and the job of others like me. We watch over you. That's what we do.'

'You're mad. Again, the stupid riddles. My friends here will kill you and I will help them. We will roast you on a spit… You left me to the Praetorian Guard, you vulture. The Praetorian Guard no less! So, you didn't you get your reward money? You've come to try again?'

The old man had stepped forward a little.

Jacob had hissed. 'That's far enough. If I shout, then you will be dead in seconds old man… D'you know what the soldiers do to Jews? Do you?'

'And yet here you are,' the old man had said opening his arms wide as if embracing the tent. 'Safe and sound. And yes boy, I know very well what they do to Jews.'

'I escaped the enemy only because I can run fast.'

'I know you can run.'

Once again, Jacob had seen the pale, greenish glow around the old man's head and shoulders.

'If they'd caught me, scum, I wouldn't be here. I would be on a wooden post, naked, crucified and probably upside down with my innards being pecked away by birds. You set me up.'

'No, the Guard arrived by chance. They were not looking for you or for me. They were just there…You can put your sica down.'

'Thank you, no. Go away. I have nothing for you. You have nothing for me. I don't need… watching or whatever nonsense it is you think you do. I am amongst friends here.'

'You have always been watched… And I need to talk to you.'

Jacob had said nothing, not knowing what to do. It had been late and he'd been very tired. And alone.

He'd asked the old man, 'You know the Bedouin?'

'Yes of course I do,' the old man had replied with a shrug.

'How do I know you aren't working with the army? How do I know you're not out to catch a Sicarii daggerman?'

'You don't, but I am not.'

'How in the name of Mercury's heels do I know that though?' Jacob's head had begun to ache again.

'I need to talk to you and then you can sleep. And I shall leave.'

'The elders will be back and they will kill you.'

'I don't think that they will be back yet and, no, they won't kill me. Sit down.'

'I'll stand.'

The old man had sat on one of the highly decorated hide cushions which surrounded a low table. A woman had come in and, to Jacob's utter surprise, had smiled broadly at the old man. She'd brought two bowls of hot mutton stew along with several large pieces of flatbread which she'd put on the low table and had encouraged both the old man and Jacob to eat. Jacob's mouth had watered and he'd begun to eat greedily.

The old man had poured some camel's milk from a small jug into a clay cup and had taken a sip. He'd looked at Jacob eating fast and disgustingly. 'You remember what I told you boy?'

Jacob, still angry and confused, had nodded slightly, his mouth full.

'Repeat it then.'

Jacob had said nothing.

'Repeat it, boy.'

'I will not,' Jacob had spat, spraying the old man with food. 'The elders will be back and I shall tell them that you are their enemy.'

'The elders will not think of me as an enemy. Repeat what I told you. Talk and listen. Then I shall leave.'

Jacob had looked up at the old man and had decided to play

along. As sarcastically as he could manage with his mouth full, he'd repeated what the old man had told him almost word for word.

'And you will not fail?'

Jacob's head had still ached, but he had stared at the old man for a moment. He'd been trying to work out how to kill the old fool without disgracing himself amongst those who had been kind to him.

'Why is the top of your head green?' Jacob had asked.

The old man hadn't replied.

'Give me more money,' Jacob had said petulantly, stuffing a large piece of gravy-covered bread into his mouth.

'No. We have little time, so listen and then I shall leave. I am a Watcher. Watchers have been looking out for your safety since you were born.'

Jacob had said nothing.

'You hear me?'

'I hear you. I'm not stupid,' Jacob had mumbled, his mouth full.

'Some of your friends among the Sicarii are Watchers too. You will reach the age of thirty years and age no further. You may live for all time. Disease and poisons cannot harm you. But you can be killed... by a knife like the one that you keep fingering now, maybe a sword, an axe, a stampeding bull, a kick from a horse, a rock, a stone from a sling... a spear...'

Jacob had carried on eating.

'But not by any disease, poison, illness or age.'

Jacob, his mouth full, had finally lost his temper and once again sprayed food over the old man as he'd spoken, 'By the teeth of ancient and withered camels, what stories of sorcery and witchcraft are these?'

The old man had nodded as if expecting such a retort. 'Why is it then that the ague in the days of fever that struck down others one year ago, did not strike you?'

Jacob hadn't answered. It had been true. For some reason, while all around him in the city had been ill, he'd been fine. Had that been luck?

The old man had continued, 'And how is it that the red illness that carried off the Christians near the market three years ago did not touch you? All around you perished, but you did not.' This had been true too. He had helped a family that had the disease, a rash of some kind that ended up covering a body in sores. But he'd not been affected at all.

'How do you know that, old man?'

'And how is it that the belladonna potion that you drank in error as a small child did not harm you? The hemlock leaves and petals that you ate thinking them elderflower? The black fever that did not find you. The contagion that killed many - yet did not affect you even when others suffered. The disease of boils with breath so foul; you touched these people but were not touched by the illness.'

Jacob had stopped eating, his appetite dwindling.

'You have powers,' the old man had said, 'that you cannot possibly comprehend. No, don't interrupt again for the sake of any god and I beg of you eat with your mouth closed.'

Jacob had shut his mouth.

'You will do as I ask and collect the artefact from the hills of Qumran.'

Jacob had been worried that the elders would return at any moment and wonder why Jacob had brought a stranger into their encampment without permission, something that they would have regarded as a great insult. However, he had thought, the woman who'd brought the food had obviously known and liked the old man.

'You should leave,' Jacob had said more calmly. 'If you are found I promise you death will be your reward. They will feed you to the hyenas... Why me?'

'I told you. You are special...'

Jacob had stared at the old man and had snorted.

He'd shouted, not caring who heard him. 'Special? You play games with me? This is dung!' Jacob remembered he had stood up. 'I'm not special. I can fight with a knife. I can run fast. That's all.'

The old man had said nothing but had just looked up at the boy.

'You should leave, old man. Please. You're old and... They will harm you. I don't think you're evil. You're just stupid or drunk. These people are my friends. They have been kind to me. Save yourself, just leave. I'm not special, old man.' He'd paused for a moment. 'Why don't you collect the thing... this artefact, yourself?'

The old man had sighed. 'I cannot collect it. You must. My job and the job of all Watchers is to make sure that no harm befalls you and others like you. That's what Watchers do. I am a Watcher and mean you no harm.'

'I told you. I don't need a bodyguard. Now I will leave and we'll see what the Bedouin have to say.'

The old man had stood up. 'You shouldn't leave,' he'd said.

Jacob had taken out his sica. 'Or else, what?'

The old man had stepped forward and his left arm had shot out. In one smooth movement, he'd grabbed the boy's knife and had thrown it down pinning a scuttling lizard to the tent's carpet.

'Or else nothing,' the old man had said.

Jacob had picked up his knife. He'd shrugged. 'You did that last time. You dislike cockroaches and lizards? Not bad with a knife though old man, not bad.'

'Be respectful boy and just listen. For a short time only, then I shall leave you. There is so little time.' Something in the man's look had made Jacob shrink a little.

'My job is to protect you, to keep you safe,' the old man had said quietly. 'That is what Watchers do for Silver Greens. People like you. We have done this for as long as history itself.' The old man had paused suddenly as if listening out for something.

Jacob had still been able to see the pale green light surrounding the man's head.

The old man had noticed Jacob staring. 'All Watchers have a green aura. Yours is silver…'

'What in the name of Venus and Mars is an aura?' Jacob had asked, believing that the old man really was totally crazy or drunk. Or both.

'Sit down,' the old man had instructed.

'No, I prefer to stand.'

'An aura is a field of energy that surrounds every one of us.'

Jacob had looked at his own left arm, then the other. 'I don't have an aura,' he muttered.

'You do - and you can see mine.'

'The pale green around your head? That is your aura?'

The old man had nodded. 'We all have an aura.'

'Does an… aura hurt?'

'No. An aura is the hidden energy that each of us has. Inside.'

Jacob had been more than a little anxious about the elders returning to the tent to sleep. He had always believed that someone was an enemy until they had proved that they were a friend. And friends, in his opinion, were very scarce. Jacob had always thought that trust was a rare commodity, a luxury almost. Perhaps it was best, Jacob had considered, to keep the old man talking. Then maybe he'd leave anyway. Or the elders would escort him away. Or just kill him.

Jacob had asked, 'An aura is magic? Like alchemy?' He'd always known about Trivia, the goddess of sorcery and witchcraft. He had always known the stories about her haunting crossroads and graveyards. It had been said since his childhood that the goddess travelled never by day, only at night and the only way to tell her presence, people had always said, was by the barking of dogs. He remembered that it was then when he'd heard dogs barking.

'No, not magic. Or alchemy,' the old man had replied. 'Neither is it anything to do with Trivia. It just is. You are powerful and more powerful than most with your… condition.'

'My condition? I'm not ill! I can run and fight. I do both well. That's my condition. Nothing more.' For a moment Jacob had felt hollow.

'I don't mean that kind of power.'

'Are you unwell old man? Too much arak maybe? I'm sorry that you've come all this way to speak your riddles, but I'm sure that there is a good wife somewhere wondering where you are? Best to go back to her now. She'll look after you.'

Now, as he watched the boy on the other side of the gorge tending the goats close by the glittering waterfall, he remembered vividly walking as a very small boy through the city's lanes hand in hand with someone. His mother maybe? He couldn't remember. Whoever it had been had held his hand tightly when drunk or mad people passed by muttering to themselves or singing loud songs, their hair matted with animal grease. They were usually filthy and went about naked except for a loincloth. Sometimes without a loincloth. They were often covered in sores and wounds from beatings, or worse. Sometimes they were old soldiers with dementia and sometimes they were clerics turned mad by some horror or other. Sometimes they were religious maniacs or simply lost souls or souls who had lost everything.

'You have been chosen to perform a task,' the old man had said, 'but it's a hard task and will test you.'

'You keep saying that.'

The old man had put his head to one side as if again listening out for something.

'I do things,' Jacob had said, 'because I choose to, not

because I am told. And, again, you talk in riddles. But,' Jacob had said playing for time, 'tell me more, do.'

Still the old man had been listening out for something. All Jacob had been able to hear were the general noises outside the tent - the low wind, women talking quietly, children calling or giggling, an occasional goat bleating and dogs still barking.

'We have so little time,' the old man had said. 'Dangerous people are looking for you - and others like you. These people are killers. Don't smile. Better killers than you. The Guild is a group of men and women with money and much influence. They are everywhere in the world. If Guild people find you, they will take what they seek from you and then... death. Their auras are the colour yellow or orange. Do you know the colour orange?'

Jacob had smiled at the old man's senility and had shaken his head. The man had taken a small blood orange from his tunic pocket.

'This is an orange.' He had tossed it to Jacob.

The boy had caught it and sniffed at it. 'Even if I believe you, which I don't, what must I do then?'

'You must do what I ask.'

The man had again listened out for something. Jacob had only heard children's laughter, a woman's gentle voice, the clatter of a pot being disturbed. And dogs barking.

Then the dogs had suddenly stopped barking. Immediately the old man had stood, his face pale but his hands steady.

'We must both go now,' he had said quickly, pulling Jacob up none too gently. 'You to the east and the caves. Tonight. You must go and remember all that I have told you... and I...'

But the old man had said no more. A sudden look of pain and resignation had come over his face before he'd collapsed forward on the floor with a terrible thud. The boy had seen a large bone-handled knife in the old man's back and the green glow around the old man's head had gone as had his own headache. More importantly - much more importantly than anything else - was the fact that the tent had filled with legionaries.

5

Rome, Italy, 1492

In the confusion, Gabriella was one of the last to have squeezed through the closing doors of the palazzo.

Looking about her now, she could see that wherever she might have considered hiding, there were just too many people. It was also far too bright with the coloured glass lamps casting a flickering and festive look around the street. There were people who'd just come out of the palazzo rushing away as fast as possible, some running or hobbling along as best as their ages or outfits would allow. Carriages made off, a few even leaving behind those people whom they were meant to carry. Everywhere was busy and loud.

Gabriella knew that by standing still she would bring attention upon herself. She knew that she had to get away. But where? She was confused, frightened and unsure as to what she should do. The guard had given her the ring, apparently belonging to the Pope and clearly it was of some great value or importance given the fuss that had been made over its loss. The guard had also wanted her to leave urgently so obviously her having the ring was important. But why?

Gabriella had absolutely no idea what the ring was or why she'd been given it. What was she supposed to do now? Where was she meant to go? What would her parents have done? She quickly blanked out that course of thinking.

The street was emptying now and it was obvious that she couldn't stay where she was. She knew that at any moment she'd be spotted and caught. Where was this Maria person she was supposed to meet?

She took the ring out of her jerkin pocket and studied it for a moment then put it back and began walking away from the palazzo. As to where she was going, she had no idea.

She thought that the whole evening had been frightening in every respect. First, there was Cesare and his horrible suggestions. Then the disgusting Pope Alexander who stared and looked surprised when he saw her as did Cesare's beautiful sister and other people too. And the death, no not just the death, but the murder of a prominent duke. Gabriella shivered. The sister and the Pope had seemed afraid of her. So too had the old woman with the terrible teeth and the revolting man sitting at the table. Why? Because she was black?

She stopped musing and focused. Any minute now there would be people coming out of the palazzo looking for her and the ring. People with lit torches and swords. Very angry people. They would think nothing of dragging her away if they thought that she had something to hide. And then she'd be killed. Forget the dragging away, she thought, she'd just be killed. Nervously she patted her jerkin pocket to check that the ring was still there.

Suddenly, without any warning, a hand shot out of an alcove, grabbing Gabriella's left arm. The girl, dragged into a gap between two buildings, gasped and, with a cold shock, knew now that she'd been caught. The awful realisation hit her hard - that the result of capture would be certain death. They would find the ring and believe that she'd stolen it.

In the shadows her captor whispered slowly in Italian, 'My name is Maria. I know who you are. Your name is Gabriella and you are also a princess of the Aro peoples. You are safe. I promise that you are safe.' Gabriella was frozen in fear.

'I will not harm you,' said the woman who held Gabriella by both shoulders. As the woman stood in front of the girl, a street lantern made of pale green glass shed what seemed to Gabriella like a green glow around the woman's head. 'But I do need to talk to you. Not here. Trust me please. I am not your enemy.'

Maria could see that the girl was terrified, her whole body trembling. 'Don't be afraid,' said Maria soothingly. 'I won't hurt you. Truly.'

The woman's reassurances, no matter how earnestly spoken, made Gabriella believe even more that this tall woman in a dark grey cloak and with a kindly face was an enemy. Desperately, she tried to shake herself free, but the woman's hold was tight.

Together they moved quickly into the street, the woman pulling and Gabriella stumbling. The girl kept trying to make her escape, but she simply wasn't strong enough and Maria's grip was vice-like.

Who was this woman, Gabriella wondered? She seemed to be friendly, but what if she meant to do her some harm? What if this was a trick? Since leaving her home in Niger, she had trusted nobody except Jereiphia and the apothecary. She certainly did not trust this woman.

After about twenty minutes - minutes during which the girl thought that death would strike - the pair came to a row of houses in the Campo de' Fiori. Gabriella knew Rome only a little, but she recognised this street. She'd been here with some of the palazzo's kitchen workers on the way to meet grain dealers at the warehouses by the Tiber. Looking around in panic, she wondered if she could escape and seek some help near the warehouses. Or, better still, hide there.

Maria, still holding Gabriella tightly, looked up and down the empty street. Nobody, it seemed, had followed them. Maria smiled at the girl reassuringly and put a finger to her lips. She waited for a moment and listened carefully. Nothing. All was silent. Gabriella steeled herself to run.

A man dressed in what had once been finery but was now dirty and ripped, leapt out of a shadowy doorway. Gabriella jumped. Maria stayed stock still as if expecting him.

'Ah, my lovelies. Sweet pickings,' the man chortled throatily. He was short and wiry with a rat-like face covered in red and yellow pustules. The man stank - of what Gabriella could not tell, but it was like rotten meat. He had an agitation that reminded Gabriella of people with madness fever that she had seen several times in her village. He kept nodding his head and had a strange gleam in his eyes. But, most worryingly, he pointed a very sharp-looking, thin rapier at Gabriella.

'The ring, sweetness, the ring,' the man said, laughing. 'Give it to me now and I shall be on my way.' Gabriella did nothing and, in any case, didn't fully understand his street accent, but she did understand his intent to harm her. Maria did not let go her hold of Gabriella. The man sighed and, without warning, swiftly struck out with the thin sword. It pierced Gabriella's jerkin and she yelped.

'Next time, it'll be your heart my sweet blackamoor. I really don't care. Alive or dead makes no odds to me. The ring! I know you have it. I saw you looking at it outside the Borgia palazzo. Rich pickings thought I. Rich pickings for me. I call myself a soldier of the night. The ring now if you please - and be quick.'

Maria let Gabriella's arm go. With a speed that defied reality, the girl was astonished to see Maria grab the young man's tunic with both hands and then immediately lift him high in the air by the throat. The man, shocked and struggling for breath, dropped his rapier and began babbling, his eyes bulging. Maria let the man fall in a heap. Dazed and whimpering, he grabbed his sword and ran off into the night.

Maria turned and smiled again at Gabriella who couldn't believe what she had just witnessed. Firmly taking one of the girl's hands, Maria led Gabriella down the road arriving at a house with huge flowerpots outside. As if waiting for Maria to arrive, the front door opened to reveal a cheerful, dark-haired young man who winked at Gabriella. That did nothing to reassure her. She turned to look down the street to see if the assailant was still around, but there was no-one.

'That man,' said Gabriella, her voice shaking in fear. 'That man - he will just come back and find me.' As she spoke, there could be heard from not far away a long, sharp scream of terror that stopped abruptly. Then, silence.

'Gabriella, he will not return. You are safe,' said the cheerful young man. 'Please, come in.'

Inside the house, Maria took off her cloak and the young man gave Gabriella two blankets for she was shivering badly. The three went into a small, comfortably furnished room where Gabriella was invited to sit.

A fire was burning cheerfully in the grate and a shy boy of about eleven came in with a tray on which was warm bread, a large piece of cheese, fruit and some hot wine into which honey had been mixed. Maria urged Gabriella to eat something. She didn't need asking twice and just hoped that what she was eating hadn't been poisoned. Seeing that the other two were eating and drinking the same, she shrugged, drank the wine greedily and attacked the warm, crusty bread and cheese, both of which were delicious.

Maria began, 'Gabriella, you are safe. But we have little time and I must explain something to you, so please listen carefully.'

'Out there. The… man. The scream. What happened?'

The young man shrugged. 'He was stopped. He threatened you. We protect you. We and others like us. It is what we do.'

'But he may come back.'

'He will not come back. Think nothing of it or him. Vermin.'

'What do you mean you protect me? Why protect me?'

'That's what we do.'

Gabriella's head was spinning and these answers weren't helping.

'What do you want from me?' she asked. 'I have no money.' Gabriella, trying hard not to cry, hoped that these two wouldn't kill her for the ring. Should she just hand it over?

Maria laughed. 'We don't want any money. Or the ring,' she said as if reading the girl's mind. Jerking a thumb at the young man next to her and then pointing to herself, she tried to reassure Gabriella. 'We are called Watchers and we are many. Our job is to protect people like you - for you are special. Yes, yes, we know that sounds strange and we'll explain. But we mean you no harm. The opposite in fact.'

'People like me? Special? What do you…?

'Listen carefully to what we have to tell you and all will become clear. By the way, this is Emilio.' Emilio grinned at the girl.

'We are both Watchers,' went on Maria. 'Ours is a venerable and old society. Outside there are more Watchers and, in the palazzo, there were others. The guard who gave you the ring for example. We are wherever people like you are.' Emilio nodded and smiled reassuringly at Gabriella.

The girl ate and listened to what Maria and Emilio had to tell her. As what she was told unfolded, her eyes widened in shock, disbelief - and then in absolute terror.

6

The Judean Desert, Imperial Province, Roman Empire, 79 CE

He stared across the gorge and watched the waterfall, enjoying the sound it made as the water hit the pool far below. The water almost seemed to be falling in slow motion.

It's strange, thought Jacob now but, at the point of any danger, everything always appears to move in slow motion. He had seen the soldiers in the tent, but his immediate thought had been only for the old man at his feet.

The legionaries, in breastplates and hard leather, had moved closer towards the boy. He had been able to smell them - unfortunately - hot, sweaty, unwashed and with foul breath. One, he remembered, had been scratching an open, raw sore on his cheek. Another, the centurion, had been running a finger absent-mindedly over a deep pink scar across his nose. A third had been urinating over the old man.

Jacob had immediately gone for his sica and, within a blink of an eye, could have made sure that the urinating soldier had bitterly regretted what he'd been doing. However, the boy had seen that now all the legionaries had drawn their gladii, those short swords perfect for close combat, worn high on their right sides. The centurion had stepped closer, looking down at Jacob who had crouched to see the old man.

'Stand up, stay absolutely still, drop your knife and, when I say so, come with us,' the Roman had ordered.

'And if I don't?'

The centurion had pressed hard with a foot on the dagger's handle into the old man's back to check that the old man was dead. One of the soldiers had shouted angrily, 'It's not a question, fool!'

With his foot still pressing hard on the dagger's hilt, but still staring at Jacob, the centurion had yelled a command to his men, 'Take the boy!'

Just then, one of the women, the one who earlier had brought Jacob the food, had rushed into the tent. All the soldiers had turned to look at her. She'd screamed when she had seen the old man on the floor lying in a spreading pool of dark blood. When the soldiers had been momentarily distracted, Jacob had darted to the back of the tent where the goatskin was furled up a little to allow air to circulate. Ducking underneath, he had run, cursing the fact that he had not been wearing his sandals.

He remembered that there'd been a strong moon and he'd been able to see where he was going. As he had run south in the direction of Jerusalem, not too fast but at a steady pace, watching out for sharp stones, he'd thought about the old man. For some odd reason that had led him to think about his own family, long gone of course.

Jacob had always known that his mother and his father had fed him, educated him and, yes, he supposed, cared for him. But had they loved him? As he ran, he hadn't been able to remember if they had or not. And his sister Esther, yes, she had loved him. Hadn't she? Probably she had. Maybe she had. Maybe she hadn't. But, one day, his mother, father and Esther had just disappeared.

Running, he'd remembered that after his family had gone,

he had stayed with other people, people who'd cared for him. And he'd also remembered the day when the gang of men had followed him home. How old had he been then? Six, seven perhaps? The small, two-roomed house had been burned down. He had been the only one to escape with the help of two passing strangers and then had been recruited straight away by the Sicarii, not least for his skill with a sica even at that age, but also because he was a fast runner and had little fear of anything much. The Sicarii had carefully channelled Jacob's hatred against those who had destroyed all the people who might have loved him. It had been a hatred that had burned in his heart and the hatred hurt still.

Again, as he had run, he'd wondered about the old man. Did the old man have a family? Had there been someone expecting him home? Had the old man made sense? Not really. Had Jacob been the cause of the old man's death? Now, as he looked at and heard the waterfall, Jacob thought that the life of someone in an assassination squad had always meant death.

Twice Jacob had hidden behind huge desert boulders, waiting to see if the soldiers had followed. Seemingly they had not, but he hadn't been sure. And anyway, where could he have hidden? The desert had dunes, gullies and escarpments, but the army had resources to find whatever or whoever they wanted and usually did.

And, he'd thought, if they had found him, then that would have been the end. The Romans had never had any time for Jews and certainly not Jewish assassination squads. Jacob had been puzzled. They could have killed him at the same time as they had killed the old man. But they hadn't. Why? He had assumed that obviously they had wanted him alive, but what for? What had he done? Well, he knew what he'd done with the

Sicarii and, for that, capture would have meant instant death. So, that couldn't have been the reason. What else could they have possibly wanted from him? And how had they known that he'd been in the Bedouin camp? Had the old man led them there? Had the old man been a bounty hunter? Had that been it?

Jacob had hurried on to the destroyed city. Although he'd been exhausted when he'd got there, he had immediately felt safer. He remembered laughing out loud because he'd gone to the Bedouin camp for safety in the first place!

His headache had gone, but his throat had burned with thirst, even though he'd eaten the delicious orange that the old man had given him. He had not been able to make up his mind about the old man. Had the old idiot been telling the truth? If so, he'd wondered, should he go to the hills as he'd been asked - no, as he'd been told? In his heart of hearts Jacob had already known the answer. He'd felt that he owed the old man at least something and anyway he'd been paid ten pieces of silver.

He had needed to collect his meagre belongings. He'd also wanted to buy new sandals and some food to take with him to the hills. His feet were tough, but had been sore from the long run, so he'd found a broken fountain that still had a trickle of water dribbling from the spout. Carefully he had washed his feet and had rested for a while.

Sitting among the ruins of a city that he'd once loved, Jacob had suddenly felt very much alone. That hadn't been a new feeling of course. He'd been alone and lonely for a great part of his life.

He had known of course that for the past few years, on pain of death, Jews hadn't been allowed within what had once been the city's walls. Since the great city's destruction, most of the synagogues, Jewish houses, places of business and markets had become ruins. Jacob had always known where to find shelter in deserted buildings or shells of empty houses near to what had been Temple Mount. But, over the years, there had been fewer places to hide.

For those years he'd kept to the shadows and had been aware of the parts of the city to avoid - like the west side where the tough 10th Legion was still encamped. Thinking of tough soldiers, he had looked hard at the shadows around the broken fountain where he had sat. That constant worry about being seen or, worse, being caught, had been at the front of his mind for as long as he could remember. It had been a constant tension and he had always checked his surroundings; for him it had been as natural as breathing.

Splashing water on his hair and face, he'd gone to where he knew he could buy a gourd of good wine and a large flatbread filled with cooked vegetables. Keen not to meet more of the governor's Praetorium Guard, he had walked carefully and, as far as possible, away from prying eyes. There had been little evidence of any military and, whenever he had seen anyone, he'd darted into the darkest of shadows, his shape melting into the black.

Chewing on the flatbread and drinking the wine, Jacob had found the temple ruins and the stones under which he'd hidden his bundle of clothes and belongings. They had been stolen. That had been no surprise really, but he'd been irritated because he'd thought he'd been clever in secreting his modest hoard.

He remembered that a skinny cat, licking its fur, had stopped to stare and then had carried on licking itself. Jacob had kicked the cat away knowing about the diseases they carried. Thinking of diseases, he'd considered what the old man had said. Could it be true, he'd wondered, that disease could not harm him? It had been perfectly correct that he'd never been ill, even though contagion had ravaged the city on many occasions. And he'd never been unwell from drinking water from suspect wells or fountains when others had sometimes become very ill or had died. And the old man had called him special. He had never felt particularly special. Yes, sure, he'd always felt special when he threw his knife further than anyone else. But that had just been skill and practice. But what about that nonsense when the old man had talked about immortality and auras? As he'd finished the flatbread and wine, he'd thought about that green glow around the old man's head. Had the old man been a sorcerer maybe? A magician perhaps? An alchemist? Jacob had known that there were such people, although he'd never met one.

But, immortality? That was absolute camel dung, he'd thought in disgust. Nobody was immortal. Again, he'd thought about death and, for a moment only, he had felt hollow.

He'd found a well that he knew had drinkable water. Although, maybe, he'd thought, the water had never been drinkable at all but foul - and it hadn't affected him. More stupid thinking. He had shaken his head and drawn up a leaking bucket of water, had tasted a little, sniffed at it, shrugged and had enjoyed a long drink. He'd then poured a full bucket of water over his head. In a dark part of what had been a synagogue, he'd covered himself with some torn, ancient religious cloths that hadn't smelt too disgusting and had slept.

He had awoken to the noise of a watchman's bell marking the change of a guard somewhere or maybe the hour. It had still been night and that, Jacob had thought, was a good thing. He'd always known that dark in Jerusalem had always been safest.

He'd counted out his money. A few weeks' ago, he'd minded some sheep for the desert dwellers and had earned a few assarii. He'd also saved a couple of denarii as well as some shekels. Plus, of course, he had the silver that the old man had given him.

At a small night market, Jacob had bought a gourd of fresh water and a smaller one of good, red wine. He had added a couple of large, folded flatbreads, two handfuls of black, salted olives wrapped in leaves, an onion, some dried fruit and a small hessian bag filled with large, fresh dates. He had tried some goat's cheese at a seller's invitation and had decided to buy a modest piece of the cheese mixed with minced meat and chickpeas, all tightly wrapped in cooked cabbage leaves.

Jacob had spoken Aramaic as it was spoken locally and nobody had taken much notice of him. Most people would have thought that he'd been just another orphan, nothing more, or an urchin or a street thief. And there had always been lots of those. His blond hair had stood out though, not surprising in a land where most people were dark, so he'd bought a shemagh scarf which he'd wrapped round his head, much as the Bedouin did, hiding his hair and face as much as possible. He had added to his shopping a soft, leather shoulder bag and a decent blanket that didn't stink too much.

Lastly, he had bought a new pair of strong sandals that had fitted perfectly. He wiggled his toes now and smiled. Then he frowned as he remembered the purchase. The sandal vendor had recognised him as Sicarii. With his head close to Jacob's and under his fetid breath, the trader had murmured, 'Pay the price I ask plus two silver denarii vermin Jew, or I will call the guard.'

Before the merchant had even finished his sentence, Jacob's sica had been at the man's throat. A tiny drop of the man's blood had fallen on a pair of children's sandals.

'I will pay what you would ask a Roman to pay,' the boy had hissed, sheathing his knife and throwing the correct money on the floor. With that he had turned away to begin his long walk towards the caves of Qumran.

7

Rome, Italy, 1492

Gabriella believed very little of what she'd been told by Maria and Emilio - and understood even less. She yawned. How she longed for the warmth and happiness of home - the sun, the winds, the land, the food, the tribe, her friends and her family. That thought burst when she remembered what had happened to her family, her tribe and her home.

She was grateful of course to have been rescued from the Borgia household and of course from the terrifying man in the street with the rapier, but she couldn't understand why these two people were talking to her as if she was important. Had she been rescued or was she just someone else's prisoner?

Emilio was talking. '… And this is why you have the Ring of Solomon. It is for you to use.' She looked at the ring as it lay on the table. Just an iron ring, an unattractive lump of metal and certainly nothing special or of any value.

Maria said, 'You haven't been listening.'

'I'm sorry, I…'

Gabriella had already made up her mind that Maria and Emilio were kind, even though they were obviously crazy. She didn't think that they meant her any harm, but she was cautious. Maybe they would let her go soon and she could somehow travel back to Africa. But it was a very long way to the Aro peoples and, anyway, were there any Aro peoples left? Was she the only one?

Saddened, Gabriella sat up straight, trying to keep awake and alert. Again, she missed a part of what Emilio had been saying.

'…and so, it's our job to keep you safe,' he said. 'It's what we and others have done since you were born… it is what Watchers do.'

'How have you done that? I come from Africa. There are… were none like you where I lived. No… Watchers.'

Emilio shook his head, slightly impatiently. 'Gabriella, please listen. We need you to help us. As I've explained, we are everywhere where there is a Silver Green.'

'Help you? How?' Gabriella asked. 'What can you possibly want me to do? I know nothing.' Apart from how to be a princess, she thought. 'I am not one of these… Silver Greens,' she added.

The young boy came into the room with a tray, smiled shyly at Gabriella and put in front of her a bowl of thick vegetable soup with rice flour dumplings and some large pieces of dark bread. Greedily, for she was still hungry, she dipped the bread into the soup and ate. She also drank some wine and was now fighting to keep her eyes open. Idly, she wondered once again if she'd been poisoned.

The sky through the wide window had turned pearlescent. She guessed that it was nearly dawn and that she'd been awake for almost twenty-four hours. A distant bell tolled the hour and other bells joined in as if in echo.

Emilio was becoming impatient. 'You were listening when we spoke of Silver Greens?'

'I think so.'

'And when we spoke about Guild matters?'

Gabriella nodded hesitantly.

'The world is in danger, Gabriella. From disease.'

'Disease?' The girl's Italian wasn't bad, but it wasn't brilliant.

'Everyone on earth, apart from a few, could die from disease.'

'Everyone? What do you mean?'

Emilio tutted. 'Apart from Guild people and their chosen followers,' he said.

'The Guild,' Maria said firmly, 'seeks power. It always has. Power over the whole earth.' Gabriella wanted to say something, but Emilio held up a hand.

'Wait, please,' he said. 'The Guild has come close to dominating the world on many occasions over thousands of years. Very close, but not yet and hopefully not ever. But it's a battle.' He checked to see if the girl understood what he was saying.

Gabriella said impatiently, 'But that's impossible. Nobody rules the whole earth. There are countries, cities, villages, tribes... so many places.'

Emilio paused. 'One hundred years ago,' he said, 'The Guild created and spread a disease that killed half the people in the world. More than half. Can you imagine such a number? The epidemic was terrible - a plague that people here in Italy called The Pestilence. Elsewhere it was called The Black Death.'

Maria took over the explanation. 'The disease was said to have been spread by fleas on rats. But that wasn't the cause. The Guild and its alchemists created the infection. Invented it. To kill people. Once a person contracted the disease, there was no cure. If a diseased person touched another person - husband, wife, friend or child - then they too contracted the disease. Skin turned black, great boils grew all over the body…' Maria stopped. Maybe too much detail, she thought, but she also knew that time was pressing and that she had to get the girl to focus.

'The Guild released the virus to persuade countries to bow to their will,' went on Maria.

'I know nothing of this,' said Gabriella, frightened and shaking her head. 'We had no such disease in my country.'

'Untrue,' said Emilio sharply. 'There was disease everywhere… Asia, Africa and the great countries of Europe.'

'I… knew of no disease.' Because you are a princess, she thought.

Emilio tapped the table to regain her attention. 'The Guild's plan was to kill everyone.'

Gabriella wondered if she'd misunderstood.

'Everyone? In the world?'

Maria nodded.

'But why?'

'Because they saw and still see people in all nations as foolish and weak.' Maria sighed. 'The Guild wanted to repopulate the world with people who were exactly like Guild people. They wanted… they still want… a race of people who are in their own image. They believe only in perfection. For them perfection was, and is, strength, money, influence and power. Imagine a world with rulers like Cesare Borgia and his sister. And his father. Bullies. Murderers. Liars. Cheats. Ruthless, selfish and greedy men and women with no kindness in their hearts. There are many like this and they are everywhere.'

Gabriella understood that.

'But,' Maria said, 'The Guild didn't actually want everyone to be the same and they didn't actually want everyone to die. They needed people who would do the dirty work, all the physical labour. They wanted people who could be disposed of when their usefulness was over. Slaves. You understand slavery, I think?'

Gabriella nodded.

'They still want slaves. The Guild's plan was to keep millions of slaves across the globe who would serve only Guild needs. Easy, they thought. Build a new race and ensure that any others were slaves. Nobody in-between. Guild people at the very top and the rubbish at the very bottom.'

'But, in the end, the plan was weak. Nobody,' went on Emilio, 'was immune to the disease. The Guild's alchemists prepared an antidote to the virus, a serum, but it didn't work at all and many, many Guild people died too.' Emilio looked for a long moment at Gabriella who became uncomfortable under his gaze.

'The Guild,' he said, 'has now prepared yet another plague disease, another Black Death, far more powerful than the first. Darker than the Black Death. It's designed to spread even more quickly than the first and will kill even faster. It is contagious by touch, air or water. If people have the disease, they will die in terrible pain and agony. There is no cure apart from a secret antidote that Guild alchemists have created. This time the antidote serum works. It has been tested and we know that it works.' He paused once more. 'You understand?'

Gabriella nodded even though she didn't believe what she understood.

'When the plague is open to the air, once breathed in, death is within moments.' Emilio paused. 'It lasts in the air for only a short time though, so its range is limited. The Guild will manufacturer enough for their purposes, of that one can have no doubt.' He paused again.

'Those who breathe in the poison immediately break out in sores the pus of which spreads under the skin all over the body. The body turns black and rots. Those affected cannot breathe properly; they vomit blood and suffer extreme pain caused by the skin's decay. Then the end.' He hesitated and looked at Maria and then at Gabriella who was feeling not only tired now, but sick.

Emilio spoke more quietly. 'The Guild must do two things to gain power. They must frighten the world and force all the great nations - Spain, France, England, Holland. Yes, Italy too - and lands far across the seas including yours - all to become subject to Guild force and power.'

Emilio drained his glass of wine and poured more. 'The Guild will do this by threatening the world with the release of the plague. They will demonstrate how the plague works in some controlled areas around the world - a village, a small town... anywhere. They will make sure that leaders see what will happen. Any country totally agreeing to the rules will receive sufficient antidote to last that country for one year only. The Guild will insist that any and every nation and state must renew its annual pledge to serve. Any that refuse will receive no further antidote. The Guild will this way ensure total order and obedience. In truth, of course, the plague will respect no borders or seas and that means that any country will try its hardest, by force if necessary, to convince its neighbours to follow any Guild demands. Remember what I said though. The virus cannot stay potent in the air for long or over distances. That doesn't matter because the threat of no antidote will still force every nation into bending to whatever Guild people demand.'

Gabriella was shocked. 'Is this really true?'

Emilio nodded. 'Be of no doubt. All nations will be the source of slavery. Think of it. The Guild will build a new world in its own image. Eventually of course, with its new world, the new population will be immune from the plague because of the antidote serum and the plague will be unnecessary. Anyone who is against Guild power and instruction will be annihilated. There will be slaves of course. And… keeping people in slavery is not a difficult task.'

Gabriella gasped. 'This… this will happen in Africa too?'

'Everywhere. Africa too, yes.'

'How do you know all this?'

'It's our business to know. We… have seen what this virus can do.'

'And animals will be affected too?'

There was no answer.

Gabriella made a decision. 'I am tired,' she said firmly. 'You have been very kind, but I must leave…'

'Your task,' Emilio went on, ignoring what Gabriella had just said, 'is to destroy the plague virus.'

The girl stared at Emilio, then Maria. 'What do you mean? I can't do that! How could I do that? I have no skills in warfare or fighting. Are you mad? I apologise. Of course you are not mad, but this business is nothing to do with me. Please just let me sleep for a short while. Then I shall be on my way.'

'Gabriella, listen,' said Maria urgently. 'You cannot be harmed by poisons and illnesses. It's just something you were born with. The snake bite that you had as a small child? The black mamba? You were not hurt and suffered no ill effects. The disease spread by mosquitoes? The one that affected the neighbouring village. You had visited there and were unharmed while others were very ill. Another snake, the puff adder, which bit your bodyguard and then you. He suffered but you did not. The Devil's Weed plant, which would normally make anyone very ill, had no effect on you even though you trod on three thorns. The Guild seeks one like you so they can discover how they too can be made safe from poisons and illnesses. Then they could walk freely without fear of their own plague or any other poison. But to do that they need you.'

Gabriella couldn't really take any of this in at all.

'There is one more thing, Gabriella,' said Emilio. 'You will not die of old age. No, wait! There is something in you that will stop you becoming older than around thirty years. Thereon you will not age… but you can be killed by a sword or knife or… any instrument, but not of old age.'

Gabriella just stared at him with her mouth open.

'That's enough for now. Perhaps too much. You must sleep,' said Maria, 'and we can talk more tomorrow. There are many bedrooms here. And you will be safe I promise. Adolpho will show you to your room. You will be safe and please know that we and other Watchers will always make sure you come to no harm.'

'Sleep? Sleep! Now?' Gabriella realised that she had shouted. She stood unsteadily and, without thinking, picked up the ring. She was still unsure what might become of her. Would they do away with her in the night? Was this some kind of dream?

She turned to see the boy Adolpho standing by the door once again smiling shyly at her. She wondered if she could just run, get out of the house and go. But she was, she knew, just too tired. Perhaps she would lie down for a short while and then leave when the house was quiet.

Walking to the door, Gabriella turned, her voice shaking, 'You think I shall sleep?'

Maria stood, 'Gabriella… you will sleep and will awake refreshed.'

'Goodnight,' said the girl, 'and I thank you for your kindness.' She thought of something. 'This ring, the Ring of Solomon that you say is special and has special properties, do you believe that it will protect me?'

'No,' said Maria.

8

Qumran, Judean Hills, Imperial Province, Roman Empire, 79 CE

The night air had been freezing cold, but now the hot morning sun was heating everything except the cave's cool interior. The cave had been marked exactly as he'd been told. But, so far, there'd been no soldiers and no-one had passed this way. Jacob, totally fed up, wondered how long he should wait. He kept saying to himself that he would count to a hundred and then leave. He'd done that twenty times already.

He started wondering yet again about the old man and tried once more to make some sense of what the man had said. Not for the first time, he wished that he had someone to advise him. Or just a friend. But of those he had none.

He began to count in his head again and had reached sixteen, when, suddenly, he heard a clatter of stones, gravel being crunched underfoot and then some voices. He retreated further back into the cave and held his breath. The voices came closer and around the corner of the pathway he could see a group made up of six legionaries led by a centurion. Bringing up the rear was an elderly man dressed in a green hooded cloak and who looked to Jacob like a scholar or a cleric of some sort. The man was muttering to himself. The soldiers, ignoring the cleric, carried long baskets in each of which were great heaps of leather cylinders, scrolls and rolled papyri.

Jacob wasn't sure what to do. The chatter of the group was in a coarse, street Latin and the talk was about battle tactics and swordsmanship as well as hand-to-hand combat. There were crude comments and a great deal of laughter about a woman and a man obviously known to the soldiers. Should he just show himself? Stay hidden? The Romans might think him a thug or a Sicarius and kill him instantly, not least just to prove their skill or just for a bit of sport. If they thought that for a moment he was a Jew, they would kill him, or torture him for fun. Then kill him. On the other hand, if he didn't show himself and if he didn't try to fulfil his promise to the old man, then his word would mean nothing. He stood up, took a deep breath and then, making himself look as pathetic as possible, walked out of the cave in front of the soldiers, his hands clearly visible. He tried to put on a poor, piteous look, smiled cautiously at the centurion and bowed his head.

'Who are you?' shouted the centurion in coarse Latin, as the small procession halted in its tracks, all conversation coming to a sudden stop. The elderly man continued to mumble, but more quietly. The centurion, obviously enormously irritated by everything, carried on shouting, but now in Jacob's face, 'Stench of a Jew's latrine, who are you?'

The scholarly-looking, older man stopped murmuring to himself and stared at Jacob. The sun was behind the cleric and lit his hood creating a soft glow of pale green.

'I was asked to receive something from one of you,' said Jacob as bravely, loudly and politely as he could, using the same coarse Latin that the soldiers used.

Three of the soldiers had eagerly drawn their swords. One of them laughed and suggested, 'Maybe a cut to the neck?'

'You mean to rob us boy?' sneered another soldier as he emptied his nose at the boy's feet. The centurion gave the soldiers a look and they stopped laughing.

'I mean no harm I assure you,' said Jacob.

'Mean no harm? What harm could you do, camel piss? Anyway, receive what?' The centurion looked curiously at Jacob as he scratched a large scab on his cheek.

'What I say,' said Jacob much more bravely than he felt. He was worried for his safety because the soldiers obviously outnumbered him. His worry was verging on terror given that they might guess that he was a daggerman. He knew very well that he couldn't run fast on the narrow ledge. He also thought now with a flash of panic and cold fear that perhaps there was nothing at all for him to collect.

'Boy,' said the centurion moving forward menacingly, 'are you Sicarii? Are you a daggerman? I see you have a prized sica. You know what we do with daggermen, boy?'

'I am not - and I curse the Sicarii with all my heart,' said Jacob spitting on the floor, careful not to hit the centurion's legs or feet. The boy looked the centurion straight in the eye, trying to sound as common and innocent as any Jerusalem street urchin although, thought Jacob, there was precious little innocence in Jerusalem.

'If I was with the cursed Sicarii,' he snarled, 'then may any god or goddess rot the world's teeth. And mine. And my family's teeth.' Jacob realised as he spoke that he was talking nonsense. Desperately and with mock indignation, he added, 'If I was a daggerman, I wouldn't be here would I? I'd be with my brethren, wouldn't I? Anyway, all Sicarii died at Masada long ago... Didn't they? Or so I heard.'

Jacob realised that he'd probably said too much. Stupid! Quickly, he added, 'And this knife, why - I stole it from a very dead, bastard Sicarius. The only good one is a dead one, eh?'

Jacob tried to spit on the floor again in a manly way, but this time only succeeded in dribbling down his chin.

'Are you a Jew?' asked the centurion slowly and suspiciously.

'I hate the Jews, centurion,' said Jacob as stoutly as he could. 'They deserve death. Like the Sicarii. Death to them all.'

The centurion looked hard at Jacob and then the cleric coughed. The centurion turned his gaze from the boy to the cleric and, looking back at Jacob, shrugged. One of the legionaries sniggered.

'Well,' the centurion said now scratching his bottom, 'we must go onwards and you are in our way.'

'Please...' said Jacob.

'Boy, remove yourself,' said the centurion pompously. 'Go. Move aside. Or die. I don't much care which.' Waving in the general direction of the cleric in the green cloak, he said grudgingly, 'We must help this... cleric. He has paid us well. And you must get out of our way unless you wish to be flung over the edge and hope that either you can fly or that the gods will save you.'

'I am supposed to collect something from one of you.'

Jacob could see the soldiers yawning and shifting. One was chewing on a piece of dried meat. Another was picking something from between his yellow teeth. Yet one more soldier was clearly relishing the idea of some sport.

The centurion glared at Jacob. 'What something?'

'I don't know,' whined Jacob trying desperately hard to sound like a poor idiot. He realised that the centurion and the legionaries were probably as tired and thirsty as he was and instinctively knew that he had little time before their patience was fully exhausted. Which must be around now, he thought and stepped back trying to keep all the soldiers in sight. He glanced towards the old man who was relieving himself near the cave.

The centurion glared at Jacob pointing his sword in Jacob's direction. 'So, boy, for the last time of asking, will you get out of our way? Or do we cut you?' Jacob, feeling foolish, angry and frustrated in equal measure, stepped to one side. As the soldiers marched on with their baskets and bundles of documents, Jacob tried once more, now affecting the tearful approach.

'Centurion. Stop. Please,' he pretended to sob, quite convincingly he thought. 'I beg of you. I am sorry to delay the best of Caesar's army, but I am to ask for Flavius Josephus. Is one of you he? Please, I beg of you, is one of you he?' There was genuine desperation in his voice and he prayed that this was matched by as hopeless a face as he could manage. He had to do something to ensure that the old man's death hadn't been in vain and, anyway, he wanted the artefact, whatever it was, to sell. If there was one.

The centurion, already leading his troop off down the narrow path with a sheer drop on one side to the valley's floor and the caves on the other, halted again and turned. 'These things,' he shouted, pushing one of the soldiers out of the way and gesturing to the full baskets, 'they belong to the man you call Flavius Josephus. But he is dead, boy... and... who told you about Flavius Josephus?'

The scholarly-looking cleric walked faster to be next to Jacob and said to the centurion in a loud, firm voice that seemed to belong to one much younger, 'Say nothing more captain. You are not paid to say anything. And certainly not to vermin like this boy... We will continue.' He spoke in Mishnaic Hebrew which the centurion seemed to understand as did Jacob. The cleric walked on but hesitated. Turning, he looked back at Jacob and said in a loud voice that could be heard by the soldiers, 'You, vermin, Flavius Josephus would have been with us but, as you have been told, he is dead. Murdered. Now, go. There is nothing here for you. Go back.'

The boy could do nothing more than look askance as the group walked on in the heat, the soldiers whistling or arguing about something or other. The cleric followed them, stumbling over the uneven stony ground and, once again, began mumbling.

Jacob stared after them, stamped a foot in frustration and swore under his breath. Should he run after the cleric and remonstrate with him? But to what end? Should he insist on asking for answers? Again, to what end? Just to be killed? Jacob was close to real tears now, of frustration, thirst and tiredness - and because he had nowhere to go. The Bedouin? No. They might not welcome him after the incident with the old, ragged man and word always got round quickly in the desert. The city then? There was nothing much for him there either and, besides, it was a ruin. The Sicarii? Not many of them were left and, truth be told, he'd had enough of being in an assassination squad. For seven years, he'd only known delivering damage and death. He didn't want that now. So, should he run after the soldiers and try again to get some information? Pointless.

Feeling sick at heart and defeated, Jacob walked back to the cave to fetch his blanket and his empty water gourd. He scuffed the gravel and swore loudly again. He knew that he had let the old man down. Well, he thought, sod it, sod him and sod the army. And sod Flavius sodding Josephus and any sodding artefact. He picked up the blanket and saw underneath it a long thin cylindrical package wrapped in brushed hide and tied with blue cord. On the hide were some markings or drawings. Whatever it was, the package wasn't his.

Excited now and, knowing that the mumbling, scholarly man must have put the package there deliberately, Jacob picked it up. It was surprisingly heavy and slightly longer than his outstretched arm. On the hide, apart from the strange lines and designs, there was one word: Dīs.

He looked around just to make sure he was alone.

Who in the name of Caesar's armpit was Dīs? He knew no Dīs and he certainly wasn't Dīs. He sat down in the cave wondering what to do next and then, thinking that perhaps the soldiers might return, he decided to go back towards what had been the city, not least because he didn't want to spend another night freezing his bones in a cave. He felt that he'd be safer in the ruins of a city that he still loosely called home.

9

Rome, Italy, 1492

For a brief moment Gabriella couldn't remember where she was. She blinked, feeling a warm breeze from the open, wooden shutters through which sunlight streamed. Refreshed, she sat up, stretched and yawned.

Maria, arranging some clothes, turned and smiled. 'Good morning. I have some fresh clothes for you. It's late and you've slept well. Get up and eat something… we have much to do… aha, I see you're wearing the ring.'

Gabriella glanced at the dull metal on her middle finger of her right hand. She looked up at Maria and any mistrust of the woman seemed to have faded.

'I thought that it was the safest place,' Gabriella said. 'But,' she smiled, 'you told me that the ring gives power to the person wearing it. The right person you said. The person who should wear it.' She laughed. 'That's not me. I don't have dominion over the winds, animals, the earth, water or… demons. Or whatever else you said that I would have if I wore the ring.'

'So, you were listening!'

'I don't remember everything you said.'

'No matter.'

'And I don't feel special,' called Gabriella as she watched Maria leave the room. As the door began to close, she called out, 'And I don't think that I can summon otherworldly spirits and make them do my bidding!' She chuckled to herself and was about to get up. She tried to remember what else Maria and Emilio had said.

The heavy bedroom door shut softly. Before Gabriella had any time to say or do anything else, it immediately flew open again, so violently that the hinges snapped and the door fell forwards with a crash. The light through the shutters caught the dust which looked like small, bright specks of gold dancing in the air.

The deep-throated roar was sudden, deafening and terrible. Gabriella could feel the bed reverberate and, terrifyingly, she could hear the snorting of an animal or some kind of beast that was just outside the room. Its tread made the floorboards shake.

She knew with icy dread and total fear that whatever it was would be in the room at any moment. And then it was. The creature was colossal and looked like a man, but a man the like and size of which the girl had never seen before. It had angry, inflamed eyes pushed back deep into their sockets and in one bony claw it held the remains of a human head. Gaunt to the point of emaciation, the monster's desiccated skin was taut over its bones. Its complexion was the colour of ash, its lips blubbery and bloody.

The monster, now in the room and crouching, was breathing heavily through its gory mouth. It turned its hairless head towards the girl who was shaking in terror. The creature fixed its bloodshot eyes on Gabriella and then, staring at her, slowly and with great relish gnawed the head it held. Gabriella couldn't scream or move. She wasn't aware that she was breathing in short, sharp breaths or that she'd wet herself.

The creature's drooling lips parted in a kind of smile. Its

hands and feet were scaly and almost claw-like. The smell of rotting meat was awful. The creature moved forwards towards the bed, the remains of the head it was eating falling from its hands. It had found better things to eat.

Gabriella suddenly found her voice and screamed. And screamed. The creature lurched forward making guttural sounds. Green slime was coming out of its nose and pink drool was slipping from its open mouth. Gabriella rubbed her hands together in shock and cried out loud, 'No, no, stop, stop. Stop!'

The last word was shouted with force at the creature whose claws were about to touch her. Its head tilted slightly as if it was examining which juicy morsel of Gabriella's head it would eat first. She could smell its noxious breath and she saw the rows of blade-like teeth. She shrieked, 'Stop,' once again and rubbed her hands together feverishly.

As she rubbed, she felt the large ring on her right hand and rubbed that too making her fingers bleed. Suddenly her ears popped and there was the fresh smell of vanilla in the room. The creature instantly disappeared along with its disgusting smell. There was no evidence of the creature ever having been in the room at all, apart from the damaged door. Gabriella hugged herself and started crying, rocking herself backwards and forwards on the bed. Maria came in and surveyed the scene.

She smiled at Gabriella and said, 'Can't raise and manage demons eh?'

Later, after much reassurance and a great deal of washing, the still terrified girl sat down in the kitchen to drink some warmed goats' milk and eat a hunk of bread with honey. Maria looked at her.

'That wasn't real, Gabriella. It was a figment of your worst nightmare. It was a test. Our test. The ring's test. In future it could be someone else's nightmare forced upon you. You must be careful. The Guild can interfere and influence. They can make you believe the worst. Untrue things may seem true. What isn't there seems to be there. What should be there... is not. With the ring, you can fight and protect, but it must be used well. Used badly and it will turn against you and your friends.' She smiled again.

'Imagination,' Maria said still smiling, 'is strange and we can all be frightened of simple things - a small sound, a shadow, a look, a shape, a face, a dream, a smell, an animal, a person, someone or something from our past... You will manage such things as in life we all must. But the ring can make such ordinary things terrifying; it can pick up terrors and make them real - not only in your head. It acts for you, but you must control its power.'

'But could that... thing have hurt me?'

'It depends. In many ways yes, because the imagined terror can become real according to the rules of Solomon. In other ways, no... if you use the ring well. The Pope, for example, wanted the ring for power and greed.

'Could the ring have given him power?'

Maria shrugged. 'He has power, doesn't he? So, who or what gave him that?'

Gabriella nodded. 'Today I shall leave for Africa,' she said bluntly and with conviction.

Gabriella began to see a pale green light behind Maria's head which gradually increased in strength. Her own head suddenly hurt with a pain that she'd never experienced.

Maria smiled. 'The pain will go. All things will pass. What you see is my aura. All Watchers have green auras. Guild people have yellow or orange, mostly orange.'

Gabriella knew the words yellow and orange.

Maria asked, 'Would you like an orange now?' She took one from a bowl and rolled it across to the girl.

Gabriella asked, 'Why did Pope Alexander have the ring?'

'Stolen from a monk in Spain who had tried to hide it so that it could do no harm. The good monk was a Watcher. He is no longer with us.' Maria paused.

'The ring - the seal - has been on few fingers,' she went on. 'It was buried long, long ago in a cave very far away from here. Only a few knew of its whereabouts. One who did know decided to take it from the cave. Watchers followed it to Constantinople where it was delivered to a merchant who sold the ring to the sultan.' Maria grimaced.

'The sultan recognised the ring for what it was and immediately had the merchant beheaded. The sultan then began to use the ring for the good of his people to start with, but he became greedy and used it unwisely and selfishly. He died a most terrible death. After that, well, the ring was sold by one of the sultan's wives to the brave Spanish monk. He had been given money by Watchers to buy it. Cesare, the Pope's son, who has fingers that reach many countries, arranged for the seal to be stolen from the Spanish monastery in Madrid.' Maria paused and looked sad.

'Did you know the monk?'

'I did. A... good man. His secret was betrayed.' Maria breathed in deeply. 'Watchers have followed the seal for thousands of years… Cesare knew what the ring was - as did his father.'

'Did you do… something to the cook who used to beat me at the palazzo?'

Maria looked puzzled. 'No,' she said. 'What cook?'

Gabriella wondered if Maria was telling the truth but there was, she thought, no reason to lie.

She looked at the ring again. 'How does the ring work?'

'I explained that to you last night!' She softened her tone, 'But you will discover. Only the wearer can really discover and understand.'

'But… I'm the only person who can use it?'

'No. Others could use it if they take it from you, but only if they truly believe or if they are a Silver Green.'

Gabriella smiled. 'I am a princess and am really not what you call a Silver Green. I'm going to leave for Africa today. Maybe you should keep the ring. Perhaps you could lend me a little money? I will repay you, once I…'

But, she thought, how could she repay anyone? She had no money and her parents were no longer… where they should have been.

Maria put a hand on Gabriella's shoulder. 'It is said that once upon a time, a demon and, yes, they do exist, a demon called Asmodeus, stole the ring and ruled in Solomon's place for forty days while the great king was away. When Solomon returned and found the ring gone, he was terribly upset and grieved at its loss. The demon, worried that he might be discovered, threw the ring into the sea, where it was swallowed by a fish, caught by a fisherman and then served up to Solomon who found the ring again inside the fish.'

'Why are you telling me this?'

Maria laughed. 'To amuse you. And because maybe it's true.' She looked serious. 'Look after the ring please. It would not be helpful if it was dropped into the sea.'

'But I will leave for Africa today…'

'Gabriella, you will not leave for Africa. Where would you go even if you did travel there? I fear that the Aro peoples…' Maria stopped as she saw tears in the girl's eyes. 'One day yes, Gabriella, you will go back, but not this day.'

Gabriella stood up, determined to leave.

'Please listen,' said Maria. 'You cannot be harmed by disease or poison. Guild plague or any plague cannot harm you. This is one of the reasons we need you.'

'I don't understand what you mean. Of course I can be harmed. I have been harmed. Thank you for your hospitality. I will leave now. You've been very kind, but I can't help you. Give this ring to someone else,' said Gabriella slipping the ring from her finger.

They both heard the front door open and close. Emilio came in looking worried and bleak. He went straight over to Maria and held her shoulders.

'We have to move fast,' he said. 'The Silver Green must begin today. The threat is getting worse and we are to hurry. Have you told her yet?'

Maria shook her head.

'Well, we must tell her now.'

'But she hasn't had time to be properly trained and she knows so little about what to do.'

'They say that's a risk we must take.'

'But...'

'No, Maria.'

Gabriella, ignored, was irritated. 'I am here, you know,' she said.

Emilio turned and smiled wanly. He walked over to the girl and took one of her hands.

'Mi dispiace molto. Mie scuse.'

'I'm leaving now,' said Gabriella.

'No, please. Wait,' said Emilio softly. He looked into Gabriella's eyes. 'We need you to destroy the plague virus.'

'Very funny. How do you think I'm going to do that exactly?' The girl wondered again if these people were crazy. Harmless, but crazy. 'I can't do things like that. I told you. You can see. I'm not a warrior. I'm fourteen. I'm not a soldier!'

Emilio pointed at the ring on the table. 'The ring makes you a soldier.'

'I don't want the ring,' said Gabriella quietly, 'and I don't want to be a soldier. I am a princess of the Aro peoples and I will return to my village.'

Emilio frowned. 'You are a Silver Green and we need your help,' he said simply.

Maria added, 'The plague virus will infect everyone. Everywhere. Except for whoever has the antidote. But you are a Silver Green and cannot be affected. And you have the ring.

We need your help!'

'But if any of this is true,' said Gabriella sitting down, 'there must be other… Silver Greens who could help you. Older ones. More… accomplished ones.'

'But you have more abilities than most Silver Greens.'

'Oh, really?'

'Yes really.'

'Like what?'

Emilio was becoming impatient. 'I'm sorry but we're wasting time! We must act.'

'You're frightening me,' said the girl standing again and making for the door. 'I told you, I really want to leave. Please let me go. I have done nothing to hurt you.'

'Alright. Help us a little then.'

'What does that mean?'

'Help us a little and then, if you still feel unhappy, leave.'

'You want me to do something in Rome? Was the virus invented here? In Rome?'

'No,' said Maria, 'near a land called Tanah Melayu. An island called Singapura. Very far from here.'

'A day's ride?'

Emilio laughed but there was no humour in his laugh. 'No. Months by sea. The island suits the purpose - a long way from prying eyes and on the island there are raw materials as well as eastern alchemists… and slaves.'

'Slaves?'

'Yes, slaves. For…'

Maria quickly interrupted Emilio and gave him a hard look. 'The antidote is made there too,' she added. There was silence for a moment or two. Maria looked hard at the girl.

Emilio said quietly, 'Help us please, just a little.'

The girl was crying. 'I want to go home,' she said in a quiet voice.

'Gabriella,' said Maria after a pause during which they heard noises from elsewhere in the house. 'I know that your village was destroyed and that… you lost your family… We know this. Jereiphia, who helped you cross continents, is a Watcher. One of us. The apothecary too. And the two people who saved you in Venice. We mean you no harm.'

Now Gabriella was openly weeping. 'Gabriella,' Maria said gently, 'the people who did what happened to your family, your friends, your village - they were Guild people or paid for by Guild people. The Guild owns the slave trade. The Guild trades in slaves. People like… your people.'

Gabriella looked up and stared at Maria. She tried to speak, but nothing came out. Maria went to the girl and put an arm around her shoulders.

Gabriella couldn't put into words what she felt. She thought about her family and asked, 'Is this really true?'

'I promise you on my life and Emilio's that it is. The Guild has been trading slaves for years. Many, many years."

'What will happen to me?' Gabriella asked Maria.

Maria said nothing and seemingly didn't need to. For some reason that she couldn't properly understand, Gabriella felt stronger. She felt that, if that's what The Guild did and had done, then maybe she could help avenge her family and others. So, Princess Iheme of the Aro peoples of Niger straightened her shoulders, walked head held high to the table and put on the Ring of Solomon.

She nodded towards Maria. 'And where must I go now?'

There was a pause and then Maria said, 'Back to the palazzo of Cesare Borgia.'

10

The Judean Desert, Imperial Province, Roman Empire, 79 CE

Jacob, tired and hungry, had climbed down from the hills of Qumran and was pondering what to do next. His plan had been to go back to what had once been Jerusalem, but now he wasn't so sure. He hadn't opened the package and he hadn't rested since he'd left the cave.

Given what he knew about the risks, he wasn't sure now how smart it was to hide in the ruined city. And, even if he did hide there, where would be a safe place? And even if he found a safe place, what then? Safety wasn't something for which the ruined city was now known. Most of the places he thought safe probably weren't. Normally he would sleep wherever the assassination squads had told him was safe or wherever he knew there was only a remote chance of anyone discovering him. Should he perhaps travel north towards Syria? Or join the Bedouin in the deserts to the south? He knew that there were some who would take him in to help with the sheep or goats, never asking him questions. Not for the first time he thought that being part of the Bedouin might be a good life.

Wishing yet again that he had someone to talk to and discuss his quandary, Jacob rested in the meagre shade that a few large juniper trees offered against the dry and pounding heat. He looked at the package and turned it over and over in his hands. Whatever was inside seemed hard and solid. Now was as good a moment as any to open it he thought and again wondered why the old man had been so concerned that he, Jacob, should receive this parcel and deliver it somewhere.

He started to undo the blue twine. As he did so, there was a slight noise nearby. Swiftly and all in one movement, Jacob was on his feet, his beloved sica in his right hand. A snake? A goat? A person? There was nothing and nobody there. But what had made that noise? There were desert foxes, but they rarely made any noise particularly during the day. Maybe a wild boar? The back of Jacob's neck tingled and he shivered. Someone was watching him.

'Good afternoon, young soldier,' said a voice from high above. Jacob looked up and, shading his eyes with his left hand, could see a man sitting in the tree way above his head.

Jacob's immediate thought was that this was strange because, ever observant, he had looked carefully around and above him before he had sat under one of the trees. He had seen nothing untoward. There had certainly been nobody in the branches. Or so he'd thought.

'What are you?' asked Jacob in Aramaic holding his knife tight.

'That's not very friendly is it, when I have food and water and you have none? When I am up this tree and have my bow and sharp arrows and you are down there with but a silly, small knife. Speak Latin.'

'I said, what are you?' asked Jacob again, this time in Latin and with as much steel in his voice as he could manage. The desert was known for brigands and thieves who regularly pounced on travellers, killing them and stripping them of everything.

'My name is of no consequence but, since you ask, you may call me Yehuda. I am not here to harm you. I was in the tree before you arrived though, so really it's me who should be rather cross that you disturbed my peace and quiet.'

'I did not see you.'

'I know. I am a master of disguise and can blend in anywhere. Even if you had looked more carefully, you would have seen a tree, not a man in a tree or a tree with a man in it.'

'Then I bid you good day, master Yehuda. I shall be on my way,' said Jacob as politely as possible, having no wish to spend any time with someone who might at any moment let loose a sharp arrow. He sheathed his knife, picked up the parcel, his blanket, his leather bag and, hoping that he was not about to be shot with an arrow in the back, began to walk off.

'Wait boy! Hold on. What do you have there?' called out the young man who now sat on a branch, holding his bow.

'It is of no concern of yours,' called back Jacob who just wanted to run. 'I will be on my way. I wish you safe travels.' His stomach churned and he felt a chill of fear run to his guts as he wondered when the arrow would come and how much it might hurt. He pictured himself in agony, writhing on the ground. The heat of the day and the cold in his stomach fought each other.

'Hold on, I said! Wait. Stay there boy,' commanded the man. Jacob, turning again, could see the man now had an arrow in his bow. Jacob stopped doing anything. He froze and put his hands in the air, one holding the package and the other with no knife.

'My knife is in my belt. I wish you no harm,' Jacob called out. I have no gold. A few silver coins,' he called out. 'Nothing else. Take the money.'

'Stand there and don't move.'

'I tell you - I have nothing worth stealing!'

Jacob felt sick and knew that he was about to die, but he would not die without a fight.

'What's in that package?'

To present less of a target, Jacob slowly turned sideways. 'It's… for someone else… I am but a messenger, a courier. I was told to collect it and keep it safe and I will do just that.' He pictured in his mind's eye smoothly taking his knife and throwing it at the stranger - all in one continuous movement. He'd done it many times before and hadn't missed yet.

'Well, master messenger, let us see then what it is that you have collected.'

'You shall not have it. This is not for you.'

'I understand. Well now, you have a simple choice. An arrow in your heart. Or in your back of course. You may decide. Or you could just unwrap the parcel and let me see what it is you have. And, by the way, I can shoot an arrow much faster than you can take out and throw your sica.'

The man was speaking in an easy, calm voice as if discussing the weather and he smiled as he said, 'But let's get on with it, shall we? I can see Roman horses beyond that wadi. I believe that the soldiers will deal with us both very poorly if we are found. Me because I am running from all things Roman and you… well I don't know, but I suspect that you are Sicarii and they're always running from something.'

Jacob looked off into the distance. He too saw the horses.

Jacob thought that his life was going from bad to worse. While he could see some horses, most were hidden behind dust clouds, so he couldn't tell how many Romans were approaching. He looked back at the man who he was astonished to see was no longer in the tree but was now standing a few pedes from Jacob pointing his bow and arrow straight at the boy. Jacob looked down at the parcel and began to undo the blue twine.

'Stop,' said the man called Yehuda. 'Can you read?'

Jacob stopped undoing the twine and nodded.

'Then what is the word written there?'

'It says Dīs and there's a diagram,' said Jacob.

He started again to undo the twine's knot.

'Stop,' said the man again, but now more urgently and with some concern in his voice. Jacob could hear the horses getting closer; he was either going to die from an arrow or a hundred hooves.

'Dīs is short for Dīs Pater. Dīs Pater is another name for Pluto and Pluto is one of the gods. The god of death. Ruler of the underworld,' said Yehuda. 'Brother of Neptune and Jupiter. Husband of Persephone. What you have there is a map...'

Jacob could hear the horses getting louder. There must be hundreds of them, he thought. He was about to run in the opposite direction from the cavalry, but to where he had no idea. There was nowhere to hide. Nowhere.

'But this can wait,' shouted Yehuda. 'The cavalry cannot! Follow me boy if you value your life.' The man turned quickly, picked up his own bag, slung his bow over his shoulder and ran.

Jacob quickly grabbed his own belongings and, panicking, ran after Yehuda. He wondered again where they could hide from experienced horsemen, who even now must be able to see the two figures running towards an outcrop of rock. This lot could be Praetorian Guard, considered Jacob as he ran and he well knew how ferocious they were. Yehuda stopped suddenly and looked at the ground, then shouted, 'That hole between the two rocks. Down there!'

'Are you enormously stupid?' yelled Jacob.

'Down there,' repeated Yehuda. 'We'll be safe down there.'

All Jacob could see was a dark gap between two huge rocks. If they went down the narrow hole, he thought, they would not get out. And, also, the drop might kill them.

Jacob realised that they had little choice. He glanced up and could see the decurion, the cavalry leader, ahead of his men - maybe forty or so horses in a line. Were they chasing him? Or this bowman? Or someone else? He thought no more about it because now he had to follow Yehuda who had just jumped down the hole.

11

Rome, Italy, 1492

It had been raining and the Via Piazzola was glistening in the occasional moonlight. No longer were there any lit lanterns or torches outside the great Borgia palazzo. When the moon peaked out from behind clouds, the faint light gave the street and the white marble of the palazzo an eerie glow. The windows were dark and there was no sound from within - a big change from the bright lights and party atmosphere of the Pope's recent visit.

Two armed sentries stood, bored and yawning by the huge front entrance out of which not long ago Gabriella had fled. Either side of the big front doors were huge, dark marble statues of men carrying spears, shields and swords. On the doors were strong iron bars ensuring that entry would be impossible without a small army. Gabriella didn't have a small army. Maria and Emilio were with her though. Each of the three were dressed in dark clothing and, as they crept along, made no sound.

The shadows around the palazzo were black and the now limp flags, so bright in a variety of colours during the papal visit, were now just shades of grey.

Gabriella now knew that, not only had she to gain entry to the Borgia palazzo, but she also had to find the chamber in which the deadly plague virus was stored. And then somehow she had to destroy it. She shrugged at the sheer enormity and stupidity of all of this. Again, she considered that she had no clue as to how she was going to achieve anything, ring or no stupid ring, special powers or not, whatever they may, or may not, be. But, if Guild people really had been destroying her people and her family, then she knew that in her heart she had a duty to fight back.

On the other hand, she thought, she was a princess. She wasn't a warrior. She was a king's daughter. That was all and that was enough. She was a monarch in waiting, not someone about to damage a powerful and dangerous organisation. But she knew that a king's daughter had duties and responsibilities. But, princesses, she thought, didn't save worlds. Well, maybe in stories they did, but this wasn't a story. She suddenly wished that she had kept to her idea of going back to Africa.

The three figures crouched down behind a wall on the other side of the street facing the large palazzo doors.

A booming clock close by chimed three. People like her, thought Gabriella, should be asleep. Suddenly the two soldiers outside the doors stiffened to attention as a tall, cloaked figure approached. The figure raised his hat and said something to one of the soldiers who nodded and took a large key from his tunic. The soldier and the tall man walked away briskly from the front of the building to a narrow passage adjacent to it and disappeared into the shadows.

Almost immediately, a group of well-armed men appeared at the front of the palazzo. Commands were shouted and some of the men went one way and others another. Those who remained stayed at the front.

'Guild men,' whispered Emilio.

Maria nodded. Then she whispered to Gabriella, 'Remember all that you've been told. Solange will help you in. She is old, but don't be fooled. She will see your silver aura. Only Silver

Greens have a silver aura. Don't worry. We will be here and will protect the front - and you. Remember, the virus can never harm you.'

Gabriella nodded although she had no clue what Maria meant and didn't believe it anyway. But, she reminded herself, if what Maria had said about slavery was true, then she had a duty. The Guild was her enemy.

Taking a deep breath and copying the other two, she pulled up her soft, black scarf over her mouth and nose.

Emilio immediately stood and threw a lit cannister towards the front of the palazzo and, as the cannister burst, thick, dark, acrid smoke streamed out causing the armed men to gasp and wheeze. Shouts could be heard as more men arrived. Emilio threw another lit cannister which exploded with a crack and a flash. More smoke. He looked down at Gabriella, but she wasn't there.

As soon as the initial smoke from the first cannister had appeared, Gabriella, as instructed, had sprinted towards the narrow passageway down which the soldier and the tall man had gone moments ago. She didn't know this part of the palazzo. Before she had been anxious. Now she was terrified. Wasn't she meant to be watched and kept safe? Isn't that what she'd been told and promised? To be watched? Well, who was watching out for her now?

Her thoughts came to an abrupt halt as she saw before her, at the passageway's end, a door and in front of that door was the soldier and the tall man. They turned as one and stared at Gabriella. At the same time, she heard a scraped footstep behind her. Whirling round, she saw an old woman with a large basket packed high with fresh flowers the smell of which was wonderful in the cool night air when the only other smells were cordite and drains.

The old woman was smiling a gummy kind of smile. Gabriella looked back at the soldier and the tall man in the black cloak. The tall man was grinning and had drawn his sword, as if in welcome.

Gabriella was startled for a moment to see an orange aura around the tall man's head, like a halo. The Guild! She stood still, not sure what to do. Flee? No. Fight? With what? She remembered the ring and was about to rub it, roll it round her finger, look at it, kiss it - do anything to get it to work. Then she remembered what Maria had said. She had to think what she wanted the ring to do. She had to think precisely how she wanted the ring to behave - and she had to think about whether she wanted water, winds or demons. For good or for bad. But she had to be careful, Maria had said, otherwise the ring could turn on the owner. It had all sounded very complicated and a total load of rubbish.

'Hello, my dear,' said the gummy and wheezy old woman who was now very close to Gabriella. The smell from the flowers fought with the odour that came off the old lady's unwashed body and clothes.

'I am Solange. Very early for a small thing like you,' said the woman kindly.

The soldier shouted at the old woman. 'You,' he snarled. 'You stupid, old bitch. Get away.'

'Bon giorno, maestro,' called back the old woman as calmly and as pleasantly as her croaky voice would allow. She held up her large basket to show that she was delivering flowers.

The tall man had suddenly stopped grinning and was trying

desperately to get the soldier to stop walking towards the old woman and the girl. Gabriella wondered why.

'I said,' shouted the soldier, spittle flying from his dark toothed mouth. 'I said, piss off, you old whore.'

The old woman didn't move, but merely smiled and nodded stupidly.

The tall man was waving his arms trying to attract the soldier's attention.

'Nobody's allowed in here this morning,' said the soldier 'and that includes you, you miserable old witch. You can go and drown yourself in the Tiber for all I care, but the girl stays. Step forward blackamoor.'

'Don't the Borgias want any of my flowers then this morning?'

'No, they don't you old hag,' shouted the soldier, taking a sharp knife out of its sheath, the blade glittering in the moonlight. He waved the knife in the direction of the old woman who, with some alacrity, handed the long basket to Gabriella.

'Look after this for a moment please dearie,' she said softly to the girl.

The soldier sneered and was looking forward to slicing the old woman somewhere and then watching her scream and bleed to death. It would be something to brag about later back at the barracks.

The tall man was now shouting at the soldier, but the soldier either chose not to hear or couldn't. He was very close now to the old woman and the girl. Gabriella stepped back holding the basket of flowers with one arm and put her other in front of the old lady. The old woman pushed the arm away and Gabriella could see that the gummy grin had gone.

With a speed that shocked Gabriella and certainly the soldier, the old woman straightened up her bent back and grabbed the man by the throat and pushed him back against the wall. So sudden was the movement that one of the soldier's shoes came off as did his hat. Solange squeezed and the soldier's eyes bulged. The old woman kept hold of the man with one hand and with the other grabbed the man's hand holding the knife. The soldier was desperately trying to break free from the stranglehold but couldn't. The hand at his throat squeezed more. The soldier began making awful gurgling noises, drool coming out of his gasping mouth and urine covering his leggings. His eyes were wild with terror as the old lady took the man's hand holding the knife and in one swift movement made him stab himself in the stomach. The old lady let go of the soldier's throat and he slipped to the ground. She took the knife and, with one flick of her wrist at the man's throat, it was all over. She looked at Gabriella who could see a green aura round the old lady's frail-looking shoulders.

'Thank you, dearie,' said the old woman calmly as she threw down the knife, wiped her hands on her grubby pinafore and took back the big basket. The tall man had disappeared into the building.

'Be careful my dear,' called the old woman casually as she walked towards the side passage door. 'They want you, you know.' She smiled at a very confused Gabriella who was staring down at the dead soldier.

'Come on dearie. Get a move on. You're coming in, aren't you? I go left to the kitchens. You go right, as you've been told. No slacking now.'

Gabriella followed the old woman. As she reached the door, she turned. The dead soldier was gone.

Inside the palazzo there were two corridors. The old woman took the one on the left and said nothing more to Gabriella who began walking the other way.

The corridor was dimly lit with only a few sputtering lamps burning the last of the night's tallow. Gabriella walked carefully for a few minutes, listening out for any sounds. She came across the small door of which Maria had spoken. She pushed it and, surprisingly, it was open. Suddenly, there were the sounds of voices and marching, steel-heeled footsteps. Heart hammering, she went through the narrow doorway, shut the door quietly and waited in pitch black.

The space she was in was very small and she could see nothing. However, she could feel that there was another door behind her although it wouldn't open. She heard the voices and footsteps get closer and, to her horror, they stopped right outside the door behind which she was hiding.

She could hear the conversation which was in a strange regional accent of Italian and therefore not all of what was being said was clear to her. But she understood the gist. One of the men was a scientist and he was arguing with the other two or, maybe, three people about the safety of transporting the plague material and antidote without packing the jars carefully and using carriages with special springs. Someone was adding that, even then, the carriages could only go molto, molto lentamente. Or something like that.

A woman's voice added to the discussion by saying, 'We haven't time to go slowly!' There was no answer from the scientist. Someone then said, 'She's right, signor Zhang Wei.

We must get the material out tomorrow night at the latest, as instructed.'

The conversation was in whispers for a while and then Gabriella was sure that she could hear yet another voice.

'Let me show you,' said the other voice, 'what we've done so far with the packing of the jars. This way.'

Since she was holding tightly onto the door handle, Gabriella could feel someone trying to turn it. She had her foot against the door and now in desperation grabbed the handle with both hands. She pulled as hard as she could. Someone on the other side swore and pulled hard. There was a pause and the door was then attacked even more. It would be great, thought Gabriella, as she began to sweat, if she really could summon demons. A friendly demon would be quite useful right now.

The attempts at opening the door stopped again and the voices behind the door ceased too. Gabriella pictured demons in her head. Or at least what she thought demons might be like. Were they all like the one which had appeared in her bedroom? Were they all like that?

As she thought about demons, she heard more footsteps rushing along the corridor. Rubbing her hands together in her anxiety, she tried to think of monsters from childhood stories. There was one that an aunt used to tell her which, she remembered, had a demon in it. Gabriella's heart was beating fast and she was sure that the door would be flung open soon and then whoever was on the other side would drive a sword through her.

Suddenly, there was a terrific rush of freezing air behind her. She was pushed against a wall and her skin felt like ice. Strange tendrils of what felt like pieces of cloth touched her neck. There was a breath, a freezing breath, on her face. She tried to turn but couldn't. Something was pressing against her back, arms and legs, something that made Gabriella wide-eyed with fear. She felt the skin on her neck and arms being punctured by little pricks of what felt like needles. The pain was intense.

'No!' screamed Gabriella suddenly. 'There. Go there. Them. Them. The other side of the door! Not me!' The pressure on her immediately released. The pain that she had felt disappeared instantly. Whatever was behind her drew back. Gabriella turned and could now see a figure lit from within itself - a terrifying, wraith-like shape.

The wraith was exactly as had been described by her aunt - silvery white and shimmering, never still. Its head turned to the girl and she saw what seemed to be a mask of hollow eyes, no nose, its ears flattened against its head and a thin-lipped mouth which was shaped like a perfect oval. It looked as if the mouth was screaming but she could hear nothing. She could see no teeth. The eyes were small, glowing points of what seemed like liquid metal. The figure hovered, waiting, its claw like fingers, thin and sharp, moving languorously through the air.

'Go,' shouted Gabriella firmly, pointing through the door the other side of which was now a tumult of shouts and demands for entry. 'Go and destroy them. All. All!'

The figure came close to Gabriella again and its eyes locked on hers, searching for something. Gabriella held its gaze and her breath. For no reason that she could explain, she bowed her head towards the demon. The figure bowed slightly in return then moved away abruptly and seemed to absorb itself into the door and through it.

On the other side all sounds suddenly stopped. There was some foot shuffling and scuffing followed by muffled cries, short gasps and shouts that were cut off abruptly. Then silence again, but only for a moment. Because out of this silence came screams of utter terror and pain. Gabriella felt the door open and someone rushed inside trembling, sobbing and gasping for breath. The door slammed shut and Gabriella heard nothing more on the other side. She waited for a moment, resisting the urge to turn to the person next to her in the pitch-black space.

The door opened slightly and then a little more - seemingly of its own accord. She could see nothing but the empty corridor. No wraith, no people. No sign of anything. Except there was something on the floor - wide pools of blood, torn clothing, ripped shoes, a broken ruby brooch and what seemed like hair.

Letting go a breath, Gabriella turned and, with the light from the corridor's lamps, now saw a man inside the tiny vestibule staring at her. It was the tall man she had seen outside the building.

The first thing she noticed were his oriental clothes. The long, dark cloak had gone. Gabriella had seen such clothes on people when there had been a visit to her village. Those men had been mystics and magicians, or so her brothers had said. At first the visitors to her village had seemed kind and had beseeched her father to let them have some minerals and other materials in exchange for gold to which her father had agreed and, later, regretted. The second thing she noticed about this particular man, tall for someone from the orient, was that he had begun moving towards her. And the third thing was that the door to the corridor had slammed shut.

12

The Judean Desert, Imperial Province, Roman Empire, 79 CE

Luckily, the hole wasn't deep. The small cave had just about enough room for two people, although Yehuda and Jacob had to crouch. Dust and sand fell in a steady trickle from the cave's roof and Jacob worried that the whole thing might collapse at any minute and provide a ready-made tomb.

The only light was from the shaft of bright white that shone down from the gap through which they'd jumped. Small particles of dust hovered in the air.

More than anything, Jacob was relieved that the drop had been short. The next worry was whether they'd been seen. Yehuda and he waited on the sharp, rocky floor with bated breath as they heard the horses and shouts of the men almost above their heads.

Sounds of complaints, laughter and the horses breathing heavily were close and clear. The smell of the sweating animals and soldiers made Jacob gag and he had to put a hand over his mouth and nose. He heard legionaries dismounting. If the two fugitives had been seen going down the hole into the cave, thought Jacob, then they would be done for. They must have been seen! The Romans would simply throw straw and a small amount of pitch down the hole and anything else inflammable. Then they'd light it. He'd seen them do that before many times.

Jacob could hear conversations, sometimes close by and then further off. Suddenly, a stream of yellow liquid came down splattering as it hit the ground. Jacob wanted to sneeze and held his nose so tightly that he thought it might bleed.

It was suddenly quiet above as if everyone was listening under an instruction. Even the horses seemed to have stopped wheezing, neighing and stomping. Jacob could feel his heart racing, but he kept perfectly still as did Yehuda. He prayed that he wouldn't sneeze. Then, much to his enormous relief, he heard a sharp command and the sounds of the soldiers mounting their horses and, after a few moments, thundering hooves. Soon the desert was quiet once more. Jacob breathed out and sneezed twice, enjoying each one.

Yehuda whistled. 'That was close,' he breathed and grinned.

'Were they after us?'

'I don't think so. Well, not after me anyway,' smirked Yehuda. 'They could have been after you of course.' Jacob looked sharply at Yehuda. He had said nothing to the man with the bow and arrows about his fleeing the legionaries. Yehuda, sensing a moment of discomfort, laughed awkwardly. 'Let's get out - I'm baking. And it stinks in here.'

They climbed out of the hole and went back to one of the nearby trees, Yehuda sharing what little food, wine and water he had with Jacob.

'May I see the parcel now?' he asked Jacob after he had watched the boy eat some bread and dried goat meat.

'What if you take it and run off?'

'Very funny. Where do you imagine I'd run? And, anyway, you could catch me. You can run fast.' Yehuda paused. 'Probably,' he said hastily. 'I mean you look as if you can run fast. Strong legs. Long. And,' he said waving a hand in the direction of wadis, escarpments and sand, 'as I say, where in Caesar's teeth would I go?' Jacob stared off into the distance, wondering if this was a person to be trusted.

'Look, I can shoot an arrow straight,' said Yehuda, 'but I am no athlete. Come on, open it. Aren't you curious?'

'It's not mine to open,' said Jacob quietly. 'I was asked to collect it.'

'And...?'

'And to keep it safe. And to give it to someone.'

'Who?'

'I don't know.' Jacob felt uncomfortable and foolish. He looked at the package and then thought about the old man. Well, at least he'd done what he had promised. So far, anyway. He shifted away from Yehuda, so that there was a little distance between them, then undid the blue twine. The soft, pale hide with the map and writing on the outside was tight around whatever was inside.

Jacob very carefully removed the hide to find underneath a tube of firm, harder leather. This tube had a piece of cork at one end. Removing the cork Jacob could see that there was something wrapped in a clean white cloth and removing the white cloth revealed a spearhead fitted onto a broken, wooden spear shaft. The shaft looked as if it had been snapped in two and it seemed that the blade was made of some metal Jacob didn't recognise. He could see that it was razor sharp and glinted strangely in the sun.

Yehuda saw the spear and smiled, but said nothing. Jacob studied it and, looking closely, saw that there was something like dried blood on the tip. He looked again at the word written on the wrapping: Dīs. The diagram seemed to be made up of random lines and arrows with occasional words, some in Latin, some in what looked like Greek and a few in Aramaic.

'You have half a spear there I see,' said Yehuda, grinning. 'Will you use it?'

Jacob looked at the man. 'I told you. It isn't mine to use. I shouldn't have opened the parcel. I won't give it to you, master Yehuda, so you will have to try and take it. But, let me warn you that I can throw my sica just as fast as it will take you to let fly any arrow.' Jacob wasn't at all sure if this was true, but he had to get away somehow.

'My bow is not in my hands. Look… See? Unarmed. What's your name?'

'Ya'akov… just Ya'akov.'

'Well, just Ya'akov, I don't know what you've done to annoy the Roman army but, truth be told, they don't care much for me either so they might have been after you or me… or maybe someone else. Who knows? Who cares? My family has been an enemy of Rome for a long time… Where does your family live?' Seeing that Jacob was not going to answer, Yehuda changed tack. 'May I look at the diagram?' he asked. 'Please? You can keep hold of the spear.'

Jacob didn't pass over anything. He looked down at the spear and was once again puzzled that Yehuda should think that the Romans were after him. How would or could he know that? Or even think it? But the Roman cavalry had obviously been after someone, hadn't they? And, anyway, it was true that the Romans hunted all kinds of people… He was suddenly aware that, even in the day's blistering heat, the spear shaft was cold in his hands.

'May I look?' asked Yehuda again. 'I will not harm you. Or it. My bow is down.'

Jacob looked hard at the man and made a decision.

He handed the hide to Yehuda. His right hand went to his dagger, just in case and his left held the spear. Yehuda studied the diagram for a long time. Eventually he spoke. 'I know what this is, Ya'akov,' he said. Jacob was startled, but said nothing.

'Pluto is the ruler of the underworld, the land of the dead,' Yehuda went on, 'and the underworld begins near the old, southern gates of Jerusalem. Or what were once the old gates. Not a lot left there now.'

Jacob stared at the man, then at the map. He had heard of the underworld of course but many, including himself, didn't believe that it was real. Most thought that it was just a myth that maybe had a place in children's ghost stories; but it was something in which Romans believed and, thought Jacob, Romans weren't stupid.

Jacob asked a question not particularly wanting the answer that he knew he'd get. 'The underworld's real?'

'Oh yes. Of course, it is. I think that your map shows us where to go and how to get into it.'

'Us? What do you mean us?'

'You then.'

'What? So, I have to go to the underworld and just die?' asked Jacob.

'No, not necessarily,' said Yehuda. 'People... some people... can go to the underworld. Or so I've heard. And they can leave when they wish. If they're lucky. But few are allowed in and fewer leave. Maybe you are special.'

Jacob thought about what the old man had said. Special was an odd word to use. He looked over Yehuda's shoulder at the map. 'Do you really know how to get to the underworld?'

'Yes, with this map I do.'

'Will… will you take me there?'

'What's in it for me?'

'I have no money to give you or what I have is very little. I've got nothing else and I can't give you the spear. Or my knife.'

Yehuda nodded and thought for a moment. 'Tell you what,' he said. 'If I take you to the underworld and you get me in, then I'll help myself to some of the riches from there. They say that Pluto has a hoard of gold, silver and jewels taken from the dead. A little of that will be payment enough and then some.'

Jacob stared at Yehuda. 'What are you? A thief?' he asked.

'Are you not a thief? Have you not stolen lives?'

'What do you mean?'

'You are Sicarii. I can tell.'

'You can't tell. Why do you think I am Sicarii? The knife? Many have a sica and are not Sicarii.'

'Well, maybe so but aren't we all thieves one way or another? And don't tell me that you've never stolen an apple or some dates.'

Jacob said nothing but looked down at the broken spear.

'We're all thieves, one way or another,' said Yehuda quietly.

'I was a street thief for a while, then I became a follower of Christians... We were a... group of friends. It all went wrong though.'

Jacob was agitated. 'You think of me as a daggerman then?'

'Well, aren't you? You do have a sica and you're on your own and you run fast... I mean I expect you can run fast... and it was clear that you didn't want to meet the Roman cavalry.'

'Nobody wants to meet Roman cavalry. You didn't! Neither of us did. Are the Romans searching for you?'

'No. I don't merit forty armed soldiers on horseback. If anyone's looking for me, it would be the Jews and maybe... followers of Yehoshua from Nazareth... Have you heard of him?'

'A bit. Not much. Son of one of the gods and all that?'

'Yes... sort of,' smiled Yehuda. 'My great uncle, Yehuda of Kerioth and Hebron, was accused of telling lies about this man Yehoshua. They had been good friends, the best. But it all went wrong.'

Jacob wasn't remotely interested in this, but it diverted conversation away from what this man thought Jacob was. How though did he know about the Sicarii and running fast and taking lives? That seemed to be more than mere guesswork.

'That's a shame,' said Jacob. 'It's always... difficult when friends argue... So, what did your great uncle do? Why did he anger his friend?'

'Well,' went on Yehuda, 'it's said that my great uncle betrayed Yehoshua for money. That he was paid money by the Roman governor or maybe the Jews to arrange for Yehoshua to be disgraced. My great uncle was a good friend of this

Yehoshua and he'd never... Well, anyway, it was all a long time ago, but people have long memories and whatever my great uncle did seems to have stuck to my family's reputation... including mine. You know what the Sanhedrin is?' Jacob nodded. 'Well, the Jerusalem elders, the Sanhedrin, felt that this Yehoshua man was becoming dangerous, causing civil unrest, preaching all over the place. The Romans wanted to make an example of him. So did the Sanhedrin.'

'And did your great uncle betray his friend?'

'No. Never. He betrayed nobody. He died for betraying nobody... I'm certain of that.' Judas paused and looked up at Jacob. 'And you? Why do the Romans want you then?'

Jacob was suddenly fed up with secrets. He was hot and tired and decided in that single moment to trust Yehuda.

'I don't know,' he sighed. 'You're right. I am... I am... I was Sicarii so that's a good enough reason to be chased I suppose... My parents died... were killed. Long, long ago. One day they were there, the two of them and my sister and then the next they were gone. I never saw them again. I lived with friends of my parents. They were kind but were killed in the house where we lived. It was deliberately set alight. I was saved by two people. They were Sicarii. They helped me... and I helped them.'

Jacob watched a dust cloud disappear into the air. 'A few days ago, I met an old man, very tall he was, in rags too and pale. Dead now... killed by the Romans. Well, he told me that I needed to collect a package from some legionaries up in the hills and to keep it safe. Then deliver it. He said I'd know what to do. That's it really, although...' Jacob stopped abruptly and cursed himself for saying too much. What a fool he was, talking about things that he'd promised not to talk about!

'Although what?' asked Yehuda casually.

'Oh...' Jacob thought fast. 'Just that the old man needed someone fit and able to collect this parcel and deliver it. He gave me some money - a little money - and I accepted the job. And here I am.' Jacob tried to smile.

'That's it?'

'That's it. Not very complicated.'

'But how would you have known where to deliver the package if you hadn't been able to understand the map?'

'I don't know. But I met you, didn't I?'

Yehuda looked around where they sat and then at the boy. He seemed to come to a decision. 'Look, if you want me to help you,' he said, glancing up at the blue sky turning a pale yellow and grey, 'we'll have to go now.' He pointed at the clouds changing colour. 'I think that there's a sandstorm on its way and we need to get into the city. Agreed?'

A noise was heard from way off.

'Dogs or something,' muttered Yehuda.

'No, not dogs,' said Jacob. 'That'll be Bedouin camels.'

'You know the Bedouin?'

Jacob nodded and looked at the man again. Desert winds were creating little spiral whirls in the sand. He knew that he would never find the destination for the spear on his own and he also knew too that he'd need support from someone who hopefully was as good with his bow and arrows as Yehuda seemed to think he was.

'Take an arrow and shoot it at that Balm of Gilead over there,' said Jacob standing and pointing to a tiny, flowering plant many pedes away. Yehuda said nothing, but looked over at where Jacob was pointing. He stood up, took a particular arrow from his quiver, fitted it into his bow, breathed in deeply, held his breath, pointed the bow skywards and let fly. The arrow, thought Jacob in disgust, was going nowhere near the plant and he got ready to run off without Yehuda. However, as he watched, the arrow climbed and climbed and then suddenly fell in a straight line. He could hear the slicing smack as the arrow hit its target.

He walked over to the plant and saw that the arrow had neatly divided it into two equal halves releasing the wonderful scent that Jacob remembered from the city's temples. When there had been temples, he thought bitterly. He walked back to Yehuda. 'It's a deal,' he said without smiling and the two shook hands.

'Do you know what you hold there?' asked Yehuda as he picked up his things ready to walk. 'That spear, do you know what it is?'

'It's just a broken spear. Sharp though. And the wood is very cold. Maybe it has value? But who would buy a broken spear? It must be of interest to someone.'

'It's special. I recognise it, I think. My family have talked about it,' said Yehuda. 'I think what you have there is what some call The Spear of Destiny. It's the spear that pierced the Nazarene's side when he was crucified. Yehoshua ben Yosef of Nazareth. The Romans put him up on bits of wood.'

Jacob was unimpressed. 'They kill a lot of people that way. And this is just a broken spear, nothing more.'

'No, it is something more. Anyway, you're right, they do kill a lot of people that way. Back then, the Romans planned to break his legs - crurifragium it's called - it's a way of hastening death during a crucifixion. Just before they did that, they realised that he was already stone dead and that there was no reason to break his legs. But, out of spite or whatever, a bastard Roman centurion, who went by the name of Longinus, well, he stabbed the Nazarene in the side with his spear and laughed. What you've got there is that spear I reckon.'

Jacob found the story uninteresting but nodded out of politeness anyway.

Yehuda stopped walking for a moment and looked at Jacob. 'The bastard viper Longinus knew the man was dead, but he stuck the spear in anyway. When he pulled it out, the spear snapped and he threw it down.'

Jacob walked on, lost in his own thoughts. Nothing was said for a few moments.

'The following night,' said Yehuda catching Jacob up, 'some of the Nazarene's followers made sure that Longinus suffered.'

Yehuda paused and looked off into the distance. Jacob had slowed down. Yehuda glanced back at Jacob. 'The followers kept the spear because they wanted to treat it as a relic and they reckoned that it had the man's blood on it - or so the story goes. Who knows? They thought that it would be a precious reminder of what had happened to the Nazarene. It disappeared I think or was stolen. Who knows? Anyway, they say that the spear has powers. Some say that the owner of the spear can... defend mighty armies... or attack them... rule the world... that kind of rubbish.'

Jacob knew that there were lots of stories about alchemists

and religious zealots who years ago and even now practised strange rituals which supposedly caused magic to happen. Or gave great powers to people. Nobody really believed the stories and he certainly didn't.

Yehuda pointed at the spear. 'They say that whoever wields that will have great power. You laugh? Well, that's what we were told. The spear, like a lot of things at that time, disappeared. Souvenir hunters.' He paused. 'I wonder why you've got it.'

'I told you why,' said Jacob, irritated. 'But I don't think that I can defend or attack mighty armies!'

'No, possibly not.'

'Anyway,' said Jacob, 'The spear's not for me. I'm just delivering it. I have to give it to someone else.'

At that very moment, and for no reason whatsoever as far as he could tell, Jacob felt an uncontrollable sadness and could not stop himself from feeling a lump in his throat. He stopped walking.

Yehuda eyed him curiously. 'What's wrong?'

Jacob shook his head, unable to speak. He wondered whether now was the time that he would be stabbed, strangled or shot with an arrow, but that's not what was making him sad. He was trying hard to fight a sudden weariness, a total loneliness that overcame him.

Ashamed, he felt tears prick his eyes and, suddenly, for all that he had missed, for the few whom he thought that he had once loved, for the wickedness that he had done to so many and for the utter loneliness he now felt as the desert wind raised sand around the two figures, Jacob wept and felt a great pain in his young heart.

'Come on,' said Yehuda, walking away and coughing to cover his embarrassment. 'Let's go. We don't want to walk in the sandstorm, do we? And by the way, my friends call me Judas.'

13

Rome, Italy, 1492

Gabriella stood stock still sensing that the oriental man was edging towards her. She shouted out, her voice shaking in panic, 'Stop now or it will be the worse for you. Believe me, it will.' This she realised would frighten nobody. She tried desperately to open the second door behind her, but it wouldn't budge.

She was aware that the man had stopped moving. In truth, he didn't know quite what to do. He had witnessed the demon that had just attacked his colleagues with a ferociousness that he'd never ever seen before and hoped that he would never see again. He didn't for one minute believe that this small girl had conjured up the demon, but he was a great believer in such things and, at the same time, was a cautious man and did not want to risk any danger. He had seen the girl's silver aura and knew what she was. He also knew full well - and with enormous pleasure - how pleased his Guild masters would be if he captured this girl. Alive or dead. No, not dead. They wanted one such alive. Was this though the one that they sought? Just think of it! The honour, the glory, the fame. The rewards. He would be revered!

Gabriella wasn't stupid. She assumed that the recent demon had come from the ring, even if she still thought that magic rings didn't exist outside of stories.

'Come any closer and you will die,' she spat with much more confidence than she felt. The man had begun to move again, reaching for a sharp stiletto knife that was sheathed under his left arm. Gabriella tried to edge away in what was a very confined space. She could smell stale spices on the man's quickening breath.

Gabriella rubbed the ring and thought of ropes that would keep the man tight and out of harm's way. Suddenly, the small space was lit by a bluish light that seemed to be coming from the ring. The man blinked, mesmerised by the light. He licked his thin lips as he reached forwards, knife in hand, his red tongue contrasting sharply with his almost white pallor. The sudden light surprised Gabriella too, but she kept thinking of ropes and a demon to help her.

Suddenly an ear-splitting scream almost shattered her eardrums. The man was being squeezed by an unseen, but enormous force and was struggling, his arms flattened against his sides.

The screaming stopped because the man had nothing with which to scream. His mouth ceased to exist. His whole body burst open much as an overripe peach might burst open if squeezed by an enormous hand.

It was over in seconds, leaving Gabriella to stare at the disgusting mess in front of her. She felt a tingle in her right hand and, looking down, she saw that the ring was now bright silver with a touch of blue. The light from the ring and its glow died away, the metal becoming its normal, dull grey colour once again.

She was spattered with blood; some of the gore was in her mouth and eyes. She spat and rubbed her face with her hands which were also covered in disgusting bits of person. She removed her jacket and tore a large strip from her blouse which she used to wipe her hands and face as best she could.

Breathing deeply through her mouth as well as carefully trying to avoid the mess on the floor, she turned and opened the door that led out to the corridor. Most of the hanging lanterns were sputtering now, the tallow being low, and several were out. Someone, Gabriella thought, could come along at any minute to replenish the lanterns. In any case, someone would surely have heard the screams. She had to hurry.

Gabriella turned back into the small room and, avoiding the bloody mess on the floor, once again tried the second door. It still wouldn't open. Then she rubbed the ring and shut her eyes thinking of open doors, nothing but open doors. She heard a click and, thankfully, with no demons or anything else horrendous materialising, the door opened slowly of its own accord.

Through the doorway was another corridor. It was quite wide but dark, although there were some lit candles in alcoves along one of the walls that gave a small amount of light. Again, thinking that surely there would be people at any moment, she walked on, stopping frequently to listen out for sounds. Nothing. She wondered what had happened to Emilio and Maria. So much for Watchers watching, she thought and not for the first time.

She hoped that this corridor would lead her to where she needed to go. But at the corridor's end, just where she expected to find a door that would open to the virus storerooms, there was nothing. Just a brick wall which matched the other brick walls along both sides of the passageway.

Gabriella stood there puzzled. This is where she had been told to go. This is where there was supposed to be an entrance, a doorway to the virus storerooms. She was beginning to panic and was worried that very soon someone would find what was left of the oriental gentleman. If nothing else, there was enough blood on the floor in the small room and outside in the corridor to cause more than idle concern. She began feeling up and down the wall that faced her in the hope that she might find a secret lever or opening of some kind. Nothing.

Exasperated, she wrung her hands wondering where the wretched door might be. What would she do, she wondered, if there wasn't a door?

She stopped rubbing her hands. Suddenly, there was a powerful rush of air and before her stood a boy about her own age. The boy was dressed in a reasonably smart doublet and hose in deep yellow with blue fastenings and a green, feathered hat. He looked slightly idiotic as if he was going to a fancy dress party.

Bowing low, he asked the girl. 'How may I help you?' The boy spoke in heavily accented Italian. Gabriella didn't say anything.

'Signorina, sono qui per aiutarla. È mio dovere aiutarvi. Dimmi cosa posso fare. I am here to help you. It is my duty to help you. You requested me. Tell me what I can do. But you must be quick.'

'I requested you?'

'Si signorina. You did. The ring. I am here for you. My duty. Be quick.'

'Your duty? Who are you? Where did you come from?'

'You touched the Ring of Great Solomon, the Seal of Power and you sought help. That is why I am here, principessa. But I cannot stay. What do you want me to do?'

'You are a demon?'

'No, no, per favore non chiamarmi demone…'

'Well, what are you then?'

'It is of no importance what I am. My job is to do as you say. Consider me a friend in need but, please, do not think of me as a demon.' Gabriella caught a tiny shadow of sadness on his face. The boy smiled. 'Shall we begin? I have other things to do.'

'You will do as I say forever?'

'No, not forever. Not forever. Nothing is forever. All things will pass.'

Gabriella looked at the boy who still smiled and had clear blue eyes and a friendly face.

He laughed. Gabriella, shocked, stepped back. The boy's teeth were longer than normal and had sharpened ends.

The boy quickly closed his mouth and, still smiling, said, 'I am in your head. I am real, but not real. I am dangerous and I am also good. I will help you. But never anger me. When you do not need me, then I will go. And I must go soon.'

'But what can you do?' asked the girl.

The boy shrugged and said, 'There is something that triggers the wall and makes it open. Guardare. See?' And he stepped firmly on one of the floor's flagstones. Immediately and without any sound, the whole of the wall facing Gabriella, that a moment ago had seemed so solid, now swung noiselessly open.

The boy, still smiling, quickly urged the girl through and the pair walked into what was a series of huge cellar rooms, each visible one from the other in a kind of star shape.

'This is what you seek, principessa?'

Gabriella nodded but said nothing. The room in which they were standing was large with a high, arched brick ceiling supported by heavy wooden beams. There were benches along each wall and, above them, large glass-fronted, closed cupboards. Gabriella looked closely at one cupboard. In it there were heavy-looking glass jars filled with a deep purple liquid. In every cupboard - and there were many - she reckoned that there must have been about seventy jars. She walked into another room and there were similar jars in similar cupboards, but in these jars the liquid was blood red.

The other rooms held similar cupboards and similar jars with either the purple or red liquid in each. In one room there were hundreds of wooden cases almost ready for dispatch, each filled with straw, soft cloth and full jars.

At one end of one of the rooms, there was a kind of alcohol still, of the type that she'd seen before where people had added juniper or genièvre to flavour spirits.

'Here,' the demon boy pointed at the alcohol still, 'they use the still to pour the plague liquid into the jars.' As he spoke, the boy's whole mouth grew and became huge and wide as well as deep. And black.

It was if the boy's head had become something terrible with a gaping maw where a mouth should have been. The illusion, for Gabriella thought that it must have been but an illusion, lasted only a few seconds, but it was terrifying since it contrasted so much with the boy's sunny smile. Then the boy was exactly as he was before, looking expectantly at the girl.

'What's your name?' asked Gabriella.

'I have none.'

'Well, everybody…,' began the girl.

'You have come here to destroy the virus?'

'Yes,' said Gabriella, 'I have.'

'You seek help?'

'I don't know yet.'

'You seek help. But I cannot stay long.'

'You keep saying that!'

'You know some of the story. The virus was created far from here. In the Kingdom of Zhonggou - the land of Chung Kwoh. But then its manufacture moved to an island called Temasek. And after that to another island, Singapura. The spring water there is perfect for the mixture. There the plague potion and antidote - and its writings - are kept under careful guard. Some of the plague is here as you see, ready for distribution - and use.' He smiled again.

'I have to go there, to this island?'

'You will go there.'

'Can't you... spirit me there? Can't this ring do that?' asked Gabriella hopefully although she didn't believe for a minute that such a thing would be possible. Although, she thought, here was a boy demon spirited out of... nowhere... out of her ring.

'Maybe... yes,' said the boy with razor sharp teeth, 'but that would be a risk because the ring might keep you and not allow you to be you again.' He shrugged as if he didn't really care either way.

Gabriella, fearing that she was still very much dealing with things that she did not understand, decided that such a method of travel was not for her.

There was a faint noise from the passageway.

She turned and saw what was happening. 'No, no! The door, the wall...' she gasped.

The boy turned but, too late, the wall had closed again.

Gabriella stared at the wall, then back at the boy. She spoke quietly. 'I thought you were meant to help me!'

The boy shrugged and smiled. 'I can only do what you ask me to do,' he said. 'Think of what I should do.' He shrugged again. 'I will do it.'

'These jars - I don't know which to destroy or how they can be destroyed. Which jars contain the virus and which the antidote?'

The boy shrugged again. He said, 'I cannot tell you what you must do or not do. I can only help you do what you decide to do.'

Gabriella listened. She could hear louder noises from beyond the entrance wall. The clanking of metal probably meant soldiers, armour, swords and other weaponry. What should she do? Where was the help she had been promised?

She walked over to the still, took a cloth and quickly wiped her hands and face which were sticky with blood. Hurrying over to one of the cupboards she flung open the door and grabbed a glass jar filled with deep purple liquid. The boy watched, still smiling.

'If I open this and it is the virus, will it harm you?'

The boy shook his head.

'Answer me! Will it harm you?'

'No, it will not harm me. I am in your head and in the ring. It won't harm you either. You are immortal.'

'Nonsense. Nobody is immortal.'

She tried to think back. Maria and Emilio hadn't said anything about the colour of the virus or antidote. Purple or blood red? Or, if they had said something about colours, she couldn't remember which was which.

She could clearly hear the voices outside now getting louder and then, shocked, saw that the wall was slowly opening again. The talking stopped as eight pairs of eyes stared at Gabriella holding a jar containing purple liquid. Gabriella looked to her left for the boy. Of him there was now no sign. In front of her though was Cesare Borgia and, looking extraordinarily pleased with himself, he stepped into the cellars and began walking slowly towards her.

14

Jerusalem, Judea, Imperial Province, Roman Empire, 79 CE

Jerusalem was dark. Even though the city was a ruin, there was still a curfew every evening once the city's gates had been closed. The gates, five in all, were huge pieces of Roman engineering and, although the once substantial city walls were now in many places just piles of stones, the gates were surprisingly intact. Soldiers of the Praetorian Guard were strict and anyone discovered on the streets after curfew would find themselves in big trouble. Death was the threat. And often the promise.

There were the beggars of course whom the Guard left very much alone and a few street lamplighters who each night still lit the few remaining oil lamps. Roman soldiers from the barracks were allowed out too, but they tended to stick to their camps unless they were on duty.

Jacob thought of the Sicarii daggermen. They had cared for him when he had nothing and no-one. The Sicarii had expected much in return. And Jacob had given much back. The Sicarii still roamed the city in small groups and, where they could, always dealt vicious murder to Romans and their sympathisers. Despite the mass Sicarii suicides at Masada six years ago, there were not only a few Sicarii groups still around but other bands of fighters as well, several led by Sicarii men and women. Jacob had worked with them all. Often were the times when he and perhaps two other daggermen had worn stolen Roman army uniforms to get close to small groups of real soldiers. Once close the rest was easy.

But he was troubled now as he crept through a city that he'd always thought of as home. Could what he did and had done with the Sicarii be called work? Was it all about helping a cause? Was it about revenge? Was it...? He didn't really know what it was. It was, he supposed, dealing death from shadows. He had never really analysed why he did what he did, but he did know that the burning hatred he felt meant that he could deal death to those who had dealt death and cruelty for years to people who very often could never protect themselves.

The Sicarii hid in shadows as he was doing now. He knew very well that if a shadow could conceal one person then it may be concealing another. On this particular night though there seemed to be nobody about.

Jacob could smell juniper in the air and somewhere someone was cooking meat which made his mouth water. Judas and he hid their meagre belongings in the wall of the ruined public baths. Jacob shoved the spear's wrappings in his bag which he put over his shoulder and held the spear with the broken shaft.

'You're going to carry that with you everywhere we go?' asked Judas pointing at the spear.

'Yes, I am.'

They crept from street to street keeping out of sight.

Judas said, 'We should eat something before going much further because we may not get to eat again for some time.'

'Agreed, but from where?'

'Follow me. I know a place.'

The pair went on and Jacob felt faint with fatigue, thirst and hunger. He'd been awake for more or less a day and a night. Despite his headscarf, his time in the desert had meant that he'd caught the sun, something he was usually careful not to do and his face felt hot and tight.

The night sky was cloudless, the stars were diamonds set in blue-black and there was no wind to cool his face and neck. Occasionally, bats beat their wings close by and he could hear some distant shouts and calls. Faint music came from somewhere and suddenly stopped. Jacob could remember when, as a very small boy, he had enjoyed lying flat on top of the house at night before bed, staring at the stars and listening to someone playing similar music. He had listened to a family next door also looking at the stars and talking about the patterns that the stars made and why some stars seemed brighter than others. He remembered seeing, from time to time, a shooting star and Jacob, aged about four, excitedly thought that these stars carried a variety of gods to earth. Nobody had ever told him any different.

Eventually, Judas and Jacob came to what had been a small synagogue. It was totally ruined of course, but there was a square of yellow light from a hole in the ground which had a grate over it - invisible unless you knew where to look.

Judas led Jacob, who was now desperate for water, to a narrow brick stairway and down they went to find three huge men guarding a small doorway. The men were talking in whispers and, as soon as they saw Judas, three swords were a fraction away from the bowman's throat. One of the men smiled when he recognised Judas and commanded that weapons be withdrawn. However, they stared hard at Jacob and, through his tiredness, the boy thought that each looked strangely fearful. Vaguely, he wondered why. He couldn't see properly, but he just made out the orange light from within creating a glow behind the three doorkeepers' heads. He felt his knees sag.

'I know him,' one said. 'He's Sicarii.' Once more the swords were out, but Jacob couldn't have cared less because, at that moment, even though he scrabbled feebly for his knife, he just slipped to the ground in a faint.

He had terrible dreams. Jerusalem was under siege. It was the festival of Pesach and people were packed into the temples celebrating the departure from slavery under Rameses II in the time of Moses. This was the moment that the Romans chose to attack people at prayer. All were put to death. In other parts of the city, he could see defeated and tortured rebels, forerunners of the Sicarii, as well as frail citizens, most of whom were taken into slavery.

He could see each of the times when he had taken a life, but he couldn't see any faces. The scene changed and he could see himself trying to explain astronomy to someone, but again he couldn't see the face. He desperately wanted to see who the person was and, crying out, he awoke.

He had absolutely no idea where he was, but could smell cooking and the smell made him feel nauseous. He felt just as tired as he had before fainting. His head ached and he had a bad taste in his mouth. He sat up and discovered that he was holding the broken spear tightly in his left hand. He immediately checked that he still had his sica. He did.

A little girl was sitting next to him and was watching him with big, brown, serious eyes. Jacob looked at her and was struggling to sit up when a deep voice said, 'Stay there. Eat something first. Here.' A wooden plate was handed to him on which was bread, some olive paste, a piece of fried fish, half a small cucumber, an onion and some dried figs. He was handed something that smelled horrible in a wooden cup which he sipped tentatively and then downed the lot, immediately feeling awake and much better. The little girl with the big eyes watched him as he ate. The man with the deep voice passed Jacob a tumbler of wine which Jacob refused and, instead, asked for more of the foul-tasting liquid.

'Ahah,' said another voice that he recognised. 'Feeling better?' asked Judas cheerily.

Jacob nodded. 'Yes... Thank you.'

'Well, as soon as it's light, we must move on. It's too dangerous at night near Pluto's home above ground.'

He gestured around the huge underground room where Jacob could see men, women and a few children. 'These are my friends,' he said. 'Yours too now. They hide because they are... they escaped the pillage and ruin of the city. There are other groups like these. They will rebuild Jerusalem. One day.'

Jacob looked about him as he ate. He didn't recognise anyone. He assumed that this cellar must have been a store at some point for the synagogue. The air wasn't fresh and the place stank of bodies, food and urine, but he felt safe. The little girl was still staring at him.

'Why does she stare so?' asked Jacob.

Judas laughed. 'She's special, like you. She can see your aura. That's what she sees. You can't see hers yet. But one day you will see everyone's.'

Jacob was so startled that he nearly dropped his platter of food. His stomach lurched. 'How do you know about me?' he asked, his lip trembling involuntarily and his right hand gripping his sica.

'I am a Watcher Jacob and I know all about you. We are many and there are more Watchers here.'

'But how did…?'

'My job was to help you if something should have happened to the old man. And something did. We protect people like you… and her,' he said indicating the little girl. 'I can see your aura and so can she. Yours is silver.'

Jacob looked at the little girl. 'What's your name?'

'Abijah,' the little girl said, smiling at him.

Jacob nodded and looked hard at her. She smiled but didn't move. Everything suddenly went very quiet in the room and he could only hear his breathing and then not even that. Everything around him became dark except for the little girl and then suddenly he saw it - a faint glow around her shoulders. Dull yellow to start with. Was that green? No, it wasn't. It was only yellow and the yellow became orange. He blinked. The colour faded and slowly disappeared. It hadn't been green. He was sure of it. He remembered what the old man's aura had been like. That had been green. This had not been green.

Maybe his mind was playing tricks Jacob thought and shrugged. Maybe he was just not seeing or thinking straight. Perhaps colours looked different down here. Maybe. He rubbed his eyes and was about to say something, but stopped himself.

Judas smiled at the little girl, nodded at one of the men and said to Jacob as if sudden departure was necessary. 'We must go,' he said briskly. 'These people have packed some food for us and we have fresh water. We can't go back to collect our things - far too dangerous - so they've given us a blanket each, scarves, cloaks, some torches, a tinder box and a few flints. Do you feel well enough to move?' Without waiting for an answer, he stood and said curtly, 'Let's go.'

'Scarves?' queried Jacob.

'Yes, scarves. Let's go,' said Judas.

As they left, Jacob smiled at the little girl and thanked the people for their hospitality. Daybreak was spreading a weak, pinkish light, the sun only just beginning to show itself. The air was refreshing and Jacob's head felt much lighter and his skin cooler.

The pair walked close against walls and rubble to avoid creating any shadows and, whenever they heard footsteps, they froze until the possible danger had passed.

'How far before we go underground?' whispered Jacob at one point when Judas stopped to study the map on the spear's wrapping.

'Not too far. Soon. A thousand pedes or so. But keep alert. The governor's mercenaries are always sharp and they're good. Or bad, depending on how you look at it.' Jacob knew the mercenaries better than most people. He said nothing.

To their joint relief, they met nobody and eventually came to an ancient site of what once had been a forum now all but destroyed. Large, black rats ran around unafraid of the humans.

'They eat bodies,' said Judas as if he were commenting on an everyday occurrence which, thought Jacob with a mental shrug, is exactly what it was.

There were huge pieces of ruined stone-works and broken

statues as well as rubble and some large, regular-shaped pillars that would have once supported a large building. Judas studied the map carefully and shortly found an almost hidden entrance to a dark tunnel in front of which was a thick and solid, iron gate.

An engraved dedication to Pluto above the entrance confirmed the identification of the gate.

'Have you been in there before?' asked Jacob.

'No.'

'Truly?'

'Truly.'

Jacob wasn't certain that he believed Judas and sincerely hoped that the man could be trusted. The pair stood for a moment looking at the dark and foreboding entrance from which they could see wisps of whitish smoke. The acrid smell of ammonia and putrefaction was strong and made Jacob's eyes sting. He could see that the cave's opening was of sufficient size to admit a couple of people side by side, but that was all. The entrance was taller than it was wide. In the poor light, Jacob could make out that there was a steep descent on the other side of the gate and, after a short pace or two, pitch-black.

'We must wrap these around our heads,' said Judas and produced two very long palla scarves which had been dampened with water. He also took two tar-covered torches from his large bag.

'We'll light these inside the cave. You must keep the scarf tight over your mouth and nose, for the air in the caves can be poisonous. Animals which have entered... die instantly. Even bulls.'

Jacob stared at Judas. 'And we're going in there?' he asked, astonished at Judas' stupidity. 'Just like that?'

'Well, we must if you are to follow the signs on your package…. Look, Pluto's eunuch priests would prove their power by entering this gassy cleft and they would come out alive by holding their breath and taking advantage of known pockets of safe air within the cave.'

'Gassy cleft?' shouted Jacob. 'What, in Caesar's buttocks, is a gassy cleft? And who can hold their breath for more than a few… We'll die in there!'

'No, we won't. Not if we're careful and you do everything I do. And keep your voice down!'

'I suppose birds that fly too close to here die as well?'

'Sometimes,' Judas admitted with not much concern.

'I was joking, Judas!'

'Come on. If we're going in, we must go in now. Remember to keep your scarf tight. Put it on top of your own scarf if you want. Double protection. Follow me closely. Speak little. Breathe slowly. Don't stop unless I do.'

'Halt. Do not move!' A deep, loud voice boomed out of the gloom stopping Jacob in his tracks as he was about to remonstrate with Judas on his seemingly stupid advice. They both turned as one, Jacob's right hand moving quickly to his sica.

'I said halt,' repeated the voice, which was not only deep but also sounded as if the owner needed to clear his or, in this case, its throat.

'I have three knives to your one,' the booming voice spoke

out without expression, 'and I warrant that I'm faster than you, boy.' The gurgling voice chuckled and then sneered, 'but I need no knife to deal with you. Either of you.'

Jacob saw before him a monster - a man, yes, and a huge man, but with an oversized head, huge chest rippling with taut muscle, sturdy legs and long teeth filling a large gaping, drooling mouth with yellowing gums. He... the man... stood half-naked, with long, grubby nails which were more like talons. The eyes were buttons of sly evil - black, sharp and beady. The thing was wearing a wide belt with three enormous, blood-caked butcher's knives attached.

The monster lurched slowly towards Judas and Jacob. As it walked, it picked its large nose enthusiastically with one finger and ate the result of the exploration with thorough enjoyment.

Judas spoke up confidently and with no tremor in his voice, 'Sir, we mean you no harm. We are entering here and you may as well let us go on our way for, as you must surely know, we shall be dead soon.'

Jacob looked quickly at Judas and wondered if he was telling the truth.

'Yes,' said the creature to Judas. 'Indeed, you will be dead soon. But here and by my hand. You might even make good eating. You have good flesh upon you. Not much I grant you, but sufficient for my simple needs.' The creature, close now, threw back its heavy head and laughed again.

'But you,' rumbled the creature now swivelling its eyes towards Jacob. 'You will come with me. I must deliver you to my masters. They want you. Alive, alas.' The creature looked again at Judas.

'Step towards me, puny Jew and prepare for death,' the

creature said to Judas.

'I shall not die by your instruction,' spat Judas and, at fantastic speed, almost quicker than the eye could see, he pulled an arrow with blue feathers from his quiver, positioned the arrow in his bow, drew back the bowstring and let it fly. Jacob groaned and the creature laughed its deep, gurgling laugh because the arrow totally missed the monster even at such a close distance. The creature threw its massive head back and laughed again, at the same time removing one of the long and wide knives from his belt.

Jacob just stared in despair as the arrow flew high and far away but, to his utter amazement, he saw it turn in a wide curve and speed back towards the monster. The sound as the arrow hit the monster's head was sickening - much like a heavy hammer hitting a huge watermelon. The creature looked mildly surprised at first, tried to reach behind, sagged, dropped the knife, staggered forward, was about to say something before its eyes rolled upwards and it voided its bowels. The stream of excrement seemed to be never-ending. Then the creature toppled forwards and, with a sickening crunch, hit the stone pathway. The smell was terrible. The monster's legs twitched a little and then were still.

Jacob was astonished. 'How in any god's name did you do that?'

'A trick,' said Judas mildly. 'Just a trick. Each of my arrows has a different quality. That one was made for me by a man who had travelled far to a place where men threw special, curved sticks which then return.'

'Magic?'

'No, I think not. Just some alchemy. Science.'

Jacob looked round nervously in case another monster should emerge. 'Science? I know nothing of that, whatever it is. But how did this… creature know we were here and why did it want me and not you?'

'You are…' Judas stopped himself. 'Things like that,' he said quickly, jerking a thumb at the dead monster, 'are Guild born and bred.' He took a few steps towards the cave, looking away from Jacob who could sense that maybe Judas had begun to say too much.

'Yes… and…?'

'And nothing,' said Judas in a rush. He took a deep breath. 'Listen to me. The Guild will try anything to capture you. The Guild seeks the secret of immortality and you can provide them with that secret. The secret is…'

'What?' Jacob was both angry and fearful. 'You say these things, but how do you know any of this?'

'When you were asleep. You spoke.'

'If you're lying it will be the worse for you.'

'Oh really?' Judas had turned away. 'And you'll do what exactly? The Guild,' he said over his shoulder, 'seeks - no, it demands - the immortality that… you have.'

'You want that too?'

'No, no, don't be silly! Ya'akov, I'm a Watcher. I'm on your side. As I said, I protect you. This… creature… was a Guild creation. Bred for purpose. I suspect that it didn't cost much either - a few people to eat and a knife or two on its birthday, if indeed it was born… Now, we must go.'

'But,' said Jacob, 'back in the desert, you threatened me with your arrows. You would have taken the spear…'

Judas turned to look at Jacob and grinned. 'And who has just saved you?' Jacob didn't answer. 'Just keep your spear tight,' said Judas curtly, 'and your scarf tighter. And follow me.' Turning back towards the cave, he swung round and announced with a mock bow, 'Welcome to the afterlife.'

'Wait,' said Jacob catching Judas up. 'That creature,' he said pointing back at the creature's body. 'Shouldn't we hide it?'

'The Guild will be here in more numbers soon. That always happens. Or… or so they say. Here, drink some water - just a little.'

Jacob sipped some water from the offered gourd and, as he did, he noticed that the morning sun was bright orange, reflecting prettily on the white rock behind Judas. It was going to be a beautiful day but, maybe, he thought despondently, his last.

As they walked to the gate at the cave's entrance, Judas said, 'You know that goats and sheep and all sorts are sacrificed to benefit the gods?'

Jacob nodded. 'That's no secret.' He paused. 'Do you believe all of that camel dung?' he asked.

'Perhaps,' said Judas. 'I'm not certain. Maybe it means something. Maybe not. I don't know. Who cares? But I do know that the underworld is real enough. And here it is! I want jewels, gold and silver. I want money - and I really couldn't give a rat's whisker about much else. Let's go.'

Following Judas' lead, Jacob tightened the dampened scarf tightly around his own headscarf as well as his nose and mouth. He hoped, on the life of anyone's god, that he wasn't making a terrible mistake. Absent-mindedly, he held the broken spear tightly to his chest. As Judas pushed open the unlocked, heavy gate and walked into the cave, they were immediately enveloped in utter darkness.

The floor sloped steeply downwards and the pair had to stop and make their way much more slowly. Footsteps could be heard outside. Jacob held his breath and stopped to listen; Judas grabbed one of Jacob's arms willing him to say nothing. After a few moments, they could hear a muted conversation and some angry comments, then grunts as the dead creature's body was obviously being hauled away.

After waiting for a few minutes, Jacob and Judas stepped forward again, the floor tilting at an even steeper angle. Jacob could hear rumbling and, despite the damp cloth over his face, he could smell ammonia and sulphur. There was occasional light from breaks in the cave's roof and Jacob could see yellow dust in the air. If it was actually air, he thought.

The path suddenly became even steeper and there was no longer any light from the roof. They both had to hold on to the slippery, greasy sides of the passageway to stop themselves falling.

Judas said, 'Wait a moment.'

Jacob could hear the scrape of the tinder box. 'Is it safe to do that?' he asked nervously, wishing not for the first time that he was elsewhere, perhaps minding goats for the Bedouin.

Judas didn't answer. His torch struggled for a moment, then flared and fed a warm, welcome light. The two looked about them, instantly recoiling in absolute horror and utter disgust at what they saw.

15

Rome, Italy, 1492

Cesare stopped walking and waved an arm as if to introduce his men all armed to the teeth. The men were sniggering and sneering at Gabriella while Cesare was smiling, a nasty glint in his eyes.

'Well now,' he drawled. 'Well, well, well. The Watchers really do have the little bitch to do their bidding. My father thought as much. My sister too. I knew of course that you were, you are, a Silver Green and I let you go. Stupid me. But, my dear,' he said sarcastically, 'how did you get in here? Who made a mess of our oriental cousin and where are three of my best alchemists? And what do you think you're going to do with that jar? So many questions Silver Green. Choose any one of them to answer.'

Gabriella just stood stock still, watching and hoping upon hope that something or someone would rescue her. Cesare had called her a Silver Green! Could he see a silver aura then? If not, how did he know? She told herself to focus. As a princess should focus. Without thinking, she squared her shoulders and stood ramrod straight.

'You have nothing to say? Very well,' sneered Cesare, 'I shall count to three and, if answers come there none, you my girl will be killed... probably... No, once again - stupid me,' he tutted. 'I do apologise. There's no probably about it. Definitely and quite slowly. After of course we've done a little work on you.' He laughed.

Gabriella clutched the glass jar to her chest. Some of the

137

men tittered.

'Come one step closer,' she said considerably more bravely than she felt, 'and I will drop this jar.'

Cesare continued to smile but slightly less than before and the men had stopped snickering. Then Cesare began laughing and, as if on cue, all the men joined in.

'I mean it,' said Gabriella trying to hide the desperation in her voice. 'The poison, the virus, will not harm me, but it will kill you.' She prayed that what Emilio and Maria had said was true.

'Ah yes, yes, yes, of course,' shouted Cesare gleefully, 'but you can still die by knife or... but we would prefer to work on you first. You have something that we want, you see.'

'I will walk out of here now,' said Gabriella. 'You will allow me free passage and everyone will live.' She realised that what she was saying was remarkably stupid and, anyway, this wasn't what she had been told to do. She had to destroy the virus. She could see the orange auras surrounding each of the men standing by the cellar entrance. She wished that she had discovered if there was another store-room entrance or, rather, exit. She also wished that the wretched demon boy was here by her side, even with his scary teeth. So much for the Ring of Solomon. The Watchers weren't much help either! She was sure that Cesare could see that her hands were shaking.

'By all means walk,' he said unconcerned. 'Hold the jar and leave my house,' he drawled sardonically, 'and we will of course just let you go.'

'Are these cellar rooms airtight?' asked Gabriella.

Cesare looked blank for a moment. Then, indignantly, he

said, 'Of course they are, you idiot. When this wall is shut and secure, no air may pass in or out. As one traitor discovered last year.' At this all the men jeered. They relaxed. This would be easy. They relished the thought of perhaps having some fun with the girl before they were allowed to kill her.

'Then,' said Gabriella, 'tu sciocco e bastardo, I will smash the jar.' She drew a deep breath. 'I will not be affected,' she said. 'But you will, Cesare Borgia. And all your ugly friends here.'

She was amazed at her effrontery and bravery - or stupidity.

There was a silence and then Cesare grinned once more showing off a few of his blackened teeth. Odd, thought Gabriella, for a good-looking prince to have rotten teeth.

'Please do,' he said slowly. 'Smash away. We are immune. We have all taken the antidote.'

Sweat broke out on Gabriella's forehead. Of course! How stupid of her! Obviously, she thought, they would have taken the antidote. She tried to rub the ring, but couldn't with the jar in her arms. Had they really taken the antidote though? Or was that just a ploy?

Suddenly she had an idea. This man Solomon had been wise, hadn't he? So Maria had said. Well, two can be wise! She stepped backwards to one of the cupboards always keeping a wary eye on the armed body of men.

The men weren't laughing now and didn't move, but watched her like hawks as did Cesare. When she bumped intentionally backwards into the cupboard, the watching men all started, ducked slightly, stepped back and then froze. She reached behind with one hand and opened the glass door. Glancing behind her she saw that this cupboard had jars full of the red liquid. Good, she thought with relief and removed one of those jars. Gently, still watching the men, she put the jar with the purple liquid down on the floor. She stood up and held the jar with red liquid aloft.

All the men, including Cesare, stepped back.

'Ah,' said Gabriella, slightly relieved. 'You are more fearful now? Well, that is good news. And the antidote that you have taken has caused you to be of comfort has it? Cesare Borgia…,' she shook her head pretending to be saddened at the news, 'you haven't taken the antidote, have you?'

Gabriella smiled. 'Embrace me now if you dare, Cesare Borgia. Clutch me close now, you bastard.' Gabriella began to shake the jar a little. The men stepped back again, this time treading on each other's feet. Cesare, she noticed, had dragged two of the guards in front of him.

'This I take it,' said Gabriella shaking the jar in front of her, 'contains the plague virus? Suitable colour.'

'Put it down,' said Cesare with gritted teeth. 'Put it down now girl and I promise that we will treat you kindly. You have my word.'

'Your word? Your word? I do not value your word! And you call me girl? Not bitch? Or whore? I'm certain that you and your… friends would treat me with the respect you feel I deserve. I'm delighted to find that you and your band of brothers are not immune. Shame.'

Gabriella walked forwards slowly, clutching the jar and watching the men in front of her. Her hands were slippery. Cesare put another guard between himself and the girl. The men didn't know what to do and some turned to run, but the exit was blocked with everyone having much the same idea.

Cesare suddenly shouted, 'Stop!' Nobody was very sure to whom he was shouting. The men stopped squirming and Gabriella stopped walking.

'Let me pass,' she said. 'Move into the cellar all of you, but very slowly and, before you do that, kindly throw your weapons on the floor. Now!'

The men hesitated and Gabriella held the jar aloft at which point all weapons clanged to the floor. One large guard was looking with a face like thunder at the girl and he held on to his sword. Cesare told him in a shrill voice to drop it. The man glared at Cesare, then at Gabriella, but reluctantly dropped the sword.

'I shall count to six,' said Gabriella. She had no idea why she had chosen six. 'At six I shall drop the jar and the virus will kill you. If the wall is still open, it will kill everyone in this house and your neighbours. And theirs. It will not hurt me,' she said. In panic, she wondered once again if she was truly immune to poisons.

It was warm in the cellar and Gabriella's hands were becoming more and more slippery. She suddenly remembered for no apparent reason that there had been a witch doctor in her tribe who had claimed to be immortal and immune from poisons, but then he had died from a snake bite.

Still nobody in front of her moved.

'One,' she said. Everyone was still. Gabriella held the jar with both hands as if preparing to throw it against a stone wall. Now one or two of the guards did walk in.

'Two.' Nobody else moved.

'Three.' A few more men moved inside the cellar. Cesare

was watching her and still had three men in front of him.

'Four.' The rest of the men moved in leaving only one in front of Cesare.

'Move over there,' said Gabriella indicating the furthest cellar. The men moved.

'Five. Cesare I will do this. I do not wish to kill you and your kinsmen, but I will…'

'I don't believe you child. You are not that brave, but merely a bitch.'

'Then, six,' she shouted, 'and perish.' At that moment two things happened. The first was that the last man who was in front of Cesare rushed into the cellar. The second was that the jar slipped from her damp fingers and fell to the floor.

Gabriella gasped in horror and stared at the glass jar which bounced a little when it hit the floor, but didn't break. Cesare turned, stamped on a flagstone and ran off down the corridor. The wall door began to close. Now all the men were in the cellar as was she and the door was closing silently and fast!

Gabriella closed her eyes and held the ring finger tight. She imagined the demon boy and could see him in her mind's eye. There was a rush of air and she opened her eyes to see the demon boy next to her, smiling. He shouted, 'Shut your eyes!' which she did and heard him stamp on the glass jar with great force. The jar crunched and burst, firing the red liquid and small shards of glass over the cellar's stone floor. Gabriella opened her eyes, didn't hesitate for a second and dashed for the exit. She made it with a fraction to spare although, as the wall closed hermetically shut, her tunic was caught and it ripped, buttons popping. She could hear screams and shouts of agony from within the cellar. So much for the antidote, she thought.

Catching her breath for a moment, she took stock. The screaming had stopped, but she could still hear desperate shouts and bouts of terrible coughing. Where had Cesare gone? Was he waiting somewhere along the winding corridor? Would he suddenly pounce?

She still hadn't destroyed the virus. She hugged her arms and put her head against the wall.

'Well done,' said a voice.

Gabriella looked round.

'You did well principessa,' said the demon boy.

'No thanks to you!'

'Really? But, lady, I was ready. I am in your head. You had but to call. You did well. You would like to destroy what is in that cellar?'

'I'm told that I must.'

The demon boy nodded, 'Yes you must.'

'Why did you disappear?'

'Shall I help you?'

'What?'

'You must tell me if you wish me to help you.'

'I do wish you to help me! Can you?'

There was no answer, but the boy took her right hand and pulled her quickly along the corridor away from the moans and shrieks. He stopped and listened. Looking satisfied, he grabbed Gabriella's finger wearing the Ring of Solomon, took her other hand and began to rub the one hand with the other.

'Stand back and rub the ring harder,' he said. 'Close your eyes. You must do this. Think only of fire. Fire of the greatest possible heat, white hot flames, fire whiter and hotter than any fire you have ever seen - and then think of the power of that fire. Think of that fire, its strength, the greatest fire that you can imagine. Concentrate!'

Gabriella did concentrate; on her eyelids she could picture great white tongues of flame shooting forward along the passageway. The demon boy pulled her into a deep alcove and she opened her eyes.

She could feel the floor vibrating. Flakes of brick fell from the ceiling. She heard a pounding sound that became louder and louder. Something heavy. Something in a hurry. This wasn't fire. Fire didn't pound. An earthquake? Now? Here? In Rome? She covered the top of her head with her hands.

A huge black bull, so enormous that it could hardly fit into the passageway, galloped past, its eyes red and its snorts accompanied by great wads of yellow mucus coming from its nose. Its pace and power were tremendous. Gabriella stepped forward a little and saw the bull charge straight at the wall door. It didn't stop but crashed straight through and disappeared. The wall crumbled and disintegrated. The demon boy pulled Gabriella back. She made to move forward again but recoiled as, without any warning, a long, thick tongue of blue and white flame roared past the alcove.

For a few minutes there was nothing but the boiling air, the raw, clawing flame and the smell of burning... something disgusting. Flesh. Then an explosion as all the virus and antidote jars burst, snapped, crackled, popped and burnt instantly. The whole cellar was incinerated by the pure flame. So complete was the destruction that nothing in the cellar remained. Everything had burned to dust, vapour or simply… to nothing.

The flame stopped as quickly as it had started, almost, Gabriella thought, as if a dragon had breathed out and had then run out of breath. There was silence apart from the small sounds of red-hot brick cooling down.

The demon boy, seemingly unaffected by anything, said, 'You must go but I may not follow. We may or may not meet again, principessa. You to your destiny and I… I to my dragon.'

'Dragon? Not really? A dragon! They don't exist.'

The demon boy smiled.

'You call me princess?'

'I do,' said the demon boy, his mouth yawning and becoming a huge black cavity framed by the sharp teeth.

Gabriella wasn't fazed. 'But how do…?' She turned to see the remainder of the brickwork around the virus cellars collapse. There was now nothing there but a gaping black hole and a few bricks. When she turned back to the demon boy, there was nobody there.

Exhausted, Gabriella knew that she needed to get away from the palazzo as fast as possible and find Maria and Emilio. She suddenly felt reasonably pleased that her mission had been achieved. Now, she could ask for a little money and make her way back to Africa. That hope lasted for a moment only because her next thought was to avoid Cesare in particular and any of his henchmen in general.

She assumed that Cesare would have some plan up his sleeve to wreak retribution upon her. The Guild would have news of what had been done to the store of plague venom and the antidote. It would be common knowledge amongst Guild people before long and she wanted to get on with her journey back to Africa. She had, she reckoned, done her bit.

Gabriella walked tentatively along the corridor towards what she hoped might eventually be the side door she had used to come into the palazzo. The corridor was very long and winding. She thought, as is often the case of course, that things looked very different now walking back the way she'd come. But she became more and more alarmed as she turned each corner and walked up several winding stairways, trying to make as little noise as possible. She knew that, without any doubt whatsoever, the way she was going was the wrong one.

The corridor narrowed and darkened. In front of her now was a black door. She had a choice, go back or open the door in the hope that it led towards the outside world or at least closer to it.

She tried the handle and slowly pushed the door open. She knew instantly that she'd made a big mistake. She knew instantly that she should have shut the door immediately and run as fast as she could, but she didn't. Instead, she screamed.

16

Underworld, Jerusalem, Imperial Province, Roman Empire, 79 CE

Jacob and Judas stood still and stared. In front of them as far as the eye could see were row upon row of skeletons, some hardly recognisable as human. Possibly, thought Jacob, because they weren't. The skeletons were mostly white, but some still had skin, flesh, clothing and even faces. The light from Judas' lamp made the vast cavern a nightmare's background.

Jacob was nervous. 'Is this the whole underworld then?' His voice, muffled as it was because of the scarves, still echoed and his words bounced about.

'No,' said Judas, speaking quietly as if in honour of the dead. He moved the torch in a wide arc to shed light as broadly as he could. 'The underworld is huge, as big as the city above. This is just the antechamber I think, where some of the bodies and bones are kept. Maybe like some sort of waiting room. If you look there you can see recently dead people, some still in shrouds.'

Jacob did not want to look, then did and felt sick. 'The smell is terrible,' he said quietly. 'Who brings them here?'

A huge voice roared, 'I do!'

They both jumped and Judas almost dropped his torch. Turning, they saw a short, wiry man of indeterminate age. He was wearing a filthy tunic and his long hair and beard were grey and greasy. He had his hands on his hips as he regarded Judas and Jacob.

Judas found his voice first. 'You are a servant here perhaps? Can you lead us to your master?' The bowman spoke with a confidence that Jacob did not feel. Jacob's left hand inched towards his knife.

'My master? Here?' The little man seemed amused.

'Yes,' said Judas. 'Your master - and we are in a hurry.'

'I am sorry that you are in a hurry.' He laughed and bellowed, 'I don't recall that you made an appointment... My master is me. I am in charge here. Yes, indeed that I am.' The small man had a voice that would have fitted a person four times his size. He spoke in an uncommon and slightly old-fashioned Latin dialect but sounded genial and friendly.

The little man bowed and any friendliness, such as it was, disappeared. 'Can I ask you two gentlemen why you are here? We tend not to receive guests or, at least, not any who have breath left in their bodies. Are you about to expire? If not, I would recommend that you keep your scarves tight to your faces should you wish to stay in a healthy state. Unless, of course, you have no need of scarves?'

There was a silence and the little man chuckled. 'But forgive me, where are my manners? You see, I'm not used to... visitors who have breath left to speak.' He bowed again. 'Now, what may I do for you gentlemen? Oh, my dear, dear boy, I would strongly advise you to take your hand away from your sica and you, take your hands away from your bow, for you would not do me much harm were you to try to put them to use. And I would do you a great deal of hurt in return. Swift and permanent hurt.'

Jacob and Judas looked at each other and then looked back at the small man who was now right in front of them. Neither had seen or heard him move. The man was grinning and Jacob noticed that he had few teeth. He noticed too that the little man had something that looked much like crusted blood around his mouth and beard.

'Come this way,' said the big-voiced little man and led them towards the back of the huge cave. As he walked past the rows of skeletons, the man occasionally patted a few of them and mumbled under his breath.

They walked through to another, smaller cave and this one had some good light coming from four huge oil lamps which burned brightly. At each corner of this cave Jacob could see that there were entrances to other tunnels or caves.

The man waved at the lamps. 'Human fat, you know. Works a treat. Fired and fed by human fat. Works very well. Always has.'

Jacob looked around and nearly gagged. The smell was appalling. He said something under his breath. Pluto turned towards him and put his face close to Jacob's.

'Listen, you miserable cur,' said Pluto with menace and breath to match, his mouth almost in Jacob's face. 'I work here and have for many, many years. I live off flesh and blood - and I need light. You are nothing to judge. So, do not! You understand?'

Jacob, terrified, nodded.

'And I offered you no invitation. You are here because... well I don't know why yet. Oh,' he chuckled again, 'you may both remove your scarves in this space. The air is safe for you here.'

Judas asked, 'You do not need a scarf?'

'I am a Silver Green.'

Jacob was astonished. 'You are a Silver Green? I am...' Judas kicked one of Jacob's ankles hard.

'You are what?' asked the man.

'I... I'm sorry. Nothing, my lord,' muttered Jacob. 'So, you are...'

'Immortal. And cannot be harmed by foul air or poisons.' He looked hard at Jacob, so hard that Jacob had to look away.

'You know what a Silver Green is?' Pluto asked.

Jacob and Judas said nothing. The silence went on for too long.

Pluto shrugged. 'Being immortal has its benefits of course, as you can imagine. It has its disadvantages too... not least because I'm losing my looks and my teeth. Silver Greens are meant to age until about thirty and then age no more, but they must have made a mistake with me!' He laughed and then stopped. 'I think that it's because... well, never mind. None of your business. But may I ask you and, probably for the last time, why are you here? What or whom do you seek?'

Judas asked a question which he immediately regretted. 'May we trust you?' The man turned slowly to face Judas.

'May... you... trust me? Your name if you please dear sir?'

'Yehuda... Judas,' said Judas quietly.

'Yehuda,' said the man almost to himself as if trying the name on for size. 'Yehuda. Well, dear Yehuda... gentle Yehuda, sweet Yehuda... I am more trustworthy than you or your namesake. You are Yehuda ben Yosef?'

'Yes, but how did you know that?'

'I know of your father and his father of the same name. I know of your great uncle. Who does not, eh? We have him here of course. And the other one.'

'Other one? You mean...? You have the Nazarene here? You mean that other one?' asked Judas.

Pluto just looked at him and said nothing.

Judas was about to say something else but had second thoughts.

'Just know... Yehuda,' sneered Pluto, 'that I am indeed trustworthy. I may not be mannered, clean or well-versed in the arts, but I tell the truth and, more than that, I know the truth. Unlike,' he said slowly, 'some.'

Judas looked around the cave as if to pick another topic of conversation.

'People believe me to be important,' went on Pluto his eyes not shifting from Judas, 'but am I more than I am? I was told that this,' and here he looked around, 'all of this was to be my lot. Oh, I argued of course, but I was eventually obliged to accept that what had to be done... had to be done.' He pointed at Jacob. 'And you will do the same.'

'What do you mean?'

'You too are a Silver Green, Ya'akov ben Maccabi.'

Jacob was astonished once again. Pluto smiled, not a very warm smile, but still a smile of sorts nonetheless, 'I can see your aura. It is silver. And I take it that Yehuda ben Yosef here is a Watcher?' Judas nodded.

Pluto nodded too. 'Yes, of course you are. A Watcher. You

brought the boy here?'

'Yes dominus,' said Judas somewhat shamefacedly now, 'and we followed a map.'

'A map?'

'Yes. This map,' said Jacob and handed over the hide which had wrapped the spear. Pluto took the leather and studied both the map and the writing, but said nothing.

'Dominus, you are the ruler of this… of the underworld?' asked Jacob of the small man.

'I am no ruler,' said Pluto smiling. 'Or maybe I am. Let's just say that I manage this… establishment. I receive the dead and help their souls on their way. Allegedly.'

Jacob didn't know what else to say and so said nothing. Pluto looked closely once again at the map.

'But,' Pluto said looking up, 'you still have not told me what you want here and I truly tire of asking. I have had enough of your company and so you had better leave - or of course stay. But, if you stay, then you stay. Understand?'

Judas nodded and stood up, ready to leave. He looked miserable and angry. Of course, thought Jacob, he has no gold.

'I have this,' said Jacob to Pluto and held up the so-called Spear of Destiny. The little man looked.

'I was instructed to bring this to someone,' Jacob said. 'As it is written there. Dīs. That's you. Look, your name is written there. It's for you dominus.'

Pluto looked at the map, then the broken spear. 'Well,' he sighed, 'be good enough to give it to me then, boy.'

Hesitantly, Jacob handed over the spear which Pluto took, peering at the broken end first. He looked closer and then looked up - not at Jacob, but at Judas.

'Do you love the memory of your great uncle?' he asked and Judas, taken aback at the turn in the conversation, nodded.

'I hope that you do,' said Pluto. He looked back at Jacob and handed the spear back. 'I was forewarned that this day would come. Apparently, you,' he pointed at Jacob, 'must do something of great importance.' Pluto laughed a full and very loud laugh. He wheezed and laughed again. 'Your face boy! Just a small task, saving humanity?' He laughed some more.

'This… this is funny? This amuses you?' asked Jacob, standing up flustered, confused, angry - his hands clammy and his forehead hot. He felt dizzy.

'Sit. Sit down boy. I can laugh if I choose. I need no permission from you to laugh. Or to cry. Be still. I don't laugh at you, but at the thought of you saving humanity. The fighters and the peacemakers, the emperors and the foot-soldiers, the honest and the dishonest, the merchants and the beggars, the good and the evil - that is the humanity to be saved. Should it be saved? Good question. Saving humanity is a big, big task and an impossible one for a boy. The Watchers have asked me to help you and help you I shall. Here, hold the spear.'

Jacob took the spear. Pluto nodded as if something had been achieved.

'Gentlemen,' he said, 'I will not offer you refreshment, for it would not be to your taste. But here is cool, fresh water. Take a gourd.' Jacob hesitated. Pluto was impatient. 'It is clean I promise you,' the little man said. 'Take it! I have not pissed in it and it has touched no more than the spring from where it comes. Drink. It's safe. I'll tell you something, so listen well.'

Jacob and Judas took a small gourd each, opened the stoppers, sniffed the contents, looked at each other and drank greedily. They heard a rumble accompanied by a great cloud of dust that belched through the lower part of the cave followed by a wave of very hot air. Jacob looked worried.

'Oh, that's nothing,' Pluto said, shrugging. 'The world far below this world coughs and farts from time to time.'

'So, let me explain,' Pluto said, scratching an armpit. 'I knew that one of the Silver Greens would come. I had been told. Watchers do share information you know.' He indicated Judas. 'Master Yehuda, you of course will know this, what with you being a Watcher and everything. And here you are, master Ya'akov. It is you. With the spear. You know about the spear and what they say it was?' Jacob nodded and looked at Judas.

'Good,' went on Pluto. 'So, they say that with it comes some power and the rest of the power comes from you. That's what they say. I really wouldn't know and neither do I much care. The spear is not yours to keep of course. Whoever claims the spear holds some kind of destiny of the world.' He shrugged. 'Or something… I forget. Probably nonsense. Who knows?' He turned to Judas. 'Do you?'

'I have not claimed the spear,' said Jacob hesitantly. 'I was told to…'

'You have it,' retorted Pluto. 'I just gave it to you. That you have it at all is a claim, believe me. A very strong claim. You don't have it by accident, that I can promise you.'

Jacob said nothing and just looked helplessly at the broken spear.

Pluto pointed upwards. 'The Romans are losing their empire,' he said quietly. 'It's crumbling fast day by day, hour by hour. The empire is losing power and has no funds. No money. No gold. I have gold, but they may not touch that.' He laughed again and Judas' eyes glittered.

'The Barbarians are strong now,' went on Pluto, 'and will, one day, overcome Rome. The Jews rise in strength once more too. And others as well. Christianity is spreading. There'll be wars and the Romans will lose some of those wars and then they will lose them all. The economy is based on plunder and looting. It produces nothing new. Emperors, all of them, even the ones who are not mad, rely on wealth from conquered territories and on tax collection that drives farmers into destitution.'

Pluto stopped to check that Judas and Jacob were listening.

'Soon Rome will burn. The Capitoline Hill, the Pantheon and Pompey's Theatre - these and more will be destroyed.'

Judas sneered. 'How do you know this?'

'I know. As I know that following the flames will be the plague. Titus will be poisoned. Brother against brother...'

'How...?'

Pluto was getting angry. 'Will you stop interrupting?'

Judas stopped interrupting.

'Rome will destroy itself - one way or another.' He paused and turned to Jacob.

'The Guild,' he spat. He paused. 'You know about these weevils?'

Jacob was anxious not to anger Pluto. 'A little, dominus,' he said quietly.

'The Guild,' went on Pluto, 'will make sure that Rome is destroyed. The empire is corrupt and its violence is legendary. Cruel. You know that? Of course you do. Let's see. What do they do? Well, they sew criminals into leather sacks together with an assortment of animals - let us say a starving wolf, a diseased monkey or hungry ants - and leave the result for a day. Or, what else - ah yes - you'll enjoy this one. A donkey is killed, sliced open and its entrails removed. The accused, perhaps a thief or some poor bugger who was in the wrong place at the wrong time, is stripped of clothing and stuffed into the animal's belly. The belly is stitched closed, leaving only the accused's head outside, preventing suffocation, but prolonging suffering. The donkey's body is kept in the sun; it decomposes while the living victim inside is cooked by the heat and consumed by maggots. Vultures peck at the decaying flesh.'

Jacob felt ill. He stood up and ran to one side of the cave, his chest heaving. He was violently sick. He wiped his mouth with his sleeve and went back to his place. Pluto looked not the slightest abashed or sorry for the boy.

'I shall refresh myself on your vomit later. Thank you.'

Pluto beamed at Jacob and carried on. 'My point is this. According to Roman belief, death is not a punishment, but a release. The torture is the punishment - and the terror that goes with it. Oh yes - and this is a good one - hammering a stake into...'

Jacob had heard enough. He stood and shouted, 'Enough! I know of this! I've seen these things and worse! I... I have seen these things.' He found it hard to breathe, not just because he was afraid, but because this place was heavy with warm air and thick smells. The huge cave and this... man... made no real sense. It was like a terrible nightmare. He wanted to throw the spear down and run from the cave and out into fresh air. He wanted to do that, but he didn't.

Pluto smiled. 'So, here we are,' he said, taking no notice of Jacob's discomfort. 'Here we are, boys. Rome is finished.'

He looked at Jacob and carried on as if teaching in a school. 'So, how will Caesar keep control over his cruel and crumbling world? What can he do in the time he has left? The Guild... you've said that you know something about these very pleasant people?' He didn't wait for an answer. 'Of course you do. The Guild, that bastion of nastiness. Those flies around the world's dungheaps.' He glanced sideways at Judas and looked back at Jacob before continuing.

'Well now, Guild coffers and brains have been used to support the empire. The Guild and various emperors had a deal, an arrangement. The Guild delivered its part of the bargain. The Guild wanted a prize in return. A Silver Green - just one little, simple Silver Green. Not too much to ask, eh? Why? So that they might have their clever alchemists experiment and extract the very juice, the very essence of a Silver Green to make an elixir, an elixir of... immortality.' He chuckled to himself. 'You seem to be the one they want. You're it.'

The little man paused again as if considering something. 'The Guild has actually wanted two things. You for the secret of immortality. And believe me, they have tried very hard to get you.' He chuckled, glancing once more at both Judas and Jacob.

'The other thing they want, a small consideration, is to rule. Not just one kingdom or a single country but the whole lot.

They made the Romans their puppet rulers of the world and the Romans should have handed over that power. That was the deal. Didn't happen of course. Never was going to happen - and, lads, I have no clue as to why any idiot Guild person would ever think that it was going to happen. The Roman rulers mucked everything up of course by being stupid, greedy or mad. Or all three. The deal involved a promise by the Romans to gather an enormous number of slaves. The Guild expected these slaves. Didn't happen. Well, it did happen. Rome did gather slaves - but kept them.' The little man picked his teeth for a moment and scratched his bottom.

'The Guild had to find its own labour which it did, but still it wanted more slaves to make its plans work. The Guild, thinking that things might change, continued to help Rome in so many practical ways. Did Rome keep its promise in return? Of course it didn't. It laughed. Not a smart thing to do. Not at all good. The Guild didn't like that. No, it did not.' He pulled at his beard. Bits of something fell from the scraggy hair. He caught whatever it was that fell and popped it into his mouth.

'The Guild,' said Pluto, 'has built a network of underground citadels - much like this, but maybe with more home comforts.' He grinned at his audience. Another great belch of hot air rushed into the cave. Jacob could smell ash and burning. Pluto took no notice. Judas picked his fingernails.

'The Guild did not get its slaves from the empire. And our emperor has not captured a Silver Green. Has not, in fact, captured you.'

The three could hear more rumbling as before, but this time it went on for longer. Pluto rubbed his face.

'The Guild, if it does not have what it was promised, will

destroy Rome.' He grinned and shrugged. 'Simple as that really. But Titus will be taught a lesson just as a last measure. One very last chance.' He looked across towards Judas and the nail picking.

Pluto turned to Jacob. 'You know what a volcano is?'

Jacob nodded. 'Of course.' Judas just picked his nails.

'Well, what you don't know,' said Pluto, 'is that volcanoes don't always erupt on their own. Did you know that? The Guild places material in them which makes the mountains explode with a gargantuan force.' Pluto made an exploding noise. 'Boom! In the old days, in Greece, people thought that this kind of thing was the hand of Zeus.' Pluto cackled and coughed long and hard. 'Those were the days, eh? When gods were gods.' He wheezed some more.

'The Guild,' continued Pluto, 'has an alchemist who made a material that can burn like the sun and it is this that sets off the eruptions. It's terrible alchemy. Not like the fumes and flames I get here. That's just the natural world. More or less. No. Volcanoes will be made to explode. Bang. The ash and heat will cause droughts, famines and death. Seas will shrink, rivers will dry, animals will expire, crops will blacken. Rome will starve. The world will starve. Everyone left on the surface will perish. The Guild has used Rome's slaves to build the citadels. The pretext was that the citadels were for the empire. What a joke! The Guild will live underground until the ash has done its worst and then they will rebuild and rule the world as they wish. In their own image. With the secret to immortality from you boy, they will live forever.'

He laughed again and poked Jacob in the chest with a bony finger.

Pluto grinned. 'Good plan, eh? They will give their slaves the immortality serum until the slaves are of no use. Or, if they complain too much.' He shrugged.

'Now then. You. Silver Green,' he said to Jacob in a matter-of-fact voice, 'you have a task to perform? Correct?'

Jacob felt faint. 'I don't know what you're talking about, magister.' He genuinely had no clue what this odd little man was saying. Desperately he wanted to stay alert but kept feeling dizzy. Pluto took absolutely no notice of the boy's plight, but looked from time to time at Judas who was now cleaning an arrow instead of his fingernails.

Jacob was about to speak, but Pluto held up a thin hand with gnarled joints. The hand was not his own.

He began to chew on it with huge relish. Jacob looked away.

Judas did not look at Pluto, but at the arrow he was cleaning. 'Excuse me,' he said arrogantly, 'but interesting as all of this is, where do I fit in? My part was to help this boy which I have done and then take some treasure from here. After all, you won't ever use it and... there must be enough gold here for a city of people to live happily for the rest of its days.'

'Quite so. You're right. A hundred such cities actually,' Pluto said pleasantly and politely as he turned towards Judas. 'There are ten caves such as this - each with jewels and gold reaching the ceiling and to feed any avarice. I could show you caves with wonders in them that would take you days and weeks to look through. However, young man, you shall have none of it.'

There was a silence and even the rumbling below them stopped for a moment. Judas looked up at Pluto and his voice had a steely edge to it as he gripped his bow. 'Oh yes - and why is that?'

'Because, you deceptive, devious, little sewer rat,' said Pluto in a pleasant, matter-of-fact voice, 'you are no Watcher.'

Judas glanced nervously at Jacob and away again, but not before Jacob saw fear in the other's eyes.

'That's not true,' said Judas quickly and was about to say more. He was not allowed the privilege.

Pluto spoke in his usual loud voice, but with slow emphasis. 'Everything you have said is a lie. Do you consider me stupid? I also know a Guild man or woman when I see one. I can smell 'em. I can almost taste 'em. And it is very hard, try as you might, boy, to hide an aura - and you have not hidden yours very well. Not from me at least. You,' Pluto said now pointing at Jacob. 'Can you not see this rat's aura?'

Jacob glanced at Judas. 'No, I cannot,' said Jacob stuttering slightly and wondering if his nightmare would shortly end.

'No?' The guardian of the underworld looked at Jacob in some surprise and tutted. 'Much to learn, much to learn. Well, you should by now know something about auras. This nasty piece of work has an orange aura that could light up a palace and only Guild folk have orange auras. Nobody else. Ever.'

Jacob looked at Judas, shocked, betrayed and saddened - but some understanding leaked into his overtired brain.

Pluto pointed at Judas with the half-eaten hand, 'You knew about this boy here. That wasn't hard. The Guild is well-informed. You knew where he was going in the hills. You knew where the soldiers were and when they would attack old Aram whom they killed in front of this boy's eyes. You took him to a den of Guild followers and pretended that they were good people. They were not.'

Judas tried to interrupt, but Pluto wouldn't let him.

'You would have killed the boy and taken the spear?'

'No!'

'Yes! You are a Guild man. Admit it at least.'

Jacob looked from Judas to Pluto. He asked quietly, 'How do you know this, magister?'

Pluto leaned towards Jacob. 'Because,' he said, 'there are Watchers always looking out for you. Always have - since you were born... And information flies when we guard a Silver Green. You are precious goods, boy. More than you know.'

Jacob looked at Judas, willing, almost pleading the bowman to deny the accusations and to prove his innocence. But Judas just stared at his feet. For a moment there was silence apart from the steady hiss from a deep fissure in the rock.

Judas looked up. 'Even if that were all true, I...' he began, smiling condescendingly. But before he could go any further, Pluto stood in front of the bowman.

'You have a choice, rat,' Pluto snarled. He pointed to a dark cave entrance on the other side of the cavern. 'That cave there leads to one of the places where I keep some treasures. They are well ordered. There's one piled high with gold ingots, another with silver bracelets, yet another with crowns and suchlike, one that has nothing but gems - and so on. Go there and take your chance. Take whatever you can carry and leave my world with my blessing.'

Judas had lost some of his bravado and his bottom lip trembled slightly. He asked, 'There is a choice?'

'Certainly there's a choice. Simply leave now with nothing. I will personally show you out.'

Judas smiled but Pluto did not. There was silence apart from the bubbling and hissing noises that came from deep beneath the ground.

Jacob watched as Judas weighed up his options.

'I choose the gold,' said Judas eventually.

Pluto nodded. 'Your choice is no surprise. I cannot say that I wish you well, but off you go.'

Judas looked at Pluto unsure what trap he had just fallen into. He wouldn't look at Jacob. With his bow, arrows, scarf and bag, Judas picked up a fresh gourd of water and walked off towards the cave's dark entrance. He didn't once look back.

'Now,' said Pluto happily to Jacob who stared wild-eyed at the retreating Judas, 'we must set you on your own journey, for you have much to do. Close your mouth boy.'

'What will happen to him?'

'Happen to him? Oh, he'll find the first cave of riches alright and he'll see the glittering piles. He'll go far inside and then fill his pockets and his bag with bits and pieces. He'll turn to leave and will see six exits only one of which will lead him out. Each exit looks the same and he'll have no clue which one to choose. I guarantee that he will choose badly.' Pluto shrugged. 'He'll be wandering about eventually without food and drink. And light. Until... well, I'm sure you know how these things end.'

'But...'

'Ya'akov, there are no buts. He would have handed you in. Of that please have no doubt whatsoever - and he would have been paid handsomely. Be wary of everyone. Many will seem believable to you. Trust nobody. Me included. The Guild is skilled and deceit is their art. Take my hand.'

Jacob looked at Pluto's offered hand in disgust but, seeing that it was the man's own, took it nonetheless, filthy as it was and stained red. His own arm suddenly felt warm and that warmth spread through his whole body. He felt sleepy and could see, quite clearly, a silvery glow around Pluto's head and then around his shoulders. The silver outline spread. Pluto let go of Jacob's hand and the silvery light went out.

'Now, I need to introduce you to my brothers, Neptune and Jupiter. And, before you ask,' he chuckled, 'they are not any kind of god either. Mind you, if they were, I wouldn't tell you, would I?' He laughed. 'Come with me.'

Jacob looked back at the cave that Judas and entered, but the bowman had gone.

'Ya'akov, follow me please. That scum was no friend of yours. Truly. Now, my brothers - well they're a different story, a good pair - very tough and talented you know. They are Watchers with a few powers added for good measure… and they are as trustworthy as the day is long. You believe me? No? Well, that's a good start. Follow close. Come along now. We must go. Watch out boy, don't slip. Careful. Mind the blood.'

17

Rome, Italy, 1492

Gabriella screamed as a knife was put to her throat the instant she walked into the room. It was held by a nasty and menacing child that had leapt onto a stool. At least the thing looked like a child and had a child's face, but the arm around Gabriella's neck pulling the girl towards the knife was incredibly strong.

Gabriella tried to pull back, but the hold round her neck was too powerful. There was a sudden shout in Italian from someone and immediately the knife was withdrawn and the child... the thing... jumped down, did a summersault and made a mewling kind of noise as it scampered off into a corner of the room.

There was another strange sound, a kind of singing, but not in any way melodic or easy on the ear. The language of the discordant song wasn't Italian or anything that Gabriella had heard before. On one side of the room, there was a small group of musicians playing strange instruments accompanied by four singers. In the middle of the room, facing Gabriella, were three men of various ages, dressed in brightly coloured cloaks and tall, conical hats bearing strange shapes. The men sat bolt upright, not moving.

In front of the men on a long table were small glass beakers, each filled with coloured or smoking liquids. Glass pipes connected one beaker to another and a much larger glass beaker containing a blue liquid turned white and back again to blue as it bubbled away. Instruments were laid out at one end of the table - scalpels, knives, various white ceramic dishes and what

165

seemed like a boiling liquid of some kind in a large pot. There was a strong smell in the air, a mix of burning cedar wood and something else, something Gabriella did not recognise, something that was acrid and irritated her throat.

Behind the staring, stony-faced men was a roaring fire in a large recessed fireplace.

As Gabriella stepped forward, the music and singing ceased. The atmosphere was malefic. Shadows flickered in the light of the fire and then grew longer and blacker. The men still stared. There was a window high up on one of the room's walls from where Gabriella could see and hear rain.

The outside world, so near, seemed distant. Lightning flashed, painting the whole room in a bluish white, tinged with flickering yellow from the fire's glare. In a flash of lightning, Gabriella saw something with slumped shoulders standing on the far side of the room, something with black eyes and great ears like horns. The creature wasn't human thought Gabriella, but it didn't seem to be an animal either. Was it a demon? But surely not hers! Had she rubbed the ring by mistake? No, she was sure that she had not.

A heavy machine of some kind began to run with a sudden lurching, grinding noise - belts turning, cogs meeting, meshing and grinding, heavy rollers rotating. Gabriella could see sharp spikes on the rollers and she shuddered. She wondered where the child-like person with the knife was hiding.

'We will kill you afterwards, of course,' said one alchemist suddenly in perfect Italian as if he was in the middle of a pleasant conversation. 'As we are bidden,' he added.

Gabriella tried to smile at the three men, keeping a wary eye on the beast in the corner. 'I don't understand, signori,' she said in Italian. 'I seek no trouble. Only the way out.'

Another alchemist spoke up, smiling politely. 'The way out? Of course. The way out. That is why you are here. For the way out. Our experiment is reasonably quick and, while it will be very painful for you, very painful indeed, the soothing calm of death will follow. Step closer, do.'

The third alchemist turned towards the creature in the corner and spoke to it in some strange language that Gabriella didn't understand. The musicians and singers were instructed to leave.

'Cesare Borgia,' said the eldest alchemist, 'and his sister, the delectable Lucrezia, have asked, no, have demanded, that we take from you some blood and... other certain... materials from your body, so that we - and they of course - can become immortal, like you. Except you won't be immortal any longer for you will be dead. But a small price to pay, don't you agree?'

Gabriella was already fingering her ring. 'Where is Cesare Borgia?'

'It is of no concern of yours whatsoever,' snapped one of the alchemists. 'He is most angry that you have destroyed the virus and its antidote but, dear child - did you think that this was the only supply? Even now we have sent messengers to the far parts of the east where the mixtures are made. It is a very long voyage, but our plans are only delayed and not abandoned. The Guild is deeply disturbed at what you have done. We have been delayed for far too long and too many times!'

The lightning continued to flash across the high window and rain drummed on the window's glass as if knocking to get in. Candles, oil lamps and the fire made the room's shadows dance. Gabriella turned to leave, but saw that the creature that had been in a corner a moment ago was now barring her exit. The alchemists, busily sorting out their surgical instruments, were more animated and clearly relishing the task ahead.

Suddenly Gabriella became angry, bitterly angry - and this was an anger that welled up, a pent-up anger that had been hidden for some time. Anger at the loss of her family, at the abuse she had suffered, at the things that she had seen, at the fact that nobody recognised that she was a princess, at the ridiculous position in which she now found herself. She rubbed the Ring of Solomon and pictured herself being immensely strong.

The creature in front of her smiled or so it seemed. Its skin was grey with yellow pustules and its head was almost too big for its bent body. It had fine hair and it wore a grubby loincloth and a strange necklace. It was stroking its face with one hand and flexing the claws on the other as if about to play the clavichord. It was solid with rippling, grey muscle and was content, it seemed, to wait patiently for instruction.

Gabriella felt a change in her body. It was as if she had been warmed from head to toe. The feeling was pleasant and she felt strong.

'Come here,' snapped one of the alchemists to Gabriella who didn't move. The alchemist said something to the creature.

The creature nodded and slouched forward, its head below its shoulders and its angry, bloodshot eyes locked onto Gabriella's.

Gabriella leaned back and, as the creature came closer, she stood on tiptoe and smashed her forehead into the creature's face with terrific force. She yelled something that nobody in the room could understand as the creature reeled, blood or something like blood pouring from its face.

The three alchemists stood still, astonished and a little bewildered. One grabbed a long, sharp, surgical knife. He was the shortest of the three and possibly the bravest, but that meant little. Gabriella was still facing the creature which now stood a little taller than before and bared its teeth. It wiped a claw across its damaged head and stared stupidly at the result.

Gabriella, in something of a haze, but still feeling courageous and strong, smiled a smile that she had never smiled before and slammed her two fists into either side of the creature's head. The strike was as if the creature had been hit with the huge weight of two pieces of Veronese marble. Its eyes rolled upwards and it fell to its knees with a thump and then, as it began to fall backwards, Gabriella pushed a finger into each of the creature's eyes in quick succession. Then, without waiting to see the result, she breathed in deeply, turned and walked slowly forwards towards the three alchemists.

Within moments, one of the three alchemists had been forced into the heavy, whirring machine that sat at one side of the room. The man was soon mangled, spiked and ground by the heavy, rotating rollers. Another had managed to climb up a huge storage cupboard filled with mixtures and concoctions. He smiled, thinking himself safe. The smile turned to horror as the girl managed to shake the huge piece of furniture and the man fell. The dazed alchemist tried to stand but, as he did, Gabriella pulled the heavy piece of furniture which crashed down on top of him. The third alchemist was still screaming in the fire. Gabriella, taking no notice of the alchemists - dead or alive - breathed heavily once again and sank into a soft chair, exhausted. She shook her head and seemed to awaken as if from a dream.

Looking in disgust and horror about the room, she knew that this had been her doing, but she had no clue as to how she had managed to do it. She tried to breathe more easily, relaxing a little in the hope that any immediate danger had passed.

The creature, blind and supine on the floor, was twitching and making hoarse, grunting noises. Then it disappeared leaving a strong smell of rot. The screaming alchemist soon stopped screaming. The only sound left was the roaring of the log fire and the raging storm. Lightning still flashed across the window and there were occasional peals of thunder.

The girl couldn't quite understand what had just happened. She seemed to have become a monster in her own right with strength to match. Where had this strength come from? And the anger? She had never felt such fire in her very soul.

As she was thinking these things, she heard distant footsteps approaching. She knew that she must leave without any delay. Further time spent here spelt danger. But which way was out? She couldn't go back the way she had come in and she didn't want to leave by the door that the musicians had used.

Looking wildly round the room for another exit, she noticed a small door that looked as if it might be nothing more than a cupboard. Quickly she ran to it and wrenched it open. In the dim light, she could see that this was a doorway to a low, narrow passageway. Silently, she begged any listening god of any description that this was not another passageway leading to yet more disaster. However, she could feel cold air that must have come, she hoped, from outside. Quickly she ran as best she could along the corridor which, though poorly lit, allowed her at least to see what was in front of her.

Ahead was a large, solid wooden door and she could hear

the heavy rain beyond. Quickly, she tried to turn the huge metal door handle which didn't move. She rubbed the ring and pictured herself on the other side of the door which suddenly swung open of its own accord. Gabriella, amazed that the ring had the power to do what she wanted, stepped outside and was immediately enveloped in the raging storm. The door blew back and slammed shut. She couldn't see properly where she was, but it wasn't the front of the palazzo of that she was certain.

Wishing that she was warm and dry, the freezing rain seemed to increase as did the wind. She shivered, hugging her arms around herself and, in so doing, rubbed the ring. Immediately, the rain stopped, the wind calmed and the sun broke through the heavy, scudding clouds. Gabriella smiled to herself as she watched the ring go from bright blue to its normal dull grey.

As she began walking away from the palazzo, Maria appeared from around a corner. She ran to Gabriella and hugged her tight but, without saying anything, pushed the girl violently away. Gabriella's smile at seeing Maria turned to fear. What was this? Had Maria become an enemy for some reason? Was this yet another twist?

Two short, but very strong, arms were suddenly around her neck. Somebody or something behind her was immensely strong. She could hear grunts and snarls as whatever it was began to strangle her. Maria stepped forward immediately and with two swift swipes of a long, thin knife, stabbed twice over Gabriella's left shoulder. The child-like person, more like a large doll, fell from Gabriella's back and, wounded, scampered off across the street only to fall under the wheels of a passing carriage.

'It was behind you,' said Maria pulling Gabriella into shadow. 'Now, it is no more. A demon. The Guild can try and manipulate the power of the ring. I've told you. Be careful. Your strength can stop them. You were lucky.'

'Lucky? You think I've been lucky?'

'Yes.'

Gabriella looked across at where the doll-like creature had fallen. 'Is the… thing… dead now?'

'It was never really alive.'

Gabriella wanted to shout at Maria for putting her in danger with no help at all from the so-called Watchers. She wanted to yell that now, this very moment, she wanted to be on her way to Africa, to be the princess that she was born to be. But she said nothing at all. She was exhausted and felt that she had done enough to ensure that Emilio and Maria would hopefully help her to go back to Africa.

Maria took one of Gabriella's hands and quickly marched the girl away from the palazzo. Gabriella allowed herself to be led away and the pair walked, without speaking, along a series of side-streets until they reached the safe house. Maria unlocked the door and led the girl in.

Within moments, holding a cup of warmed red wine and with blankets once again around her shoulders, Gabriella slumped to the floor. She wept. 'Where were you? Where were you?' Tears were streaming down her face. 'You said that I would be safe. I wasn't! I wasn't safe at all. Where were you? Where is Emilio?' asked Gabriela.

'I have something to tell you,' Maria said.

18

Underworld, Jerusalem, Imperial Province, Roman Empire, 79 CE

Breathing heavily, for the sulphurous air was making Jacob feel sick and faint in equal measure, the boy stumbled behind Pluto as they walked back towards the main entrance through which Judas and he had come. He thought of Judas and his treachery. And what was Judas' reward? To wander with all the wealth of a king and never able to enjoy it. Doomed in the dark amongst the dead. Jacob wondered if he could ever trust anyone. Would everyone lie and cheat?

The boy couldn't see properly and images kept swimming before his eyes. The damp scarf that Judas had given him had long ago slipped and fallen off, but Pluto had made no effort to pick it up and Jacob was beyond caring. He hoped that he was being guided to the exit so that he could go back to normality but, on the other hand, he just wanted to lie down and sleep. Or die.

Pluto had said something about the task. What was it he'd said? In his befuddled brain, Jacob decided that, if he got out of the underground horror, there would be no tasks; he'd had enough. If he lived, he would go off and join the Bedouin and see out his days as a shepherd. He would marry and have many children. He and his many children would tend sheep, goats and camels. That wasn't a bad life after all was it? No, it was perfect and it would be peaceful.

As he tripped and almost fell, he thought of something else. If he was truly immortal, well that was a long time to be a shepherd! How did immortality work? The old man had said that he wouldn't age beyond thirty, but Pluto was well over that age and he was meant to be immortal. Were there different rules of some sort? He'd been told that he was special. Was aging until he was thirty part of being special? If you lived forever, one day you'd have had enough surely? Would you take your own life? One day, would you beg for that? Was this all a dream?

Pluto was talking about something, but Jacob wasn't listening and just wanted to get out of the place.

'You know,' said Pluto breezily as if out for a stroll in a garden. 'Well, I'm sure you must know - Jerusalem was once the most fantastic of cities, astride two mountains amid the barren crags of Judea, everyone reasonably well off, happy and with enough to eat. You must hand it to old Herod; bit of a bully yes - psychotic, but so creative! His palaces and fortresses were built on so monumental a scale and were so luxurious in their decoration that the historian Josephus, oh he's here somewhere by the by, well he wrote that Herod's buildings 'exceed all my ability to describe them'. Now look at the city - a total mess! What's wrong, boy?'

Jacob couldn't raise his head properly. It seemed terribly heavy. He managed a shrug but thought at any moment he would just collapse. He couldn't see properly either. Maybe this was the end, he thought. Maybe this was the time when he would drift off and never awaken. In the underworld. Well, it'd be a short journey to lay his bones to rest. Jacob tried to laugh but couldn't. Maybe dying here is what he deserved for all that he had done wrong. Holding on to Pluto, he felt tears of self-pity well up in his eyes. Yes, maybe he would just drift away... that would be some payment for all the hurt he had done.

'My wife, you know, the lovely Proserpine,' Pluto was saying to a totally disinterested Jacob, 'well she first visited here - and lived. She too wasn't harmed by illness or poisons. Like you.' Playfully he nudged Jacob in the ribs.

'Now, you're not the first person to come in here alive. Not by any means. Not many come out of course. Some people come in and try to seek lost souls, against all advice, and die in the attempt. Maybe I should get a sign? What do you think? In Greek, Aramaic and Latin? What about those who can't read though?' He laughed.

'Then there are those who come to charm us with gifts, with money, gold and sometimes delightful music. All so that they can have a loved one returned. Touched as we always are by such requests, once the dead are here, well, they must stay.'

Jacob slipped and stumbled again and was about to fall, but was held up by a strong and confident hand. Jacob didn't even look to see whose hand it was, but he could smell lavender.

'This is my wife, Proserpine,' said Pluto proudly. Jacob turned with difficulty and saw a beautiful woman who seemed ageless. Her long blonde hair was plaited and her dress was of the finest yellow, diaphanous material that fitted close to her body. She smiled gently at Jacob but said nothing.

'Met her for the very first time - actually not here, but when I was out and about in the world. Long, long time ago that was. Love at first sight you know. Sometimes we meet the freshly dead together. Rumour has it that we take some to what they up there call the Elysian Fields, the so-called land of the blessed, but there is no such place, Ya'akov, no such place. The evil souls we get - and there are many of those I can tell you - are alleged to go to a very dark eternity in Tartarus, the region of torment, but there is no such place as that either. Oh, I know that the empire makes yearly sacrifices of black bulls, sheep or pigs and all sorts in night-time ceremonies, but that's just an excuse for a few drinks or an orgy. The sacrifices are done over a pit so that the blood is supposed to drip down to me here. Load of rubbish. Mind you I confess to being partial to the smell of burning cypress wood that they use at their funerals. Ah, here we are.'

Proserpine shushed her husband and said, stroking Jacob's cheek, 'The boy's a Silver Green, husband. He should not be affected by any poison. So why is he faint?'

'Dear Proserpine. Kiss me my dear. The boy is in shock, nothing much more. He's just seen someone he thought a friend go off to die. He wishes he could know more about what's happening to him and he finds the fumes here unpleasant. He is immune, but exhausted. Nice enough lad, don't you think?'

Pluto stopped and listened for a moment then, satisfied with whatever he heard, he winked at his wife and whistled a long and piercing whistle. Nothing happened. Then from the shadows there appeared two very tall and strong-looking young men.

Pluto turned to Jacob and with a proud wave of his hands indicated the two men. 'My younger brothers. Let me introduce you. That one there is Jupiter. And the smaller one is Neptune.' He cackled.

The brother called Neptune was by no means small. He was a giant of a man. Both were smiling at Pluto and they each hugged Proserpine, then looked curiously at Jacob.

'Not often you have visitors, brother. Not live ones anyway,' said the one who had been introduced as Jupiter.

Pluto looked at his brothers and said, 'This is Ya'akov ben Maccabi. You already know the detail of what must be done. See to it.' He turned to Jacob.

'My brothers, like me, are Watchers,' he said. 'Real ones, unlike that camel spit back there. My brothers have always proven their worth and have done so honestly. They move around the lands of men - up there. I cannot venture up there for very long. That is my curse. But they can and do. They watch out for people like you and... help keep order for The Watcher Authority. You may trust them with your life. But, as I told you, you would be wise to trust no-one and then trust only whoever properly deserves trust. As time goes by, your head will help you. As will this.' And he prodded Jacob's chest gently over the boy's heart. 'As for your spear,' he shrugged, 'who knows?'

Jacob was weary beyond exhausted. Physically and mentally, he was finding it hard to cope with everything that had happened recently and he was struggling to take in any new information. For the second time in the space of little time, his vision blurred, he lost focus, his hands began tingling and he felt icy cold.

Before he collapsed, Neptune grabbed the boy and lifted him up as if he were a bag of feathers. He slung Jacob, his bag, cloak and spear over his shoulder while Pluto, gently for so rough a man, dabbed the edge of his filthy tunic around Jacob's face. Pluto then kissed the top of the unconscious boy's head. The three brothers and Proserpine exchanged some brief words and, finally, with smiles and salutations, Pluto retreated into his dark domain holding hands with his wife. The others made their way towards the surface and fresher air.

Once outside the cave's gate, Neptune poured a little water into the boy's mouth. Jacob spluttered and came round, having no initial clue as to where he was. Both the big men were watching him as he lay on the ground.

Neptune spoke only as much as was necessary. 'We need to take you first to the south of another country. It is a very long journey.' He shrugged and chewed on something that had mint in it.

'A very long journey,' Jupiter repeated. And that was all he said.

Jacob, groggy and exhausted, understood nothing but just tried to nod. He didn't care where he was going and had no interest in anything but sleep. He had the spear - he could not yet call it his - and he had his knife which the two brothers noticed he kept touching. He tried to sit up but couldn't.

Jupiter picked Jacob up despite the boy's weak protestations. After a short distance, Jacob vaguely remembered being placed gently into the back of a simple, covered cart which was attached to two horses. The rear of the cart had a false bottom on which were soft blankets and that is where Jacob was put. Above Jacob a wide plank of wood covered the hiding place and on that the brothers laid out some fresh vegetables. Jupiter began singing a soft melody with words that Jacob could hear but did not really follow.

It was late afternoon as the cart left the ruined city and ventured out along the track towards the desert. There were few people about and fortunately no patrols at that time of day.

In case they met any soldiers, Jupiter and Neptune had a story about taking vegetables to sell to a Syrian merchant encamped in the desert and who was, anyway, a great friend of the governor. Jacob fell into a fitful sleep under the cart in the hidden, wooden compartment dreaming that he was in someone's vegetable garden and, despite wanting to, couldn't leave.

Every time he awoke, he wondered where he was and then before anything made any sense, he fell asleep again. There was a gourd of water next to him and a pouch of dates. Despite trying to call out feebly from time to time, the gentle rolling of the cart and the quiet voices or singing of the two brothers always lulled him back to sleep.

The journey took until near dawn when they eventually reached Sychar near Shechem and an encampment where the two big men were welcomed enthusiastically as was Jacob. He recalled falling gratefully into the arms of someone who said something comforting to him in a confusion of Arabic, Latin and Aramaic; then, once again, he remembered nothing more.

When he awoke, he could smell mint and, opening his eyes, squinted at the harsh, bright light of day. He closed his eyes, breathed in the scent again and smiled to himself. It reminded him of childhood. Why mint though? He wanted the memory, but it evaded him.

The bed was warm and he felt safe. Stretching languidly, he delighted in the fact that he had a clear head.

Suddenly he knew that he wasn't alone. Opening his eyes, he saw looking down at him a woman with clear, almond-shaped eyes and a smiling mouth. Jacob noticed that she had faint freckles, dimples in her cheeks and tied back, jet black hair. Then he noticed something that made him start. The woman only had one ear.

As if reading his mind and seeing his reaction, the smiling

woman said in a relaxed and relaxing voice, 'It happened a long time ago and I lost the ear in a fight, during the battle for the Temple, defending some people… children and old women. Many of us did that - nothing special.' She shrugged as if embarrassed.

'Most people notice the missing ear,' she said, laughing. 'I used to have my hair down to cover it, but it just gets in my way, so…' and she shrugged once more. 'Drink some of the mint tea,' she insisted. 'It'll do you good.'

Jacob sat up and propped himself up on a pillow.

He took a sip or two of the tea. 'Where am I and who are you?'

'You are in the district of Samaria. Your two friends brought you here. This place is called Sychar. You've slept for a full day. Soon you must travel to the port of Caesarea. There you will board a ship bound for Italy. It will be a long voyage. Have you heard of Italy?'

Jacob looked at the woman carefully and nodded. There was something vaguely familiar about her. 'It's where the Romans come from,' he said. 'Rome… Italy… the empire… the emperor. Enemies all.'

The woman, noticing that the boy was frowning, changed the subject and asked, 'Are you hungry?' Jacob nodded. He still didn't know the name of this one-eared woman. He was suddenly acutely aware that this was the second time recently that he'd awoken in a strange place amongst so-called friends and the last time that had happened, he thought, the outcome had been less than happy.

'You frown again. Why?'

'Am I amongst friends?' Jacob asked realising that it was of course a remarkably foolish question.

'It's up to you to decide.' She paused. Neither seemed to know what to say next. She smiled again at him - an open, wide smile. 'Your clothes,' she said cheerfully, 'are washed and are over there, along with your bag and cloak. And here is your spear. Your broken spear. Now, go and wash and wash well. You stink. Then get dressed. Eat something and then we must leave.'

'We?'

'Indeed. We.'

'To a ship?'

'To the ship.'

'And will the journey across the sea be safe?'

'That is a good question. Probably not very safe, no.'

'Do I have a choice?'

'Not really, no.'

'And who will explain what I have to do?'

'I will,' said another voice and Jacob had to turn to the other side of the bed to see who'd spoken.

19

Port of Civitavecchia, The Tyrrhenian Sea, Italy, 1492

Gabriella had been shocked and greatly saddened to hear about the loss of Emilio. Even though she had known the young man for only a very short time, she'd liked the cheeky smile and his positive manner. Death seemed so sudden here - and recently in her short life she had seen or had been close to a great deal of it. She felt bewildered. Loss weighed heavily on her young shoulders and she was confused at what had occurred over the last few days. But she kept reminding herself of what her mother and father would have said to her and that strengthened her resolve to be brave. The very thought of them made her stand tall as she knew a princess should.

Maria and Gabriella were in Civitavecchia, the great port that served Rome. Maria was seeking out a particular ship, one that was bound for the known far places of the south eastern world.

The port was a hive of bustling activity with people of all races, shapes and sizes. On the quayside, Gabriella could hear a myriad of shouted languages and she was captivated by the colours of vegetables, fruit, clothing and the plethora of goods that were on display. Fishermen, selling their latest catches, called out their best prices. Sweating merchants haggled over bolts of cloth. Urchins ran around playing games and stealing the occasional piece of fruit or handful of figs. Near the customs office three youths were being beaten by four papal officers.

The rattling boom of huge canvas sails added to the

symphony of the smacking, slapping and cracking of sails that came from the smaller vessels. Boats and ships of all sizes and types were either tethered to the three quays or moving westward across the bay. There were enormous merchant ships, sitting high in the water, heading out to sea. Maria had told her that these ships carried spices, cloth and wine. Heavier cargo vessels, almost bursting with sacks of wheat, made their way slowly as they tacked with the wind. Barges with their huge brown sails, heavily laden with dripping, light brown clay, were so low in the water that Gabriella thought that at any moment they would disappear beneath the waves.

Sturdy vessels, more angular than streamlined, carried huge crates on deck. Gabriella could smell spices, although she wasn't sure whether the welcome smell came from supplies on the quayside or from the ships. She could also smell the latest catches from a fishing fleet with nets aloft and baskets full of still wriggling fish. A Spanish galeón was anchored at the edge of the bay, full flags flying. A fast and heavily armed papal ship, with its shiny guns, huge masts and massive sails, patrolled harbour waters with shouted commands easily heard even over the sharp wind. Waves in multiple shades of green were topped by sparkles of dancing light.

Maria was talking in Spanish to two men who were dressed in dark clothing and who, from time to time during their conversation, looked over at Gabriella. There was a great deal of head shaking following which the men then stood back a little and conferred. Gabriella wondered what had happened. Maria went over and held the girl's hands tight.

'We are in the wrong place,' Maria said. 'Our ship, the ship that we should have taken, is not safe. The food onboard has spoiled and the water barrels are fouled. And there are too many Guild people about. These men are Watchers and will escort us to the port of Palos, near Huelva in Spain's south. It is a very long journey, but it is the safest way to get to a safe ship. The Guild will want to stop us but hopefully their spies will not know of our planned route.'

The journey to Palos was indeed very long and not particularly pleasant. Over the weeks, the two men accompanying Maria and Gabriella spoke little, never smiled but were ever watchful. Gabriella was quiet for much of the time, but there was important information about what was to come that Maria had to explain which she did several times and in detail.

Travel was mostly on horseback and some of it by horse and cart. Great care had to be taken as they journeyed along roads or bridleways to be sure that they weren't being followed.

But they were being followed. What none of the four knew was that there were two other travellers, acting as insurance. These two additional Watchers kept a very careful eye on Gabriella and her three companions for the whole length of the long journey.

The roads through Italy were often uneven and the dirt paths were mostly furrowed which made travelling by cart uncomfortable and often painful. In Spain the roads and paths were sometimes even worse. On occasion the way was almost unpassable, particularly in wet weather and there seemed to Gabriella to be a lot of that. Frequently, the four had to walk and sometimes they were obliged to wait under large beech and cypress trees or in deserted shepherd's huts until storms passed.

During the journey, Gabriella's questions to Maria, while being few, were repetitive. She wanted to know much more about the ring, Pope Alexander, his evil daughter Lucrezia and disgusting son, Cesare. She wanted to know more about the task ahead and why she, of all people and of all Silver Greens, had been chosen. She particularly wanted to know more about demons. Maria's answers were sometimes precise, but not always. And, on the subject of demons, Maria was vague.

'Lucrezia,' said Maria on a rainy evening in a small town outside Barcelona where the four were planning to spend the night, 'is clever, scheming and ruthless. She kills anyone who gets in her way. Cesare is a senior Guild man, although his behaviour in the past has been found to be unsavoury - even for Guild tastes. Is he still trusted? Probably, but he does what he does for himself. On the other hand, he gets results and that's all they really care about. It is he who developed the plan to create and distribute the plague virus. It was he who found the alchemists to create the antidote. He will do anything to protect the remaining virus and antidote on the isle of Singapura. Singapura is his plan. The Guild yearns for power and, even more than that, for the secret of immortality. That can only come from a Silver Green, a Silver Green like you.'

If that had been said to frighten Gabriella or to keep her on guard, then it worked. Gabriella nodded, swallowed and shuddered. She was finding it hard to accept that she was a Silver Green and, as such, was being hunted. Nervous of shadows, strange noises and people coming too close, she was becoming ever anxious.

The rain beat down on the inn's roof and windows. The wind whistled and made shutters and the inn's sign rattle. Gabriella was about to go up to the bedroom that she shared with Maria. A short, overweight man approached. He had a drinker's red nose and his clothes, once smart and costly, were now dirty and ill-fitting. The man stood far too close for comfort and leered at Gabriella, breathing into her face.

'Yours is a pretty young body,' he slurred, swaying a little as he cupped Gabriella's chin with both hands. She jerked her head away.

Maria moved quickly to the man's side. 'Let the girl be, sir.'

The man turned to Maria. 'Or what, pretty lady? I might decide to have you both tonight. I shall pay you something of course.' He grinned. 'If it pleases me.'

'I said, leave the girl alone. Sir.'

'And I say again, or what?' The man's voice was becoming louder and he leaned in very close to Maria, his breath heavy with onions and sour wine.

'You will beat me? I should like that,' said the man. 'You will punish me in other ways? That too I may enjoy.'

On either side of the man the two Watchers appeared, one holding the drunk's left arm very tightly. Suddenly, another man, tall and elegant, strode into the circle.

'Go to bed Luigi,' the elegant man said in Italian to the drunk nuisance.

'I will not…'

'Then these men will take you outside and beat you. I shall not stop them.'

'They…'

'To bed Luigi.'

Luigi giggled as he swayed. 'On my own?'

Maria took one of the man's hands and crushed his fingers. Luigi squealed.

The tall, elegant man stepped forward and whispered something in Luigi's none too clean right ear. The drunk swayed a little, looked with interest again at Gabriella, bowed low, almost to the point of falling flat on his face, tried a curtsey and left.

The smartly dressed, elegant man bowed his head slightly to Maria and then to Gabriella. He stepped forward, but the two Watchers stopped him.

The man looked at the two Watchers, was about to remonstrate but, seeing their solid stance, hard faces and knives, changed his mind. 'I apologise for that man,' he said now in Spanish. 'He is a scribe who works for one of my family. We are on our way to... He will not bother you further.'

None had noticed the second set of Watchers who had both stood and were now sitting down again in the shadows, for all the world a couple enjoying a simple supper and some wine which they were not actually drinking.

The elegant man said, 'Madam, your bodyguards can stand down now.'

Nobody moved.

'Very well.' Still nobody moved.

'Forgive me,' said the man trying to keep his composure. He bowed. 'I forget my manners. My name is Giacomo de Columbo and...'

'Sir,' interrupted Maria. 'Forgive us, but we have travelled far and we have far still to travel in the morning. We need our rest. It was kind of you to interfere with that gentleman's unwelcome attention, but we must now bid you goodnight.'

'Wait! I beg your pardon. Please. I would be acquainted with you and the night is young. The least I may do is to offer you some wine. I…I…' Suddenly, he stopped talking, stared in sudden surprise at Gabriella and took a step backwards.

'Ladies, mis disculpas… my apologies,' said Giacomo de Colombo, now confused, 'I did not realise… I did not know…' He lowered his voice to a shadow of a whisper. 'She is a Silver Green.'

The two Watchers stepped even closer to Giacomo de Colombo. The two in the shadows stood again and, unseen, stepped forwards. Maria, taken aback for only a moment, said, 'I don't know what you mean. I advise you to say nothing more. Nothing! These men here,' Maria said indicating the two Watchers now holding Giacomo de Colombo's arms, 'will wish to know more, much more, of who you are and why you are here. You will tell them, sir. Of that have no doubt. You may die as a result of what you say. Be thankful that you still live. And now truly we must retire.'

'Where are you bound?'

'It is no business of yours. None.'

'In Spain?'

'I have just told you that it is no business of yours. If you follow us, then you will die for your troubles. If you are not dead sooner. And now goodnight.' Maria nodded briefly to the man who bowed in return, but not as confidently as before. She turned and led Gabriella upstairs.

The man called Giacomo de Columbo, narrowed his eyes and watched them go. The two Watchers held an arm each as they escorted him to another room in the inn. The door was opened and Giacomo de Columbo was pushed into the room. The Watchers stepped in, closed the door and locked it. The other two Watchers, a young man and a slightly older woman watched the three go into the room. They looked at each other. And smiled.

20

Tyrus, Mare Nostrum, Imperial Province, Roman Empire, 79 CE

Captain Umero, of the naval vessel Quintus, had briefed Jacob well. The boy had listened carefully, although he'd struggled with the speed at which the captain rushed his Latin. He soon discovered though that when Umero spoke, people always listened.

The captain also loved to talk about his ship, the fifth largest in his fleet now ready to leave Tyrus, probably, Umero believed, the best port in the Mare Nostrum. He had been in the Roman navy for fifteen years, had served on several vessels and had captained many. He had seen action along most of the empire's coasts, from the freezing edges of the Oceanus Atlanticus to the Pontus Euxinos followed by a long tour of duty around Alexandria and then chasing Parthians near Apollonia. He knew the sea well and the dangers in and of it.

In truth, Umero was much more than a captain. He was one of the few praefecti - Roman fleet commanders - and he earned a great deal of money as well as respect. But Umero preferred to be known as a captain or, as many who sailed under him, the captain.

He was battle-scarred as was his beloved ship. Quintus had a V-shaped hull and a ballast which made it much more stable than most vessels of a similar size. Its stern-mounted steering oars had superb leverage and were not at all cumbersome to use. Every time the ship was in port, the huge steering blades were oiled with linseed. Double planking strengthened the ship's hull, thereby allowing heavy weapons to be transported from Italy to Judea or Syria. And the ship was fast; it needed two hundred oarsmen who were, it was argued, the best in the Roman world.

Umero had learned most of his navigational skills from the Carthaginians. They had also taught him as much about listening to ships as using them to win battles. He always took careful notice of the sounds his ships made. The gurgle of the running tide past the ship's sides, the gentle lapping of small waves created by a passing vessel, the bump and very light crunch of a ship's prow nudging the quayside and the moan of rigging in the wind. Umero had heard all these many times before, along with the countless other noises that were part of knowing that all was well. Or that it wasn't.

He loved to hear the straining of timbers each one of which worked in harmony with its neighbour, the murmur of the rowers, the rattle of the anchor and feet on the decks. He liked the sudden clangour of the drums marking out the rowers' pace. Even the smells, they too always remained with him. In particular, the braziers, burning resin, timber oil and the verbena lotion that some of his officers used. When any ship pitched a little as another vessel passed, thereby disturbing the bilges, the stench was one of decay. The Guild always reminded him of decay and that is what he thought about now. Decay.

Umero paused in his reverie as he noticed activity on the quay. There was a centuria of the Praetorian Guard. These men, he knew, were hard as nails, specially trained and afraid of nothing. He could see the soldiers in the dwindling light. Why were they there? Normally, given his rank and the power he had, he would have been advised of any troop movements, particularly any so close to wherever he might be operating. But the emperor's own guard were obliged to tell nobody anything. Anyway, this was odd because the emperor wasn't in this area, mused Umero. Or was he? He, Umero, would have known that, surely? Maybe the Praetorians were after the Jews again. Maybe that's it, he thought. A secret foray. Or maybe there were Christian revolts that the troops in Antiochia or wherever couldn't manage on their own.

Unless... he thought... unless.... He turned from his view of the quayside and beckoned a sea-serving soldier.

'Fetch Marcellus,' he said curtly.

The man returned quickly with the ship's battle captain, someone whom Umero trusted with his life, as he had done on many occasions and vice versa. Before approaching, Marcellus remained at the cabin's entrance and raised an arm out in salute to Umero.

'Domine?'

'Come in Marcellus. There are eighty or so of the Praetorian Guard on the quay. Do you know why?'

'Yes domine. They are to follow us in three ships along with the cohort that stands by.'

'Why did I not know this?'

'I didn't know that you did not, my captain.'

'I did not and am now displeased in extremis that I have the emperor's own guardians on my tail like some whore's disease. Why?'

'I can tell you precisely why,' said a deep and loud voice.

Umero turned as did Marcellus who immediately saluted once again and inclined his head. The person to whom the salute had been given this time was one of the procuratores ducenarii, the most powerful leaders in the emperor's navy. This man was one of the few who ran the Praetorian forces and he was, Umero knew, also one of the emperor's confidants.

'Ah, Tiberius,' said Umero affably, 'you arrive unannounced and it seems that you always turn up when the bilges churn a little or there's a bad smell around. To what do I owe this dubious pleasure?'

'One day, my dear Umero, you will say, or probably do, the wrong thing at the wrong time and then we'll have you hanging upside down on a wheel, naked, covered in honey and being pecked at by vultures and a variety of animals or insects attracted to the sweet feast. You will have a bird's eye view that is until you have no eyes. One can only hope for the day.'

'Well now, Tiberius Augusta, speak up if you please before I let my men throw you over the side as a good dinner for the fish. That death would be both painful for you and most enjoyable for us to watch.'

'I have troops that say that won't ever happen. And you know it.'

'Well, we could put a bet on that couldn't we? How much money do you have with you?'

'I have not come here to argue...'

'In which case, I bid you good evening and do be careful as you leave my ship.'

Tiberius Augusta sighed theatrically. 'I've come here to let you know that we have orders to relieve you of your duties. You have on board this vessel a boy. He is to come with us.' He turned to Marcellus and said, 'Fetch him.' Nobody spoke or moved. 'Fetch him,' repeated Tiberius Augusta to Marcellus louder and with menace in his voice. 'Battle captain - Marcellus is it? If you value anything at all, including your own life, and those of your family, you will fetch the boy now.' Marcellus turned to leave.

'Marcellus,' said Umero calmly, 'you will do no such thing. Walk a step in any direction and you will rue the day.' Marcellus did not move.

Umero stepped closer to Tiberius Augusta. 'Tiberius,' said Umero in a matter-of-fact way, 'you can't have the boy. I have no idea how you knew he was here, but clearly you do. I will not hide the fact. I urge you to caution, however. Yes, you outnumber me, but your crack troops will suffer. As will you. That's a promise. Your choice. But you shall not have the boy this day or any other. Not while I live.'

'Well, that's easily remedied,' said Tiberius with a sneer. 'You cannot fight the emperor's troops. That's treason. I ask you once again for the boy. No harm shall come to him.'

Umero laughed. 'We both know that isn't true. And for that reason alone, you shall not have him. Snakes like you who pretend allegiance to our emperor, but who are in receipt of Guild gold, make me sick. You get two hundred thousand sesterces a year for doing what you call your job. And additional Guild money accounts for what, Tiberius? Another couple of hundred thousand? Or more?' Umero turned to Marcellus. 'Please arrange for the fleet commander to leave my ship. He is departing our company. Now.'

'I hope you know what you're doing ducem navali Umero!' spat Tiberius. 'The emperor will learn of this. What shall I say in my report? A Roman threatening the Guard? You threaten me, you threaten Rome. And therefore you threaten the emperor. The payment for that is, as you very well know, death. Now then, the boy if you please. And quickly. I tire. It will be sunset in an hour or so and we must travel.'

Outside Umero's cabin there could be heard a scuffle and noises of metal on metal. All three men turned. The soldier on the other side of the cabin who'd had his head bowed since Tiberius had entered the room, now looked up, alarmed. There were several thuds and thumps as something heavy hit the floor. Four times.

Umero spoke in a relaxed way, 'I imagine that those four were your immediate consort? No need to answer. I can see it in your cowardly face. Concerned, are you? For your life?' The noises outside the cabin had ceased.

'Marcellus,' said Umero with cool efficiency, 'Go and see that all is well and ensure that our special guests are safe.' To the soldier on the other side of the room, he said, 'Go with him.' The soldier, greatly relieved, saluted. Marcellus nodded briskly and saluted both senior men. The soldier and he left the cabin.

'Now then,' said Umero turning to face Tiberius square on, 'the hate I bear for anything to do with Guild people and their organisation is more than you can ever know. Logic therefore has it that I also hate you. Tiberius, you have no idea how much I detest you and others like you. You are a traitor. Those outside this cabin who have just now paid with their lives in protecting you, not very well as it happens, I imagine were also Guild men. I suspect that all of your soldiers are too.' A shadow of fear crossed Tiberius' face.

'My men,' said Umero, 'are loyal only to me and to my

emperor. I take orders yes, but not from scum like you. I now have a voyage to make and I will make it. I'm sorry that I can't afford the time for you to entertain my men by dying in an interesting way, so this will have to suffice.'

Before Tiberius Augusta could reply or even move, he had a Carthaginian gladius sword blade sticking through his chest. Umero removed it as the man sank to his knees and the sword was thrust in again, this time through the man's neck. Tiberius fell backwards in a rich pool of blood, thrashed for a moment, shuddered and then lay still. His eyes, wide in agony, filmed over. Marcellus almost on cue, came back, looked at the body on the floor and, without even batting an eyelid, saluted once more and said, 'Our visitors are safe, domine. Shall we dispose of this… along with the others?'

'Yes,' said Umero. 'The visitors are five in number? And truly safe?'

'Five, yes. The boy, two of Pluto's brothers, a woman with red hair and another woman, with one ear. All safe.'

Umero nodded and knew exactly who each one was and why each was on his ship. 'Very well. We set sail now. It's sunset. I was told to sail when the sun kisses the sea. Well, we shall beat the kissing.'

'Domine. Ducem.'

Umero held Marcellus' shoulder. 'One title or other will suffice, dear friend.' He smiled. 'You don't have to keep calling me both. Navarchus will do in front of the men or in an official capacity. When we dine alone it's Umero.' He smiled grimly, kicking the dead body at his feet, 'And please have this garbage removed quickly. And the blood cleaned from the cabin floor. Oh, and you have one of this scum's guards alive as I asked?'

'Yes, ducem, I mean navarchus.'

Umero smiled at his friend's awkwardness. 'Then,' said the captain, 'I want him to take a message, with two of your best men, to the senior centurion on the docks. Separate the centurion from his soldiers and the message is to say that his master has been held up in... discussions and will be along by and by and that the Praetorian Guard is to stand easy. If anyone argues, kill them. You will have twenty men close by.'

'Navarchus.'

'See to it. I want to set sail and I want to leave port with no sound. None. No shouts, no drumming, just silence. Oh, Marcellus?'

Marcellus turned back.

'Keep these people safe. The visitors.'

'I understand.'

'Probably not, but thank you for telling me that you do.'

Well, thought Umero after Marcellus had left, if he hadn't been in trouble before, now he was. The worst. If the emperor was party to Tiberius' game, Umero considered, then no matter what his rank, he was in a mess. Whatever the emperor thought of him, killing one of the empire's prefects was not something that one did lightly. He stared out at the gathering dusk. But, he wondered, while he felt no guilt at disposing of any Guild pig, on whose side was the emperor? The emperor owed Umero his life, but then the emperor could have owed Tiberius his power base. Life or power base? Both, he knew, amounted to much the same thing these days.

Umero wondered what the emperor knew and whether the man was a Guild player or an honest leader. Another thought troubled him. Someone had betrayed their position and their task. How had Tiberius known about the boy?

For some reason and out of nowhere, he thought of his wife and children. Time to retire soon, he thought. If they let him. But maybe now he'd be a hunted man. Once the Praetorian Guard discovered what had happened to one of their leaders, a chase would be on.

He nodded as people came in to remove the body and clean the cabin.

Umero looked at his world map on the cabin wall. He could hear quiet preparations for the ship's departure. Thank any number of gods, he thought, for his crew. His naval colleagues had always acknowledged that Umero was superb at co-ordinating his rowers and, it was said, he had not only the best rowers, but the best drummers too. Well, sighed Umero, someone always wants to be best. You were only as good as your last battle or, indeed, your last sailing and he never allowed himself to forget that there were younger, excellent commanders who were jealous of - and craved - what he had.

Umero knew that he had his enemies of course and several had already tried to usurp his authority. They only tried once. But things were getting worse, much worse. The empire was crumbling. Money was tight and lives were even cheaper than they had ever been before.

He turned and saw that the cleaning team had removed most signs of the recent murder. Was it murder, he wondered, or pest control? He shook his head. The smell of pine essence was strong and, while it removed any stink that had been left by the mess that had once been Tiberius, it wasn't Umero's favourite perfume. The pine essence always reminded him of death and the smell of death always reminded him of… what exactly?

Umero had been asked personally by Imperial Notice to oversee this particular voyage. The five senators, three of them Watchers, had counselled him well in the task he had to perform. He'd assumed that it had the emperor's blessing. But he wasn't certain now if this was so. He also knew that he was beginning to be mistrusted by all those in power who were not Watchers. Guild influence did that. Guild power was building where Rome's power was diminishing and Watchers could do only so much. Theirs was a role of minding Silver Greens, not of running empires.

He smiled as he listened to the men readying for departure. He knew every single part of each ship under his command like the back of his hand. Particularly this ship. This ship's hull could carry ten thousand amphorae - the tall and elegant, commercial storage jugs that were always used to transport grain, spices, wine… and often other, more secret things. And Umero knew, almost to the jug, precisely when there were either too few or too many on board. And he was good at defending cargo as much as he was at defending the empire. He'd had as many battles with pirates as he'd had with any of Rome's enemies.

Umero saw Marcellus returning from his task and, such was his trust in the man, he knew that anything untoward would have been reported immediately. He knew therefore that his twenty or so troops would have returned unharmed. All was well. So far.

Umero liked his emperor - Titus Flavius Caesar Vespasianus Augustus. He was straightforward and understood the navy, but once again Umero wondered whether the man could be trusted. Was he Guild infected? The Guild had helped Rome in so many ways, so surely it would be impossible not to be swayed. Was the emperor being blackmailed? Maybe. Umero sighed and shrugged. He had no idea what the result of this voyage would be. He just knew that the boy had to be transported. And protected at all costs. That's what he had promised and, as a Watcher, that's what he would do.

The fiery, deep red and yellow ball of sun touched the dark blue and darkening Mare Nostrum. Umero thought that you could almost hear the hiss as the sun met the sea. The wind was calm and the rowers, all of them free men, began to pull in perfect harmony and in absolute silence.

The Quintus' three sails were down as the vessel edged its way slowly and quietly out of port. It passed a huge military trireme which lay at anchor. Its sailors stopped what they were doing and, much to Umero's irritation, saluted his ship noisily as it slid by, such was his reputation.

Everyone on the ship heard the warning trumpets from the shore's garrison. The alarm was accompanied by a massive, lit brazier that turned the quayside night into day. Umero thought that whatever lay ahead it was too late to do anything different. The voyage was underway and he and his ship would now be regarded as the enemy.

The offshore wind freshened and blew a cooling breeze over the visitors. Jacob had been in a small cabin which was divided in two, the women in one half and Jupiter, Neptune and Jacob in the other. But now that they were on open seas, they had been allowed on deck to get some air, watched carefully by four legionaries.

'Are we prisoner?' asked Jacob.

'Not at all,' replied Jupiter. 'We are among friends and are being protected. Especially you.' Jacob thought of Pluto's advice not to trust anyone. He didn't as a rule anyway, but still felt miserable at the thought of what Judas had done, even though he should have guessed. His misery was compounded by the fact that he had badly wanted to trust the bowman.

He glanced around, but could see little. No lamps were lit. The only light was from the rising half-moon and the brazier on shore, although that was becoming smaller and smaller by the minute. He noticed the smell. The bilges had shifted with the ship's movement and the stench was powerful. On the breeze, however, he sensed something more pleasant, the smell of the dry desert as it met with the aromas of the sea. Jacob didn't know anything about the sea and had no knowledge of winds, clouds, waves, tides and storms. And he was feeling a bit seasick.

The two women were talking quietly together. Jupiter and Neptune were lost in their own thoughts, one looking out to sea and the other searching the sky. Jacob wondered what they were thinking about. They had said little since his exit from the underworld, but he had noticed that they always kept close to him as they were now.

The soldiers watching and guarding the visitors, him in particular, were all hastati in rank, junior legionaries. Each had been recently trained but, although probably not yet much battle tested, they'd fight to the death for Rome and certainly for Umero without any hesitation.

The sea was pitch black. In the distance Jacob could see the disappearing port. Lamps and fires on the shores of Caesarea, Sebaste and Ashkelon twinkled and then, as the ship sped onwards, one by one, all the shore lights disappeared over the horizon. Everything was dark save for the luminous water of the ship's wake lit by the moon.

The slap of the water as it hit the hull and the very quiet plash of oars, along with the muted drum were the only regular sounds of the night. Occasionally, there was a soft voice of command, but that was all. The air onboard became sweeter.

The vessel, being the fastest in the Mare Nostrum fleet, increased speed once the sails were up, each one cracking like a whip as it filled with the cold wind. A few lamps were lit, but none on the top deck. The rowers were instructed to stop and most went off to find food or stayed where they were and slept.

The waves buffeted the ship making it rock a little. Jacob had been told by Jupiter that the sea was not best travelled between November and March because of the terrible storms that frequented those months, but obviously this voyage was deemed important enough to ignore any warnings of possible danger. The boy hoped that he wouldn't have to learn to swim the hard way.

The spear felt comfortable in his hands and he looked again at the blade. Suddenly, he heard someone step up behind him and he whirled round, his free hand already holding his sica.

'No need for that,' said the woman with red hair calmly. 'How are you?' she asked.

'Fine,' he replied, 'a little seasick I think, but nothing else.'

'We won't stop now until we reach Italy and then we have to travel south by road. There we'll find our contact who will lead us close to where the explosive material is kept under Guild guard…'

'I am fourteen years' old and have no training in these things, let alone explosives under guard! I've said this many times and nobody seems to think that it's a problem. Well, it is a…'

'People believe in you.'

'That's very nice of whoever these people are, but things don't always turn out as planned. I know that very well indeed.'

Jacob wasn't particularly angry but was genuinely keen to know how seemingly intelligent people, including the captain of this very ship, believed that one person, a boy, with no relevant skills could do what was required. It was almost funny. Except that it wasn't.

The woman with red hair smiled. 'We need to be careful,' she said as if Jacob hadn't said anything. 'The Guild's agents are everywhere. The Praetorian Guard back on the quay for example.'

'The Guard, they were all Guild?'

'Yes. Can you see auras yet properly?'

Jacob nodded. 'I think so,' he said. Then shook his head. 'But not always.'

'The Guild has some followers who are able to hide their auras. It's hard to do but some can do it. You… must be careful.' She smiled at him once more.

'What if I simply refuse to undertake this task, run away when we arrive at wherever we're going and somehow get back to Jerusalem.'

The red-haired woman shrugged. 'You won't do that. Anyway, who would welcome you in Jerusalem?'

Jacob was about to say something very rude and then thought despondently that she was probably right. His thoughts were interrupted by loud shouts from the starboard watch. Eyes turned and in the dim light behind the ship Jacob saw the outline prow of a huge ship, closing in fast.

'Bitches teeth!' spat the woman. 'That'll be the Praetorian Guard giving chase. They were quick.'

'Classis Misenensis,' shouted Neptune. 'It's a quadrireme, part of the senior fleet. Heavily armed and fast. Based out of Portus Juius, which isn't far from where we're going. That ship will be fully loaded with weaponry and men.'

This was the longest speech that Jacob had heard the massive man make.

Jacob snorted cynically. 'And you know this how?'

'Because I once ruled these seas,' Neptune said calmly. 'These seas were mine.'

Astonished at that piece of news, Jacob heard another shout, this time even more urgent and from the ship's port side. Everyone on deck turned to look and Jacob could just make out the outline of yet another vessel - a huge, dark, menacing shape, flying curious flags. He could see the massive steel spikes that surrounded the bow and several round things on the end of tall poles.

'Human heads,' said Jupiter softly.

'Pirates!' said the red-haired woman less quietly.

21

Palos de la Frontera, Huelva, Andalusia, Spain, 1492

The green leather chair on which Christopher Columbus sat had a lion's motif on each arm. Maria sat opposite him. The heavily decorated room in the navigator's rented house close to the centre of Palos was airless.

'Maria, I simply cannot help you,' he said in Portuguese. 'I would, but I cannot. My brother - the one you met on your journey here - pleaded your case and he wants to help - we all do, but I must lead my three ships out of this very port in five days. The Spanish queen has allowed no further delays. In the name of the Crown of Castile, I dare not change my plans. They would have my head!'

Maria nodded sadly and smiled. 'You plan to voyage until you reach riches of gold, pearls and spices? Wherever that may be?'

'Yes. No. Maybe. I seek lands yet undiscovered. I shall travel west and the voyage will be very long. My plan is to find a new route to India, China and the Spice Islands. The world as you know is round and by sailing west instead of east around the coast of Africa, I will still reach my destination. But it is a gamble.' He paused. 'You ask about riches? Yes, these are expected by the Queen, but she also wants dominion over new lands… Maria, I may not arrive where you want to go, indeed I may not arrive anywhere. It would be futile to take you, only to find that your mission would come to nothing. And I cannot alter mine.'

'What are we to do? We have travelled so far from Rome hiding on the way and being careful to avoid the enemy Guild. The Guild is nearby now, of that I am certain and its people are undoubtedly waiting for a chance to take the girl. We have to get to Singapura.'

Christopher Columbus, not always a kindly man, was kind now. He smiled.

'You know that I have three brothers and a sister. We will help where we can, of course we will; it is our sworn duty to do so. And if The Watcher Authority instructs me to take you now, why then I must do my duty above all else. Even if that means angering Castile.' He pulled a face, drew a hand across his throat and grinned.

'But listen. One of my brothers,' he said, 'Bartholomew, is setting sail in eight days. He attended the school of seamanship in Sagres, south of here. As did I. Mapmakers, geographers, astronomers all gather there under the leadership of Henry, Prince of Portugal, Duke of Viseu. He instructed my brother well and, I hate to say it but, of the two of us, Bartholomew is the better navigator. This is my point. He is the best. Don't tell him I said that, otherwise his head will swell.'

Columbus smiled again. 'Seriously though, he sails towards the Hindustan lands to find trade routes. He goes east. Señor Vasco da Gama competes, but my brother will try to be the first.' He sipped some wine and turned to Gabriella who had not understood a word and gave her the biggest smile yet. Shyly, she smiled back.

Maria asked anxiously, 'Will he take us? Would he deliver us to the island of Singapura?'

'Nobody knows this Singapura island. I do not. My brother

will not know it either, but my family owes you and your family a great debt Maria. We also owe many Watchers a great debt too. And while I know nothing of your plans when you arrive at this island of which you speak, I do know for a fact that it's important. I will arrange for you to speak to Bartholomew. I'm sure that he will take you. Rest assured.'

'Thank you, Christopher,' Maria said, getting up and kissing him on his cheek.

Gabriella smiled with relief when she saw that something good had been agreed. Christopher Columbus gave her another big grin and then opened his arms and gave her a hug. Nobody, thought Gabriella, would have ever dared touch a princess like that back at home. Home... wherever that was now. Hugs in her current world were scarce and she knew that the big man genuinely wanted her kept safe. She could just tell. That, she thought was very often the case. One could just tell.

The next few days were busy. Bartholomew did agree to take Maria and Gabriella, as his brother had promised. The two Watchers who had seen the ladies safely to this point, bade them farewell knowing that from now on there would be other Watchers to take on the duty. Of the other two, the man and the woman, who secretly had been following the travelling group thus far, only one was instructed to join the ship - as the cartographer charged with creating a map of the sea voyage. The other went to France where she had other duties to perform.

Gabriella was constantly concerned about her safety.

'There are always Watchers close by to protect you...' said Maria for the hundredth time. 'Yes, I know you felt alone in the Borgia palazzo but, if necessary...'

'If necessary! If necessary? It was very necessary! And I was very much all alone!'

'No harm befell you.'

'Only because…'

'Yes, I know you were in danger, but you managed, you survived, you used the ring. And wisely too.'

'How could you possibly know that I would ever be able to make the ring work? And how could you know that I would be safe? If I hadn't been safe - and I was definitely not safe - how could you have helped me?'

Maria said, 'The ring kept you safe and, Gabriella, so do we,' then ignored any further questions on the subject. Preparations for the journey ahead kept them busy. Gabriella had no clue what a long sea voyage entailed and Maria's knowledge was limited. There was a great deal to buy and pack. Their dunnage included oiled sailcloth jackets and leggings for wet weather, cool clothing for hot climes, warm clothing for any cold they might meet, a large bundle of candles, a whole string of dried sausages, a wheel of some very hard cheese, strips of dried fish, a great deal of carbolic soap and a wooden box of thin, but hard, biscuits that they were told would last for years. And much else.

Bartholomew was a young, excitable but clever adventurer convinced that his voyage would benefit trade. His belief was solid and he felt that his venture would prove much more useful than his brother's. Maria knew that they were rivals, certainly, but that they also adored each other.

Thankfully for Gabriella, Bartholomew spoke in Italian almost all of the time and asked no difficult questions about why the two ladies wanted passage to some unknown island.

Bartholomew, a Watcher, knew that there would be other Watchers onboard but, even under pain of death, he would never have divulged who they were, even if he knew. He was troubled though because he was aware that some Guild people, the more experienced ones, could hide their auras as could some Watchers. That made him worry about his crew and officers, all of whom were handpicked. But any one of them could be a double agent. However, he was reassured a little that hiding an aura was very hard indeed to achieve and it was rarely possible to keep an aura hidden permanently. He grinned to himself as he thought about his chosen path in life. Yes, his path was full of risks and this voyage, in more ways than one, was possibly the biggest.

Bartholomew warned Maria about the dangers of the sea - storms that could last for days, pestilence, pirates, rocks that could tear a ship in half, monsters of the deep and a wide variety of other terrors. She nodded and accepted that the journey may not be plain sailing. He laughed and she curtsied in acknowledgement of the joke.

Maria told Gabriella of Bartholomew's intention to find a sea route to Hindustan that would give Spain access to lucrative trade in the east.

'Bartholomew,' she said, 'has the experience to keep his ship safe - and us. The crowns of Castile and Aragon would not fund this venture if they thought that he could not achieve results. They believe in him as they do his brother. He has voyaged south along the west African coast trading in gold, silver, cloth and spices. Others have also traded there in those things and...' She paused for a moment, '...and... other things. But... the southern extent of the continent remains unknown to anyone in our part of the world. Opening a trade route is important. If

Bartholomew can do that, why then fortune is his.'

Gabriella, stony-faced, asked, 'You said other things. What other things?'

Maria said nothing for a moment. 'Yes,' she said quietly, 'Other things. Trade in the world is growing and some always want what one nation has that they have not…'

Gabriella was about to say what they both knew. But she didn't. Instead, Gabriella simply cried.

Two evenings before sailing, over dinner at Bartholomew's home with some of the ship's officers, Maria watched Gabriella sipping wine and fiddling with a small mountain of sugared almonds, occasionally eating one.

'Bartholomew,' Maria said trying hard to sound confident, 'you have told us of the southern coast of Africa. The coast there is perilous. It is said that this passage has waves higher than… than the Ca' da Mosto in Venice. Is there no other way?'

Bartholomew nodded at the question and then shook his head. 'Alas no. There are two great oceans that meet - the cold western waters of the Atlantic and the warmer waters of the Eastern Ocean. Well, where they meet - that is the Cape of Storms. The seas there become, what's the word…? Yes. The seas become mad.'

Bartholomew laughed as he peeled an apple, then sliced and ate each piece from the point of his small pocketknife. He saw Gabriella struggling with a walnut and passed a nutcracker to the girl.

One of the officers said to Maria, 'Mi scusi, signora… what you say is true and the Cape is treacherous. But we must go this way. There is no other. Le navi del capitano… our captain is correct and the waves can be dangerous. But many seas are like this.' The officer poured himself some wine. 'Our journey will be a success!' The other three officers all raised their glasses as did Bartholomew.

Nodding, Bartholomew said, 'There was a man - Pedro da Covilha was his name - who travelled overland to Hindustan. Took him three years. Disguised as an Arab and, speaking fluent Arabic, he gathered information about the east African and Hindustani coasts. I have that information. Covilha spoke of many islands near to the land mass of Tanah Melayu. Yours could be one of those.'

Gabriella, not used to much wine, was sleepy and Maria excused themselves and led the girl off to her room. The large house was quiet for it was late and, after having received a candlestick with a freshly lit candle from a servant, the two made their way upstairs. Maria was suddenly aware that at the top of the stairs there was a woman wearing a thin chain mail tunic standing on a higher landing. The woman was looking down.

Maria stopped walking and froze. Gabriella was aware that something was wrong and she looked up to see what seemed to be an apparition. The woman beckoned them up, but Maria began treading slowly backwards down the stairs still facing the woman and calmly urging Gabriella to do the same. The apparition began walking down the stairs towards them. As Maria held the candle aloft, she saw that the ghost had a terrible scar running from temple to neck. The woman, expressionless, was able to walk down faster than Maria and Gabriella could walk backwards. And then Gabriella tripped.

22

Mare Nostrum, Roman Empire, 79 CE

The ship was full of movement, shouted commands and men taking up positions. Despite the commotion and activity, there was, thought Jacob, an absolute order to the organisation of these battle stations. Without fuss, men grabbed armour and collected weapons. The braziers, now lit, had on top of them big iron tureens containing black pitch the smell of which Jacob liked.

The ship's sixteen massive catapults were stretched and loaded with huge rocks, great iron chunks and the pitch. The sails were full, cracking like guns and bellowing out as huge sheets in a rising wind which seemed to have come from nowhere. Anything loose had been battened down and all openings had been shut. It was clear to Jacob that Umero was going to try to outrun the enormous Praetorian ship that was closing fast. It was also clear that he would fight if necessary.

'Their quadrireme is fast and manoeuvrable enough to attack us by ramming,' shouted Jupiter. Jacob couldn't see Neptune. 'It has a sharp-edged corus as do we,' Jupiter yelled above the noise. And to Jacob and the women he shouted, 'It's safest if you take cover. Go now!'

The woman with red hair was about to protest.

'Don't argue. Safest on deck. Go aft. Find shelter. Take the boy with you.'

The woman nodded, grabbed Jacob and ran to the front of the ship. Suddenly several soldiers appeared on deck and surrounded the visitors. There was a short command. Quickly, a testudo - a tortoise - was made. The soldiers raised their shields and joined them together, creating a tight enclosure with a strong roof. Just in time because iron bolts and heavy, round rocks were being directed at the ship. While most fell in the water, some hit home and were soon littering the decks. The damage they caused was insignificant so far, but, from the shouts and yells, Jacob could tell that a few had reached their targets.

Umero and Marcellus were on deck wearing armour and battle helmets, yelling precise commands. Umero ducked under the roof of shields and spoke to the woman with red hair.

'They will use hot pitch, heated resin and boiling animal fat. We will return the favour. We will also use smoke to confuse them. For a while. And we have quicklime and sulphur should the need arise.'

'But what of the pirate ship?' shouted the woman with red hair as she nodded in the direction of what was an ominous and threatening shape now closing fast on the quadrireme.

'That,' said Umero smiling grimly, 'is mine. It is here to protect us. Shortly we will run and make a break. We have the pace. The pirate ship will take our place. It is heavily armed and it has Greek fire. If my enemies see Greek fire, they will retreat and quickly. If they do not retreat, why then their ship will burn as will all within it.'

Jacob, crouching as low as possible at the feet of soldiers and, protected by their strong shields, had no real idea what was going on. Not for the first time, he fervently wished that he was meandering around the ruined city of Jerusalem or, much better, roaming the Judean hills with a flock of sheep and a few dates in his pocket. He would learn to play a lyre or a pipe, he thought. Maybe help to spin wool. He knew that some men did that and were good at it too. Maybe not very exciting, but that at least was a life that he sort of understood. Wherever he went now, he thought, there was the danger of death and he'd had enough of the danger of death.

He was cold and wet from the sea spray. When they arrived at wherever they were going in Italy, he'd already decided that he would escape and make his way back to Jerusalem. Somehow. Enough of this Silver Green camel dung. Enough of the immortality rubbish. Enough of running somewhere or nowhere. Yes, that's what he would do - join the Bedouin. That would be his life and he smiled at the prospect. But how to escape and get back home? Anyway, where in Vulcan's nostrils was home? Did he have one? The woman with red hair tried to take his hand, but he pulled away sharply and edged further from her.

Another hand patted him on the back and he was about to get very angry at whoever had done that. He looked up with his sica in his hand and saw a centurion with a kind, but grubby face, marked with the smoke that was coming from the braziers. The face grinned at him. Jacob tried to smile back, but didn't quite manage it. The soldier thrust a crust of bread at him which Jacob gratefully took and ate. The red-haired woman watched him, nibbling on her own piece of dark bread.

He could see that the soldiers were all chewing on something - bread, dried mutton, hard cheese - which must have been difficult while ensuring that the umbrella of shields was solid and left no gaps.

The noise was intense as the pirate ship headed for the Praetorian quadrireme. The Quintus fought with vigour too and it was soon clear that the quadrireme had no heart for a lengthy battle with Umero's vessel and the pirate ship which was obviously fast and extremely dangerous. The drum beat on the quadrireme changed, indicating that the Praetorian commander had ordered a retreat and the quadrireme began to turn, making a long semi-circle as it headed back towards safety.

A cheer went up but most of the crew were instructed to keep at their stations. Just in case. However, the soldiers surrounding Jacob were told to stand at ease and went off to their various posts as the boy mumbled his thanks. The woman with red hair had gone off somewhere too. Suddenly, he was alone.

The wind was now very cold and Jacob could see that the waves were much higher. Picking up speed again, Umero's Quintus rolled heavily as the pirate ship went past. Shouts from both ships were swept away in the wind. His spirits lifting a little, Jacob wondered if the pirate ship would eventually accompany them all the way to Italy. He hoped so.

The huge Praetorian quadrireme was now heading away and its rear outline was clear in the moonlight. The braziers and smoke added to the eerie picture enhanced by a ghostly sound as the wind whistled through the ropes and rigging.

It seemed to Jacob that very powerful gusts of wind and rising waves were pushing the Praetorian ship broadside so that it listed slightly, but quickly righted itself. Then, as if from nowhere, there arose a huge wave starboard of the vessel. Jacob stared at the wave with utter amazement and in absolute awe. The wave was enormous. He could feel the spray from the almost vertical and sleek wall of deep, black water as it rose smoothly higher and higher.

To Jacob the only noise was the rush of the wave as it climbed. In one single moment, when the wave reached a point far higher than any of the quadrireme's masts, it seemed to pause and hold, spray flying off the peak and then crashed down with all its intense might onto the retreating ship. Jacob could feel the heavy surge of water beneath him and nearly lost his footing.

Where the Praetorian quadrireme had been but a moment earlier, there was now only boiling, white froth. The sea settled and the wind calmed. Jacob stared out but couldn't see any sign of the quadrireme or those who had been onboard.

Jupiter appeared at Jacob's shoulder. 'Alright?' he asked, seemingly exhausted.

Not answering, Jacob looked up and was aware of Neptune appearing at his other shoulder. The huge man was soaking wet and he too looked worn out.

Jupiter asked him, 'Are you well, brother?'

Neptune crouched down, catching his breath.

He nodded and then said, 'Yes… Now.'

'Why is he so wet?' asked Jacob.

'He's been in the sea,' was the only answer that Jupiter gave.

23

Cape of Storms, Southern Coast of Africa, 1492

The woman walked with great purpose downstairs towards Maria and Gabriella, no expression on her face. Gabriella, having picked herself up after her stumble, could feel Maria tensing by her side. They both stopped walking backwards now that they had reached the bottom of the stairway.

Maria could see no aura at all. She asked, 'Who are you, madam?' Taking no notice, the lady carried on walking towards them. Gabriella held the Ring of Solomon and was about to rub it, when Bartholomew threw open the doors of the dining room, looked at the woman and shouted with surprise and delight. Gabriella turned to look at him in alarm. Maria continued to watch the woman coming downstairs.

Bartholomew shouted with happiness. He laughed, 'Mama, hello!' The woman walked slowly towards him as the young navigator ran to her, arms outstretched.

Bartholomew looked over his mother's shoulder and spoke to Maria and Gabriella. 'I apologise. My mama has just now returned from France where she goes sometimes for special treatment. She was attacked three years ago and robbed. She received terrible injuries as you can see. She does not speak and rarely smiles. Since she recovered her wounds, she has always worn this kind of clothing. Unnecessary of course now, but she sees it as protection. She may even sleep in it. I don't know. Strange I grant you. But she is still my mother.' He said all this in something of a rush, a big grin on his face. 'And,' he said, 'she will join us on the voyage. I promised her.'

Having hugged her son to within an inch of his life and having greeted the officers who had come out to see what all the fuss was about, Bartholomew's mother turned towards Gabriella and Maria. She stepped forwards, nodded at Maria then held Gabriella's hands in her own. She looked deep into the girl's eyes seemingly to peer right into her soul. And she smiled.

Maria found out very quickly that seafaring was tough. Like all sailors, none of the crew were pleased to have women onboard even if one of them was the captain's mother. There were eighty-eight people on the ship including the sailors, the galley cook, a surgeon, a parson, the master gunner, two boatswains, a scrivener, the cartographer, a master carpenter, his assistant, the quartermaster and several officers.

Although it was very clear from the outset that Bartholomew ran a tight ship, little was seen of him. He spent much of his time with his charts and on several occasions, in calm weather, he and some of his officers took a rowing boat around the ship to assess the Santa Barbara's seat in the water. Whenever Gabriella overheard any of Bartholomew's conversations, the topics seemed to concern themselves with violent currents, land mass, the seas ahead, stores but, mostly, the wind.

Occasionally, in the evenings or at dinner with the officers, she noted that he loved to talk about the sea's dangers and in particular the Cape of Storms, that rocky headland at the very tip of the vast lands that were Africa. Her Spanish was not bad now and she smiled at the amount of times Bartholomew mentioned Cabo das Tormentas. However, whenever Africa was mentioned she would look down at her plate and think of what life had been like once.

Bartholomew was by and large sensitive to Gabriella's

heritage and he never deliberately said anything untoward, but he did love to tell long tales of derring-do in African lands and of creatures that made the company around the table smile and often laugh. Gabriella did not smile and certainly did not laugh at hearing such things. She would have liked to have stood up to explain exactly what life in the lands of the Aro peoples had been like. She would have liked to have explained what it meant to be a princess, but now she wasn't sure what it meant at all.

Bartholomew delighted in pointing out that the Cape wasn't the real end of Africa at all. That honour apparently belonged to Cape Agulhas. Gabriella thought to herself that any Cape by any name was not the real end of Africa. The real end of Africa for her was quite different. That terrible day of bloodlust, terror and hate when she had lost her family, her friends and her world. That for her had been the end of Africa.

On most days, the first mate, a grizzled Venetian, was pleased to chat to the girl about seafaring and he didn't mind at all her dozens of questions. In answer to Gabriella's querulous enquiries about the dangers of the Cape, he was happy to explain.

'We must,' said the first mate, 'keep a good distance away from the shelf of Africa that hides under the waters where the oceans meet. You may ask why.' He waited until Gabriella asked why.

'A very good question if I may say so! Well, this shelf,' said the first mate with a twinkle in his eye, 'has sudden hollows and depths that can fashion rogue waves big enough to sink any vessel. Of course, the converging currents around the Cape do make whirly pools down which ships can be sucked, never to surface again.'

Gabriella found this kind of storytelling terrifying. Because she had no experience of the sea at all, she tried to keep awake at night as much as possible, 'just in case,' as she reported to Maria, 'they met a whirly pool.'

Her habit in times of nervousness was to check that the Ring of Solomon was safe on her finger. Sometimes she would rub it absent-mindedly and then quickly stop if she caught herself thinking of monsters of the deep or just the deep itself.

'Tell me where we are now master mate, if you please,' she said on another occasion.

'Why child, we are now in line with the very Cape of Storms. This is where the fun starts! Mark my words.'

Gabriella and Maria awoke at the same time that night when the ship reared up. Both of them fell off their bunks. Books, bottles and chairs crashed about the cabin as did anything that was not fixed or tied down. A sailor burst in without the usual courtesy and shouted that Maria and Gabriella should put on their waterproof sailcloth jackets and leggings and be on deck where it was safest, something which Gabriella very much doubted. He yelled that they must be tied securely to something solid and threw them two lengths of rope. Gabriella doubted the wisdom of that advice too.

Maria shouted that they should dress, difficult given the slip-sliding floor.

Outside the cabin, everything was in absolute ferment. They fell on the water-soaked and slippery deck and then hung on tight to the closest rigging.

The mighty swelling of the sea beneath the ship felt, thought Gabriella, like the deep breathing of some great animal lifting and then dropping the vessel. The waves, angry, black and flecked with white, grew so large that the vessel was dwarfed, riding up and then violently down the swollen sea. There was no longer any grace in the waters - only anger.

The wind was furious and whipped huge washes of dark, frothing water over the decks. The rigging screamed as if it was being murdered. The sea, which Gabriella felt could get no more terrifying, became more terrifying in its sheer weight, height and might. The ship, one minute almost vertical, seemed to cling to and then climb a wall of water. The next moment it was being dashed back into the depths of great valleys of boiling froth from which Gabriella knew that there was probably no return. She tried to say something to Maria, but that just resulted in a mouthful of saltwater.

Within moments from exiting the cabin, she was soaked and could only nod weakly when the ship's cartographer, himself trying hard not to slip, tied both Maria and her securely to a mast. Gabriella was certain that this night was to be her last. Time passed, but the storm did not and she just waited, ever colder, for the ship to sink to the bottom of the ocean. People crawled by her hanging on to anything, with ropes around their waists attached to masts or other fixed parts of the ship. No-one took any notice of either Maria or Gabriella, apart that is from two officers and the cartographer who were firmly strapped to railings close by and watched out for Gabriella as closely as the elements would allow.

The ship heaved and yawed, twisted, climbed and fell, everything creaking. Lengths of rope whipped past Gabriella and Maria like angry snakes and stores that had been only loosely fastened on deck flew over the side. Once again, Gabriella felt that some huge animal was carrying the Santa Barbara on its back.

As the ship rolled almost to the point of no return, Gabriella calmed, shut her eyes and rubbed her ring. She thought of Africa, a land not so far away from where she would surely drown. Then, determined, she thought of other things and screamed with all her might for the storm to cease. She yelled for all she was worth for the huge animal on which the ship was being carried to disappear.

24

Port of Apollonia, Senatorial Province, Roman Empire, 79 CE

Umero docked for a short while in Apollonia, a stronghold of the Marmaridae district. He hadn't wanted to stop, but the ship needed fresh water. The pirate ship, his pirate ship, hove to a little further down the coast in a hidden inlet. The commander of the Apollonia garrison gave instructions that Umero and his crew were to be welcomed and fed. Hot baths were arranged and the ship was restocked not only with water and wine, but with dried meat, bread, olives and fruit. A few live goats, chickens and pigs were added, much to the crew's delight. Marcellus ensured that the pirate ship was afforded the same courtesies. All provisions were paid for and nothing was taken for granted.

Jacob, Neptune, Jupiter and the two women were given a large room in the garrison and were put under protective guard. They were, Jacob was told, only staying for two nights and Jupiter explained to Jacob where they were heading next.

'We'll steer north and the captain may or may not decide to restock once more with water. Then to Misenum in Italy and onwards to your task. The last stretch will be tricky because the weather is very poor at this time of year, but my brother will help us.'

Jacob wondered what that meant and which brother Jupiter had in mind. He looked at Neptune who was talking to the red-haired woman while munching a huge hunk of black bread that he held in his left hand and a large piece of hard cheese that he held in his right.

Jacob asked, 'And then what?'

'And then,' said the woman with one ear. 'And then,' we must escort you to Pompeii. There the Romans will be shown the error of their ways. You will stop that happening.'

Jacob bristled at the presumption that he would do what these people wanted without question. He'd had enough of being told what he must or must not do and wanted to object and refuse. However, he thought, now was not the time for that conversation. Anyway, when he found the right time, he would just escape and leave no warning. He would just leave.

He asked, 'And from there?'

'To the east, as you know very well,' said Neptune, his mouth full. 'To destroy Guild fire.'

Jacob had to keep a hold on his temper so fed up was he with vague answers to his questions. He counted ten in his head.

'And how,' he asked disinterestedly and just to pretend to sound curious, 'is this Guild fire different from Greek fire?'

'Guild fire,' said Jupiter after checking with the women that it was alright for him to speak on the subject, 'is a power from the heart of the earth, from deep underground. Deeper, much deeper than the underworld. In the earth's depths can be found molten rock mixed with sulphur, thunder stone and pyrite. There are other ingredients…'

Jupiter went on listing the other ingredients, but Jacob wasn't listening. He wished that he hadn't asked the question. Anyway, he thought, he'd absolutely made up his mind to escape as soon as he could and somehow get to the Bedouin.

That was the plan. Jupiter was clicking his fingers to attract his attention.

'Attend, boy!'

Jacob gritted his teeth. How dare he be told to pay attention!

'The Byzantines created the weapon known as Greek fire,' Jacob said, playing along. He thought that it would be safest to give no clue as to his plans. 'Correct? To protect Constantinople during some Arab siege or other?'

'That's what is believed,' said Jupiter, nodding then shaking his head. 'But it's not correct. Greek fire was a Guild invention - nobody else's. Not the Greeks. Not the Byzantines. Guild alchemists called this invention of theirs naphtha.'

It was only when Jupiter had finished speaking that Jacob was aware that the red-haired woman had been staring at him. He turned away quickly, irritated at the woman's presumption. Who by Caesar's nose hair did she think she was? Once again, he had to try hard to keep himself from losing his temper.

He thought to himself that he was a warrior. But, he wondered, was he? Assassinating people didn't make him a warrior. He knew that. Was he special as they kept telling him? He hadn't done that well in recent days, skulking under things, hiding under soldiers' shields, fainting twice, making mistakes about people. Not much bravery or being special in any of that. Well, maybe it was time, he considered, to flex his muscles.

They all heard the buccina being sounded, indicating an early sailing in the morning. Jacob and his four comrades were ordered out of the garrison and back on-board ship, a day earlier than planned.

The pirate ship had moved as unobtrusively as a pirate vessel could next to Umero's ship and was already readying itself for sail. The pirates were held under suspicion by the Roman garrison's command, but such ships and their bounty were occasionally captured by Rome's navy, so it wasn't necessarily such a strange occurrence and few would ever dream of questioning Umero.

In his cabin, Umero was worried. He had witnessed the sinking of one of Rome's biggest ships with all hands onboard. He had killed one of Rome's naval chiefs. The emperor would know about this soon if he didn't know already. Rumours would fly as rumours always did. There would be searching questions about where Umero's loyalty lay. And, Umero knew without doubt that Guild tentacles were still reaching out for the boy.

Umero unclenched his jaw. Someone, he thought, knew of his plans. Someone onboard his ship was a traitor. He just knew it.

Once back onboard, Jacob asked Neptune, 'Do we sail with the tide?'

'This sea has no tide boy, but we sail at dawn,' said Neptune, 'Umero suspects foul play I should think so he will want to make haste now. Best get some sleep because the seas will be rough tomorrow and sleep will be beyond you.'

Jacob wanted to be on his own and think. 'Can I take a walk around the ship before I sleep?'

Jupiter was about to snap back that he couldn't, when the woman with red hair said, 'It's fine. I'll walk with him.'

Jupiter looked doubtful.

The woman with red hair said, 'It will be safe. A short walk.

No more.'

Reluctantly, Jupiter nodded, but immediately regretted it. Too late. The red-haired woman and Jacob went off towards the prow of the ship which was pointing out to sea. Turning, Jacob could see that the garrison was lit by night flares and braziers which made monstrous shadows of men and women as they passed its walls.

Umero, who had stepped out of his cabin for air, saw the two go on their walk around the ship and shouted for Marcellus.

He yelled, 'Who in the blue smoke of Apollo's breath let them walk?' Marcellus could only apologise in a low voice and said that he had thought that permission had been granted.

'That woman,' shouted Umero, 'is always doing as she pleases. Marcellus, go after them. Now. Bring them back. Put four more of your best legionaries and a centurion on guard all through the night. Go now. I trust her Marcellus, but she puts herself and the boy in danger, even on my ship.'

Marcellus was about to argue that little harm could come to the woman or the boy on the ship but, after a brief glance at Umero's expression, he simply nodded, saluted and left Umero's cabin, shouting instructions as he went.

Jacob looked at the woman with red hair. 'What's your name? I have asked you often, but you have never said.'

'My name is Shoshana,' said the woman. 'It's not important.'

Jacob glanced at her. 'Why did you want to walk with me?'

The woman shrugged. She looked at the boy. To her, Jacob, carrying his bag and spear, suddenly seemed to her to be very young. She indicated that they should stop for a while. Both looked up and stared at the stars. The sky was a rich velvet, dark blue, almost black but not quite. The stars, a myriad of small, sparkling white diamonds that looked as if they had just spilled out on a dark blue table, provided a picture that Jacob could have watched all night long. It was his huge, curved lid on the world.

Without looking at Shoshana, he asked, 'Do you know the stars?'

'A little,' she said and nodded abstractedly as she pointed to the heavens. 'I did, but have forgotten most. Long, long ago I used to watch them each night… Do you know the heavens?'

Jacob, still looking upwards, murmured, 'I do.'

'That formation there,' she said pointing. 'You know the name?' Jacob knew that what she was pointing at was The Road of Milk, Via Lactea. He was about to explain when three loud legionaries passed, one bumping into Jacob and another jostling Shoshana. The soldiers each apologised profusely and hurried on.

Jacob, puzzled, watched them go, thinking that Umero would have never allowed any drunken behaviour onboard his vessel. But, watching them go, he wondered if they were actually drunk. He'd seen many drunk people in his time and knew how they behaved. Something wasn't right. The body language was wrong. Something was missing. He saw them rush off the ship, pushing away the deck guards. He thought little of it until he noticed that one of the fleeing soldiers was carrying his spear.

He choked. 'My spear!' Enraged, and without thinking of any consequence, he ran for the quayside, dodging obstacles and people on the way. The deck guards tried to stop him, but he was a fast runner and he'd dodged many Roman soldiers before now. Besides, he was angry. As he jumped onto the quay, there were shouts behind him and he recognised some of the voices. Nonetheless, he ran on.

The three thieves were good runners too and they were definitely not drunk. The one who held the spear was in the middle and the three kept a steady pace along the quayside pathway that rose on an incline above the water's edge. Luckily the pathway ran against the garrison's walls and therefore it was well lit, but Jacob knew that the lights were only along this stretch and soon the thieves would be able to disappear into the night. He suddenly realised that this whole thing must have been a ruse to lead him away from safety.

He picked up speed and took out his sica without pausing. One of the thieves slowed and turned to look back and that was his big mistake because in the next second the sica was embedded in the man's left ankle severing the Achilles' tendon. The man yelled and fell forward in agony. As Jacob ran past, he hardly slowed to retrieve his sica and kick the man hard in the ankle wound. The man shrieked in pain. The other two slowed slightly, hesitant and unsure what to do. This hadn't been part of the plan. This wasn't what they'd been paid to do. Being knifed for a small bag of silver had not been the idea.

The man with the spear ran on, but Jacob kept him in his sights. As he passed the second man, Jacob tried a trick that he'd learned from the Sicarii. He reached out as he ran and, with one hand, grabbed the man by the neck and drove the heel of his other hand straight into the man's nose which broke on impact. The man yelped, reeled and fell to his knees clasping both hands to his bleeding face.

Closing now on the spear-carrying thief, Jacob realised that he was now almost outside the port's boundary and long past the garrison's walls. Here the pathway narrowed and was very high above the water. The light was poor, but there was at least a little from the moon.

The man with the spear slowed, stopped and turned. He faced Jacob, breathed heavily and grinned, waving the spear aloft as if to tease the boy. Jacob, seething with anger, stepped towards him. How stupid he'd been, he thought. Stupid and careless.

He noticed that the man had been joined by two others who had appeared from the shadows. All three had their backs to the pathway's edge. Not only had he lost the spear, but Jacob knew that he was now about to be captured.

His anger grew. He decided that this was not how it should all end. He also decided that he would not be taken without a fight. That's what he was good at, he told himself. He had nothing to lose and so with his arm outstretched, he pointed his sica towards the man with the spear. Slowly he walked forwards. The three moved back and stopped. One looked over his shoulder and realised that he and his two friends were only a few pedes from the pathway edge that led to a vertical drop down to the sea. In fact, they could hear the sea crashing against the sea walls and rocks.

Jacob kept walking towards the men. Suddenly he jabbed forwards with his knife and the man with the spear wasn't sure how to proceed. The man stopped, looking nervously left and right. Jacob took another step forwards. One of the men decided to flee and dashed past Jacob, but in so doing received a very deep, long cut on a forearm for his trouble. Whimpering, the man ran on, his arm dripping blood.

Jacob was determined to get his spear back. Taking a chance, he rushed forwards, pushing the second man hard in the chest with a fist. Totally surprised, the man squealed, stepped back, lost his footing and disappeared over the edge. The scream seemed to last for a long time.

Now Jacob was face-to-face with the man who'd stolen the spear. The man looked fearful but then grinned and pointed the spear towards the boy. Jacob didn't think twice. He moved forwards, dodging the spear's sharp point and at the same time grabbing the spear's shaft. The man wouldn't let go.

Holding onto the spear with all his strength and with only one hand, Jacob walked the man backwards to the precipitous edge. The only thing that was stopping the thief from falling was the fact that he was holding on to the spear. Jacob brought his sica upwards and instinctively the man let go of the spear to protect his face. Now, with all his remaining strength, Jacob pushed the blunt end of the spear into the man's chest. The man looked into Jacob's eyes and now it was Jacob who smiled grimly. As the man fell, he didn't scream, but Jacob did hear the splash.

Exhausted, but holding the spear, Jacob turned round and saw four more Guild men each heavily armed and mean-looking.

Suddenly figures approached. More Guild men? He couldn't fight four on his own, not now. He certainly couldn't handle four plus the newcomers. But the newcomers were not Guild men. They were Shoshana, the woman with one ear, Jupiter, Neptune, Marcellus and five legionaries. His heart lifted. The four men suffered terrible sword cuts and each tried to escape, but the wrath of the fighters was dreadful to see, even for a Sicarii daggerman.

Jacob looked about him relieved that he and his friends had survived. Shoshana came up to him and asked him if he was unhurt. He nodded. Marcellus marched up to him, his anger fierce.

'You,' Marcellus shouted, 'you put the ship, my captain and these people in jeopardy. Such foolishness is worthy of the utmost punishment. Be grateful that you have friends in powerful places!' Jacob tried to apologise but Marcellus was having none of it and continued his tirade.

Humiliated and ashamed, Jacob knew that Marcellus was right to be angry and he knew too that Umero would be disappointed. These people had cared for him. They had protected him. He knew that, but he also knew that the spear had been entrusted to him and he felt that he'd given his word to look after it. Had he given his word to do that? He wasn't sure. Anyway, he thought, what should he have done? Should he have just let the spear go? Maybe that's precisely what he should have done, he thought.

Head held high, he faced Marcellus and accepted the vitriol that was directed at him. In disgust, Marcellus turned away and waited along with the legionaries. Jacob looked at Jupiter, Neptune and the women for what, he wondered. Support? Forgiveness? He didn't want all this conflict and he hadn't asked for any of it. They all said nothing.

He glanced again at Shoshana. There was something that had, at that very moment, suddenly and without any warning whatsoever, occurred to him to ask her, something that he dared not ask in case what he was thinking might be true. It was a question the answer to which might make his current misery complete.

25

The Coast of Madagascar, The Sea of India, 1492

The storm stopped with a suddenness that surprised everyone onboard the ship except for Gabriella. The Guild could apparently control her ring. Not always perhaps, but sometimes and only when she wasn't careful. Maria had told her this on many occasions. Had her secret fears of the Cape and its deep, dangerous waters been manipulated? Had the ring done the bidding of others?

Pale, scudding clouds revealed stars and the moon shone on a now silent and calm sea. Staring over the starboard rail Maria and Gabriella could clearly see a trail of something huge under the water disappearing in a white wake away from the Santa Barbara. Maria made no comment and Gabriella offered none either.

The following weeks saw the crew making repairs to the damage the storm had caused, but Bartholomew was keen to find a port somewhere to get help for five injured seamen and to refresh the ship's supplies. There were now endless, sultry days and nights of little or no wind as the ship made its way slowly to Madagascar, a huge island off the coast of Eastern Africa. There the ship was restocked with food and fresh water. The injured were put ashore and into care, gold was paid for their safe passage home and any damage that had not been repaired at sea was made good.

There was still no wind. The first mate told Gabriella that weather with no wind was named the doldrums. The girl couldn't have cared less what anything to do with the sea was called. She'd had enough of the sea.

Once docked, five new crew members were found, all of them Spanish. The remaining ship's crew were allowed onshore each with a small purse of silver coins allowed from their pay. Bartholomew insisted that everyone had to remain in small groups and be accompanied by an officer. They were commanded to be back within twelve hours otherwise, Bartholomew warned, the ship would sail without them.

Gabriella was not allowed onshore, much to her disappointment and, for the first time to the girl's knowledge, she noticed that Maria showed some signs of strain.

Once underway again, albeit slowly because of the tranquil weather, the Santa Barbara met few ships and those that were seen seemed far away. 'Deliberately,' said Maria to Gabriella, 'because Bartholomew never knows which ship is friend and which is an enemy. The Guild has its tentacles everywhere and there are those who would wish Queen Isabella's adventures to fail too.'

Almost at the same time as she said this, there came a cry from the topsail lookout that there was a vessel coming close by. Bartholomew shouted some orders and most of the crew took to fighting stations. Others crowded to one side of the Santa Barbara to see a long, dark ship very low in the water travelling fast with no visible crew. Despite the very light sea breeze, the stench from the passing ship was awful.

The first mate said to Gabriella, 'That's a slave trader that is, taking men, women and children from Africa to be sold. You understand the word slave? Eight hundred souls I reckon on board there. Good money for someone. You can smell the stink for a very long way no matter how the wind blows. Half of the cargo will be dead now and many of the remainder will be dead by the time the ship reaches land, God help them.' Realising what he'd said and that what he'd said was too much, the first mate mumbled something of an apology.

Gabriella said nothing because she could not. She stared at the passing ship and looked at the vessel long after it was but a speck in the distance. She had wanted someone to wave at, but there had been nobody. She wanted to understand but could not. She wanted to cry the tears of one who had lost everything that had been dear to her, but she did not. She wanted to cry for the loss of her parents, for her brothers and, she thought, for her small, short history, but did not. But she did eventually weep because she knew what the word slave meant in any language.

Gabriella was rarely left on her own, but on this occasion as the girl watched the slave trader disappear, Maria had gone to discuss something with Bartholomew, leaving the girl alone. Another Watcher, the cartographer, was in the shadows, always ready. However, just then four sailors chose that moment to unravel heavy, tarred ropes right in front of the cartographer, obstructing his sightline and blocking his way.

Someone approached the girl as she continued to stare after the low, dark ship. He spoke words of comfort in Italian and gave her a reassuring pat on her shoulder. Even though she would have preferred her own company, Gabriella turned to look at the person who'd interrupted her thoughts.

The man smiled. She stepped back one pace and asked, 'You came aboard from the island I think señor?' The man nodded. 'Welcome,' she said knowing full well that she needed to be careful of strangers, 'but I will bid you good day...'

The Spanish seaman was kindly and seemed eager to talk about himself and his adventures. Her Spanish was sufficient for a simple conversation and she thought that the man seemed pleasant enough. She could see no aura which was a relief even though she was aware that auras sometimes could be hidden. He wore a range of earrings in both ears and had the smell of someone who rarely washed, something that most sailors sought to avoid for fear of disease and being ostracised.

His name he told her was Francesco Anissa and he said that he'd visited Africa several times, speaking about the land in a way that enchanted the girl and allowed her to remember her happy childhood. He talked to her about slavery in an effort to reassure her and promised to teach her about seafaring. He was pleasant enough and, although Maria had said that the girl should not talk at any length with any of the crew, this sailor seemed almost paternal. By the time that the cartographer could see Gabriella again - once the sailors had finished their task with ropes - she was alone.

Gabriella pondered what Francesco Anissa had said. He'd explained how slavery wasn't really slavery at all; he had told her that Africans had wanted to travel across the seas to seek a better life. The Spaniard had tried to be convincing but, while she'd listened politely, in her heart, she couldn't reconcile what he'd said with what had happened to her village or what she had seen. He had explained that the stories of terrible conditions on the slave ships were myths and that the smell was just the result of rotten bilges, very common, he said, on long voyages. And, of course, he said, nobody really died. That too, he said, was nonsense.

A week or so after the slave trader ship had passed and, as the Santa Barbara sailed closer to the coast where the winds were brisker, Francesco explained to Gabriella how the depth of water was measured. Watchers were on hand not far away. Francesco urged Gabriella to look underneath one of the cannon placements where the plumb ropes were kept. Dusk was beginning to settle over the sea and the sun was a fireball lowering itself upon the horizon. There were few people on deck.

Francesco then urged Gabriella to come with him to see how the anchor worked. The Watchers stayed close by. The Spaniard began to explain the leather fathom marks on the measuring rope and he invited the girl to take a closer look. That meant leaning over the side of the ship, but he promised to hold her legs as she did so.

'Oh, I think you'll find that the girl won't do that,' Maria's voice was ice cold, loud and hard as flint. On either side of Maria were two Watchers, one of them an officer, the other the cartographer. Both held pistols and each was pointed at Francesco.

Francesco quite calmly turned his head to see who had spoken. 'Ah,' he said, 'No?' Sneering, he pulled Gabriella up and snatched her left arm in a vice-like grip.

'No,' said another voice - a calm, deep and melodious voice - that belonged to the tall and wide cook.

Gabriella looked down over the side and could see the rushing water and the spume; it was mesmerising. Frightened, she tried to pull away, but Francesco held her arm tightly and turned fully towards Maria, the two Watchers and the burly cook whose constant smile never left his face.

The Spaniard beamed and looked around the small group. 'I am outnumbered I see. For the moment. No matter. What do you propose to do about this situation precisely?' Without waiting for any answer, he said, 'Look out there.' He pointed at a ship heading now towards the Santa Barbara, its silhouette black in front of the setting sun. There was a yell from two of the lookouts and Gabriella could see that what was coming closer was a large warship. The crew immediately recognised it as an old Dutch-built man-of-war which they knew would be heavily armed with row upon row of cannon.

'A hundred cannon,' whispered the officer still pointing his pistol in Francesco's direction.

'Or more,' whispered the cartographer.

As the man-of-war came into proper view, it was easy to see that the vessel had three masts, each with four huge but filthy, rust-coloured sails. The ship was wide, long, menacing and closing fast.

Another shout from one of the Santa Barbara's lookouts alerted the Santa Barbara to the fact that the warship meant immediate harm as it turned slowly broadside on. Everyone could now see the gun ports being lifted. Gabriella heard shouts and commands from Bartholomew and his officers.

Francesco, still sneering, said, 'Presently, I will take the girl and leave. A boat will come for us. She is now my property. Mine alone. The Guild and all who support Pope Alexander claim the girl.' He made to bow low, still holding Gabriella's arm tight.

The cynical bow was a mistake. What happened next was very fast. The big cook rushed forward amazingly quickly for a man of his size, brandishing a long carving knife and stabbed down on Francesco's left hand - the one that was holding on to the ship's rail. Almost at the same time a pistol shot could be heard and Francesco grunted, clutching his left shoulder. The girl was free and, in one smooth movement, the cook tipped the astonished Spaniard over the side.

Gabriella leaned over and could see the man hanging on with one hand to an iron hoop that was just below the railing. However, the hoop was slippery with green, slimy algae and the girl knew that the man couldn't hold on for long. He was also bleeding heavily from the wounds in his shoulder and free hand but, even though he must have been in terrible pain, he was grinning and, with the damaged hand, was waving frantically at the dark ship that waited with guns readied.

The man laughed. Suddenly his laugh was cut off with a choking sound as he and everyone at the rail could see shark and barracuda drawn by the scent of blood in the water.

The Spaniard now stared up at the girl, fear on his face. Gabriella automatically put out an arm to help him. But he couldn't hang on to the iron hoop with his damaged hand and it was impossible for the girl to stretch her arm further. The man reached up and tried to grab the girl's hand with his good one which meant that he had to let go of the iron hoop. Their hands touched, but only briefly and neither could get a proper grip. The man fell, desperately trying, but failing, to catch hold of something on his way down to the sea.

Francesco didn't scream as the first lunging shark attacked him, but the water became red and he did scream after that. A pair of strong hands grabbed Gabriella underneath her arms and pulled her back. The big cook clasped the girl and then let her go to Maria. The Watchers slipped back into the ship's shadows and their duties, one of them pocketing the marlin spike that he'd had ready to use.

The Spaniard, or what was left of him, was being buffeted by the feeding frenzy. Puffs of grey and white smoke could be seen which were followed by loud bangs as the enemy ship opened fire. Most of the cannon balls hit the water but a few landed on the deck, wood splinters flying out like lead shot.

Thankfully, the wind was up now and the Santa Barbara turned fast, sails cracking until it too was broadside. Gabriella heard more shouted instructions and then a huge cacophony of sound as the Santa Barbara's own guns were fired deck by deck. The man-of-war was hit and a fire could be seen at the stern.

'That's the galley burning,' murmured the cook. 'It's near the gunpowder locker room so they will need to put that out fast.'

Nothing happened for a moment, but Gabriella could see that the fire on the man-of-war was spreading. She could also see that there were people running with pails full of water to stop the blaze. Gabriella saw the man-of-war turning slowly, its gun ports closing as it began to make its way back towards the coast. A cheer went up among Bartholomew's crew as the Santa Barbara righted its course and continued on its way.

Several of the crew and Bartholomew approached to see if the girl was unharmed. Gabriella went up to the cook and bowed her head mumbling thanks, but the big man shook his head and it was he who bowed his head before the girl.

'Sir, why do you bow to me? I have done nothing. You saved my life.' But the cook just smiled shyly, turned away and went back to his galley.

Gabriella looked up at Bartholomew who nodded and ushered any gawping crew away.

To Maria he said, 'I am told that this cur who now provides dinner for the fish talked of the Holy Father and the Borgias.

My financier, the Queen of Castile is close to the Pope. This troubles me. I have long known that the Borgias were not to be trusted, but the Queen of Castile? I doubt that her intent is anything positive towards the Pope and the Borgias, but we shall see. The Guild grows. I shall find out and then… we shall see.'

'Thank you, Bartholomew. For the risks and…'

'You have nothing for which to thank me. My duty is my duty and here we are… still safe!'

Of the warship there was now no sign at all and Gabriella, standing next to Maria and Bartholomew, wondered if she would ever see again the land that had been her home and was somewhere not that far, she judged, over the horizon. All three stared out at the darkening sea each with very different thoughts. There was no sound at all except for the gentle slip-slopping of water against the ship's sides and the sudden, blood-curdling scream that came from Gabriella.

26

Pompeii, Campania, Senatorial Province, Roman Empire, 79 CE

Umero had given a stern lecture to Jacob and accepted Jacob's sincere apologies. Privately, Umero wondered if he would have done the same in his youth. Marcellus reluctantly agreed that he would have done the same but expressed his concern to Umero that the lad had put everyone else at risk, not just himself.

Various members of Umero's crew had been castigated for appalling security with the threat of dire consequences should something similar ever reoccur. Umero, still very concerned that he had a spy onboard, gave the order to set sail immediately.

Marcellus, still unhappy at what Jacob had done, had a brief meeting with the garrison's commander and his centurions about the previous night's altercation and the commander in turn agreed to carry out a search.

'Not just a search. Search and destroy. Succeed in this,' Marcellus had urged. When the commander raised an eyebrow, Marcellus reminded him of Umero's connections with Emperor Titus and no more eyebrows were raised.

Shoshana had sustained a wound to her forehead which was washed and ointment smoothed onto her bruises. Jacob watched her and wanted to talk but didn't know how. When she caught his eye, he looked away.

Jacob, exhausted, fell asleep on a blanket on the floor of the cabin he shared with Jupiter and Neptune, his bag clutched close to his chest and the spear by his side. The two women watched him for a minute or two and then left to talk for hours in low voices.

In four days they reached Pompeii without further incident. Jacob was briefed again on the tasks ahead and what needed to be done. He pretended to be interested, but he wasn't and knew that, when the chance arose, he would be off and back to the land that at least he knew.

The whole idea of a peaceful life with the Bedouin really appealed to him now. He'd had enough - enough killing, enough fighting, enough running somewhere, enough running away. He didn't want to hide or lie or have to steal. There was nowhere he could call home - a proper home - and he'd spent much of his life looking over his shoulder. All this dung, he considered, about auras, Silver Greens, Watchers, Guild this and Guild that, immortality, saving the world, volcanic eruptions, death around every corner - he was fed up with the whole lot of it.

He had no idea why he had the spear or what it was supposed to do but he had never believed in magic and wasn't about to start now. And these strange people who had suddenly come into his life - the tall, old, ragged man, the mumbling cleric, Pluto, Jupiter, Neptune and Umero. And what of Judas? What of the two women? What of the one called Shoshana? Yes, he thought, he wanted to talk to her, but didn't know how.

Not so very far away, Emperor Titus, a military genius and the man responsible for Jerusalem's ruin, was offshore on the imperial quinquereme which was surrounded by fifteen support and defensive naval vessels. The quinquereme was enormous with its three banks of oars and metal-plated armour at the prow. At the prow there was also a wooden statue of Mars.

The vessel was festooned with flags and the woodwork was painted red and white. Titus occasionally went ashore for banquets and to meet a variety of foreign dignitaries who sought an audience with him. But, overall, he felt safer aboard his ship.

This evening the emperor was feeling sour, partly because of some oysters he'd eaten the evening before and because now he was talking to a very dull man. The Guild's representative just would not leave.

'We had an arrangement, my emperor,' said Vassily de Souza in an oily voice.

'I am not your emperor.'

'Of course. My error, emperor. The Guild, emperor…'

'Yes, I know. The Guild expects.'

'Indeed emperor… and well put if I may say so. The Guild always expects. We have great expectations. The Guild is also concerned about these expectations. Very concerned indeed. We have no Silver Green despite assurances from you. In addition, we have no slave workforce despite… ah, assurances from you. We have been most patient.'

'Do you know what we do to people we dislike? We cut out their tongues, then do away with their hands, then their feet and, after that, we throw them into the sea. That's an easy death. Would you care to hear more adventurous ideas? Ask the Jews. If you can find any.'

Vassily fidgeted as he stood before Titus. He knew that within earshot were several men who were Guild through and through. Roman soldiers yes, but Guild men first. However, he didn't know how many there were, but nonetheless he felt reasonably safe.

'Emperor,' he said in a wheedling voice, 'please see the matter from… our point of view…'

'Bugger your point of view. I'm not interested in your point of view,' retorted Titus, his voice loud and tight with anger. 'You speak of patience, but you and your… friends know nothing of patience.'

His Praetorian Guard, seven seasoned soldiers, stepped forward in unison one pace hearing the tone of their master, but Titus waved them back. 'You shall have nothing,' he said, wincing as his stomach grumbled. 'We cannot take hold of one of your Silver Green bastards. We've tried. I'm not very interested. And the empire is my empire. The slaves are my slaves. Not yours and not the… Guild's. Now perhaps you would care to leave? I shan't invite you in such a kindly way again. Livius!'

A Praetorian prefect saluted.

'Livius. Escort this… gentleman out and, if you see him once again after today, kill him. Once dead, I shall see his head on a plate. Understood?'

'Emperor,' said Livius smartly and saluted.

'Emperor please,' whined Vassily de Souza.

'Goodbye. Please offer my… regrets to your friends.'

'Emperor, they will be most displeased. They will wish you to know that there will be retributions… consequences on a scale that my… that you… that the emperor will find… hard to explain.'

Titus stared at Vassily. Then looked up at Livius. The

emperor nodded only very slightly at Livius who in turn inclined his helmeted head a fraction.

Titus said, 'You have overstepped your mark. I did warn you...'

'Emperor it is I who must warn you. The price for angering us is very high. But,' said Vassily de Souza now anxious to leave having seen quite clearly the red in the emperor's eyes, 'I see that you are not to be moved. I beg your indulgence and am grateful for your time. Good day.'

Titus watched as Vassily de Souza left the chamber followed by Livius and the six legionaries all dressed in red, white and gold. Once outside, Vassily's servants moved to collect their master, but they were stopped by guards. Any Guild members of the emperor's military retinue dared not give themselves away and they had received no instructions to interfere. They assumed that this little, nervous man was expendable. And so he was. Vassily was hoisted off his feet, screeching protestations. As he was hauled away to the death that Emperor Titus had just promised, his shouts disappeared into nothing.

When Umero docked at Pompeii's main quay, he gave instructions that none of the five passengers were to leave the vessel under any circumstances whatsoever until he personally gave his permission. He needed to discuss next steps with the pirate captain whose ship had stood off the coast with all flags lowered and small sails in evidence only.

As Umero was rowed over to the pirate ship, he saw the emperor's quinquereme and he knew that soon there would be some kind of moment of truth. The Guild either owned the emperor or it didn't and Umero needed to know. He was also unsure whether he himself was now an enemy of the state or still one of Rome's loved sons. He thought he knew the answer to that.

The town of Pompeii, located about five thousand pedes from the mountain called Vesuvius, was a flourishing resort for Rome's most distinguished and wealthy citizens. Elegant houses and elaborate villas lined the well-paved streets. Tourists, townspeople and slaves bustled in and out of artisans' shops, taverns, brothels and bathhouses. People gathered in the large arena to watch plays and fights or lounged in the open-air squares and marketplaces.

The day after the meeting with and demise of Vassily de Souza, Emperor Titus was now beginning to tire of the area and wanted to be back in Rome. He was about to give orders to leave when he had another Guild visit. This visitor had expressly wished to meet the emperor on board his quinquereme.

The Guild and its visitations had by now thoroughly bored Titus. But, because this man's colleague was now at the bottom of the sea providing healthy meals for fish, he thought it would be prudent to meet a Guild representative one last time.

'Emperor Titus, vale,' said Julius Marcatto casually. The Guild had a few very senior people who were heads of various parts of the organisation around the world. Julius Marcatto was Guild head of this part of the world. He smiled at the seated emperor who could see immediately that this person was far more reassured and relaxed than the fool de Souza.

'I knew your predecessor,' said Julius Marcatto casually, 'may his soul be revered by the gods - and we must all pray that many more statues will be erected for the world to see such a... great man.'

'Yes, I expect you did, I expect it will and I'm sure there are already more than enough. Your... arrangement was with him. Not with me. Be brief.'

'Ah yes, emperor, but the... ah... long-standing arrangement passes of course down the chain of command - that is most specifically written - and I am afraid, as my colleague Vassily will have explained, that is also part of the contract, the signed contract... I wonder where he is by the by. Well, not to worry, I am sure that he's safe.' There was a pause and both men looked at each other without flinching or blinking.

'Magno imperatore terrae, great emperor of all the earth,' continued Julius Marcatto, smiling mirthlessly, 'the penalty for unpaid debts to us, imperial status notwithstanding, must still apply. And, emperor, should you consider a fate for me that might be like that of others... well you may wish to reconsider.'

Julius Marcatto's voice turned from politesse to steel. 'May I bring your attention, most gracious emperor, to the fact that within earshot there are, oh... twenty-six men who are actually my men, not yours. They will be more than a match for your small unit of Praetorian Guard, strong and brave as indeed they are. Be of no doubt whatsoever, my revered and most honourable ruler of the empire, you will be dead before my body hits the ground. My men have specific instructions and, I promise you, it would be best not to test those instructions. Oh, and just in case, I have other Guild fighters nearby on a vessel who at a signal will invade your ship and kill everyone onboard - rowers, crew, attendants, the lot. And you. I trust that we're clear. No, please don't stand, for I have not yet finished.'

Julius took a seat himself, something that was forbidden without the emperor's permission. Titus glared, seething but saying nothing.

'Now,' said Julius. 'To business.'

'In a short time, dear Julius,' said Titus drily, 'I shall have to ask you to leave because I have guests for a formal dinner and I am afraid that an invitation was not sent in your direction.'

'No matter - and of course I quite understand, but I do fear that your dinner will have no guests and, alas, you will have no dinner.'

Titus' irritation was growing. 'Your meaning?'

'My meaning? Well, grant me a moment to teach you some history. The Vesuvius mountain… look you can see it from here… no, I insist, please look… well, it's a volcano. How can I explain better? It is a mons igneus. My scholars say that the mountain has been erupting since… well, the beginning of time. Two thousand years ago an unusually violent eruption shot volumes of superheated lava, ash and rocks high into the sky. That catastrophe destroyed every tree, animal and person within sight of the mountain and far, far beyond. Oh… trust me, I will get to the point my emperor. You tap your fingers in irritation? You shrug? Do bear with me please.'

Titus, increasingly angry and certainly unused to being addressed in such a way, held his temper but only just. He was looking forward to killing this worm himself.

'You know,' continued Julius, 'that the mountain grumbles and roars a little from time to time? People look at it then in trepidation and, what's the word? Well, fear will do. Yes, fear.' Julius smiled. 'And in such a pleasant, sunny spot as this.' He stopped talking and gazed happily at Vesuvius.

'Even after the terrible earthquake that struck the Campania region ten years ago,' he continued with a smile, 'your people still flocked to the shores of the bay here, as indeed they do now, emperor. Pompeii has grown more crowded every year. Much more.' Titus was becoming ever irritable and his close courtiers wondered at the fate of this man who dared to speak to their emperor in such a way and indeed for so long.

'Well,' continued Julius softly, looking at the emperor as if addressing a child, 'three emperors gave an undertaking... as you know of course, in writing, to honour a number of unbreakable promises each of which, alas, has been...hmm, what's the word? Yes, that's it. Broken. By you.'

He beamed at Titus as if they were best friends discussing a game of some sort. 'Weapons, ships like this one, roads, waterways - all that and much, much more. We gave you these things as part of the bargain. No, please do not give little signals to your men for mine are so close by and this ship will become a slaughterhouse I promise you. And you, my friend, will be the prize pig.'

There was absolute silence.

'Now,' continued Julius after a long moment, 'you have inherited the debt. You know this perfectly well. No Silver Green for instance and, emperor, what a mistake and huge shame that is, because there has been one very close to your own Praetorian Guard in recent days and it would have been so simple to... well, never mind. What is done is done. Or not done in this case. But with all the might of Rome, you could not achieve this small favour. We are disappointed.'

The emperor was staring hard at Julius who could see anger and vitriol in the eyes of the man who ruled most of the known earth. Or, rather, thought Julius, who ruled in name only.

'Even now,' said Julius totally unconcerned, 'the same Silver Green is here in Pompeii. Yes, right now. Heavily protected of course, but still... I believe that with some thought and resource, you might have seized him and handed him to us... but don't be concerned, because we have once again taken matters into our own hands.' He clapped his hands and walked about the room as if it was he who owned the ship. Titus clenched his fists and his teeth.

'But,' said Julius, 'we will have him I believe this very day. And then, dear me, there are all those slaves we were promised... so many slaves from all over the empire. Each nation state was to offer slaves. That didn't happen either, dear emperor. Not one slave. Why? Because you kept them all.' Julius paused and relaxed. He gazed across the water again as the sun was just beginning to set.

'The Guild always keeps its promises,' he continued, still looking out to sea. 'Always. Consider this, emperor. We have something called Guild fire. You may know Greek fire. How stupid of me! Of course you do. You are a soldier and a good one at that. But we invented Greek fire and we have now created something far more powerful than anyone can ever imagine. Guild fire can destroy and consume on a vast scale. It will ensure that Guild power is complete.' He looked sternly at the emperor.

'Power,' went on Julius, 'is a wondrous thing is it not? With it you can do anything! But real power, power that lasts, well that kind of power requires an ingredient that has eluded us for centuries. Real power requires immortality. Can you imagine such a thing? Just think about it! Hence our need for the Silver Green. The elixir we shall produce will be for Guild men and women and,' he paused for emphasis, 'those whom we choose to support… for as long as they prove useful. Any intake of elixir will last for but one year and, if it is taken, repeatedly - say our alchemists - then immortality is a given. Alas, emperor, you will now not be among the chosen.' He sighed theatrically and turned again to look at Vesuvius. 'Pity,' he whispered.

Julius pointed towards the volcano. 'We promised to support your empire and, by any god, we have supported it! Now your empire crumbles. You promised to help us and yet you failed. As you know, your people have helped us to create underground citadels. Many of them. You thought that the citadels were for you. But, alas, no. Not one. They are all for Guild use.' Julius smiled. 'Soon,' he said calmly, 'as you gaze across the water and then inland to the mountain, the volcano, yes… see… that very one over there, well it will shortly erupt and disgorge. People's blood will boil emperor and their bodies will just evaporate.' He stood up suddenly for dramatic effect. 'I can't think of other words to describe what will happen, but your poets might. If there any left alive tomorrow.'

Titus was now listening and gripping the arms of his golden chair.

Julius went on as if he was describing a marvellous party that he'd arranged. 'I'm glad that you're listening properly now. There will be an explosion the sound of which has never been heard on earth or made by any god. You will remember it, this noise. It will frighten you. It will ruin ears, blind eyes and it will kill. The Guild will have created this explosion. The volcano will erupt and will sink some of your fleet here. You will think that is all. No. It is not all.' He paused to make sure Titus was paying full attention. He was.

Julius talked as if giving a lecture. 'There will be a hard rain of red hot, fine-grained ash and pieces of burning white pumice

- you know, the stuff that they use to scrape your feet? People will believe that the world is coming to an end and in a way it is.' He laughed. 'You shake your head? Oh, I promise you, what I'm telling you is the absolute truth.' He paused. Within earshot, the members of the Praetorian Guard and other soldiers weren't sure whether to drag this man away or let him carry on. They saw no sign from their emperor.

Julius still looked unconcerned. 'More and more ash will fall, clogging the air. People of high and low birth will be affected. Buildings will collapse. Finally, a very fast surge of heated, poison gas and liquid rock will crash down the side of the mountain and swallow everything and everyone in its path.'

There was silence. Julius smiled.

'Emperor, your world will suffer drought, flood, famine and dust. Then, if we still do not get what we want, and I must tell you that our requirements will have increased, we will do the same with every volcano in your empire within one year. You and your world will be destroyed as will everyone in it. Not only everyone under Rome's rule. I mean everyone on earth. People will experience a perpetual ash winter and will starve if they are not poisoned or crushed. The Guild will live underground until the ash has fallen and the sun once again shines. With our new immortality, we will become immune to poisons and will rise up to build our new world above ground.' He paused for breath. 'There,' he said cheerfully. 'How's that for a dinner time story? Shame that you won't be able to tell it tonight.'

Titus stood, breathed deeply and looked out. He could see the villages of Stabiae and Herculaneum and he could see some grey smoke coming from the mountain top. He glanced sideways at his guest and saw the man put something in both of his ears. He was about to laugh at that and probably strangle his visitor himself, but, turning back to Vesuvius, he saw a huge plume of white and bright red flame shoot out of the mountain's top, flame that reached high into the blue sky immediately followed by a tremendous jet of white steam.

A moment later there was a deep growling roar which grew and grew in volume, vibrating and shaking everything, buildings, the sea, his ship, the earth. And the noise grew. It was this unbearable sound that made the leader of the Roman Empire clamp his hands to his ears, but not before they had begun to bleed.

27

South East Asian Sea, 1492

The loss of the ring was the end of the world for Gabriella and ruin for Maria. The two had agonised how the ring could possibly have come off the girl's finger, but it was obvious that the only conclusion was that the Spaniard had inadvertently or maybe even deliberately pulled the ring off Gabriella's finger when the girl was trying to help him just before he fell.

Gabriella was inconsolable and for the most part lay on her bunk facing the wall. A regular visitor to Gabriella was Bartholomew's mother who, still dressed in a thin chainmail tunic despite the heat and, even though she didn't speak, sat with the girl just holding a hand or applying a cool cloth to the girl's forehead. Gabriella could see the green glow around the woman's head and shoulders and wondered what had really caused her terrible scars. She liked this strange woman who always seemed so calm and reassuring. Gabriella also knew beyond any doubt that, not only had she lost her family, she had also lost the trust of those who had invested hope in her. And she had lost the Ring of Solomon.

The ship's damage from cannon shot had been repaired with hardwood, bitumen and tar and the few wounded gunners, mostly from cannon recoil, had been patched up by the ship's surgeon. However, while the ship still had a plentiful supply of fresh water and other essentials, sea water from the holed hull had spoiled some of the stores. The dried beef, hard biscuits and cheese were now inedible. These were thrown overboard.

As he helped dispose of the spoiled food, the first mate

noted that a huge shark was floating, dead, alongside the ship and he wondered what monster had killed the shark which had been partly eaten. Even now he saw that there were a variety of fish frantically nibbling at the frayed flesh.

The ship's cook, despite his ready smile, was concerned that the foodstuffs they had left might now not last until they reached land. He was adept at creating all kinds of delicacies out of next to nothing, but even his excellent skills were becoming sorely tested. The crew had begun to complain. The cook explained to Maria that fish might have been an obvious solution, but all seafaring folk knew that it was impossible to catch fish from a fast-moving vessel. Or even one that wasn't moving that fast. Moreover, they knew that fish were not plentiful in the deep ocean because there was little food for any fish to eat.

The cook often visited Gabriella, with permission from Maria of course and he always brought with him small, bite-sized cakes or tiny cinnamon biscuits still warm from the oven. He would talk about his family who still lived in the Indies and spoke about things that he hoped Gabriella, coming from Africa, might understand. He would also sing deep-voiced songs in a strange patois which gave solace and pleasure to whomsoever was listening and these songs soothed Gabriella.

Bartholomew ordered that all the sails be struck. Becalmed in warm weather and soft seas with dwindling food supplies, the ship's company was becoming agitated. In some desperation, nets were thrown over the side to see if fish could be caught. This activity lasted for two days and two nights with no results. There were open mutterings and Bartholomew was about to break out arms for the officers when there was a sudden and excited shout from the lookout. Everyone stared at where the man was pointing. The dark mass that was approaching fast seemed enormous.

As it got closer, the mass became silvery, glinting in the sun. Whatever it was seemed to be not only flying, but dipping in and out of the water. One of the sailors voiced his fears that this must be a sea serpent of huge size with evil intent and that the ship was about to be sunk. Some sailors crossed themselves, knelt and said prayers. Others just stared. Gabriella had no interest and stayed in her cabin with Maria.

The calm sea rippled white as the cloud of silver skimmed the surface, dipped under and leapt over the waves. Everyone could now make out that the mysterious mass was an enormous shoal of flying fish. Vast numbers of dark blue, silver and green flashes of light flew, dipped and leapt straight towards the ship. Sailors and officers alike ducked as many of the fish fell on the deck which soon became a deep, squirming, wriggling mass. On the first mate's instructions, the men, relieved that this had been no monster of the deep, went about collecting the fish and putting them in saltwater barrels.

A great stew of fish and vegetables was prepared that evening. The cook beamed as he created what he called a Tamil mixture in a spicy sauce which he declared would be delicious. Word spread that the flying fish would be the ship's dinner that day and possibly for many more days to come. The cook laughed and sang to himself as he considered many different ways of serving flying fish.

The crew and officers alike admitted that the spicy fish stew was delicious and everyone had more than one helping. Some had three.

There was a sudden clamour from the galley and the

sweating cook clambered out and ran to Bartholomew's cabin with a huge grin on his face. After the cook had shown Bartholomew what he had found, the captain grinned a big grin too and hurried to Maria's cabin. After knocking politely, he barged in without waiting for an answer and saw Gabriella on her bunk, facing the wall.

He nodded towards Maria and then spoke to Gabriella's back. 'Good evening, child,' he said simply.

Gabriella did not answer, but Maria said sharply, 'Gabriella, turn and face the captain. You will not be discourteous.' Gabriella rolled over and sat up. Her eyes were sore from crying and she looked wretched.

'My pardon, sir,' she said quietly.

Bartholomew smiled tentatively, stepped towards her and held out a fist. He uncurled his fingers. 'Here is your ring,' he said softly. There was no sound for a moment or two and then Gabriella screeched and shouted in delight and relief. She took the ring, hands shaking, stared at it and sobbed. She rushed to Bartholomew and hugged the now embarrassed voyager. He smiled and gently extricated himself.

Maria asked how the ring had been found and Gabriella wanted the same information.

'It was found,' said Bartholomew, 'in the largest of the flying fish. I can only imagine that the shark or barracuda that consumed the hapless Spaniard, died and other fish feasted on the carcass, one consuming the ring.'

Gabriella, engrossed in the ring, slipped it onto the middle finger of her right hand.

'Thank you, sir,' whispered Gabriella.

'No, no. Fortune be thanked, not me. But please listen to me,' said Bartholomew. 'If what you have said is true, with the ring you will be able to charm the winds to give us favour and speed. I know that you are not a witch, but I don't want my crew to think that you might be. Sailors are suspicious and it was hard to persuade them that there should be women on board.' He smiled at the girl pointing at the ring.

'You are a Silver Green,' he said, 'a special Silver Green, and I have no doubt that you have powers. There must be some reason why the ring has been returned to you. The oceans are big and the chances of one small item being found are… but I am glad that you have it again. I ask you now though if you can bestow upon us some aid. If you can, then I beg you to give us the winds we need. I ask nothing more; without wind, we will drift. And inevitably perish.'

Gabriella smiled at the captain and nodded. She closed her eyes and rubbed the ring. She let her mind drift and thought of winds, great gusts from east to west, scents in the African air, the billowing of a plump sail, waves on the sea, spray from water caught by warm winds, scudding clouds crossing new moons, tempests she had imagined, storms she had seen, grass waving and trees whispering. She kept her eyes closed and rubbed the ring again. Nothing happened. She began to imagine stronger winds, huge gusts, winds that created waves and winds that howled in their menace.

Bartholomew looked hard at Maria. Maria looked at the girl. Gabriella stared at the ring, anger rising in her chest. It was, she fumed, not for her to create winds. It was not for her to be responsible for the ship and its voyage. It was not her job to destroy the plague virus. She was no magician. She was no apothecary, no scientist, no soldier and no slave. Yes, she had the ring again and, yes, she was pleased and relieved, but if everyone had great expectations of her, then she would rather the ring and herself were in the sea.

Still nothing happened and nothing further was said. Bartholomew left the cabin without saying a word. Gabriella could hear him shout some orders as he stomped off and that made her angrier still. The air remained motionless, the heat was draining and the silence on the ship was heavy. Still there was no wind.

And then, suddenly and without any warning whatsoever, there was. A cool breeze fast became a buffeting wind that shrieked through the ship's rigging. A sudden and great crack and crackle came from somewhere in the sky - a noise full of volume, reverberation and echo across the heavens that now darkened, reflected in the almost black sea.

The winds that Gabriella had brought forth from the Ring of Solomon were like none that Bartholomew had ever witnessed and he knew with icy fear that he might have made the biggest mistake of his life. His brother Christopher had always said that explorers on land or sea, no matter what the predicament, should be careful what they wished for because everything had a consequence - and some consequences were terrible.

Bartholomew's thoughts were interrupted by a terrific crash of thunder which made any conversation or concentration impossible. The rolling thunder that ran across the sea made his ears ring as he watched yellow and white lightning split the almost black sky and caused the sea to sizzle where the fiery forks hit the water.

Bartholomew ordered most sails to be brought down and

instructed that the main mast be made sturdier with heavy hawser ropes. The winds were not just full of force now but seemed to be coming from all directions. They were so powerful that nobody could stand on deck even if attached to something sturdy. Coils of rope were whipped away from the deck and flung overboard as if they were silk ribbons. The cook and two of the crew fought valiantly to ensure that the galley stoves didn't fall, each of which had embers sufficient to cause the whole ship to be consumed in flames. A dislodged cannon smashed against the ship's sides as if trying to escape, causing damage to the hull.

The Santa Barbara was tossed about in a wild sea. The winds ran as if they'd been restrained in chains for years and had suddenly been set free. They sped across the waves, howling through the rigging like ghosts and angry, baying dogs. The masts groaned and all the ship's woodwork creaked as if in terrible pain. Rain hammered the cabin windows like an impenetrable salvo of musket shot. Waves, now vast mountains, black and green with streaks of white, reared up like cobras readying themselves for attack. Through the cabin porthole Gabriella could see lightning forks each one much brighter than the last. Maria, tight-lipped and pale-faced, gripped her bunk's rails.

Bartholomew, initially so very keen on a traditional wind to help the Santa Barbara on its way, was terrified that his ship and all onboard would now be lost. His crew ran unsteadily forward and aft below decks, trying as best they could to keep up with his commands and at the same time desperate to hold on to something.

After two long hours which seemed like two long days, the storm abated and the wind reduced to a warm sea breeze that gradually dried out the ship and the exhausted people on it.

A relieved Maria said soothingly to the girl, 'In time you will control these things better. Have a care though. Be careful what you imagine. True, time is not with us. Even so, have a care.'

Gabriella, looking at the ring as it turned from bright blue and silver to its normal dull metal, nodded and said firmly, 'I have no need for such care. None. The winds were exactly as I imagined.'

28

Mare Nostrum, Roman Empire, 79 CE

The escape from the Pompeii coast had been swift. In the general chaos, after the first violent and eye-searingly bright flames that had shot out of the volcano, Umero had set sail immediately as had the pirate ship. Before the eruption, he had already given orders to soak all the sails and decks in seawater. Calmly everyone had been instructed to cover any bare skin with wet clothing, to put wadding and candle wax in their ears and to wrap heavy, dampened cloths around their heads. In addition, everyone on deck wore a battle helmet. Each person had been ordered to turn his or her back to the volcano as it exploded.

Despite precautions, everyone's ears were still ringing and many of the crew had headaches and a few suffered minor burns from winds bearing red hot cinders. Care had to be taken to avoid hot debris which fell on the sea and vessels like a molten waterfall. Umero's crew had covered most of the decking with metal shields tied together and it was this covering that saved the ship. Even though the explosions and eruptions were diminishing now, rivers of hot rock and cooling magma were still rushing to the sea. The sky still rained huge boulders of red-hot rock. Everyone was tasked with looking out for any spark or fire that might spread.

Huge jets of scalding steam and boiling liquids streamed out from fissures in the volcano and arced across the bay, covering hapless ships that were too close to the shoreline. Some of these vessels, particularly those nearest Vesuvius, were burning and enormous boulders that had shot from the volcano's summit had sunk others.

The world in and around Pompeii was grey with patches of angry colour. Fluid lava overran villages, farms, animals and people. Olive trees became immediate, grey statues. As Jacob watched the horrific scenes, he wondered if, like the trees, people had become statues too.

There was a smell of sulphur in the air mixed with that of burnt wood, cloth and something else that some onboard recognised.

Once safely underway and out on the open sea, Umero called an urgent meeting which included Jacob, the woman with one ear, Shoshana, Neptune and Jupiter as well as his trusted Marcellus and a few centurions.

He addressed the group. 'Emperor Titus, if he escaped which I suspect he did, will be both angry and afraid. I know him. However, he is a soldier and his bravery will overcome his fear. He will want terrible revenge but, alas, it is too late for that. If what we have witnessed was Guild work, which I know it was, then the empire is doomed. Nobody could have stopped what we have seen today or saved the lives that the spectacle will have cost.' Umero paused and glanced at Jacob who met his gaze directly.

'The Guild,' went on Umero, 'means what it says - it always does - and its followers make no threat which is ever idle. Unless Titus, if he still leads Rome, makes good each of his broken promises, then every volcano will be fired - north, south, east and west - all of them. That will create…'

'Parched earth, dried rivers, spoilt crops, polluted air, foul water, huge waves… and certain death,' said Shoshana.

'Exactly so,' nodded Umero. 'Exactly so. And the earth will be ruined for years. The Guild will have temporary citadels underground and also expects to have the key to immortality.' He glanced at Jacob again, who this time looked away.

'But now,' said Umero, 'we must help this boy destroy Guild fire.'

Jacob had heard enough. He wanted to stand up and shout out that he was not going to do anything of the sort. He was going to do nothing whatsoever about Guild fire or Guild anything. He wanted to shout out that he'd already seen enough of Guild fire and he liked none of it. He wanted to yell that it was ridiculous to expect a fourteen-year-old to destroy another powerful enemy. He'd already been trying to do that for seven years hadn't he? He wanted to shout that he would go back to Judea and become a Bedouin goatherd. But he didn't shout out or say any of these things.

Umero was still talking. 'We must make sure that the boy gets to where Guild fire is made and stored.'

'Yes, we know, to the east,' said Neptune impatiently.

'No, not there. Not the east. Jerusalem,' said Umero.

Jacob sat bolt upright. 'Jerusalem? But I thought…'

'It has always been Jerusalem,' Umero said calmly. 'Never in the lands of the far-off east. We could not speak of it. The Guild had to be led away.'

Umero looked round the group as if daring anyone to say anything different. None did.

'One of the reasons that Jerusalem was destroyed and so many Jews tortured most horribly, killed and crucified in disgusting ways even for Rome, was because Guild fire needed protection and secrecy. The destruction, the war, the chaos - all of that focused minds on other matters and we Watchers could not get close. We tried, but we failed. A man, a leading alchemist, by the name of Flavius Josephus, knew of the exact location of Guild fire manufacture, but…'

'He was the man I was meant to meet in the Qumran hills,' called out Jacob. He stopped and felt embarrassed. He spoke more softly. 'He was the one I was meant to meet in the hills, but I was told that he had died.' Shoshana put a hand on his shoulder, but he shrugged it off impatiently and looked resolutely at Umero.

'He did die yes,' Umero said. 'He was a decent man. He…' Umero looked at Shoshana for some reason and Jacob could see that she shook her head very slightly. Umero blinked in acknowledgment and went on.

'The Guild wanted his knowledge. He was forced to provide it and, when they had taken from him what they needed, they crucified him. The Guild so instructed it.' He paused. 'Jerusalem must be our next destination… But I cannot carry us to Judea. It's too dangerous. Titus will know that I am rogue now and I think he always did, although I have always served all my emperors well.' He shrugged, stared at his hands for a moment, sighed deeply and briefly looked wistful. Some of those in the group glanced at each other. Nobody else spoke.

'But,' said Umero, in a brighter voice, 'while Titus will be busy on other matters, basically saving his future, I must take my loyal people and… disappear for a while. I must return to my family and we must leave our home and hide. Perhaps go far off to another country, although perhaps none of us will be safe wherever we may run.' He stopped talking again and Jacob could see a flicker of sadness in the great commander's eyes.

Umero looked in turn at Shoshana, Jupiter, Neptune, the woman with one ear and Jacob. 'You five will go with my pirate ship. I promise you that they will see you safe to land and the men are strong. They will protect and help you in your task. You will have nothing to fear. May the gods go with you… Marcellus, see to the arrangements.'

Everyone went their separate ways. Jacob went up to Umero and touched an arm. Umero stopped and turned.

'Well?'

'I… I want to thank you,' replied Jacob.

Umero's stern face softened and he smiled as he put a hand on Jacob's shoulder. 'You have no need to thank me. It is I and others who must thank you. In any battle… there is only one victor and we must always hope and think that the victor will be us. Believe that. I know you dislike your task and don't understand it. It is written all over your face. You want to run away. I can see that too. But you… you have much to do and it is a huge burden upon your young shoulders. Maybe it is too much. I don't know. But be strong. Think of that which is just and never forget the enemy that is evil. I know that we will all have much for which to thank you. We won't meet again in this world and that is my loss. I hope…' He stopped and whatever it was that Umero hoped Jacob did not discover. 'Whichever are your own deities,' Umero said, 'may every single one go with you.' With that, he squeezed Jacob's shoulder, looked at him in the eye for a moment, nodded once, turned abruptly and marched off.

The process of transfer from the ship to the pirate vessel wasn't at all easy because the waters were choppy and the ships could only be adjacent to each other for a short time. The transfer was to be immediate and, after collecting what meagre bits and pieces they had, the five made their way to the starboard side of the ship. The pirate vessel was close, but Jacob couldn't see how he or any of the others were going to cross the gap between the ships. The swell made the gap wide for a moment and then narrow but, even when narrow, the gap seemed far too wide to jump. Jacob was aware that if he or any of the others fell, then they would be crushed or drowned or both.

Without any warning, Jupiter grabbed Shoshana and Jacob, one under each huge arm and jumped. He and they were met by three grinning, fierce-looking pirates who hauled them aboard. The process was repeated when Neptune grabbed the woman with one ear. Strangely, noticed Jacob, when Neptune jumped, the swell stopped and the two ships steadied.

The group waved and many of Umero's crew waved back. Marcellus looked hard at Jacob, eventually smiling and then saluting him. That meant a lot to Jacob and he grinned at the tough warrior. He looked out for Umero but of him there was no sign.

The gap between the two ships became wider and soon the pirate ship tacked east heading for the coast of Carthago, their first stop on their way back to Judea. Jacob watched as Umero's Quintus became smaller and soon but a dot on the horizon. He wasn't sure if it was the sea spray that was blurring his vision or something else.

The pirate ship was well-appointed and the captain, a small man with a long beard covered in remnants of food and his few teeth stained brown, made the group welcome. He was coarse, loud and blunt, but he was also kindly and had a hearty laugh. The pirate crew spoke a Latin dialect with flavours of Greek and some other tongue that Jacob could not understand but, apart from meals and short walks on deck, there was little opportunity for much conversation anyway.

The journey to Carthago took four days and, during that time, Shoshana and the woman with one ear briefed Jacob repeatedly. Jacob, for his part, listened and understood, but, despite what Umero had said, he was still planning to get away as soon as he could. And now, of course, he thought, he was being given free passage to Judea! That was, he smiled, a great bonus. One of the gods must be helping him, he thought. Idly, for a fleeting moment, he wondered which one.

He often examined the spear, wondering what it could do, if anything. Considering all the nonsense he'd been told, he couldn't really understand why someone would go to so much trouble to make sure he had the thing. It was only half a spear in the first place and acquiring it, then looking after it had become not only dangerous for him, but lethal to others and a stupid waste of time.

The pirate ship anchored off the coast of Carthago with as little fuss as possible. After some argument and a few threats, fresh food and water was bought fairly and taken on board, after which the vessel made its way for Creta. This was the final stop to freshen supplies before Yapho on the Judean coast which was where the ship would find land in a secret cove. That made Jacob's heart lighter because he'd once been to Yapho and knew that the town was situated on the Roman road from Caesarea to Jerusalem. That would make it easy for him to escape.

After Carthago, the seas became less smooth and the ship passed through a few storms which on several occasions tipped the prow downwards and worryingly a few times. None of the pirates seemed at all concerned. Some looked with great respect at Neptune and Jacob couldn't understand why apart from the fact that he was a formidable size and strong. Once the seas had quietened again, there was a shout from a lookout high up on the main mast. A body had been seen aboard a small coracle which seemed to be floating aimlessly, bobbing about on the waves.

It turned out that the body was alive. It was a Syrian who apparently, the pirate captain discovered, had been travelling with cargo to Sparta on a commercial voyage. According to the Syrian, his ship had been overturned by a sea serpent, with most hands lost. A few, including himself, had managed to escape into the sea.

The man had lost some fingers and was very weak. The pirates debated as to whether they should simply throw the man back into the sea as a liar and a wastrel or tend to his needs. After some consultation, the captain, having quickly noticed that the rings on the man's remaining fingers as well as two brooches on his chest were real sapphires and pure silver, decided to keep the jewellery. He also decided to keep the man on the basis that, at some stage, he might be worthy of a ransom.

One evening, as the sinking sun glowed deep red and the rowers were resting while the sails took up most of the effort, Jacob found himself on deck with Shoshana. There was no conversation between them. The man rescued from the sea had recovered now having been washed, fed and reclothed. The man was also on deck looking out at the sunset. He sidled over to Jacob, waved his bandaged hand towards Jacob's spear and spoke in Aramaic.

'Your spear, is it special?'

Jacob ignored the question and looked out at the setting sun.

'Your spear, let me see it, for I can tell that it is an antiquity of some value and I will buy it from you.'

'It is not for sale, sir,' said Jacob politely and turned to leave.

'I am wealthy. These idiot pirates have no idea how wealthy I am and I will offer you a great deal of silver for that spear, for I shall have it. Name your price.'

'The boy has said that he has no wish to sell it.' Shoshana took Jacob's arm which he immediately shrugged off.

'Hold your tongue woman,' spat the man pushing the bandaged hand in her face. 'You dare to speak to me so? You don't know who I am. I have said that I have wealth. Only some of it has gone to the bottom of the sea, but I still have much. And land too. Some silver shall be for the boy and maybe a little for your pains if I find you… satisfactory.'

Jacob stepped forward, but Shoshana quickly pulled him away and they hurried below without another word and joined the others for a supper of a goat meat broth, figs, black bread and warmed red wine.

Afterwards, much later, from his bed of straw and a blanket, Jacob awoke on hearing shouts and thuds from the deck. He assumed that the pirates were trimming the sails or maybe letting them out. Or perhaps the weather was deteriorating again. The running and yells increased. Shoshana and the woman with one ear sat up. Neptune and Jupiter were not there. Jacob suddenly felt that something was wrong. He got up and removed his sica from his belt; with the other hand he held the spear tight. The two women stood on either side of the cabin door knives in hand.

The noise of shouting and clash of metal from above was getting louder. Suddenly, the cabin door burst open and, for a moment, Jacob thought that it was Jupiter, but it wasn't. This man was even bigger. In one hand the man held a scimitar the blade of which dripped with blood. In the other hand was the pirate captain's head.

Jacob threw the knife and it hit the intruder in the arm. Bad shot thought Jacob who normally could skewer an ant at thirty pedes. The man glanced at his arm, looked up at Jacob, dropped the captain's head and laughed. He pulled the knife out of his arm and threw it to the ground. He turned to Shoshana. The women each grabbed one of his arms and stabbed hard. For a moment the man was nonplussed, but not for long. Shaking the women off and about to use the scimitar, the huge man suddenly lurched, screamed in agony and crashed backwards, clutching Jacob's sica which was now embedded up to the hilt in his forehead. Jacob picked out his sica from the intruder's head. He paused for a moment and wondered why he hadn't used the spear.

Jupiter rushed in and saw the dead man. He looked at Jacob and then the women to make sure they were all well.

'Pirates fighting pirates,' Jupiter said breathlessly. 'The ship's been overrun. We are taken and must surrender. The man, the Syrian whom we saved, he has betrayed the ship… and us. His pirates found our ship probably through some signal. Did you see his aura?'

Jacob shook his head.

'Well, he managed to hide it then. Some can. He is Guild through and through and has admitted as much. I fear our venture may be doomed… We must go on deck now and they will want you… and they will want that,' he said pointing to the spear. 'I will protect you all to my last breath as will my brother. But there is something you need to know…'

At that moment, two of the invading pirates barged past Jupiter, making way for someone else. Jacob gasped in relief and smiled when he saw that the someone else was Marcellus.

29

Singapura, South East Asia Peninsula, 1492

'The Guild will attack you if possible through the ring. Always. Anywhere. I've told you this many times. If your belief in the ring is not as powerful as theirs, they will use whatever you have tried to raise from the ring to work against you. Or against those you wish to protect.'

Gabriella was bitterly sorry that she had put the ship and the crew in such terrible danger. 'How can they?'

'They can and will,' replied Maria. 'They've done it before many times… with the ring and with other… things.' She stopped and softened. 'Gabriella, they meddle in dark arts and I confess that we don't know everything about the ring. The Guild, given any chance, any opportunity at all, will attack you and their enemies. And here their enemies are your friends. I did warn you that the ring can work for you and it can work against you.'

'But I don't know that I can always do the right thing. I just don't.'

'I think you do.' Maria smiled. 'Isn't that what a princess of the Aro peoples would do? The right thing?'

With sensible winds, the Santa Barbara had gained good speed and was now lying offshore by Singapura, one degree north of the equator. According to Bartholomew, there were over fifty smaller islands nearby, but he thought it was this one that Gabriella and Maria wanted. The fact was confirmed when an Indian vessel hove to and its captain exchanged food for twelve boxes of used cutlasses. Onboard the Indian merchant ship was a Portuguese comprador who confirmed that the island facing them was indeed Singapura, although Bartholomew was advised in no uncertain terms that it would be a mistake for any stranger to land there. The comprador had heard tell of fearful stories about what went on. Bartholomew and the first mate kept this to themselves.

The Santa Barbara had arrived in what Bartholomew called The Straits - a narrow strip of sea between various islands including Sumatra and Melaka. Addressing his assembled crew, Bartholomew's excitement was contagious. He spoke about his vision of future traders using this new route. He also explained how sailing around the southern coast of Singapura to reach the South China Sea or the Ocean of Hindustan would benefit the great seafaring nations. Speaking in a mix of Portuguese, Italian and Spanish, he told his crew again what they already knew, that with the royal silver of Castile they would buy spices, silk and pure linen, medicinal potions, tea, perfumes, salt, dried-herbs, antiquities and local artefacts.

'You know,' he said, 'you all know, when sold, these will fetch a thousand times their original value. More than a thousand times. Your share in a percentage of the profits will keep you for years.' There was a cheer.

'And I will give each of you one gold castellano on behalf of my queen and her king, Ferdinand. And on behalf of me.'

After the quarterdeck resonated with cheer after cheer, Bartholomew went on, 'And the Cape, my friends. What of that?' Bartholomew went on to explain that the Cape, as they had all witnessed, was too dangerous for most vessels beneath a certain tonnage.

'But,' he said, 'with a good navigator,' and here he received another loud cheer, 'why then the Cape will be safe enough and, as I promised you all, I will chart it as Good Hope!' He received yet another cheer. He asked for sherry wine to be given out and toasts were made to their worthy navigator, their future wealth, Castile and Aragon, Cabo da Boa Esperança and each other.

Bartholomew had the ship go as close as he dared to Singapura's shore. He explained to Maria that the island was surrounded by shoals, sandbanks and rocks the tops of which could be seen just above the dark brown water, all perilous to the Santa Barbara. The edge of the wide Singapura river inlet looked like dragon's teeth, thought Gabriella.

Gabriella and Maria made their farewells to Bartholomew's mother who hugged Gabriella fiercely to her clothing which hurt the girl, although she knew that the hug was well meant. They then said farewell to the cook who wept openly, much to everyone's embarrassment. With a shaking and tear-dampened hand he presented Gabriella with a new, sharp stiletto knife sheathed in soft leather. He also gave her a small, carefully wrapped bundle of his little cakes.

Maria and Gabriella said their goodbyes to many of the crew each of whom nodded and shuffled their feet, not knowing what to say. Then the hands of officers were shaken and to the first mate they also said farewell and he, unknown to any, swallowed hard and, with considerable effort, stopped his own tears.

The Watchers onboard had a whispered farewell with Maria. They were going onwards with Bartholomew.

'You know that there'll be other Watchers to care for your safety on the island,' said Johannes, the cartographer, 'but be careful at all times.'

Lastly, they saw Bartholomew in his day cabin. He said very little but smiled a great deal and kissed Maria on both cheeks.

She asked, 'Dear Bartholomew, will your voyage be safe? Are you convinced that your queen and king are of truth and valour? Not Guild?'

The navigator smiled, 'I am certain that they are honest. They know of Watchers of course. However, I'm also sure that the Pope and the Borgias will try to persuade Castile and Aragon to harm my brother and me. The Pope will not succeed. Neither will the Borgias.'

Turning towards Gabriella, he stood awkwardly, fiddling with his jacket buttons. Gabriella rushed up to him and gave him an enormous hug and he, surprising even himself, hugged her back. Then, without saying anything further, he turned and walked out of the cabin complaining that he perhaps had something in his eye.

Gabriella and Maria were given two leather shoulder bags containing wrapped food and small water containers. They were helped down into a rowing boat on board of which were four armed men, two officers and four oarsmen.

Maria felt languid in the heat and found the breeze on the way to the shoreline welcome and cooling. If she was anxious, she didn't show it. Gabriella was relieved to get off the ship, but her stomach churned at the thought of what she was here to do. She told herself again that, if she succeeded in her task, then that would be part payment for what had happened to her family and her home. Part payment not, she thought grimly, full payment.

They disembarked near the deserted banks of the river as

the waterway began to narrow from the sea. After ensuring that Gabriella and Maria were safely on a solid tree-lined shore with their leather bags, the rowing boat crew and officers bade them an awkward farewell and made their way back to the Santa Barbara.

By the sheltered river-mouth there was some evidence of habitation and one roadway along which were a few wooden commercial buildings, some trading posts and three small houses. Maria assumed that there were not many people about because it was midday, humid and hot.

She was immediately and acutely aware that they were being observed and followed. She also had a feeling that whoever was doing the observing and following were not friends.

On the road leading inland, she could see now that in front of them there were three angry-looking men, each armed with wide, curved swords and sharp cooking knives. The three men made no secret of the fact that they were waiting for Gabriella and Maria. One of them withdrew his sword from the wide belt he was wearing. Maria stopped walking. Gabriella stopped too and, unafraid, hoisted her heavy leather bag onto her back and held her hands together.

To one side of Maria and Gabriella was a bullock pulling a cart and plodding its way slowly along the muddy riverbank. The animal kept stopping to enjoy an occasional piece of grass and the driver with his three passengers were seemingly dozing in the midday heat.

On the other side of the road was a Javanese trader leading his horse-drawn cart carrying four people. None of these people filled Maria with good cheer. Where, she wondered angrily, were the Wushu fighters she'd been promised? Why were there no Watchers?

The bullock cart did not stop, but the Javanese trader and his horse-drawn cart did, its occupants now on the ground, alert, armed, facing Maria and Gabriella and ready to fight.

The river had on it several Tong'kang boats with their painted eyes making the vessels look like ferocious animals ready to pounce. One of these boats nearest the river's left bank slowed down and five heavily armed men stepped out and approached Maria and Gabriella from behind. The women were now surrounded. The bullock cart trundled on, the occupants unconcerned and still dozing.

Gabriella calmly looked at the circle of cut-throats closing in. She shut her eyes and rubbed the Ring of Solomon. One man, clearly the leader, shouted some phrases which were obviously commands. Maria could see that all the men had orange auras. Each man was grinning, relishing the prospect of an easy conquest. The leader reached Maria and stared into her eyes. He was breathing heavily and she could smell his sweat and an abundance of yesterday's garlic. Without warning, he shouted something and grabbed the top of her blouse. Laughing, he ripped it down.

His laughter was cut very short as if his lungs had been emptied. He clutched his chest and staggered back, a look of shock on his face. At the same time there was a rush of piercing, ice-cold wind that seemed to come from the water. The very air was being sucked away and everyone began to gasp, including Maria.

A shape formed. Gabriella, breathing easily, opened her eyes to see a phantom, light blue in colour but also iridescent. It swooped towards the girl and came close as if searching for something. The girl nodded gently and the phantom whirled noiselessly around the whole group of terrified men. Maria held one of Gabriella's arms to steady herself and found that immediately she could breathe normally again. Not so the men.

Suddenly the phantom flew close to the brigand leader who was lifted as if weighing nothing more than a bag of feathers. Higher and higher he was taken and then dropped to the ground where he fell in an unnatural-looking heap. Most of the thugs started yelling as much as their breathlessness would allow. Each turned to run, but the phantom soundlessly followed and surrounded them in the blue gossamer. They were lifted together, fighting for air, gabbling and pleading, higher and higher - a pause for a beat and then they too were simply dropped to the ground.

The phantom, whose shape was still growing, turned to the men who'd stepped from their boat onto the riverbank not five minutes ago. In absolute panic, they tried to turn back, but found themselves staring down at the apparition which was now spreading itself wide over the mudbanks at the water's edge.

Gradually each of these men sank into the soft, oozing and stinking mud which became still softer as it began to swallow them. Slowly they were sucked down. Gabriella watched dispassionately as the men began to slip below the surface of the gulping mud and, much as they tried, there was nothing for the men to grip or grasp. She suddenly felt that she could not allow more death. She'd seen enough and she had caused enough even though her own life had been threatened, as it was being threatened now. But it wasn't the answer.

Gabriella ran to the phantom and pleaded for the killing to stop. The phantom began to lift itself and the sinking men out from the mud so that they could scramble to safety. The men were dazed but safe. All of them ran away.

The phantom, now in the clear shape of a woman of middle years stood or, rather, hovered before Gabriella and bowed low to the girl. Gabriella instinctively bowed back and then, looking up, noticed tears in the phantom's eyes. Gabriella glanced at Maria and, turning back, the apparition had disappeared. The Ring of Solomon changed colour from blue back to its normal dull grey.

The men from the bullock cart, now a fair distance ahead, hopped down and ran back, smiling at Maria and Gabriella. Maria, sorting out her clothing, saw that each had a green aura and quickly established that the language the men spoke was Mandarin.

'Friends, we are very pleased to see you,' she said fluently in Mandarin and then proceeded to give vent to her anger at not having been better protected. The Watchers' explanation was that, once they had seen the apparition, they thought it best not to interfere. There was another collection of smiles and a few shrugs. The men all looked at Gabriella with great respect, awe almost, as if knowing full well that the girl was more than capable of defending herself and others. What they had witnessed was something that they had never seen before, even from the hands of the old alchemists in Xi'an where they had once lived.

Watching the scene from a safe distance and hidden by an ancient Angsana tree, was a tall, well-dressed man called Demang Lebar Daun. He sniggered to himself as he watched what had gone on and then turning sharply on his heel, walked away.

30

Coast of Alexandria, Imperial Province, Roman Empire, 79 CE

'I bid you good morning,' Marcellus lied as he slowly surveyed the cabin. 'Well, well, well' he said, grinning and enjoying every syllable. 'Here we are once again.'

He was no longer dressed as a senior officer in the emperor's navy, but was now in a bloodied, white, linen shirt, a soft leather jacket and very loose, black balloon trousers with dark blue, low ankle boots. He had two large knives at his hip stuck into a wide belt.

He bowed towards Jacob. 'Master Ya'akov, greetings. What a pleasure. For me that is. Not so much for you and your friends here. Yes, yes, I know what you're thinking. I'm a traitor. Yes, I know. I've let myself down and the Roman navy too and, of course, the great Umero. Dear, wonderful but stupid Umero. Worry not; he's safe... for now.'

He looked hard at an astonished Jacob. 'I have you now boy... and you are worth to me the largest imaginable crate of pure silver. I have what nobody else could get. But, dear me, where are my manners?' He paused and grinned again at everyone. 'Let me show you the scene of what has been a most enjoyable battle.'

When the five reached the deck, the sight that met them was horrific. There was blood and gore everywhere and it was hard to walk without slipping. Bodies had been hacked and some, still alive, had been crucified and crudely affixed to masts. The newly arrived pirate ship, now tied alongside, was low in the water, evil-looking and filthy.

'Ah, my friends,' called out the Syrian, who looked gaunt, grey and tired. The man's missing fingers were unbandaged, dirty and green in colour.

'Welcome,' he said with difficulty, coughing for a full few minutes. 'I do apologise that my associates have made a mess of this ship, but shortly it will burn with all who remain on board, so no matter.' That seemed to exhaust the man and he sat down heavily on a wooden chest. Jacob could see that food, water, weapons and bedding were being removed from one ship to another.

Jupiter made a move forwards, but three crossbows, a few swords and several knives were close, so he stopped, breathed heavily, bared his teeth and restrained himself. Marcellus pointed at Jacob. 'I am duty-bound to hand over this boy to Emperor Titus,' he said somewhat pompously. 'The Guild will receive the boy from the emperor. My duty will be done and I shall be rich and…'

'You were duty-bound to save this boy's life and help him, you scum,' shouted Shoshana. 'You traitor.'

Marcellus nodded and did a pretend curtsey. He continued unabashed. 'I decided some time ago that there was easier money to be made than to sail the seas and risk death day after day. The Guild, may the breath of Mars save all who serve, will pay me handsomely for the boy. As for the rest, you two,' here he pointed to Neptune and Jupiter, 'you may join my people and enjoy the spoils that piracy will bring. Or you may die. I really don't care. As for you women, you may join us too, but I suspect that you will enjoy that experience not at all.' At this, many of the Syrian's pirates guffawed and made lewd gestures.

Jupiter snarled at Marcellus, 'Gloat now, but you may find that your plans come to nothing.' He spat. 'What happened to Umero and his crew?'

'Oh, they live. When we made land, I absconded and joined my friend here,' he said indicating the Syrian who was staring at the two women and licking his now dry and flaking lips.

'My old comrades,' said Marcellus, 'will not consider me anything but a loyal Roman who has maybe met with an accident and death. They will have searched far and wide, such was their love for me and they will have asked questions. People whom I bribed handsomely will say that they saw me attacked onshore by an animal at night and that I am presumably no more than a few chewed bones. Umero will be sad, for he loved me as a brother and, for what it's worth, I respected him. We owed each other our lives.'

Jupiter sneered. 'And you have no shame now? You decided that the opportunity to betray his affection for you was too great?'

'You have it on one, my friend. Well done,' said Marcellus smiling happily and bowing.

Neptune stepped forward. 'The Guild followers whom you've killed in your time, what of them? The Guild accepts what you've done?'

'Of course! Sacrifice, big man, sacrifice. For the greater good. Much as we cut three fingers from that Syrian's hands. To fool you... and it's so easy to fool fools.'

'Take me, take my brother,' said Neptune, 'but let the boy go and the women. Put them in a small boat with a sail and some food, but let them go.'

'Oh, such heart-warming and pathetic sentiment,' smiled Marcellus and then shouted, his face very close to Neptune's, 'You don't seriously believe that I've done what I've done to fail? You think this is a game? You really think this is a game? People are expendable. The greater good is what matters.'

The ill-looking Syrian, feeling brave behind Marcellus, decided to join in. 'You think we are imbeciles? We know who this boy is and we know what he is worth. Why do you think I tricked you?' He mimicked a child. 'Poor Syrian man, half-dead in a small boat. Rescue him because our hearts are warm.' His breathing was laboured and they could smell the gangrened stumps where his missing fingers had been. 'You could have killed me,' he said, 'but these dead or dying pirates, like all of their ilk, are greedy.' He waved in the direction of the dead and the dying. 'The new crew here are deserters from the Roman navy and none are stupid. None will fall for any tricks, so beware. There will be no warnings and no mercy.' He folded his arms in a self-satisfied way.

'Enough, Syrian,' said Marcellus. 'This chatter of yours wastes time. The Guild will receive the boy from Emperor Titus and what is needed for immortality will be extracted. The deliverer of the Silver Green is me. Immortality is... ours.'

'I shall of course take the spear. Give it to me, boy,' said the Syrian.

Jacob, curious at the state of the Syrian's poor health, did nothing. 'I shall not,' he said.

'As the boy says, he shall not,' said Marcellus. 'The spear is Roman and stays with me.'

Several of the new crew surrounded Jacob and, with little

difficulty, one of them took the ordinary-looking, broken spear from him and handed it to Marcellus. The blade glittered. Marcellus weighed the spear in his hands and made stabbing movements with it.

'That is mine, Marcellus,' wheezed the Syrian. 'It's what we agreed.'

'Well, Syrian. Then you shall have it,' said Marcellus, turning slowly and then driving the broken spear into the Syrian's chest. The Syrian staggered backwards, his head turning upwards towards the sky as if in some silent prayer and collapsed heavily against the ship's rail. Nobody moved or spoke; the only sounds were those from wounded men as well as the sea slapping evenly against the hulls of the two ships.

Indicating that the Syrian's body should be thrown overboard, Marcellus wiped the spear's tip on his shirt. As he lowered the spear, the blade caught on his belt, slipped and sliced into his right hand. Ignoring the deep wound, he turned towards Jacob and demanded, 'How does the spear work, boy? How does it become powerful as they say it should?'

Jacob, who had been staring at the Syrian's body being thrown with no grace over the side, turned towards Marcellus, but didn't answer. One of the men grabbed the woman with one ear and put a knife to her remaining ear.

'Tell me how this spear works, boy,' said Marcellus testily as he sucked on his hand, the wound bleeding freely.

Jacob considered his options and realised that they were few. 'I truly don't know,' he said honestly, 'and it has never worked for me yet, but I was told that you must believe in an outcome and, if you do, why then the spear will help you to achieve that outcome. But I fear this it will only work when whoever holds it is in mortal danger. You Marcellus are not... not yet.'

The Roman glared at Jacob. 'Brave words, urchin. Soon you will be dissected and then dead. I am glad, for you are an irritant. I am promised the immortality they say you have.'

Some of the Roman deserters looked hard at Marcellus. Quickly he added, licking his lips and then the wound on his cut hand, 'We will all be immortal and shall smile when you become worm food.'

The groans and shouts of pain coming from the various wounded and dying men strewn over the ship or attached to posts and masts were diminishing. Some of the crew were already pushing the dead over the side.

'And the wounded too. Throw them all into the sea,' yelled Marcellus. Turning back to the group of five and addressing Shoshana, he shouted, 'Persuade the boy to tell me how the spear does whatever magic it does. You all have two days to tell me and then one by one you will die. Except the boy. He shall be hurt, but not killed until my masters have done what they need to do with him.'

Jacob spoke up for Shoshana, 'I told you Marcellus. I truly don't know how it works or even if it works...'

Marcellus was losing his temper. 'Hold your filthy mouth, boy. I wasn't speaking to you. But know this. I also seek Guild fire and therefore we will continue onwards to Judea. You shall help us in our task.' He paused for effect and, looking around, smiled in satisfaction.

'The Guild? You will deceive your... friends?'

'Certainly. Power comes to the one who holds power.'

'What nonsense is that?'

'I will trade you and be rewarded. I shall be one of the first to be granted immortality once you are…' He grinned. 'I have the spear. And I shall find Guild fire and use it for my own purposes. Power. Mine.'

He looked at each person daring anyone to smile or disagree.

Not one of the five or the surrounding crew members moved or spoke.

'I ask again, boy. How does the spear work?' Marcellus stared at Jacob, venom on his face. Moving close to Jacob, he screamed, 'Tell me how!'

Jacob didn't flinch. 'I've told you Marcellus and it is the truth as any god may care to bear witness, I truly do not know.'

Marcellus nodded and smiled. 'Very well. Remember this then. Our Emperor Titus, when he was a great general in Judea, commanded an army of four legions - sixty thousand soldiers including some of my men - all under instruction to deliver the final blow to a broken city that was Jerusalem. The Guild gave that instruction! Within the walls, half a million starving and scum Jews survived. Some were fanatical religious zealots, some were freebooting bandits, as were you boy. Scum like you flittered around the place like rats. Most were executed. Vermin need to be annihilated. Vermin like your friends here.'

He grabbed the woman with one ear by her good ear and pulled it hard and then let her go so that she fell and cut her cheek. She did not shout out.

'You will die for that,' said Jacob quietly.

Marcellus laughed as did some of his men.

'Oh really? Me? Die? How will that be? I have you, I have your spear and I have your sica and I have your pathetic friends.

I will sell you boy. And I shall be rich… and immortal.' He licked his hand which still bled profusely. 'Think of that! I shall live forever. And I shall have Guild fire.'

He kicked the one-eared woman hard. 'Maybe some work on this bitch will make you tell me what I need to know? You.' He pointed to Neptune and then Jupiter. 'You both - gutless goats the pair of you - will go below and my men will bind you until we decide - or you decide - on your fates. You are strong and we can use strength like yours. But I really don't care. Join us or not.' He shrugged and Jacob could see that Marcellus' cut hand was still bleeding badly.

'You, woman,' Marcellus said to Shoshana, while sucking on his hand again, 'be part of my voyage or accompany the boy. I care not one way or another. One way will end in death and the other way may end in death too and will certainly be… a little arduous.' He smirked and some of his men sniggered again.

'I will go with the boy,' said Shoshana putting an arm around Jacob's shoulder which he immediately shrugged off. Marcellus said something to two of his men who dragged away the one-eared woman. Jacob moved towards her.

'I need you to live, you bastard boy,' Marcellus said to Jacob, but I will harm you and cause you considerable pain, unless you do as I wish. Two days.'

'I see,' said Jacob through his teeth, 'and will the emperor and your… friends be so pleased with you for bringing in damaged goods? I should be very careful what you do, Marcellus.' He spat at the Roman and a glob of spit and mucus rested on Marcellus' forehead.

Wiping his face with a sleeve, Marcellus spoke with steely calm. 'Very well. You will not do that again and my temper is short,' he said. His hand was still bleeding freely. He shouted for a cloth to bind the wound and marched away.

On Marcellus' command, Umero's pirate ship was set alight and pushed away with poles. Rowers and pirates such as there were left on the burning ship all shouted and yelled for help. Most jumped into the sea, some there to drown; others hung on to pieces of wood while a few stayed with the doomed vessel. Marcellus barked out an order and Jupiter, Neptune, Shoshana and Jacob were taken down to the ship's bilges to be locked in a small room full of old rope and rotten matting.

The filthy vessel, now under full sail, turned slowly away from the burning pyre that was Umero's pirate ship and began the long voyage back to Judea.

After two days had passed, there was no news of the woman with one ear and Jacob and the others feared the worst. Occasionally, Marcellus would visit to ask Jacob if he was ready to tell him how the spear worked and each time Jacob explained that he truly did not know. He had thought of making something up, but Marcellus was anything but stupid. They all noticed that Marcellus' cut hand was bound, but they could also see that a great deal of blood was still seeping through the cloth binding the wound.

It was stifling in the small bilge room, with little air and even less water. From time to time, one of the Roman pirates would open the door and look in. Occasionally one or two would deliberately spill the meagre food that was delivered or urinate on the floor, or on the food.

Nobody in the bilge room talked much and the mood of the group was morose and bleak. At nightfall on the third day, the woman with one ear was pushed into the room. Bruised and pale, with cuts on her forearms and neck, she said nothing of her ordeal. Jacob said nothing either for there was nothing to say. He smiled at the woman who smiled weakly back.

Very early on the fourth day, an irritable Marcellus came into the room and made it clear to Jacob that, unless he explained how the spear could be used this very day, then deaths would be meted out. His patience, he said, was running out and he declared his magnanimity in already allowing more time than he'd originally promised. The group noticed that there was a raw rash on one of Marcellus' arms and blotches on the man's neck which he kept scratching. His hair was matted, his gums were raw and the whites of his eyes were yellow.

Shoshana demanded that the group be allowed to go on deck in order to breathe some sea air after days of being stuck in the malodorous, hot bilge room. This was reluctantly allowed under close guard. Once on deck, Neptune went aft and stared at the ship's wake. The others strolled about not talking and were mostly ignored by the men working the ship. Some ogled and tried to touch Shoshana and the woman with one ear.

Jupiter stood next to his brother, looking skywards with his arms held above his head. Some of the men laughed at this, but others nervously looked upwards to see what was there, apart from sky, that the big man was looking at. Jacob had no clue what was going on and wondered not for the first time if Jupiter and Neptune were sane.

Neptune suddenly turned to look at Jupiter and quickly shouted over his shoulder that the women and Jacob should retreat immediately back below decks. However, just as they were about to leave the top deck, Jacob could hear Neptune call out as if to someone far, far away, his great voice cracking with the effort.

Jacob and some of the crew looked out to sea and again at the sky, but none could make out anything unusual. As the prisoners and their guard made their way to go below, they heard something, halted and turned. They couldn't at first identify the noise. When they could, the thunder became louder and louder as it neared the ship. There was wind, almost immediately powerful and cold. Huge waves, coming as if from nowhere, crashed against the ship which seemed to shrink even lower in the water. Sails ripped and wood splintered.

Marcellus' men looked fearfully at the sky which, moments before, had been light blue and was now dark grey, with low, sweeping clouds almost black at their edges. The sea's rolling waves, as large as hills, had changed colour too, from its white flecked green to pure black. The ship swayed, rose and fell. Marcellus, still holding the spear, shouted commands, most of which nobody could hear and those that were heard were ignored as rowers and crew tried to hang on to something.

Freezing wind kicked all those on deck in the face. Water smashed the whole length of the vessel, compressing men against anything upright and overwhelming some pirates, several of whom were swept overboard. Marcellus was wild-eyed and stared at Neptune who smiled towards the mountainous seas.

'What have you done?' Marcellus shouted at Neptune. 'What in Caesar's teeth have you and your brother done?' Neptune said nothing. The ship was at the point of keeling over on its starboard side, its ruined sails almost touching the sea. Barrels, ropes and crates slipped on carpets of water and slid over the sides along with more men. Fingers tried to grip any support, mostly with no hope of success. Jacob and the two women were jammed into a doorway and it was this that probably saved them from being swept away.

The ship, with some supreme effort, righted itself and Marcellus shouted at nobody, 'We will outrun this! We will survive this.' His face was red raw from the rash and open sores that now covered his skin.

Jacob tied one end of a double width of rope onto a large cleat and the other end to the women's waists. The ship was beginning to turn steeply one way and then another, at one point losing a spar and then a sail. Hearing shouts from Marcellus, Jacob made his way carefully, holding on to anything.

'Boy, you have powers. Stop this, I command you.'

'Marcellus you are dying.' Jacob had to raise his voice to be heard over the noise of the storm. Marcellus was holding the spear but was visibly weakening. 'The spear cut your hand and infected it with the Syrian's blood which was already poisoned. He was dying. Our pirate captain had instructed that the Syrian be given amounts of hemlock, lead, arsenic and phosphorus in his wine. The pig drank copious amounts and tasted nothing. You were tainted with that blood. The poison is quick. Your hand would not and will not heal. You will die. Do you feel death creeping up on you? The spear if you please,' shouted Jacob, holding one hand out.

Marcellus turned and stared wildly at the boy. 'Use it to save us then!'

'I cannot save you and would not.'

The former Roman naval hero screamed, 'You could save me!'

'I doubt it. And if I could Marcellus, why would I wish to?'

'Save me. Please! I promise with all that I hold dear that I will never harm you or your friends.'

Jacob grabbed a large, broken piece of wooden spar. 'Hold this and take your chance in the sea. If you perish, then justice is done. If you somehow survive, then Mars or one of his friends will be looking out for you. If you decide to stay, I will not use the spear on you, but you will die. Horribly and painfully.'

Weakly, Marcellus raised the spear as if to strike Jacob who just held his hand out.

Handing the spear to Jacob, Marcellus shouted as best he could, but barely loud enough to be heard above the storm. 'Now save us I beg you. Think of…'

'And my sica. Throw it down.' Marcellus threw the knife half-heartedly at the boy but, in the wind and with no force, the knife just fell to the deck.

'I told you the choice,' Jacob said. 'To the edge, Marcellus. Your time has come to decide.'

Marcellus stared at Jacob with wild, pain-filled eyes. 'Save me, boy,' he groaned. 'You promised…'

Jacob looked at the man and wondered why such a trusted Roman who had been loved by Rome and befriended by Umero should be turned by… by what? Power? Greed? The promise of immortality? Guild fire? Fear perhaps? All those things, he thought.

'I promised nothing,' Jacob shouted above the howling wind. 'I have no power Marcellus and you deserve no promises. What choice have you given others? What choice did you give Umero? What choice would you have given me? I've given you a choice.' Marcellus made to grab Jacob, but the boy just stepped back. Next to him were Jupiter and Neptune.

'Jump Marcellus or stay,' yelled Jacob. 'What was it you said days ago about my friends? You said that you didn't care either way if they stayed or not. I truly don't care what you decide, but decide something.'

Jacob looked up at the sky. 'The storm is calming and we must be on our way,' he said looking back at Marcellus. But Marcellus and the broken spar were no longer there.

As fast as it had started, the sea and the winds calmed. The ship had taken in a great deal of water and the remaining rowers cowered below decks waiting for death.

Jacob turned. Some of the crew, holding onto masts or each other, had been watching what had happened, but were in no fit state to remonstrate. Jacob picked up his sica.

Of the ninety crew there were about sixty left alive and able to work. Jupiter and Neptune immediately took control of the vessel since they knew navigation. Those close to Marcellus were put in chains and kept in the bilges or, if they caused any trouble, were thrown over the side. Various wounds were tended and a great tureen of hot barley broth was made for all.

Jupiter made it plain to everyone onboard that the ship was bound for the Ashkelon coast with no delay. He also let it be known that anyone could be part of that voyage or they could take their chances in the sea. A few chose the sea and were immediately set adrift in coracles with some supplies and what little water that could be spared. The remaining crew were evenly distributed about the ship so that each person had a role. Everyone was searched as was the whole ship and all weapons were collected and locked away. Jacob, with his spear and bag always on his shoulder, worked as hard as anyone to help the damaged ship limp onwards through the now calm seas.

The boy was exhausted and wondered what would happen next in this adventure that he had not wanted in the first place and did not want now. Wearily, sitting on a barrel staring out to sea, he reflected that he clearly still wasn't in charge of his own destiny and maybe, he thought, the time had come to take charge. Too many things kept happening to him and he decided that from now on any direction must be his choice. His life was his own, he thought, not someone else's to play with as they wished.

For no reason, he remembered some moments of his childhood - looking at the stars at the age of four, playing knucklebones and dice with his sister, staring in horror at prisoners being paraded along streets, laughing with his father at some silliness. He tried to remember names of people, other children he had known. There was Shimshon and, yes, there was Ovram too who had taught him about the stars. He smiled as some vague memories came back. There was someone else. Who was that someone else? With a sharp jolt and a feeling of ice in his stomach that hurt with a pain that he'd not ever experienced, he no longer needed to ask Shoshana the question that had been worrying him for some time. He now knew precisely who Shoshana was.

31

Singapura, South East Asia Peninsula, 1492

After a long walk and as Maria was beset by mosquitoes while Gabriella was not, the two were taken by the group of Watchers to a large, shabby-looking house, set back from the road. There they were to spend the rest of the day and some of the night.

The girl and Maria washed and sat down to eat a bowl of rice and spicy vegetables.

'You will be safe here I promise,' said a Watcher to Maria speaking in Portuguese. She could see no aura on the man.

'I have learned to hide it. My aura… I have learned that,' the man said looking Maria in the eye.

'They were waiting for us and you did nothing. The Guild… how did Guild vermin know we were here?'

'You know how it is. They always know…'

'No. They do not always know. And I don't know how it is!'

'Spies, signals, eyes everywhere and people talk,' said the man sipping some coconut milk. 'The Guild will have been on board your ship,' he said, unconcerned. 'One, two, possibly more. Just as there were Watchers.'

Maria nodded, looking carefully at the man who began fiddling with the bowl of milk. 'There will have been times when it would have been easy to pass a message… somehow,' he said.

Maria just nodded.

'Anyway,' the man said, 'it's good that they know we are ready. This will make them nervous and it will expose weaknesses.'

Maria was surprised. 'Are there any weaknesses? What are they?'

Ignoring both questions, the man excused himself and left the room.

The Watcher leader passed him as he left.

'You should have helped us,' Maria said. 'Watchers do not let their friends and other Watchers struggle. You knew...'

'No, we did not know. Many Watchers in this part of the world have learned to hide their auras. Guild people too. I've tried but...' he shrugged. 'You and the girl must sleep now...'

'That man who just left...'

'Don't worry about him. We know.'

'Is our plan still good? We have come a very long way...'

'Yes, it is.'

The man looked at Gabriella and then back at Maria. 'You have my word as a Watcher and one who hates Guild villainy as much as you do, that we will make sure you two are kept safe - as far as we ever can. That is our pledge. My duty.'

Maria sighed. She had heard such pledges before. The man smiled and said, 'But, now we must sleep a little, for shortly we must leave.'

Gabriella did not fall asleep easily. She felt as if she was still on board the ship and, although it wasn't, the bedroom seemed as if it was rocking gently. In the same room, an armed Watcher, his aura clearly green, sat and another would be on duty all night outside. Gabriella suspected that there would be still more elsewhere. They would not risk anything going wrong now. She worried, however, as Maria had worried, that their arrival on the island was not as it should have been. Something or someone wasn't quite right.

She listened to the noises of a strange land. Everything that had happened had been strange. Was it to end here? She was only a girl and she'd suddenly been thrust into a role which was extraordinary and unfair. No, she wasn't just a girl she thought. She was a princess. That was her role too and she must always remember that princesses behaved bravely and with fortitude.

Gabriella wished that her brothers and friends were with her now. And her mother and dear father. Without realising it, she was touching the Ring of Solomon... The images of her family's faces were suddenly clear in her head - all of them were there including grandparents, uncles, aunts, friends - all smiling at her, saying things that she couldn't quite hear but desperately wanted to hear. Were any still alive she wondered and, if so, where were they? She had talked about this with Maria and of course Maria had no answers. Maria was kind and caring - Gabriella knew that and she thought of her as a mother figure, big sister and great friend all in one. But Maria wasn't her mother or her sister. She was, however, her friend and for that Gabriella was grateful.

She'd been asleep for what seemed only like minutes, when a terrible scream woke her up and made her sit bolt upright. It was still dark.

'Up, now. We must go. It is time,' said Maria urgently.

'What happened? The scream?'

'We must go, Gabriella. Now!'

'The scream? What was it?'

'A traitor's death. Get ready. Now.'

Gabriella dressed quickly making sure that she had the long, thin and razor-sharp knife that the ship's cook had given her. Outside, the moon was hidden behind clouds and there were few lamps, but she could see on the veranda at the front of the building a group of six men and four women, a mix of Malay and Chinese Watchers wearing sarongs or tunics. All of them nodded at Maria and the girl in greeting, but nobody spoke or smiled. Gabriella noticed that some auras were visible, but some were most definitely not.

Everyone was given a few rice cakes and a small flask of hot rice wine. Gabriella munched the rice cakes but didn't touch the wine. The group leader gave the signal to move.

Quickly and silently the group led off, Maria and Gabriella in the middle of the single file. As they left the compound, Gabriella clearly saw something that glistened on the pathway. The clouds shifted allowing a spill of light and Gabriella could see that what was glistening was blood. She stopped for a moment, but someone behind her gently pushed her onwards.

From time to time, Gabriella touched her ring. It was almost second nature now. Just checking that it was there. She felt, or imagined that she felt, an invisible something walking next to her. A demon? If it was a demon, was it, she wondered fearfully, a good one or bad? Was it a Guild trick? Or was it just her vivid imagination? There was obviously nothing there. Nerves perhaps? That could be it, she thought. Her stomach felt tense and she shivered. Maybe it was a result of being onboard a ship for such a long time. Yes, probably. Of course. People had said to her that the motion of the sea took a long time to get over once you reached land. She hoped that whatever this thing was, real or imagined, it was not just at her side, but on it.

Eventually, the group came to a vast swamp. The strong smell of sulphur and rotting vegetation hit the back of Gabriella's nose and throat. The line leader halted the group and talked quietly to Maria. Nobody else spoke. Maria came back to Gabriella and whispered, 'We will cross the swamp. It's treacherous but he,' pointing to the leader, 'knows this area well. However, there is only one narrow path of stones. We must cross by that path. There is no other way.'

Gabriella said nothing. The leader, with gestures rather than speech, beckoned the group to hold on to the person in front as they crossed the swamp single file.

The going at first was slow, but straightforward. After a while though, due to the moon's limited light, one or two of the group missed a step and on occasion someone's foot would suddenly disappear into black slime and reeds. There was no shouting, but the smell as the foot was retracted from the swamp was disgusting and Gabriella wondered what else, apart from vegetation, was rotting down there.

After a few hours of focussed concentration, Gabriella began to tire. She felt exhausted and everything around appeared unreal. The very narrow stone path weaved in curves and bends, never actually following a straight line. Huge lilies and vines sometimes obscured corners and that would slow down the procession to a standstill until those at the front found their bearings. No speaking was allowed and that of course made the journey even more difficult.

The arching roots of the red mangrove trees were obstacles

on which some of the group would sometimes trip and were only saved by the alert person behind. Sometimes one of the group would tread on a barnacle or oyster shell that was on the path and the crunching sound would be strangely loud. Occasionally and worryingly, Gabriella was certain that she could hear light sounds which seemed like oars dipping gently in and out of the water. She could also hear something else - a splash, a snort or a grunt. She couldn't tell what caused the noises but, once or twice, she did see pairs of yellow, unblinking eyes.

Suddenly, the man in front of Gabriella stopped dead so that she bumped hard into his back. The man turned quickly and grabbed the girl's arms. The grip was strong and, while Gabriella's instinct was to keep her balance, at the same time she tried to pull free. However, the person behind Gabriella grabbed hold of the girl's shoulders. Between the person in front and the one behind, Gabriella was certain that she was about to fall. Panic mingled with sheer terror rose in her chest and, as she fell sideways into the swamp, she felt utter despair and absolute fear of what was to come.

The noise that her body made as she fell into the cold slime and sludge was slight but, even so, she could immediately hear several things thrashing their way towards her. Was that an animal or - surely not - was it the sound of oars? Mud, along with roots and rough tendrils, seemed to be pulling her down. This is the end, she thought. Despite the heat of the night, the cold water mixed with fear began to numb her nerve endings. To die here? In a deep swamp, very far from Africa? She struggled to stay above the surface and she knew, she just knew, that she could not stay afloat for long and that her splashes and struggling would attract the attention of many things with teeth.

Suddenly she was jerked upwards with force. Something or someone was pulling her. As she broke the surface, she took a huge intake of breath, a gasp of air. She was hauled upwards so that she was standing, safe again on the stone pathway. There were two closely spaced splashes of two heavy objects falling into the water. Gabriella didn't see what had made them.

Someone helped her to stand steadily as she breathed more easily.

'Thank you, thank you,' she managed to whisper through shivering lips. She wasn't thanking anyone in particular, so she assumed that the leader or Maria had helped her out, but nobody said anything.

Gabriella whispered angrily in Italian, her teeth chattering. 'Who pushed me?' There was no comment. 'There were two of them. Who was it? Where are they?' She looked around with fists clenched. The group was still.

'They are gone,' said Maria.

'Gone?'

'Yes, gone. Gone.'

'Who pulled me out then?' Gabriella whispered.

'Nobody,' said Maria, pale in the moonlight.

'Nobody?'

'Nobody.'

'I also heard oars.'

'Oars?'

'Oars.'

'Guild oars maybe. Enough now.'

Gabriella stared at Maria then looked round at the group, still in line. The group's leader indicated that they should hurry and continue. There was no effort to console or help Gabriella who took her place back again in the line, still shivering. She took the wet kerchief from her neck and tried to wipe her face and hands as best she could. After only a few paces, she was shocked to see two bodies face down in the swamp, each gradually sinking into the mud surrounded by large bubbles. One body was being jerked and pulled down by some creature.

Still confused, cold and relieved in equal measure by what had just happened, she wondered why Guild plans would involve killing her without trying to capture her? She was wanted for the immortality elixir, wasn't she? Not much good as a decomposing body in a swamp. Was it desperation perhaps? Because she was so close? Were Guild people actually afraid? Maybe what she'd heard really had been oars, maybe Guild oars as Maria had said. To take her alive and then… But who had rescued her? Why would nobody admit who had pulled her up, so that she could thank whoever had saved her life? And who had killed the two people who had pushed her into the swamp?

Gabriella had a sudden urge to flee, to turn round and run back along the thin path. She wanted peace and quiet, she wanted to be away from violence and evil. She wanted to be safe, to be warm and free. But, she thought, she'd come this far and… and what? And nothing she thought miserably, as she walked on in her wet clothes.

As the line of people eventually reached the swamp's edge, Gabriella could see by the light of the half-hidden almost lemon-coloured moon, what looked like a deep and wide river, that had a gently swaying rope bridge across it. The group's leader indicated that everyone should stop and rest for a short while. At the river's edge, Gabriella rinsed off as best she could the slime that was still stuck to her. She stepped back in alarm when she noticed several huge, dark creatures moving close to where she had her hand in the water.

Turning back to look at the way they'd come, Gabriella could see swamp grasses and weeds. The path of stepping stones wasn't clear now and she wondered what the return journey would be like. If the tide was high on their return, then the stones would be invisible. If the stones were invisible, then she would not be able to escape. Turning the other way, she could see an assortment of logs, boulders, tree stumps and skeletons - whether of people or animals she couldn't be certain. The smell of decay was making her feel sick.

'The results of their experiments,' Maria said simply as she joined Gabriella and nodded her head towards the mass of bones. 'They kill and deposit bodies here. As they develop the poison and the antidote, they try them out.'

Gabriella shuddered. 'On slaves?'

'Maybe,' said Maria quietly.

In the distance, on the other side of the river was a large, white building lit by moonlight, surrounded by trees, but no wall.

'That's it,' said Maria nodding at the temple.

'It has no wall around it. You can see the doors and windows.'

'It needs no walls. It is protected by other things.' In the occasional moonlight, the large, gloomy building appeared shut up, unused and dark.

'Over there,' said Maria pointing, 'is the maze through which we must go to reach the temple. They won't expect visitors through the maze at night. It's well-guarded.'

'By many armed guards? They are hidden?'

'No, not by guards. By animals. And they are hidden. Also, the hedges are full of poisonous plants. I'm told that any thorn on any of these bushes has poison enough to cause paralysis or death. If it's paralysis, then we… I may be eaten alive. You will not be affected.'

'I hope that's true. But I would not let anything harm you Maria.'

'You and I will go to the temple. These men will stay guard and help manage our escape.' She looked at Gabriella who stared back.

'We will escape I promise.'

'You can't promise. Could some of these Watchers come with us?'

'There can't be too many through the maze at any one time,' said Maria, 'and we need to watch out for other possible attacks by Guild people. What happened in the swamp… maybe there are more traitors.'

Gabriella stared at her.

The group's leader approached Maria. 'It is time,' he said softly, handing her a package in which he explained were the agreed explosive materials. Maria put the package into Gabriella's bag.

'In a few hours,' said the leader, 'it will be dawn and we must make our exit before the tide turns and water covers the path of stones.'

Maria looked the leader in the eye. 'You are all true? All Watchers?'

The man looked back at Maria. 'We are now. See the auras.'

Maria glanced at the tired face, looked around at the group and nodded.

'You'll wait for us?'

'Yes, of course and that is our duty.' The man bowed slightly. 'But we may not be alive to help you.' He looked behind him and, turning back to her, said, 'Remember, once the water brought by the tide covers the stone path, there is no way out.' He paused, looking at Gabriella. 'For anyone,' he said.

32

Ashkelon, Judea, Imperial Province, Roman Empire, 79 CE

The ship's depleted crew worked hard. A new sail was made from small pieces of old canvas to replace the one that the storm had ruined. Bitumen was used to repair holes in the hull, but the vessel still leaked and the going was slow.

A careful watch was kept over the crew and rowers to see that nobody tried to retake the vessel. Jupiter made sure that food and water were distributed fairly. Sometimes flagons of rich, red wine were shared out, but drunkenness was not tolerated and neither was even a minor infringement of discipline.

Jupiter also regularly made sure that all weapons were still securely stowed away and he carried out random checks on the crew.

Shoshana set up a clever apparatus which collected rain and condensation to provide drinking water. She also built a system that filtered sea water through many layers of muslin which took away the salt and mineral taste. This water was used for washing which Neptune insisted that everyone did once every other day.

As the ship neared the coastline, small groups of the crew discussed with Neptune and Jupiter what they would do when they found landfall at Ashkelon. According to Jupiter, the town was regarded as a safe bet because there were fewer Roman outposts there. The local garrison, he said, was small and ill-equipped. It was decided that the landing would be at night and that the ship would be scuttled once everyone was off and away.

Jupiter commanded that they should all go ashore a little further up the coast at a safe cove that the two brothers knew to be there. Once the ship had been sunk, he told everyone, the crew would go their own ways taking with them what they wanted. He emphasised that everyone would be on their own from then on. The brothers had already agreed with Shoshana and the woman with one ear that it would be best to get some distance away from the crew as fast as possible.

As it turned out, Ashkelon was hosting a feast and they could hear the noise from a long way out. Probably, said Jupiter, the celebrations were for fresh troops and some newly arrived senior army people. Maybe, he muttered, a legion or two. If that were so, thought Jacob, then with an influx of between five and ten thousand troops, the Romans might be building up for something big.

Neptune decided that to go closer to any part of the coast might be a risk and so the ship was anchored a distance out at sea. Everyone would have to make their own way to the shore by swimming or using something wooden or lightweight as a float.

Many of the crew were not particularly happy with this arrangement not least because most couldn't swim, but Jupiter would have it no other way. So, the ship's lanterns were extinguished while the vessel's sails were struck and the two masts were unstepped and stowed. The anchor cable and mooring lines were tied to heavy lead which slowed the vessel. People who could not swim arranged to work in small groups to tie together empty barrels, mast spars and wooden crates. Some packed hessian or leather bags with food and even stoppered small amphorae of wine. Neptune warned that anything heavy would create difficulties as they made their way to shore. Few took any notice.

Nobody was much looking forward to braving the water. The sea where the ship had anchored wasn't rough, but it was deep, the currents were treacherous and it would take some time to swim the distance. Some were worried at what might be in the water and that worry was made worse by the fact that the night made it impossible to see what could be lurking beneath the surface. Jupiter had secured a tiny coracle for the women and Jacob which they filled with some sacking, blankets, a little food, a few gourds of the remaining fresh water, some silver and a couple of swords. Then the ship was sunk.

Almost as soon as everyone had left the sinking ship, each group or individual was lost in the dark. Neptune had forbidden any lanterns or talking; the last thing anyone wanted was an alert Roman sentry to hear strange voices from the sea. Even so, there was laughing and loud talking from some of the men.

The journey to shore, with Jupiter and Neptune in the water swimming and pushing the coracle, was uneventful. When they landed, Jacob jumped out to help pull the coracle out of the water. Jupiter instructed everyone to keep still while he checked if there were any Romans on or near the beach. He soon reported that all seemed to be clear.

Shoshana whispered, 'We need to find somewhere to wait until dawn. Daylight may be safer for travelling.' Jupiter nodded. Having hidden the coracle under palm leaves and shoreline detritus, he led the group off towards the Jerusalem road, not to follow it, but to avoid it. Vison was clear because of the fires burning from the garrison's braziers. There was no cloud and the air was cold. Everyone was soaking wet.

'If we can get to Ashdod tonight,' said Jupiter, 'I know a place where we can hide in safety. It's a cave that our brother sometimes uses when he surfaces from… but ordinary men and women can't normally enter. The air isn't that good for all. We can wait in part of the cave where the air is acceptable for a short time, but it will be sufficient… if only for a while.'

Jacob, vividly remembering the adventure with Judas, did not like the sound of that at all. 'What does he mean? The air isn't good? And ordinary men and women can't enter?' The woman with one ear was about to answer. There was a shout that came from the top of the sand dunes. It was an oarsman who was shouting out his own name and whooping with glee at having reached the shore. One of his companions was trying to quieten him and a third was running away. Jacob could hear shouts from further down the beach as others from the ship celebrated their arrival on dry land.

'Fools,' said Jupiter. 'Let's go. Keep together. But we must hurry and get away from these idiots. Most will be dead before dawn.'

The five moved off, keeping to the shadows as much as they could. The moon occasionally slipped out from behind clouds and it was easier to see but less easy to keep hidden. The journey was long and tiring because it was mostly on loose, shifting sand and Jacob found that walking in cold, wet clothes was uncomfortable, particularly with sand rubbing his skin. Soon they came to a track which ran parallel to the sea. Because of the hour, there was nobody about. Suddenly a low, but clear voice in street Aramaic came out of the dark.

'Who walks there?' asked the voice.

Out of the shadows came six heavily armed Bedouin. They

said nothing for a moment, but looked carefully at each of the five. Then one, the one who had spoken, saw Jacob and his face split into a big grin.

Jacob ran up to the man and embraced him warmly, so delighted was he to see someone who had always shown him kindness. He turned to the others. 'These people are Bedouin from the desert strips,' he said happily. 'I've helped them with their sheep and goats on many occasions and they have welcomed me… when I needed… when I…' He hesitated. 'They will help us now. And I trust them with all my heart and with my life.' Jacob spoke at length with the lead Bedouin. There was a great deal of nodding.

'The garrison soldiers,' said Jacob to the others, 'are nervous. They fear…'

Shoshana interrupted as she looked about her. 'Fear what?'

'They fear uprisings and there have been violent reprisals already over the past few days. There are patrols about each day and night. These Bedouin will walk with us to Quiriat Mallakhi but that means we must go further east. They believe it's the safest way. They will also hide us there until tomorrow night - daytime is too dangerous to travel - and they also say that the cave where your brother Pluto sometimes hides may not be safe.' Jacob allowed himself a smile. 'From all points of view,' he said. The lead Bedouin whispered something else to Jacob.

'He says that there are also many soldiers in Jerusalem, protecting the remaining Herod tower, where the temple used to be.'

Jacob was secretly delighted. He kept grinning to himself. Here was a chance to go off with the Bedouin! Here was the opportunity that he had longed for all these weeks. At last, he could become one of the desert people and live in peace.

The senior Bedouin talked a little more to Jacob in hushed tones.

'He… wants to know who you women are.'

The woman with one ear said with no hesitation, but with some irritation, 'Tell him Jacob, that my name is Esther and that I am your sister. Tell him, as you well know, that this woman is called Shoshana and she is your mother.'

Jacob whirled round and for a moment said nothing. Eventually, he found his voice. 'What? What did you say?'

'You heard what I said and none of this is a real surprise to you is it? You've known for some time,' replied Esther in a cold voice.

Jacob wasn't shocked at this declaration about his mother because what Esther had just said was true, but he was shocked to the core to learn that Esther was his sister. He was also embarrassed that Esther had decided to declare what she'd said right now. He stumbled slightly and was aware that everyone was looking at him. He had no idea what to do or say. Understanding a little of his friend's embarrassment, the Bedouin leader quietly indicated that they should make a move.

Led by three Bedouin with three at the back, the group kept to narrow tracks and shortly veered east and away from the sea. No talking was allowed for which Jacob was grateful. When they reached the outskirts of the small settlement of Quiriat Mallakhi, the Bedouin led the group to a well-hidden camp. The Romans tended to leave desert dwellers alone, but the Bedouin were still careful and cautious.

The five were given some water with which to wash and

some fresh goats' milk to drink. As they ate some vegetable stew and cheese, they warmed themselves and their clothing by two small fires which were well hidden in deep holes. Then they were put into two tents, the women in one and Jupiter, Neptune and Jacob in another. Both tents were well guarded.

Sleep eluded Jacob and he whispered to the men. 'Did you know about these women?'

'It is not our business. We are here only to protect you. But, as you have asked the question and we do not lie, then yes,' said Jupiter but, before Jacob could ask anything else, both Jupiter and Neptune were fast sleep.

Jacob was awakened urgently just after dawn by one of the Bedouin who told him that there were Roman patrols close by. The leader thought that news had leaked out about the landing, probably through one or more of the captured crew. It was thought that the five would have been described.

The others were already awake and were ready to leave in minutes. It was decided that Shoshana would go with Jupiter and Jacob while Esther would travel with Neptune. Neptune and Esther were to be the support once the task had been completed. Jacob knew that as much help would be needed to escape, if escape was ever an option. Neptune and Esther had devices which would hopefully help that escape. Four of the Bedouin would go off to their desert encampment where their camels and goats were, while one would travel with each of the two groups.

Jacob had a decision to make and in his heart of hearts he knew that he could not leave his mother and sister now if indeed it really was them. He knew that he had so many things to ask and know. He wanted to say something to his mother and sister, but wasn't sure what or how. And anyway, the time was wrong. But, he wondered, was this a trick perhaps? Was this really his mother and long-lost sister? How could that be? There'd been so many deceits in the last few weeks - and throughout his whole life - that he was unsure who was a true friend and who was not. His head was spinning with doubts and he had no idea who was lying and who was telling the truth. Had it been, he wondered, ever any different? Was there ever a time when he'd felt totally safe or free from lies? He thought that there had been such a time, but he couldn't remember what that time had felt like.

The early morning was cool and Jacob's clothes were still damp and uncomfortable. He felt more confident now that he'd decided to stay rather than run off, but had no real explanation as to why he had come to such a conclusion. It would have been so much easier to have disappeared to the desert and forget his so-called mother and sister.

He tried to focus on the task in hand and followed at the back of the small group. He knew that if they were caught, then that would be that. It was likely, he thought, that the Romans, particularly if they were edgy, would kill them all without needing much excuse. Or torture them for fun and maybe crucify them for sport. For some reason that he couldn't work out, he was determined now to see through the task he'd been set. That meant, he convinced himself, that he must concentrate on the job that he'd been asked to complete and therefore he tried very hard, with some difficulty, to stop thinking about anything else.

They travelled across a long stretch of desert towards Beit Shemesh. The sun warmed them and their clothes dried, but the salt on their skin still chafed. The journey was slow though because there was a strong headwind and some of the sand made speedy walking difficult.

The Bedouin guide gestured towards a small oasis and that's where they headed, but he stopped suddenly indicating quickly that they should fall to the ground. Hiding behind a low escarpment, Jacob could see the oasis quite clearly. A number of legionaries along with a centurion and their horses were taking water. He licked his dry lips.

Shoshana whispered, 'They will leave soon.' She paused and just asked, 'Ya'akov?' Jacob looked at her and she smiled nervously at him. He had no idea how to respond and awkwardly looked away. They waited until the soldiers had left the oasis and then walked quickly towards what they hoped was fresh water.

Not only was there a water spring, but there were four palms with a few remaining low-hanging dates which the small group grabbed and ate hurriedly. They were sitting by the water pool washing their legs and feet, when from around a dune came a single legionary leading his horse. He saw the group and initially seemed unconcerned. After all there were all kinds of travellers in the desert lands. However, as he got closer and saw the group in more detail, he looked to where his comrades had already ridden off, then drew his sword, dropping the horse's leather reins.

Jupiter stood as did Jacob who drew his sica and in the other hand held the spear tight. The soldier, realising that he was outnumbered, decided to run. However, Jupiter was having none of that. He sprang forward just as the soldier turned away. Jupiter tried to grab the man, but the incline and the fine sand didn't allow for speed. All Jupiter could do was smack the horse which galloped off with the legionary safely in the saddle.

'A mistake,' said the Bedouin guide. 'We should have done nothing and pretended to be nomads.'

'Yes,' said Jacob. 'Now the soldier and horse will follow the others, and then the centurion will know something is wrong.'

Water was swiftly splashed around faces and gourds were quickly filled. Nervous that the other soldiers might return to look for desert wanderers who dared chase a Roman soldier, the four travellers strode on in the heat barely talking, focussing mostly on putting one step in front of another.

Jacob turned to Shoshana and fully intending to be firm in his speech, what came out was low and stammering. 'You. You really are my mother?'

Shoshana nodded. 'Yes.' Desperate to hug her son close, she couldn't. She was about to say something else, but Jacob asked, 'And what of… my father?'

'The Guild took your father,' said Shoshana, 'when you were very small. They wanted him because he was known to understand science and the power of certain metals. He was a man of knowledge - a great teacher too. And… he loved you.'

She hesitated, struggling. 'He loved you Jacob… very much. Never doubt that. The Guild wanted him to help with their plans to create a much more powerful Greek fire. He never returned. The Guild employed many who never returned. Your father's name was Flavius Josephus.' Jacob's mother couldn't speak for a moment so much did she want to hug her son close, but dared not.

Jacob was incredulous. 'Flavius… Josephus? You mean…?'

'Yes, he was a Roman… a good man… a great scientist… one who converted to Judaism.'

'Killed?'

'Yes.'

Jacob absorbed this new and astonishing information and found it all strange and unbelievable.

'How do I know this is true?'

'You don't.'

'But what happened? You and my father disappeared!'

'Like your father, I too studied alchemy, secretly,' she said hesitantly, 'because women weren't encouraged. The Guild was an organisation that I wanted to join only if to find your father. But... well, there was no interest. Not then anyway. Your father was useful to them because he understood the practical use of science - catapults, explosives, machines of war - that kind of thing.' She looked at Jacob who stared down at the sand as he walked showing no expression.

'Long before Guild scum found your father, an engineer from Rome - Sextus Julius Frontinus - had heard about him and sponsored your father's work. Frontinus was powerful - a consul and a general too. He told your father about the rich chemical that lies deep in Germania, a land not too far from Italy, and gave some to your father for experiments. It is that chemical that's at the very heart of Guild fire - bright as a thousand suns and more dangerous than anything ever made or discovered. The Guild wanted that and that's what they have.' Glancing over at Jacob, she paused to wipe her face with a cloth, but he just looked at his feet as he walked.

'Go on... please,' he said quietly.

'The Roman governor of Syria wanted me to be in his household. Doesn't matter why. Before I went, under guard, to what I thought was certain prostitution and then death, I asked friends to care for you... and for your sister. These friends looked after you and loved you, but they were thought to be enemies of Rome and so their house was destroyed with them in it. Esther escaped to join my sister in Tyros. You ran away and I thought that you... were no more.'

Shoshana paused, controlling her emotions. 'Well, I escaped from the governor and was recruited by Watchers...'

'Enough talking,' snapped Neptune. 'We must hurry.'

'And what of you, Neptune,' shouted Jacob focusing his distress and anger at Neptune and ignoring the instruction to be quiet, 'What are you? Your brother is master of the underworld. What does that make you? In some way, I don't know how, you have power over the seas... and your other brother the skies.' Jacob couldn't see properly because of the tears and he didn't much care about anything.

'I'm talking to you Neptune,' he roared. 'What... are you? What... are... you?'

Neptune ignored him and walked on.

Stumbling as he tried to catch up, Jacob shouted, 'I asked you a question! You! I... asked you a question! You will answer me. Answer me! What are you?' He stood, both arms by his side unable to control his confusion - his bag in one hand, the spear in the other and his sica at his belt, his eyes filling with unaccustomed tears. He looked only at the sand twirling at his feet in the wind.

'I am,' said Neptune over his shoulder as he carried on walking and ignoring the boy's tears, 'I am your friend.'

33

Singapura, South East Asia Peninsula, 1492

Maria and Gabriella entered the dark, high-hedged and menacing maze, having crossed the river's lightly swaying rope bridge without mishap.

The girl was instantly aware of two things. One was that the hedges were both much thicker and higher than they had appeared from a distance and the other was that the maze smelled strongly of animals. Of what kind of animal, she had no clue.

They walked silently and carefully, the moon only occasionally allowing them to see the pathway clearly. Wary of going too close to the hedges where they knew the vegetation had sharp and poisonous barbs, Gabriella went first. She was immune, or so she hoped, but Maria was not - and the girl suddenly felt very protective of the brave, young woman. Being immune to the virus in the Borgia cellar was one thing. Even then she wasn't sure if she'd inhaled any of the plague. Out here the poisonous vegetation was another test that she hoped upon hope she would not have to experience.

They were making good progress when, suddenly, they heard footsteps, like the patter of a dog.

It wasn't until Gabriella almost tripped over the massive crocodile that she became fully aware of the beast. She put out a hand to stop herself falling and felt the animal's armour plate, hard and rough like rock to the touch. She could see the whole creature by the irregular light - the large head, wide snout, long muzzle, its sheer strength, length and width. And teeth.

There was something about the creature that revulsed rather than frightened her. She stopped walking and took a huge, very quiet intake of breath hoping that the animal would pass by. Maria had stopped walking too and stood still. The crocodile, the width of a big tree, lazily stepped forwards and Gabriella could see only cold menace in the animal's unblinking, yellow eyes. The crocodile, clearly sensing something interesting and less strong than itself, stopped - absolutely nothing of its body moving at all.

Gabriella nodded at Maria and both edged forwards tentatively one by one, stepping as close to the sides of the hedges as they dared. The crocodile still didn't move. Gabriella stepped past the huge beast and so did Maria. Just as they had moved behind the crocodile, each of them let out a breath at the same time and began walking faster, relieved that they had got past the animal.

Suddenly, the crocodile whipped round at incredible speed for such a large animal and, lunging forwards, snapped once, catching Maria's left leg. Maria screamed in agony as the crocodile clamped its powerful jaws and immediately got a better hold to drag the woman away. Gabriella could see the terror and pain in Maria's face. Shocked and terrified, the girl rubbed the Ring of Solomon and closed her eyes praying for Maria's release and safety. Nothing happened. Gabriella almost ripped the ring from her finger in despair but kept rubbing it. Maria was shouting and Gabriella had no idea what else to do. Rather than do nothing, she opened her eyes readying herself to try and release her friend's leg from the crocodile's jaws.

She took out her stiletto knife that she had sheathed at the back of her belt and, in one movement, threw it hard at the crocodile's soft underbelly. It was a good throw in the circumstances and pierced the softer skin but clattered uselessly to the ground. The girl groaned.

Behind her there was a sudden rush of warm air as if a Shamal wind was approaching. It hit her in the back as if she'd been shoved hard by someone with enormous strength. Then a vague shape surrounded the ground in front of the girl. The shape became a monstrous beast, a mix of all the animals that the girl had ever seen, but its shape kept altering. What did not alter at all were its huge snout and rows of knife-like teeth glinting in the moonlight.

The creature looked for a tiny moment at the girl and, giving a short bow and a strange kind of bark, attacked the crocodile in utter fury, causing the animal to forget about Maria. As the crocodile was pulled away by the furious phantom, the sound of the fight between the two beasts was terrifying. Gabriella ran over to Maria and could see clearly that the woman's released leg had been very badly mauled from the thigh downwards.

'You go on!' said Maria through gritted teeth. 'You go on. Leave me here.'

'But I can't do that! I'll stay with you. I must fetch help. Your leg…'

'No Gabriella!' said Maria vehemently. 'You must go. Silver Green… you must go.'

Gabriella could hear the receding noise of the ring's beast and the crocodile as the animals grappled. Hedges were destroyed, trees were uprooted, dust was everywhere and the ground shook. She wondered if she could conjure up something to help Maria, but she knew that she could only ever use the ring for one thing at a time, never more.

'I said go!' gasped Maria more urgently now with a

desperation that Gabriella had not heard before. 'Remember the explosive material. You know how to use it. Just think carefully of what I instructed you. Use the ring. Go!'

Gabriella nodded, took the scarf from her neck, dipped it in water from her flask and bound Maria's damaged leg as best she could. Looking at the woman's strained face once more, she gave her friend a hug, picked up the knife, left her own water flask and walked on.

She walked purposefully and carefully to the end of the maze and, while she was aware of noises from the hedges and the undergrowth, she focused only on getting out as fast as she could. She knew that any guards would have heard Maria's cries of pain and, even if they hadn't, they would have certainly heard the fighting beasts which she herself could still hear in the distance.

The clouds had moved on and the moon was now out in full, so she crouched low to take stock of what lay before her. The huge, double front doors to the old temple were ahead, but she could see that they were guarded by at least two large Malay men, bare-chested and rippling their muscles for fun. Each held a cutlass along with a wheel-lock pistol. There was also a tall woman who was wearing knuckle dusters and had a crossbow slung over her shoulder. Of the three, the woman looked the most ferocious and seemed to be snarling at one of the men. Around the property there were a great number of canon and a range of arquebus guns on supports.

Gabriella needed to get inside fast. Turning, she could see very faint thin spokes of pink sky way off on the horizon. Dawn, when it arrived, would be swift and then the tide would turn, covering the stone path across the water. She wondered about Maria and then tried to shut her mind to everything except the task in hand.

It seemed that the guards were looking out at the maze arguing about who should venture out to see what was going on. Without wasting more time, Gabriella crawled towards one of the verandas away from the front of the building. She rubbed her ring and visualised herself safely inside where she needed to be. As she continued to massage the Ring of Solomon and as she tried to focus on getting inside the building, from the direction of the maze a terrible cry rent the air - cut off in mid-scream.

Too late Gabriella realised her dreadful mistake. To her utter horror and shame, she realised that she'd been trying to use the ring when it was already in use. That meant that the monster she had mustered must have disappeared leaving Maria to the mercy of the hungry crocodile. One use of the ring at a time! That was the rule. And she knew that rule! How stupid and selfish she'd been. How could she have forgotten? Her hands were shaking and she sobbed in frustration and anger at what she knew would have happened to her friend.

One of the guards said something to the other two and hurriedly left his post to go into the maze.

Gabriella wiped away tears and tried hard not to think about Maria. She crawled under the veranda and could hear scrabbling sounds. Rats, she thought. Or something else. She pulled herself along on her stomach through the narrow gap between the base of the building and the ground, trying hard not to inhale the dust and dried animal droppings. The stench was terrible. She soon found what she had been told to look for, by touch if not by sight. Above her were some loose planks of wood which she pulled down and, along with them, a mouthful of something disgusting. She tried hard not to cough and squirmed to see better. Yes! There was a gap up there for her to crawl through.

She found herself inside a storeroom of some kind and could see a thin line of light from under the internal door to another room. She tried the door which surprisingly swung noiselessly and smoothly on its oiled hinges. In front of her was a large auditorium with rows of seats and a stage at one end. On tiptoe, she made her way to a double door and stopped mid-stride. Footsteps!

Quickly she hid behind a tall wooden cabinet, hoping that her breathing would regulate before anyone came in. But nobody did. The footsteps went by and receded until she could hear them no more.

Cautiously, opening the auditorium's main doors, she stepped out into a hallway. From the long hallway she found yet another door which thankfully opened quietly to some kind of counting room and, shutting her eyes, she went in and leaned against a wall to gather her wits.

She opened her eyes and gasped. In front of her on the other side of the room, his face clearly outlined by candlelight and staring straight at her, was Cesare Borgia, a thin rapier at his side and accompanied by two of the guards she'd seen outside the house.

Cesare had been studying a large, leather book which he now snapped shut and slammed down on a desk.

'Welcome,' he snapped. 'I will not have a long conversation with you, figlia del diavolo. You have meddled enough - more than enough - you and your filthy kind. And I have had to travel half across the map to amend the mess that you have caused!' He slammed a fist into the desktop. 'Cagna interferente.

Interfering bitch!'

He spat on the floor and glanced out of the window before picking up a stone statuette of an elephant. He examined it for a moment and then hurled it across the room where it smashed into a large mirror close by where Gabriella was standing. The guards didn't flinch, but Gabriella did.

'Did you think that coming here would help you? Did you? Did you and your Watcher brethren really think that the king and queen of much of the Catholic world would support a venture without discussing this with my father, the Pope? Did you?' Cesare was breathing heavily.

'Who do you think paid for your passage and the stupid voyage that the adventurer Columbus embarked upon? And that of his brother?'

He paused for breath. 'Ferdinand of Aragon and Isabella of Castile,' he shouted. 'And who do they look to for money and support? My father!' He slammed a fist on the desk again. 'Your benefactor who sails off without you will pay dearly, that I promise you!' Again, he slammed the table.

'I think not,' Gabriella said, surprised at her own bravery. 'I know that it is your father who is the villain. And you!' She was sick and tired of Cesare Borgia. She was angry that she had travelled the map as he put it only to be thwarted now - and she was beyond anger that her true friend was probably now lying dead not far from where this evil man stood.

Cesare smiled. 'Oh, really? You think not do you?'

Gabriella, beside herself in anger and grief, shouted, 'I do Signor Borgia… and I also only pray that your fate and that of your family, including the Pope, is awful and painful beyond pain itself. It will happen. I hope so. I hope… so!'

A small flicker of doubt or fear washed over Cesare's face.

'We shall see,' he said hesitantly. 'I think though that you will be doing no further harm to my reputation. The Guild will be well rid of you. The virus is ready in bulk now as is the antidote.' Cesare spoke with more confidence and quiet menace. 'It will be transported tonight to our ships which will set sail the day after tomorrow for distribution.' He laughed without any mirth. 'You should have had a taste of slavery perhaps - much as others of your ilk did. It would have done you good. Ah well. As I say, many will be very happy to be rid of you.'

Gabriella said nothing, but behind her back she fingered the stiletto knife's sheath.

'So, my dear,' smirked Cesare, 'shortly my scientists will slice you up and they can do what they do best. The Guild at long last will own immortality.' He tapped a finger on the table. 'I will be immortal.'

'And now, if it pleases you and even if it does not, I shall take that ring. Give it to me. It belongs to me more than it does to you, I believe.'

Hurried footsteps and some shouts could be heard and the doors burst open. The well-dressed man, Demang Lebar Daun, who had languidly and arrogantly watched Maria and Gabriella arrive on the island, rushed in. He made no apologies for his interruption and ran to Cesare Borgia. Grabbing his master's arm, he was smacked across his face for his impudence. Falling on his knees, he begged forgiveness. He had not noticed Gabriella.

'Signor,' gasped Demang Lebar Daun, still kneeling, out of breath and nursing a sore cheek, 'forgive me, but there are four ships at anchor in the bay, at the river's mouth - an armed

Spanish merchant vessel and three Portuguese men-of-war.' The man stopped for breath.

Gabriella understood his Italian very clearly. 'Most of those who have come off the ships,' Demang Lebar Daun said, 'are well-armed and wear green auras.' The man, realising now that he'd interrupted something, turned and saw Gabriella. He sniggered.

Cesare looked hard at the man, spat on the floor again, swore violently, kicked Demang Lebar Daun and said to the guards, 'Bring the girl.'

One of the guards, the woman, grabbed Gabriella in a vice-like grip and dragged her back into the hall and along a corridor. The woman opened a door, pushed Gabriella inside, locked the door and then ran off.

There was no light inside the small room. Gabriella sank to the floor, her head in her hands. She could hear a great deal of commotion and people running out of the building. She assumed and hoped that something had gone wrong with Cesare's plans. Portuguese warships the man had said. She knew of course that meant cannon and a lot of fire power. People with green auras? What did that mean? Was this her rescue or support or both? Or something else?

She breathed deeply, composed herself and felt a little more confident. She knew that the great store of virus was still in the temple somewhere as was the antidote. That meant that all was not yet over.

She found the lock and door handle by touch alone and could tell that no light came through the keyhole. That meant that either there was no light on the other side of the door, or the guard had left the key in the lock on the outside.

Gabriella took out her very thin, sharp stiletto and tried using it to get the key to turn which it didn't. She put the knife away and calmed herself, holding her right hand with her left and visualising the outcome she hoped to achieve.

The Ring of Solomon glowed blue, but nothing happened. She pictured the door opening and sure enough and to her surprise and delight, she heard the key turning. With a click the lock was undone and Gabriella quickly opened the door. To her amazement, the vicious-looking guard was standing outside. Gabriella was certain that death would now be forthcoming at the hands of this terrifying-looking woman with a crossbow, a knuckle duster, villainy in her manner and hate on her face. Gabriella stepped back in frustration and anger, ready to fight. She took out her knife and held it high.

'I am a Watcher,' said the woman impatiently, but in a low voice and with something of a smile. 'I have just freed you. My aura is hidden. I have learned to do that - as will you, if you live, Silver Green. Go now. It is your only chance to escape. And one day I hope someone teaches you to hold a knife properly.'

Gabriella, still shocked, could see a faint green around the woman's head which then immediately disappeared. She put her knife away and said firmly, 'I cannot leave without trying to do what I have been asked to do. I have come a very long way to do this and do it I shall. If I can.' She didn't have much faith now in succeeding, but she knew that she must try. For Maria's sake. For her family's. For people.

'Then,' said the woman, 'I wish you well, Silver Green, but I must go. If I can help you escape, I will. You…' The woman stared hard at Gabriella for a moment but, hearing shouts and calls from outside the temple, ran off.

Gabriella stood still for a moment. She could hear Cesare barking out orders. She needed to find the virus store and fast. But all the rooms that she dashed into were filled with furniture, religious artefacts or exotic wall hangings. At the end of the great hall was a brass door which was wide open. Gabriella found herself in a vestibule and before her was an enormous wooden door which was also open. She just knew that this was the right place.

The room facing her was vast and deserted. There was row after row of open wooden cases with glass jars lying on beds of straw and what looked like soft cloth. The shelves on every wall from floor to ceiling were packed tight with jars the same as the ones that she had seen in Rome. But here there were a thousand times more jars - all neatly lined up and looking quite pretty, she thought for a moment, as they caught the light.

Relieved at least to have found the great store, Gabriella stepped forward. The door to the room slammed behind her. Cesare coughed and she swivelled round to see that he stood with a glass jar full of blood red liquid held high above his head. He was tapping the fingernails of one hand against the jar's glass and this time he was not smiling.

34

Jerusalem, Judea, Imperial Province, Roman Empire, 79 CE

Even though dusk was approaching, the heat was still relentless. The old, ruined city was under curfew and empty.

Jacob knew most of the streets inside out. He was often reminded of the scenes he'd witnessed as a very small boy and the vivid stories he'd been told over the years by some who'd survived. Thousands of bodies putrefying in the sun, the unbearable stink, packs of wild dogs eating human flesh joined sometimes by starving people.

Titus, a general in those days and on the instruction of his father Emperor Vespasian, had ordered all prisoners, most of whom had committed no crime, to be crucified, up to five hundred each day. The vast majority had been Jews. The Mount of Olives and the craggy hills around the city had been so crowded with crucifixes that there was scarcely room for more and anyway there were few trees left to make them.

So desperate were many citizens to escape the city with their meagre savings that, as they left, they swallowed their coins only to be butchered when caught and their bowels cut open to retrieve the money. All prisoners were eventually gutted for this reason, sometimes the Romans eviscerating them and searching their intestines while they were still alive. Jacob ground his teeth and shut out images like these as best he could.

He tried to focus again on what he had to do. While travelling, it had been hard to put away any thoughts about his mother, father and sister. Repeatedly he had kept wondering if what he'd been told was true. Was this woman really his mother and Esther his sister? These questions and a hundred others had occupied his thinking for the many hours that they had walked. But now he had to focus on one thing alone and it wasn't family and it wasn't what the Romans had done in their destruction of Jerusalem and its people. Did he want to go ahead with such a suicidal task? Not at all, he thought. He was determined to be in the desert, but he felt that he owed something and maybe, he felt, this was a way of paying a debt. Some kind of atonement, he thought.

The Bedouin escort had left Shoshana, Jupiter and Jacob well before the ruined city wall. The man had given the trio some bread as well as a few pieces of dried mutton, a handful of figs and a half-full water gourd. Jacob didn't know what to say to the man or how to say it - other than his muttered thanks. Part of him just wanted to go off to wherever the man was going. It would be so simple. The man held Jacob's head one hand on either side and looked straight into the boy's eyes. Then he nodded and smiled. Surprising himself, so did Jacob.

Jupiter, who knew Jerusalem as well as anyone, led the other two through the Cedron Valley, past Hezekiah's Conduit and on to what had been the Hasmonean Palace, now a dusty ruin where sand had piled up against what once had been proud, now fallen, statues. Looking across at Shoshana, Jacob could see that she was troubled and was walking, not blindly, but almost hopelessly. She stumbled and Jacob put out an arm to steady her. She looked at him and smiled tentatively and then gratefully. Jacob, without any effort at all now, smiled back.

What had once been King Herod's palace was at the rear of the First Wall which, of course, was no longer much of a wall.

But one of the palace towers still stood intact and that was where they were heading.

'Here is where we'll wait until dark,' said Jupiter in a whisper. 'There,' he pointed, 'where the big stones are, underneath is an old cellar. Where that statue lies, the one that looks like the head of a lion. See? The stairs are steep, so go carefully. But we should be safe there. For a while.'

The three made their way to the fallen statues and sure enough there was a stone grate which Jupiter quickly pulled up without making a sound. They climbed down into what was a space that perhaps had once been used for storage. At least that's what Jacob thought until he saw four skeletons manacled to one wall. Several had missing bones and one had nails still in what had been the hands. The smell in the dungeon was foul, but at least it was cool there and they all breathed through their mouths. They ate the small amounts of food they had, drank a little water and settled down as best they could to wait.

Darkness fell quickly and Jupiter said that he wanted to see if there were random patrols and to gauge the defences and guards around the tower. Shoshana was worried that such a big man would be easily seen or discovered, but Jupiter just shrugged and said that he'd done this kind of thing many times before and that he hadn't been caught yet.

Once Jupiter had gone, silence fell and Jacob was uncomfortable. He didn't know how to have a conversation with Shoshana and right now he didn't want to think of her as his mother. She didn't try to force a conversation either. What she did do though was to go through the plan once more with the boy and insisted that he repeat every single detail, even though the detail was already etched in Jacob's head. After that, she suggested that he sleep for a while, but he refused. Despite his refusal and determination to stay awake, within moments he was fast asleep.

He dreamed of fighting strange, vicious animals on behalf of someone he didn't know. There were so many beasts to fend off and he was struggling, even though he had the spear and his trusty sica. His sica was useful but for some reason he couldn't use the spear. Someone called out for him to help, but he had no idea who it was and, anyway, he was occupied with fighting beasts. Suddenly though, the beasts disappeared and he could hear another voice calling him by name from a long way off. He wanted to find out who was calling him, but couldn't go because he was being pulled back. He wanted to hit out at whoever was pulling him. Jacob awoke with a start to find Jupiter tugging one of his arms.

'It's time,' Jupiter said.

Rubbing his face with his hands, Jacob nodded and shrugged away the dream. He and Shoshana gathered their things, following Jupiter out into the now cooler air and streets. They kept to the shadows and moved slowly and carefully, always stopping if they heard any noise, no matter how small. Soon they were close to the tower which once had been part of Herod's Palace. Now, hiding behind huge, white marble blocks, the three watched and waited.

Every few minutes, groups of heavily armed, disciplined and highly alert guards marched around the tower. There were even more soldiers on the tower's battlements. Jacob could see the crossbows which were obviously loaded, ready to fire. A few centurions on horseback made slow circuits of the tower, keeping a watch over the legionaries and looking out for any unusual activity. Occasionally, a command was barked. In addition to the military presence, there were also armed individuals who were clearly not Roman military, but who looked fierce. Their weapons were in their hands and they were clearly ready for whatever the night held.

'Barbarians,' whispered Jupiter. 'They're more dangerous than all the others put together.'

Jacob nodded. He knew the reputation that these fighters had. 'Do they expect us?'

'No. This is just their way,' replied Jupiter quietly. 'They're the best of warriors and always alert. They earn much payment - jewels, silver, coin of any sort. They only do what they do for money and take no sides other than that of whoever pays. These men are mercenaries. They will also kill anyone who does not pay their dues for services rendered. Rome fears them.'

'Are we ready?' asked Shoshana, impatient to get on.

The other two nodded.

Shoshana breathed deeply and stood straight. Suddenly she seemed younger again and more alert. The weary look had gone and she focussed now on what had to be done. Jupiter took some carefully folded clothing out of his bag which Shoshana put on, the result of which made her look scholarly. Jacob was astonished at the transformation.

Her attractive hair was covered by a deliberately unattractive, formal, clerical hat and in only a few moments her general demeanour became one of seniority, severity and certainly of someone who commanded immediate respect. Once ready, Jupiter handed her some scrolls to complete the image. Pushing her shoulders back again, Shoshana looked straight ahead and, without any further conversation, walked out in the open straight towards the tower's main entrance.

There were a few labourers in front of the tower working on some wall repairs and defences. Other than those men and the guards, the only other people around were merchants steering carts and livestock in or out of the building's great courtyard.

The queue of deliveries waiting to gain entrance was long and delayed because each person, horse, bullock and cart was being thoroughly searched. Pockets, bags, boxes, barrels and packages were examined. Questioning took time too and, if there were doubts about anyone's purpose or identity, then admission was refused. There were no arguments because it was well known that to argue with a Roman soldier here would lead to imprisonment or another punishment. Either way, death would be the result.

Even though it was night, the area around the tower's perimeter was well lit with braziers and a multitude of large oil lamps. Shoshana walked on and, just as she arrived at the open gates, a centurion on horseback barred her way and shouted something. Jacob stopped breathing for a moment, but couldn't hear what was being said; it looked as if there was some kind of argument.

It was clear that Shoshana was trying to explain something, but the centurion was obviously not impressed or convinced by whatever she was saying. He called some legionaries over but, before they reached Shoshana, a man also dressed in the clothes of an academic appeared from the guards' gatehouse and shouted something at the centurion. The soldiers stopped and the centurion immediately nodded towards the academic who, upon reaching Shoshana, bowed low and escorted her to the gate where she was not searched but was welcomed in.

'Do you believe…' began Jacob, breathing out slowly in relief that Shoshana was inside the building now, 'Do you really believe that she is a Watcher?'

'Oh yes,' said Jupiter, 'she is a Watcher, of that you must have no doubt boy. Believe it. She is also your mother. Believe that too. And she is one of the bravest people I have ever met.'

'But she has no aura.'

'The Guild has been made to believe many times that she is Guild through and through. That isn't easy, believe me. She's also taught herself not to show her aura. Hard to do. Her big task now is…' Jupiter cleared his throat. 'But enough nonsense and prattle; we must move.'

Keeping to the shadows, Jupiter led the way. Nodding at Jacob, the boy went right while Jupiter went left. Jacob ran soundlessly to the east side of the tower. He was confident that he'd not been seen and that he had timed his short run to be exactly in the gap between the patrol guards' circuits.

Jacob knew that once there had been three towers each made of pure white marble, two used as soldiers' barracks. The third and remaining one, the tallest, Herod had named the Phasael, in memory of his brother who had committed suicide while in captivity. Latterly, the building had been called the Tower of David because it was presumed to have been built on the site of King David's palace and it was also said that this was where King David's remains had been buried. Jacob knew from his briefings that the tower was extremely well-protected inside and out. He also knew the layout of every single part of the building and could find his way blindfold to the very deep cellars which is where he had to go now. Once there, he also knew exactly what he had to do.

He thought about Shoshana. He just couldn't help it. Was she really a double agent, playing a very dangerous game? Was she really and truly his mother? The Guild was a clever organisation. Could she fool Guild people? Would they still believe that she was still faithful and still a follower? Would she be safe?

He forced himself to snap out of any reverie. Pointless waste of time, he told himself. He had to concentrate on what he had to do if the plan was going to work. Focus. Afterwards - if there was an afterwards - he could think of other things. But not now. Now he had to make the plan work.

He was waiting for six big, heavily laden carts to go through the tower's gateway. The queue was in the dark because most of the lamps were close to the building's walls and entrance, but that suited the plan perfectly.

The heavy carts, each pulled by four bullocks, moved forwards painfully slowly towards the tower's entrance gates. At the huge gateway, legionaries from the crack XII Fulminata legion were still checking every person, every item of clothing - disgusting as some of these items were - and every cart, horse or bullock. Every barrel, amphora and any container, no matter how small, was opened or probed. Every cart was examined from top to bottom. Except one. On the fifth cart were three enormous jars, each taller and wider than three men. The jars were each marked with one word: venenum. Jacob was now inside one of these jars.

The three jars, he knew, contained various mixtures each one deadly to anyone but, thankfully, he thought and prayed, not to him. These poisons included mandrake, hemlock, deadly nightshade, belladonna and henbane cantharidin - an odourless, colourless, fatty substance secreted by blister beetles. There was bull's blood, essence of salamander, salts of lead, mercury, arsenic and antimony. Datura was in there too as was aconite from monk's hood, colchicum from the autumn crocus, yew extract, opium and hellebore. There were packages of pine resin, quicklime, calcium phosphide, sulphur and saltpetre. Each separate ingredient was carefully wrapped or bottled and clearly labelled. Jacob knew all this and more such had been his briefing.

The fumes within the jar in which Jacob now crouched were almost over-powering, even though there was sufficient air to breathe - just. He was also acutely aware that if all the chatter about him being immune to poison was untrue, then he would not see beyond the next few minutes.

The legionaries were about to tackle the cart with the huge jars when a centurion on horseback stopped them with an urgent and nervous command.

'Stop! Now! Leave those! They contain poisons and the release will be death. Can't you read, idiots?'

The legionaries recoiled and the cart was hastily waved on. It trundled through the gateway and into the inner atrium which had three huge wings. On those three sides were columned colonnades and there was an implivium of blue marble sunk in the corner to collect rainwater.

Each of the huge carts were directed to a prescribed area for unloading. The massive jars, each of which took five men to move and then with a struggle, were carefully stacked upright against a wall.

Once emptied of their cargo, the six now much lighter carts departed with a great deal of shouting, rumbling of wooden wheels and commotion. There were to be no more deliveries that night, so the entrance gates were slammed shut and barred. The yard was deserted now apart from the guards on either side of the walls. The occasional quiet conversation from soldiers and barbarians were the only sounds in what had only moments before been full of noise and bustle.

After waiting for a few minutes, Jacob struggled to loosen the jar's tightly fitting lid and eventually managed to push it open a fraction. Despite the quiet, he knew that everywhere in or near the tower would be carefully guarded. He also knew that, where the jars were positioned, none of the guards would have sight of that part of the atrium and anyway they would be looking outwards, not in. Sure enough, he could see twelve soldiers nearby, each spaced out a few pedes from each other. They were talking and, just as he thought, were not much interested in anything. They were there in case someone managed to break in - or tried to break out. However, each soldier had one hand on his sword and Jacob knew from experience that these men would be very good and very fast at reacting to anything. Battle ready, he thought. He turned his head and could see more legionaries and a few academics or alchemists wearing brightly coloured cloaks, walking across the yard from one part of the building to another.

Just as Jacob expected, a gentle breeze started up which was refreshing to begin with. Jacob quickly closed the lid of the jar, pulled it tight shut and smiled. He could hear the wind increase in temperament. Then he heard the beat of heavy raindrops. Soon there were shouts and the sounds of running feet. He heard objects falling, some of them very heavy and then a big crash as if something had dropped from a great height and smashed. He heard and felt one of the large jars next to his slip a little. That had always been a risk. He hoped upon Caesar's armpits that it hadn't cracked or broken and he prayed that his own jar would not slip or split.

The wind gathered in its ferocity and he could hear it whistle and whine. Jacob smiled again. The downpour was now torrential and hammered heavily on his hiding place like a deafening drum. He could hear the splashing as the implivium filled with water and presumably, thought Jacob, would soon overflow. What had started as a soft breeze was now a screaming wind that had travelled from the east and the lands of Persia. What had begun only moments ago as gentle rain was now a monsoon.

Jacob raised the jar's lid a tiny amount once again. The lid was very nearly ripped from his hands. There was nobody about at all now and it was obvious that anyone who'd been outside was now taking cover inside.

He checked once again that there was nobody about, then struggled out and pushed the lid back in place, but not before stuffing six small containers from the jar into his battered, leather bag. He looked round while pressing himself against a wall and holding on tight to an iron ring on a wall usually used to hold horses.

Within moments he was soaked. Several helmets were on the ground along with a shoe or two and a few parchments and cloaks were flying about like disoriented birds. He knew that he had little time because the wind would die down soon. Quickly he ran to a doorway that had, until just now, been guarded by three legionaries and a pack of slavering dogs.

The door, amazingly, wasn't locked. He pulled it open and went inside. There was a large passageway and in a recess were three relaxed legionaries sitting with the dogs. Swiftly, he threw a small, thin package that he'd been holding. It hit the stone floor right in front of the surprised soldiers. There was a hiss, the recess and passageway filling immediately with dense, grey smoke. One dog had become free and was now charging, teeth bared, straight for Jacob. He could see the drool hanging from its teeth. As the sleeping draught took effect, the dog yelped, arched its back, fell and lay still, snoring softly. The soldiers and the other dogs were now scrabbling on the floor and within no time they were all asleep too. Jacob breathed in the smoke a very little just to check that he was untouched by the drug and, realising that he was fine, rushed along the passageway to find the stairs that he'd been told to expect.

He bounded down the winding steps three at a time. At the bottom, there was another door behind which Jacob could hear noises. Suddenly, the door opened. A tall man wearing black cleric's clothing and a red cleric's hat stood at the doorway and behind him Jacob could see more similarly dressed men and women.

'Ah, Ya'akov, my boy, my boy, welcome. We have been expecting you. But where are my manners? Please do come in. You are damp from the surprisingly torrential rain. And you have come far, so the least we can do is to show you our work. You look tired if I may say so - and a little out of breath. Come in, please. Goodness! You really are very wet I see. The storm I expect. Listen to it up there. Quite sudden wouldn't you say? Unusual. Come in...'

The man stepped to one side.

'Please... enter. Shall I take your bag? No? I believe that you will know at least one of our... group.'

The man laughed mirthlessly and the other men laughed in a similar fashion as well. The man held up a hand and any laughter stopped instantly.

Jacob was about to hold up his spear, but the cleric held his hand out.

'Oh, I think we'll take that shall we? We wouldn't want anyone to come to harm and I fear that you'll have little use for it after today. After a few hours. You see, young Ya'akov,' and here the man's demeanour changed from false friendliness to one of nasty spite, 'we plan to experiment on you. You know of course that you have something we want, something we need. After our experimentation, you will die. I'm glad. I have never met you, but I don't like you… you have wasted our time. The spear. Give it to me. Now.'

Jacob held the spear high as if to use it to attack the cleric, but the cleric was fast. The man shouted something that Jacob didn't understand and leaned forwards at incredible speed, grabbing the spear and using the shaft to strike Jacob on the head.

'Now,' said the cleric bringing his arms down slowly, 'let us be sensible.' He indicated that one of his minions should take the spear. 'Simple Washu methods, you know. They are methods of unarmed combat started by the Yellow Emperor from China. But I can tell that you're not much interested in the history of Chinese combat. Come in and let us make what will undoubtedly be most unpleasant for you, a little… easier. Ah, your hand creeps to your knife I see. Your sica please.' Jacob hesitated. The man stepped forward and with two movements had hit Jacob very hard in the face and at the same time had taken the sica from Jacob's belt.

All along one side of the cavernous room there were men and women wearing thick leather aprons and masks of some kind covering their noses and mouths. To Jacob they looked like creatures from bad dreams rather than people. They seemed to be mixing paste or some semi-liquid material and putting the mixed material into what looked like sausage skins. Jacob glanced behind him and to his side. There were shelves of bottles and open flasks of all kinds of fluids, some marked with words like acidum sulphuratus, aqua regia and aconitum, all deadly as Jacob well knew.

On another wall there was a long bench on which were glass tubes supported at various heights by metal stands. The tubes had coloured liquids which ran slowly into various sizes of containers which already had some black substance in them. Yet more people were carefully sealing the jars once they were filled and taking them to where the paste-makers were working. Any spillage, of which there was a fair amount, was cleared up immediately by people who Jacob could only deduce were slaves, so servile and ill-looking did they appear. They wore no masks.

'Welcome to our world,' said the cleric. 'This is where we manufacture Guild fire. The little Vesuvius demonstration was mild by comparison to what we can deliver. Yes, I forget, you were there of course, weren't you?' He wasn't expecting an answer and looked in a self-satisfied way around the room.

'Do you know how many volcanoes there are in the world?' he asked Jacob mildly. 'No? Well, would you hazard a guess and say one hundred, maybe two? Three? No? Not playing my game? Never mind. Let me tell you. Almost two thousand. We will explode each one if necessary. That will make a great display, don't you think? Like a party, a celebration. Explosions and fire that will fight the sun for power.' The man imitated a large explosion with his mouth and his hands.

'The Romans believed that we were doing all this for them so that their rule would continue. A new weapon for them! Pah! Their rule? It's a joke. Don't you agree, hmm? They do nothing without us. Nothing. Their so-called rule is finished.' He looked around at the people working and fiddled with his own mask that was hanging from his neck.

'Think of it, boy,' he said as if describing something to a child. 'One hundred volcanos will be exploded at the same time three months from now. There will be no need to explode more than that. The empire will crumble faster than it's currently falling. The world will be at our feet. Nations will beg us to stop. We will have our slaves. Of course,' and here he bowed his head to Jacob, 'with your kind permission, we will gain the secret at long last to immortality. Immortality! Think of it! Well, of course why should I say that to you? You are it.' He chuckled and paused looking at Jacob with a hunger just as a tiger might look at a tethered goat.

The man snarled. 'You've led us something of a dance, haven't you? And many have perished in seeking you and the immortal essence. But here we are now. And here you are. At last!' His face became a mixed picture of glee, exuberance and malice. He shut his eyes as if in ecstasy.

'Then,' he went on, 'we can give the immortality serum to anyone we choose - and certainly all those loyal to us and our cause.' He half-turned and waved a hand, carelessly indicating the huge laboratory. 'You should feel proud that your... you will have supported so many worthwhile lives.'

He looked straight at Jacob. 'Of course, as you'd expect, anyone betraying us will be killed and naturally anyone who is useless will be given no new immortality serum so they will die. We will control the earth's population. And our new temporary citadels below ground are now complete so everything's ready Ya'akov! There's a citadel far below here as a matter of fact and I would show it to you if we had time. Which we don't.' He smiled, but there was no humour in the smile.

'Now to business. Oh, by the way, my name is Chang Tao-Ling and I have much power. The Guild is my life. I am also a Taoist prince if you're interested, which I suspect you're probably not. I speak seven languages and can speak Latin if you prefer that to my Aramaic. You don't answer? My home is far from here, but this is where my alchemy and I have been needed. Jacob collected as much phlegm in his mouth as he could and spat directly in the man's face.

Wiping the mess from his forehead and nose, Chang Tao-Ling said with a voice full of menace, 'You must learn some manners! It's never too late to learn manners, although in your case perhaps it is.' He chuckled nervously, but only briefly. Turning to two of his people, he barked in Mandarin, 'Prepare him.'

Chang Tao-Ling began to put his mask on but stopped and turned back to Jacob, 'Oh, I do apologise,' he said softly. 'I almost forgot. Would you like to see your mother? Of course you would. As I'm sure you will have realised by now, she was a double agent. But naturally we knew the stupid game she and her Watcher colleagues were playing. We are not idiots. Naturally we were grateful to her in the same way we were most grateful to your father who, alas, also cannot join us, not least because he is... how shall I put it?... no longer able to join anyone. Never mind. Such is life. Or death.' He giggled and then shouted, 'Take him!'

Jacob was pushed roughly to the far side of the room. He still had his leather bag over his shoulder and he pretended to stumble. As he fell, he grabbed something from inside the side pocket of the bag.

35

Singapura, South East Asia Peninsula, 1492

'I have the antidote of course,' Cesare said calmly, continuing to tap his long fingernails on the virus jar. 'And you do not. So, I have no fear - not this time. And I know the antidote works. Of that I am very sure; it has been tested most thoroughly. On this very island. But what if you are not immune, you interfering little bitch? Oh dear, what then? Either way, we shall find out. And, also either way, your death is certain and near. We need something from you first of course. I shall laugh at last, for you have been in my way too much and too long and my friends are displeased.'

Gabriella had a strange feeling that someone was standing close. She glanced quickly over her shoulder. There was nobody. Turning back to Cesare, she rubbed her ring.

Cesare screamed out. 'Stop! I command you.'

Gabriella did not stop. Cesare hurled the flask with the red liquid to the stone floor, but it never got there. Something had stopped it in mid-air, as if it had been caught. Cesare gawped for a moment, looking in fear at the jar which seemed to be floating and then stared at the girl. He swore, swore again, turned abruptly and ran. The flask was gently lowered to the floor as if by an invisible hand.

Gabriella had no time to ponder what had just happened. She knew that she must do what she was there to complete and, like Cesare, she ran knowing that time was not on her side.

Outside, early dawn was magnificent in its pinks, lavenders

and pale yellows. She could see what her mother had always called a god cloud - the sun sending sharp shafts of pale light through breaks in the still dark night clouds. She could hear sounds of battle going on in the distance and the ships' guns firing intermittently. It was obvious that the gunfire was getting closer. Of Cesare and his cohorts there was now no sign. Explosions shook the ground as the artillery, presumably aiming at the building behind her, quickly began to better gauge distances.

Suddenly and totally exhausted, Gabriella stopped for a moment and just didn't know what to do. Her anxiety was almost physical. Should she go forwards to the swamp and certain death either from the creatures in it or from drowning? Or maybe even from cannon fire? Or should she go back into the building and at least try and destroy the virus even if it meant smashing each bottle? Before she could answer any of these questions, she realised with a jolt that her bag with the explosives had been left in the room in which she'd been locked.

The ships' guns couldn't quite reach the temple yet, but the explosions were loud and ever closer. Gabriella could hear some explosions from a distance away and she wondered if that's where Cesare's ships were docked.

She came to a decision and ran as far as the entrance to the maze and turned to look back at the temple. Shutting her eyes, she also shut out everything around her. She imagined a great fire consuming the building. She visualised the virus and the antidote, almost jar by jar, case by case, being destroyed with no trace left. She could see the storage areas. She could see the great leather-bound alchemy books holding terrible secrets. She could imagine white hot heat. She could imagine the most powerful of flames, flames that would destroy everything they touched. She could see…

From behind her, a pair of strong hands gripped her neck, powerful hands that instantly began squeezing her throat. She knew that it was Cesare. She could sense him. Unable to speak, she still tried to keep the images of fire in her head as she struggled against the desperate strength of the man. The fingers at her throat squeezed harder and harder. Gabriella couldn't breathe properly and felt that she might faint. Or die.

She forced herself to keep the images of fire firmly in her head. Cesare kept a hand round her throat and still squeezed hard, his nails cutting into her skin. With the other hand, he tried to reach the Ring of Solomon.

'Give it to me. It's mine,' he grunted spitting into her neck and trying to grab the ring. 'The Guild will own you. We do own you! You will not destroy our work! You will…' Without any warning at all, Cesare Borgia stopped talking in mid-breath, gasped in horror, let go of her neck and staggered back as the sun came out.

36

Jerusalem, Judea, Imperial Province, Roman Empire, 79 CE

As Jacob pretended to stumble so that he could take something from his bag, the two men pushing him stood still for only a moment to allow the boy to regain his balance. It was enough. Jacob swivelled round and, with one hand, threw a small cylinder hard onto the floor. There were two bright flashes. Eyes watering with the acrid smoke, the men closest to him shouted in alarm as they tried to see anything. Others made for where they thought that Jacob stood, arms flailing uselessly waving staffs and knives in wild abandon. People working at the benches turned in concern to try and see what the commotion was, their eyes half-blinded by the smoke. There was a shout of pain as one cleric was stabbed inadvertently by a colleague.

Jacob ran to where he knew the door was that led down to the vast sub-cellar, the massive Guild fire storage room. He found the door, but it was locked. Frustrated, he realised that he had little time before the smoke cleared. Suddenly a hand touched one of his. He whirled round ready to hit the person very hard and realised with a jolt that it was his mother. Her nose was bleeding and she had a shoulder wound. She was exhausted, distressed and had been crying. She held a large key and, without saying anything, put the key in the door's lock with a shaking hand. Jacob moved to help her, but she impatiently pushed him away and unlocked the door.

'Hurry,' she said in a hoarse voice, 'there is little time. Here.'

She held the Spear of Destiny in her hand. Jacob looked at her. He wanted to talk to her, learn from her, listen to her talk about everything and anything. He wanted to understand her life. He wanted to know all the things about her and his father that he didn't know. More than anything, he wanted to hold her tight.

'You must hurry,' his mother said urgently.

Jacob nodded, turned to the door, dragged it open and rushed down a set of steep steps at the bottom of which was another door made of heavy iron. This one was open and led into a vast area filled floor to ceiling with shelves of crates stamped with symbols. He looked round and saw that near him were more glass flasks on shelves marked with labels showing that each contained various dangerous acids.

Before he did anything else, he checked, as he'd been instructed, to see that the key to this door was on the inside. He heard sounds from the stairway and, in his haste, didn't lock the door. Quickly lifting down one of the crates, he opened it and saw the sausage-like packages inside - each with a label which read: Forum Ignis. He smiled grimly. Guild Fire.

He opened the second cylinder that he'd taken from his bag and placed it on the floor. Then with his left foot, he pressed gently on the cylinder until he heard a click. He kicked the cylinder under a workbench.

There were sounds of many footsteps and urgent shouts. Too late, Jacob realised the door was unlocked. A centurion charged in followed by four legionaries and the clerics. Seething with anger and frustration, Chang Tao-Ling pushed his way forward to the front. Gone was the self-assurance and calm menace. The man was upset, very upset indeed and recently he'd lost his hat and his mask. In front of him he held Shoshana.

She was weeping, either in pain or distress or both Jacob didn't know, but the sight made him cold with rage. Chang Tao-Ling smiled, his leer and self-satisfied smugness returning.

Jacob stepped back so that he could feel behind him the shelves on which he knew were various mixtures in different sized beakers. With one hand behind his back, he felt carefully for the smallest beaker which he'd noticed contained acidum sulphurates.

The cleric motioned the soldiers to step back behind the entrance, but left the door wide open.

'Now then, all this fuss and bother for nothing,' said Chang Tao-Ling breathlessly. 'All this bravado and these little tricks you have. All of them are most entertaining, but so… childish and,' he screamed out, 'a waste of my time!' He paused to get his breath back.

'Let me explain something to you,' he went on. 'Two things,' he breathed heavily. 'First, whatever you do or try to do, we will always win. The Guild always wins.'

Jacob asked, 'But does it though?'

'And second,' said Chang Tao-Ling ignoring the interruption, 'the most valuable chemical that makes Guild fire will not be destroyed. It cannot be destroyed, do you hear?' He stared with malignant hatred at Jacob.

Smiling again, Chang Tao-Ling said, 'The essential ingredient comes from the land of Germania. You may know this perhaps. No? The material is rare and dangerous as the world will soon discover. A brilliant but very stupid scientist, a man called Flavius Josephus, helped us to create the fire. Your father I believe? Your stupid, dead father. He could have been a great scientist within our organisation but chose otherwise so…' He pressed hard on Shoshana's wounded shoulder and her screams made Jacob clench his eyes shut as if in pain himself.

Chang Tao-Ling went on, not remotely concerned at the woman's distress or Jacob's reaction. In fact, he was enjoying both. 'This material is a metal. You know what a metal is? I don't mean like iron or silver, but something quite different found in rock deep within the earth. The Guild can harness the power that radiates from within this material. In case you have an interest, it's called uranium.'

'I have no interest. Only in your death. Which will come - and soon.'

'Brave words, but untrue words, nonetheless. We will have you and we shall have immortality. Now then… your mother here, this traitor…'

Jacob stepped forward, moving quickly round the man and bringing up the spear ready to strike. The cleric squealed and flinched. At extraordinary speed, Jacob kicked the cellar door shut with as much force as he could. The soldiers and other clerics were outside now. Jacob turned slightly and shoved the spear underneath so that it wedged the door tightly closed and then he turned the key. There was a brief silence followed by hammering on the door and shouts.

Chang Tao-Ling's voice rose and he sounded hysterical. 'Open the door, you fool. If you don't, then…'

Jacob was shaking with rage. 'Then what?'

Jacob stepped closer to Chang Tao-Ling. Without further warning, the cleric took a knife from his pocket in his cloak. It was Jacob's sica and, without any hesitation, he put the knife against Shoshana's throat. She gurgled and stiffened, then thrashed while small spots of blood seeped from where the knife pricked her skin. Chang Tao-Ling snorted in delight.

'Open the door or she dies,' said the cleric. He raised the knife, ready to strike. Without any hesitation, Jacob took two steps forward and, reaching out, grabbed a handful of the man's hair and pulled his head back violently with a jerk. Jacob's mother fell to the ground.

'Silver Green, your powers have nothing against me,' gasped Chang Tao-Ling as he squirmed. 'Nothing!' He tried to turn his head to the cellar door as he shouted for help. The hammering increased.

Jacob stared at the man for a moment. As he held on to the cleric's head with one hand, he smacked the man hard across the face with the other and then grabbed the man's left wrist which he twisted until it snapped. The cleric screamed and writhed in pain.

The instant that the sica dropped to the floor, Jacob reached behind and grabbed the small beaker of acid. He still held the man's head back.

'Open your mouth,' commanded Jacob. He could hear that the door was beginning to scrape open.

The cleric wriggled and clamped his mouth shut tight.

'Open your mouth,' shouted Jacob again.

Shoshana, with very little strength, grabbed the sica and drove it into one of the cleric's legs. The man shrieked. Jacob continued to hold the cleric's head back with one hand and with the other he poured the clear liquid into the man's shrieking mouth. All of it. Jacob stared into the man's panicked eyes.

The cleric shut his mouth instinctively, but he had already

swallowed a great deal of the acid. Jacob let the gasping and convulsing man fall to the floor. Clawing at his skin, face and body, the cleric was bent in total agony. Already his face had become red with a mass of yellowing blisters. The man's screams were horrific.

Without watching more of the horror he'd created, Jacob picked up his sica and then his mother who was faint but still breathing. He looked round and saw at the back of the cellar another door. Jacob knew that at any moment the main door would burst open.

He ran to the rear door and thanked any god in any heaven that it opened. In front was a steep, spiral stairway. Suddenly he heard a hissing noise and could see flashes and sparks coming from under the bench where he'd kicked the cylinder. Clutching his mother close, he made his way up the winding steps.

He froze. Now he could hear footsteps coming down. He couldn't go backwards because that would mean certain death and he couldn't just stand still. He put his mother down on a step so that he could use his sica to fight. This, he thought, was the end, but he was determined not to resign himself to death without fighting. Raising his knife ready to strike, he heard someone shouting, but he couldn't make sense of what was being said. His only focus was to defend his mother.

Suddenly he recognised a voice. 'Jacob, stop!' It was Esther and behind her were Jupiter and his brother. 'Jacob, stop. It's us.'

Jacob looked up at his sister as she came round the corner of the stairway, but he felt no joy, only a desperate and bleak sadness. His energy disappeared and he just wanted to stop.

Jupiter pushed him to one side and grabbed Shoshana. Jacob

realised that he didn't have the spear but instantly believed that what Jupiter held was more important. He gently took back his mother and held her close.

Neptune shouted, 'Jacob, move. Upwards. Now!' Jupiter and Neptune led the way, while Esther brought up the rear.

As they arrived at the top of the stairway the exit was barred by soldiers. Jupiter walked forwards as did Neptune, both with huge swords in one hand and big hunting knives in the other. As often as the two giants beat back or disposed of one lot of soldiers, more filled the exit. The fight moved away from the doorway because of what the brothers were doing or by chance, Jacob had no idea. But it gave some room for escape.

'Keep going Jacob,' cried out Esther. 'Keep going. Just run.'

'Neptune and Jupiter,' he shouted. 'What of them? We can't just leave them there! What of them? They're trapped. Esther, stop!'

Esther didn't reply, but continued to run. Jacob could smell smoke and heard a low thump which caused the earth to vibrate, like a mountain moving. As they ran out into the large atrium, Jacob stopped.

'Jacob, we must run,' cried Esther.

But Jacob stood and waited. There was another thump which was much louder than the first, followed by a sheet of pure white fire that streamed out of the doorway from which he'd just come. The soldiers ran and Jacob couldn't see what had happened to Jupiter and Neptune. An explosion ripped through the heart of the cellars and bright red flames flew through the roof and shot high above the ruined city. A burst of white-hot light followed and blinded anyone who looked upon it. It lit up the sky as if night had suddenly become day.

A huge fireball swept upwards from the ground beneath, tearing through the earth, rock, marble and brick and only then did Jacob run holding his wounded mother. And how he ran. Soldiers and barbarians scattered in confusion only thinking of escape. Many were swept up in the conflagration. The very air seemed to burn. Everywhere there was fire and chaos. The Tower of David began to crumble, the explosions continuing to rent the air and light up the tortured Jerusalem sky, so brightly now that Jacob thought, as he and his precious cargo fell to the ground, that a new sun was being born. And for him, he thought briefly before everything went dark, it was.

37

Singapura, South East Asia Peninsula, 1492

When she thought about it, Gabriella realised that she had never seen the colour of vermillion as vivid as this. The enormous explosion had ripped through the early dawn air. Angry flames had devoured everything in their path. Gabriella had never heard a sound so loud with echoes so terrifying. Huge pieces of masonry and great slabs of heavy wood flew in all directions as blast after blast rent the early morning. What had been a large temple was now nothing but a deep crater with smoke rising from it and simply nothing else at all.

Gabriella turned to see that Cesare had fallen backwards into the maze entrance and its hedges. He began to get up, a maniacal gleam in his now mad eyes. He was covered in a fine dust and had a deep gash on his forehead. As he rose, Gabriella could see that his arms and legs were stiffening and that the man couldn't move properly. He fell back, once again into the hedge's poisonous embrace. As he lay there, unable to move, hungry creatures of all kinds came out of the undergrowth to investigate. She heard Cesare plead for help and then the screaming took over.

Behind her there was a strange rustle and, fearing a dangerous animal, she whirled round to see a huge, white shape which was unrecognisable, but also which looked vaguely familiar. The shape moved towards her, burning the air as it floated. It stopped in front of her and somehow seemed to bow before it gently disappeared. The Ring of Solomon, having turned bright blue, was now its normal granite grey.

Without thinking further, she ran past Cesare's body and the frenzy of animals surrounding it. She ran past the remains of poor, dear Maria, but then stopped. She went back to kneel by what had been her good, kind friend. She took one of Maria's cold hands and hesitated for a moment, before saying something under her breath and covering her friend's remains.

The ships' guns had found their range and all around her explosions were throwing huge amounts of dust and rock into the air. Gabriella became confused with the noise and not knowing where the next explosion might be. Her head ached and she was desperately frightened that the swamp might be impassable.

A huge explosion came close to hitting the rope bridge she was now crossing and, turning, she could see that some of the ropes had been severed. Behind her, as each rope gave way, all the planks of wood began to fall one by one. Crocodiles and other large water creatures began swimming towards the centre of the river in the hope of something tasty to eat.

Gabriella ran as fast as she could and only managed to get to the other side of the river just as the whole bridge collapsed almost in slow motion into the deep, dark water. She ran past the now dead, brave Malay and Chinese Watchers who had accompanied her through the swamp on the path which was only now just visible below the rising tidal waters.

Another close explosion from one of the Portuguese guns threw Gabriella to the ground. She got up shakily and stumbled forwards on to the vaguely visible, narrow pathway across the swamp, her ears ringing. She could see the tide pushing water gently over the stones. Now, between each round of pounding cannon fire, from the river's mouth she could hear yells, commands, clashes of steel and musket shots.

Gabriella rose again, shaking her head and began to rub the Ring of Solomon, but another huge explosion pushed her backwards and the ring simply came away from her middle finger on her right hand. Dazed and unable to keep her balance, she knew now without any doubt that she was about to topple into the syrup-like, stinking mud. Time seemed to stand still and she could no longer hear anything. Now she knew that the swamp would embrace her and, in a way, she knew that she'd had enough and was ready to go. Her task had been achieved, but on the way she'd lost so much. Too much. She had lost everything. The Ring of Solomon fell and she watched dispassionately as it disappeared beneath the surface of the liquid mud with just a hint of small bubbles.

As she fell, a strong hand grabbed one of her arms and hoisted her upright. Someone will kill me now, she thought. Turning, she saw in front of her on the pathway a man aged about thirty, tall with a scarred leather bag over his shoulder and a warm but searching smile on his face. His blond hair looked silvery with dawn's light behind him, she thought.

'Who are you?' asked Gabriella, her voice hesitant and thick with tiredness, tears and pain.

'My name,' said the man still holding onto Gabriella's arm and steadying the girl, 'is Jacob.'

Epilogue

Gymnasium Schule, Freiburg im Breisgau, Germany, 1938

Micha stood very still. As did his classmates. The tall, straight-backed officer who strode into the classroom was terrifying. His shiny, black, metal-heeled boots made a sharp, doom-laden sound across the wooden floor.

Micha's teacher, a tall, thin man looking older than his thirty-six years, wearing a grey woollen jacket and a dark blue bow tie, smiled nervously and stood up as did the boys. He clipped his own heels and bowed his head sharply as was the required etiquette. The officer gave Micha's teacher a dismissive, cold glance.

The headmaster, Herr Professor Aldous Metzheimer, his bald head shining and his small eyes glittering coldly behind his rimless glasses, looked stern as usual. He was dwarfed by the tall officer next to him and another grim-looking man in a pale grey double-breasted suit with a swastika band on one arm.

'This,' said the headmaster proudly indicating the tall officer to the class of thirteen-year-old boys, 'is SS-Oberführer Kammler and also visiting us today is Gruppenführer Dr. Karl Genzken.' Micha noticed that his class teacher's hands had clenched at the mention of the doctor's name.

'Good morning, SS-Oberführer Kammler, good morning Gruppenführer Dr. Genzken, good morning Herr Professor Metzheimer,' the class said as one in a low, monotone voice.

The boys were motioned to sit which they did with the usual

scraping of wooden chairs on the parquet floor. Professor Metzheimer looked anxious, his glasses flashing in the light. He went on to explain that The National Socialist German Workers' Party and, of course, therefore the Führer, wanted a number of children who were exceptional at science to work on a special project. He stood back nearly tripping over a wastepaper basket and the officer stepped forward.

SS-Oberführer Kammler, in his crow-black uniform with vivid red insignia, briefly but firmly explained the project and told the children that a lucky few would be chosen to help the national cause and particularly the Schutzstaffel which the class knew of course was the SS.

He explained that the lucky chosen few, five in all, would live away from home for several months, maybe longer. Micah didn't quite understand the nature of the project, but it seemed to have something to do with scientific research which was, the officer said, vital to the Reich. To make the project a success, it needed young, fresh and brilliant minds. The officer mentioned the doctor's name several times, although the doctor in turn, standing almost in the shadows, said and did nothing, apart, that is, from looking round the room. His eyes kept alighting on Micha.

Micha was nervous. He didn't really have a clue what the officer was talking about, but this wasn't the first time that very bright pupils had been offered opportunities to go and study in Berlin, Frankfurt or somewhere.

Micha began to sweat even though the room was cold. He noticed that his teacher was uneasy. The officer was explaining to the class that it was a scientific fact that some people in Germany were special and pure - and the rest, well, they weren't as intelligent and needed to be... managed. He asked the boys if they thought that this was a good idea. Nobody spoke so the officer frowned irritably and asked again in a louder voice.

The headmaster, also frowning, stepped forward. Immediately the boys all shouted out in unison, 'Jawohl, SS-Oberführer Kammler.'

The now appeased officer said that the project would be a great deal of fun although all the boys including Micah's teacher felt that there was nothing fun in anything that the officer said. The officer explained that the children would be working with other boys and girls from around Germany, alongside well-respected university professors. It would, he said, be an honour to work on the project. Parents, the school and the whole of Germany would be proud.

Once he had finished talking, the officer clipped his heels sharply, gave a Nazi salute and shouted, 'Heil Hitler,' fully expecting everyone in the room to do the same and everyone in the room dutifully stood, chairs scraping again, and did. Micha saw that his teacher had stood and saluted almost half-heartedly. Then the headmaster slowly called out five names as if what he was doing was offering a treat as one might do at a children's party.

The headmaster's smile was sickly and his thick, red lips glistened with spittle. After each name was called, the class was encouraged to applaud the chosen boy who was made to stand. The last name called out was Micha's and his heart sank. He was to go to Berlin the next day. He was aware that, once his name had been called out, the doctor's eyes never left his face.

Maybe it was the weak winter sunshine suddenly streaming through one of the classroom windows, but Micha was also aware that just behind the doctor's head, part of the framed and glass-fronted black and white photograph of Adolf Hitler seemed to be slightly orange.

About the Author

Simon Maier has always been fascinated by the idea of witnessing at close hand history as it happens. What were the adventures that people had to reach a particular moment or course of action? What was the intrigue, excitement and danger on the way? He wrote a book about it – The Other Side of History. That book gave him the idea for Silver Green which mixes real historical fact with what may have gone on behind the scenes. History is scattered with loads of significant, amazing or terrifying moments that changed, or could have changed, the world - and it's exciting to wonder what the history books don't tell us.

Simon was and is also interested in what science can do. What if people could actually stop aging and be free of disease? Could that really happen? Science says that it could. One day. Is that day now?

Secret organisations are fascinating and there are several worldwide secret societies that exist today. Are they really secret? What do they do? And do they do what they do for good... or for evil?

Silver Green is an exciting mix of all these things and it's a rollercoaster from start to finish.

Simon is a communications expert who has helped corporations around the world. He's a storyteller and has used storytelling as a way of helping people communicate better. He's lectured in Shakespeare, managed international communication agencies and has delivered global events. He writes articles, opinion pieces and blogs on all aspects of communications.

Simon is just finishing off a whodunnit and has started the second book in the Silver Green trilogy.

CPSIA information can be obtained
at www.ICGtesting.com
Printed in the USA
LVHW010248241220
674973LV00002B/104

9 781800 940956